BOOK OF THE DEAD

Also by Dean Fetzer

The Jaared Sen Quartet
Death in Amber
Death After Midnight
Book of the Dead

Edited with Gordon Butler
Fancyapint? In London

BOOK OF THE DEAD

Dean Fetzer

First printed in this edition 2012

GunBoss Books, 3rd Floor, 207 Regent Street, London, W1B 3HH, England

www.gunboss.com

ISBN 978-0-9561581-4-7

To my beautiful wife Debra –
I couldn't do this without you.

BROODING IS NOT GOOD FOR THE SOUL

T he House broods.

Yes, inanimate objects aren't supposed to do things like 'brood', but this one is definitely brooding.

It has seen over a hundred and thirty years of human activity, watching the comings and goings, the happy occasions and the dark hearts of the men that have occupied it over that time.

The good things have been rare in this House, the walls gradually soaking up the misery and pain of generations.

For that is what it was built for. Pain and misery.

From the outside it looks as if it were just a normal dwelling, part of a Victorian terrace. But the exterior is black.

The House isn't painted black or stained by London's heavy pollution. The very fabric of it seems tainted, absorbing the light and making it difficult to see.

To all appearances it's made of the same brick as the rest of the terrace, but a brick of a much darker shade. Even the windows seem dark and dull, showing little of the surroundings in stray reflections. At night, no light escapes them.

The House has a 'reputation', on the street, as a bad place.

Children say it's haunted and the Care in the Community victim suffering from long-term schizophrenia living at Number 34 claims to have seen reflections in the windows of people in out-of-date clothes – people who are not behind the windows or in the street.

Pets disappear frequently in the area of the House, most recently Snowy, the cat from Number 58. People tend to avoid it, if they can.

Menace bleeds from the very substance of the House. Its maker made it for one purpose and it has been waiting for decades for a new master – one who understands the needs and wants of an inanimate creation of brick, mortar, wood and steel. *One is coming*, that much the House knows.

The one is coming soon and then the House's purpose will be revealed.

One can detect an air of something about the House – waiting perhaps – if one steps too close to its black bricks. And yes, the House is waiting. It waits for the one to come who will surpass its trials and break through to the treasure chamber.

The House guards its possessions well and closely.
And waits.

THERE ARE TIMES I WISH I COULDN'T SEE

I look down at the figure stuffed into the corner of the vacant loft. The whole place is littered with garbage, but the part where he lies is nearly clean – not even much in the way of dust. Part of the body is hidden by a box, but Forensics is nearly done with it.

Dead junkies don't normally get the full investigation this one is currently enjoying. There are two SOCOs going over the body and the surroundings with sniffers and imagers, recording as much as they can before moving him. My internal Heads Up Display, or HUD, flashes behind my eyes, confirming what I already suspected – they aren't finding much.

The novelty of being able to see a crime scene has still not worn off.

It's been six months since my surgery and I'm still getting used to the colours, the vibrancy of everything. My friend and Medical Examiner Alicia Sampson tells me it'll wear off, in that 'I'm a Doctor, I know what I'm talking about' voice, but after so many years of darkness I'm like a starving man devouring everything I see. And there's still issues with using my eyes to get around, a disconnect sometimes causing a stutter, or falter, between what I see and my movements.

I've only been allowed out from behind a desk in the last few weeks, our perpetual shortage of Contractors making every available body important to the Company.

This crime scene is at once familiar and, with my newly returned sight, strange.

"What have we got?" I ask the attending Contractor, Grade II, Timson.

"Looks like a dead junkie, Commander," he responds, still treating rank with the respect that it doesn't always deserve. A Grade II isn't a full Contractor yet; judging by the sharpness of the creases in his trousers, he's newly appointed from the academy.

God he looks young, I think before turning my attention back to the body. My HUD, installed in my skull, alongside my phone since the return of my eyes, flicks in and I start to get input from the tests the techs are conducting.

I dismiss the HUD, as it can be really distracting. I'm sure I'll get used to it, but it's taking longer than I anticipated. "Right, so what are we doing here if it's a dead junkie?" I ask.

He looks nervous for a moment but doesn't hesitate very long. "Member of the public saw someone suspicious with the body, sir."

"Initial tox screen?"

"Says that heroin's in his blood," another of the techs answers. "I can only find one puncture wound on the back of his neck."

"Odd place to inject yourself," I mutter.

"Was... was-n't a junk-ie," stutters a voice behind me. I turn around to find a PC with one hand firmly around the bicep of a cadaverous looking young man. As I watch, shudders run through his frame, symptoms of advanced snap use.

"Wasn't he?" I ask, already of the same opinion.

The figure shakes his head violently from side to side, his lank, dirty blonde hair flopping in echo of the movement. "Nah... took a bit of snap... you know... now and then, but... nothing like heroin." The scarecrow wipes its eyes, I guess from some affection rather than just side effects.

Heroin isn't common anymore, it's true. And the body in the corner doesn't have the look of your average user: too much body tone and skin colour, clean hair and not that far from his last shower.

Timson makes an effort to pick up the threads of the investigation. "Do you know his name?"

Scornfully, the man wipes his mouth again. "Yeah, course I do – he was my frien'." He turns to me. "Name's John Tyler."

Central flags a hit almost instantly, but I didn't need the reminder. He'd been all over the news a few weeks back after a very public argument with his father, James Tyler, the third.

That's all I need, another shit-storm over a famous asshole's kid. And his father is an asshole. I've met him.

I reach in my pocket and pull out the cigarette case Skeet gave me. An antique, it's art deco patterns sparkle in the light from the big, industrial windows. I pull out a cigarette and light it. Hey, this is a dump, not an office building.

I turn back to the snap user. "Okay... what's your name?" I ask, going for friendly.

"S-sammy. Sammy Martin," he replies. "And 'for you ast, I live here," he says waving at the junk-filled space.

"Okay, Sammy-who-lives-here – when did you see John Tyler last?"

He rubs at the grime on his chin. "Dunno, he pops in real regular-like." Another moment of hard thought brings him, "Maybe yesterday? Yeah, it was yesterday, 'cos he brung me some soup and a loaf a bread. I still got some of the bread… Yesterday…" he trails off.

"Sir!" a voice calls from the area of the body.

"Yes?" I respond. "What is it?"

"Part of the body's missing, sir," the young tech in her paper suit informs me. *I know I haven't been seeing for that long, but everyone looks so damn young…*

"And?"

"It's his hand – I think it's been gnawed off…" She trails into silence.

I turn back to the kid. "So Sammy, did you get hungry last night? Think John Tyler's hand was a Big Mac with all that *special* sauce?"

The kid cowers in front of me; now I'm starting to scare him. Good.

"No! I never done nuffink to John's hand – I tole you, he brought me soup and bread! I don't eat that much…"

I believe him. I turn to the PC hovering by him. "Take him to the shelter and see if you can't get him cleaned up. We'll need him to give a statement later and I don't want to have to turn the vents up on high."

She salutes. "Yes sir!"

God they're all 'yes, sir', 'no, sir', 'three bags full, sir' – was I ever that deferent? Hell, I probably was, but again, it was a long time ago.

I nod and turn back to the SOCO. Langley? Lawford? "Anything else you can tell me?"

"No sir… there's a strange odour on his clothes the sniffer can't identify conclusively. Have sent it to Analysis." He turns and jumps when he sees me looking at him – obviously I'm not the only one getting used to my new eyes. "The ME should be able to tell you more," he says, stuffing items into his kit box.

The ice blonde hair reminds me, and then I notice it in the notes on my HUD. "Thanks, Larsson." I turn back to Timson. "I think I've seen enough."

"Very good, sir," he replies and leads the way back to the street and my car.

THE LIFE OF A BOOKSTORE OWNER IS NEVER DULL

Wolf entered the bookshop with the usual twinge. It wasn't quite the same since the fire – rebuilding is all well and good (and thank the god of fuck for decent insurance) but it doesn't bring back the character of a place.

He sighed, his dark eyes sad for a moment, remembering Stanley. A typical Londoner, Stanley had been average in so many ways, but Wolf just remembered the piercing hazel eyes and the grey hair at his temples. Oh, and his smile. Wolf would have done anything to make Stanley smile – and often did.

His mentor and the only father he'd ever known, Stanley had left him the bookshop – *Hopkins' Rarities & Antiquities*. Running that shop was the only thing he'd ever been good at. Besides finding things.

Wolf's assistant Janey thought the two went hand-in-hand; his talent for finding things brought a first edition of *IT* to hand or that Very Nice Edition of *The Great Gatsby* in leather, which would be ideal for that little old lady who comes in every other Saturday morning like clockwork.

Closing the door behind himself, Wolf was surprised to see someone sitting in the chair in the back office. Janey was looking at him from behind the counter and mouthed "tax inspector" before grimacing. "Morning Wolf," she greeted him.

"Ah, Mr Woffe?" the little man in the office said, standing up. He was quite rounded and not very tall. A strange comb-over and tiny moustache made Wolf think of someone famous. *Wait – Hitler?*

Realising he was yet to respond, Wolf replied, "Morning Janey." He stepped towards the counter.

"I'm Pocock Woffe," he said to the serial killer in the office. "Most people call me 'Wolf'."

"Yes. I'm Tax Inspector for London, sub-region 2. Mr Jessop." He held out his hand and Wolf shook it, startled at the flaccid collection of digits at the end of Mr Jessop's arm.

"Pleased to meet you. What's this about?" Wolf asked.

Glancing at Janey, Mr Jessop turned back to the office. "If you'll come into the office, Mr Woffe, I can explain the situation to you."

Wolf glanced over at Janey as well, who shrugged, shaking her head. Following Mr Jessop, Wolf felt for a moment like a child being sent to the headmaster's office.

What felt like hours later, Mr Jessop was as satisfied as he was going to get about the state of the shop's finances, without conducting a full audit, and left with a final limp hand press, promising to come back the following month for further excavation.

Slumped behind the desk, Wolf felt drained and like he'd been through the ringer. He was shocked to realise it was barely lunchtime.

There was a short rap on the door and Janey entered with a cup of coffee in her left hand. "Large Soy Toffee Nut Latte, no whipped cream, heavy on the sprinkles – just the way you like it," she announced, placing the polystyrene cup in front of him with a flourish.

"Thanks Janey, you're a star," Wolf said appreciatively, the pressure on his temples easing slightly at the thought of caffeine.

Janey pushed a stray strand of blonde hair back from her elfin face, eyes large behind the small glasses she wore. "You're welcome, boss – thought you'd need it after Hitler's visit."

Wolf grinned. "It wasn't just me, then – I've been trying not to giggle all morning!"

"Well, a short, fat version of Hitler, anyway," Janey said dryly. The sound of the bell on the door made her look over her shoulder into the shop. "Graeme's here," she reported.

Wolf stood, picking up his coffee. "I've had enough of the office for now," he declared, stepping to the door. He took a sip. "H'lo Graeme, what's up?"

The big man with thinning hair, mutton chop sideburns and a severe glare was standing just in the door. "Morning, Wolf, had a call from ol' Rat Sphincter this mornin'. You'll never believe this – he's heard about a *book* you're looking for," he said, smiling.

"That's strange, Rat's not one for reading – even doubt he can, to be honest," Wolf replied, his interest piqued. "Which book?"

"He says it's old and pronounces it..." He paused and consulted his voda notes. "'*Deee temporium sinoos*', as far as I can work out." Graeme's brow was furrowed with concentration, being more of an antiquities man than books.

Wolf stopped cold. "Really?" he squeaked. He fought to keep calm. *It had to be a forgery – the original was lost hundreds of years ago.*

Janey and Graeme were looking at him now. "Do you know the book he means, Wolf?" Janey asked quietly.

"No... Well, yes, but it's lost..." Wolf started. He sighed, best to tell them and get it over with. "If it's the book I think it is, it's by Giordano Bruno, a heretic burned at the stake in Rome in 1600. The Latin name is *De Temporum Signis,* loosely translated as *On the Signs of the Times."* He shook his head. "It has to be a fake."

Graeme held up his voda and poked it at Wolf. "He sent me a photo."

Wolf took the voda and stared at the tiny image on-screen. Well, it looked right, but it was hard to tell from a photo. He sighed, knowing he would have to see it, even if it was a counterfeit. "Go on, tell him to bring it in. But if it's bent, I'll have his ears."

He turned back to the office, feeling a sense of foreboding. Even after all these centuries, just a brush with Bruno's work felt like it had a touch of the darkness that had seen him burn.

MORE DARK TALES FROM THE MORGUE

Alicia looked up at the door from John Tyler's body which had just been placed on the slab in Room 1. "Yes?"

"Got another fresh one on the slab in Room 3," Jack, her assistant, announced. "White male, forty-five to fifty, average height, brown hair, multiple lacerations and contusions – oh, and a broken neck."

"Car wreck?" Alicia asked. She was Head of Forensic Pathology for the Company's offices in the City of London and they often played this game, trying to guess causes of death before they had seen the body. It wasn't something they shared with the families or officials of the courts, of course, but a bit of morgue humour helped them cope with the horrors they regularly got in.

Jack smiled. "Too obvious; you're not trying," he complained.

Alicia shook her head and leaned back in her chair. "Any type of crash involved, so I can avoid going through other permutations?"

"Nope."

Thinking about it, Alicia conceded it would have to be some kind of multiple incident cause. "Frenzied knife attack followed by a fall down the stairs?"

Jack grinned, loving it when he stumped the boss. "Not even close – give up?"

Alicia tapped his chit with one of her own, conceding the bet. Only five credits, but it kept them on their toes. She stood up. "Show me."

Jack led the way to Room 3, the main examination room, and took great delight in unveiling the corpse.

From the way the head lolled, the neck was broken, not just fractured. There wasn't a lot of bruising on the neck, so it might have been post-mortem. The cuts, however, were definitely antemortem and quite precise.

"Wait a minute…" Alicia squinted. "Are those words?"

Jack nodded. "Yes, Central's identified it as Latin: *Nulla est lex quae omnia regit.*"

Alicia looked at him. "And in English?" she enquired.

"'There is no law governing all things'," he replied.

Alicia swore. "Shit, don't tell me we've got a newbie serial killer running around out there."

Jack's thin face looked serious for the first time. A lock of blonde hair fell across one eye, which he pushed back. A nervous tic. "I hope not, boss – they drive me round the twist!" He carried on. "There was nothing on the body, other than these." He held up two coins, old ones, by the look of things.

Alicia took them, rubbing the faded surfaces with a thumb. It was dull metal, not gold, and looked positively ancient.

"Roman perhaps? Or Gaulish?" offered Jack.

"Neither, actually. From Belgae, I'd say. First century BC."

"How'd you know?"

"I followed my father around metal detecting when I was a kid – he had a pretty good collection," Alicia boasted.

"Never would have thought it, boss," Jack replied.

Smiling, Alicia looked more closely at the body. "ID on the body yet?"

"Still waiting for Central to work her magic," Jack said.

"'She'?" Alicia queried. "You're of the opinion the Company's Central Artificial inTelligence™ machine is female?"

Jack shrugged. "I'd say CAT definitely qualifies – she has moods."

Alicia shook her head again, her short dark hair slightly wavering with the movement. She fixed him with her most penetrating gaze. "And you're the only one who calls it that, you know." A thought hit her. "I think you're in love, Mr Sullivan!"

Looking chagrined, Jack tried to smile. "No! It's not like that," he protested. "She's... different... that's all."

Putting on her most sympathetic tone, Alicia said, "I think you need to get out more, Jack. Go to the pub with your mates, or visit a museum, or something." A sudden thought hit her. "Or better yet, escort me to the Company's Christmas Ball. It's on the fifth."

Jack looked like he'd rather eat nails – sharp ones.

"Now, don't look like that. You'll know people there and you don't have to stick with me all evening." Jack still looked apprehensive. "You'll have a good time."

"Isn't Commander Sen taking you?" he asked.

It was Alicia's turn to look away. "No... Jaared... I haven't seen Commander Sen for a couple of months now."

Jack was quiet for a moment, and then turned back to the corpse. "Okay, I'll go. Company pays for tux hire, right?"

Alicia nodded, relieved to be on safer ground.

"He doesn't know, does he?" Jack asked quietly.

The ground lurched again, and Alicia felt it in the pit of her stomach. "No, he doesn't," she replied softly, and then mentally shook herself. "Anyway, I'll let you get on with the PM on this one – shout if you need me."

THINGS TO DO IN LONDON WHEN YOU'RE DEAD

Madeline stalked into the silence. She was sure he was somewhere in the labyrinth of service tunnels around her – she just wasn't entirely sure where.

A whisper of cloth on concrete, a stifled sigh, and something else very faint came from her left. Circling around, the killer came to the fore in Madeline. There was a time when the killer didn't go away, doing its damnedest to destroy everything possible. But that was aeons ago.

Stopping against a pillar, Madeline's eyes glowed for a brief second in the light reflected from the distant exit sign.

Madeline's head snapped around at another hint of movement ahead of her. There.

With a single long leap combined with her blow, the prey's head snapped against the pillar he'd been hiding behind with an audible crunch.

"Too slow – and noisy, youngling," Madeline murmured, not even out of breath.

Nicholas Sebastien Louis Duchesne swore softly, rubbing the back of his head. There was no blood on the pillar and no sign of the impact on his flesh. The pillar hadn't been quite as lucky.

He punched the pillar in frustration, which creaked alarmingly. "I'll never get it!" he hissed.

"Yes you will, Nicholas – this is not something you learn overnight," she reminded him. Madeline looked at him with hooded eyes, her son.

It was an odd thing to become a mother at her age. No, one doesn't ask a lady's age – but she remembered kings and kingdoms that no longer existed and hadn't for many years. Louis had been her favourite, with his wonderful palace at Versailles. But his children hadn't been smart enough to keep the people happy. To say nothing of that horrible Austrian his grandson took up with... *Magda? Marta? No, Marie. Awful woman. Guillotine was about what she deserved.*

How times change, to now have a son of her own – it was not something she had ever imagined, much less planned for. At least with their kind there was no extended baby period, full of nappies, chicken pox, wiping faces and bottoms... Oh, they still had youngling angst, even Jaared suffered from that, so he probably had a few centuries to grow out of it.

And yet, she found herself feeling what must be love towards her Nicholas. Madeline gazed at him: tall, dark hair cascading around his shoulders, that pale skin, those lavender eyes. Although not the same colour, his gaze was just like his father's.

So caught up in looking at him, she was startled when he suddenly vanished. A flicker in the corner of her eye told her where he'd gone.

Damn the boy, she thought with a predatory grin. *He might turn out all right after all.*

WORKING FOR THE MAN

I fumble for the light switch as I enter my house. You could call the light switches in my house a recent acquisition, as I never had much cause to use them when living here on my own for the last handful of decades.

"Mwwwrrrr?" I get from the floor. Dickens, a Seal Point Siamese and probably twenty years old now – I honestly can't remember when I got him – blinks up at me from the floor. Central probably knows, but I don't care enough to ask it.

And I don't like being in its debt.

"I suppose you think it's tea time," I reply. I've talked to him for so long, I don't worry that Central will find it odd. I've done much more peculiar things in my time.

The big tan and dark brown cat leads me into the kitchen area. I make a harrumphing noise and go to the cupboard where his food lives. "Well, guess what? You're right!" I put fresh food in his bowl and while he's noisily crunching away at his biscuits, I put down a bowl of fresh water for him.

Because I can see it, I make a face at my reflection in the chrome of the large fridge. I'm not a big eater at the best of times and when I'm on my own, I tend to drink.

The bottle in the cupboard is mostly empty. Housekeeping hasn't been in yet this week, and it appears I've finished my ration.

"I'll be back in a minute," I say to the cat before heading out of the house, leaving the light on. There's an offy just around the corner and I know the proprietor well.

As I walk down the lane to the main road, I get the feeling I'm being watched. I look across the road and see a dim figure in a doorway. After a moment I realise it's glowing. I glance both ways down the lane and step across the road.

Almost instantly, I realise it's Stel. She smiles at me before slowly fading. Like the Cheshire Cat.

Weird.

"I'm sorry, Stel," I whisper as I turn back to the main road.

The first time I saw her, I thought I was having problems with my new eyes.

It is *her*. Of that I am sure. And she is dead, too.

It's Stel. I've been seeing her ghost since almost the first day they removed the surgical seals from my new eyes.

I caused some consternation with the surgical team when I asked them if they'd performed the calibrations on my new eyes correctly. This was mainly due to the fact that I couldn't make out her features when she first appeared to me. I also had never seen her in person before. I had to look up her photo via Central to confirm it, although why I hadn't done this before, still escapes me.

She's not solid, she's quite pale and translucent – if she's against a bad background, I can hardly see her. She doesn't move much, either, so it's not always obvious she's watching me.

I've checked the logs with Central and nothing's registering there, either; by my reckoning, this means she's a ghost only I can see.

So she's my problem. Or my burden. I haven't quite decided which.

The Thai people have a concept, which ties into their version of Buddhism, of a person's spirit not being allowed to reincarnate for some reason or another and so wanders the earth, often appearing to people known before death. They call this wandering spirit a *phii*.

The Chinese have a similar being called a 'hungry ghost', which is some kind of unappeased spirit that can't rest because of a bad death or poor burial.

From what I can gather these spirits have unfinished business in this world, so they can't pass on to the next.

I'm hoping my ghost is not one of these.

I don't honestly know if there's any communication between the living and the *phii*, but I've had little luck communicating with Stel's *phii*. Maybe it's me.

The last time I saw her clearly she just looked very sad and gave a small smile. I could have sworn there were tears in her eyes, but don't know how such a thing can manifest in a ghost. I do get the impression she's watching me. I don't know why, but she is. I hope she's just watching over me, not expecting something to happen or for me to do something.

What's she waiting for?

It only takes a moment to get a new bottle of whisky and return to the house. As I step up to the door, I realise it's open. I know I shut it. My trusty Glock appears in my hand and I use it to push the door open a little further.

"Mwwoar?" Dickens asks, taking this opportunity to question my sanity, although he doesn't deny the door is open – he's half out of it.

Shhh, I implore, although I know you can't really tell a cat anything. And whoever it is who's inside probably heard him already.

The door opens further and a tall woman with short blonde hair stands behind the cat, her leather jacket gleaming in the light from the room.

"What kinda welcome is that, Mr Sen?" she drawls, looking pointedly at my gun hand.

"Skeet! What the—how the…? Dammit!" I realise I'm still holding a gun at the ready. The Glock disappears and I step forward and put my arms around her.

There's a moment of stiffness before she allows herself to relax, her leathers creaking softly. I'm glad to see her – it's been too long.

"Does that mean you're glad to see me?" she murmurs in my ear.

I nod. "Oh yes, you can count on that," I reply.

She leans back. "When'd you get your ol' eyes done?"

I drink her in, the short, spiky hair, the thin, but not too thin face, and those piercing green eyes.

Skeet's almost as tall as I am. A slightly Roman nose. She's perhaps not conventionally pretty, but her features suit her. And the mouth… I remember that mouth.

"About six months ago." She starts to feel self-conscious under my scrutiny. "You know I've never seen you before?"

Skeet relaxes. "I know," she says softly. Then a shyness I never expected creeps in. "Whaddya think?" she gestures downward.

"You're beautiful," I reply. "Although I never needed eyes to know that."

"You're still a charmer, then," she says, her grin strained. A tear runs from her eye, down her soft cheek.

"Hey, what's that for?" I ask softly.

She buries her head in my shoulder. "I was afraid you'd… forgotten me," she mumbles, a sob escaping her. My big, brave Skeet.

"Shhhhh… how could I do that? You know I've been waiting…"

Nodding, her arms tighten around me. "I know… Sorry…"

"Hey, enough of that – you did what you had to do and all I care about is that you're back now." I realise we're still standing in the doorway. "Shall we go in?"

Skeet nods again, and pulls away enough to let me step forward into the hall and close the door behind me.

Don't you just hate meetings?

T he meeting with Rat Sphincter didn't take much to set up. Wolf had Graeme call him shortly after the bookshop's closing time and moments later he was at the front door.

Sitting behind his desk in the tiny office, Wolf exchanged looks with Graeme, who leaned against the counter. The kid was keen.

"You hanging around out there or somefink?" Graeme asked when he'd let him in. "You don't normally turn up that quick, Sphincter."

"Don' worry, I ain't stalkin' you or nothin', Gramps," the skinny teenager replied, with a sarcastic look. Well, he looked like a teenager. They'd both known him far too long to believe he was still below the age of thirty.

As he entered the office from the darkened shop, the light made his pointy – yes, 'ratty' even – features worsened by the typical gauntness of a snap user, not to mention the row of craters across his cheekbones, evidence of a brush with the last plague. He wasn't tall, either, although his legs and arms seemed long for his body. A messenger bag hung across his thin chest, seeming to divide it in two. And he had that smell about him.

Wolf sniffed. Yep, that rotten-egg smell that always seemed to develop with long-term snap use. How he'd lasted this long, no one knew. Maybe he was one of those functioning users who coped with the drug and just carried on.

"Whaddya got fer me?" Wolf asked, holding his hand out.

Sphincter shook his head. "Nuh-uh. What you willing to pay?"

Wolf sighed. "Sphincter, you know me – I pay what it's worth. If it's garbage, yeh get garbage. Like normal."

The kid looked at them both suspiciously for a moment before removing an envelope from the messenger bag. "Only a sample," he muttered.

Shit. Hopefully it was intact. Some codexes weren't bound, merely clamped together, but they tended to be a lot older. *If the little fucker has damaged it...*

The envelope contained an archival sleeve. Good sign.

Wolf slipped the sleeve out of the envelope and let it lie on the desk for a moment. The age-spotted paper was printed with slightly faded text.

Wolf up-ended the sleeve, allowing the page to come to rest on the mat on his desk. Paper looked right, laid rag, faint impressions of the mesh used to contain the paper during making just visible. It looked smaller than what was called 'duodecimo' – or a twelvemo sized page, roughly thirteen centimetres by nineteen centimetres. There was a hint of mildew on one corner of the thick paper. To Wolf's fingers, used to modern wood pulp paper, it felt like it could have been made out of some kind of skin.

"My Eye-tie's a little rusty," Graeme quipped.

Wolf picked up a magnifier and held it over the small text. "It's Latin, actually. *Est qui depinxit gallos gallinaceos, Qui quoniam non est omnino imprudens...*" he read, remembering Stanley's Latin tutorials. After a moment, he threw the sheet down. "Sphincter, this isn't the text you promised me."

The kid looked worried. "He said you wouldn't know..."

"While it is undoubtedly a text by Giordano Bruno, Sphincter, it's not the text of *De Temporum Signis*. If I'm not mistaken, it's the text to *De Umbris Idearum – The Shadow of Ideas*." Then the paranoia kicked in. He was *not* going to be taken in again. Casually, he stood up and stepped around the desk.

It was a small office. In one step, he had Sphincter pinned to the wall by the door with his left hand, the muscles bunching in his shoulder. "Who sent me this, Sphincter, ol' buddy?"

Sphincter's ratty features almost twitched with agitation. If he'd had whiskers, they would have been on the go by that point. "I—I never seen him before – honest!"

Wolf's blue eyes burned into the pink-tinged ones in front of him. "What'd he look like, then?"

"I don't know!" He started to shriek as Wolf's other hand came up. "Honest! I never seen him before he came in *The Crown*, day afore yesterday, and ast me if I knew you... Said he had somethin' for you!"

It was just as well that Sphincter liked his own skin best. Wolf didn't really have to threaten him very much to get information. "What were you supposed to do when I bit? Sell me the rest of the book?"

Sphincter nodded. "Not—not exactly." He started to relax. "He wants to meet you."

Wolf wasn't finished. "He contacted *you*?"

Starting to look like a bobblehead doll, Sphincter's head kept moving. "He wants to meet you in *The Crown* at seven."

"Okay. Go." Wolf released him. He stared for a moment before poking him in the chest with a finger. "You'll be there, too, Sphincter. I don't see you, I walk out again."

"Okay, Wolf, okay." Sphincter scampered out of the office.

"What was that all about?" Graeme asked.

I wish I knew, Wolf thought. "I'd say it was a test — someone's after my abilities, not trying to sell me a priceless manuscript." At least, that's what he hoped.

"A test? To see if you spotted the change from that... that first one..." Graeme glossed over his lack of comprehension on the titles. He waved at the page on the desk.

"And they just happen to think an orphan from Glasgow with a successful trade in antique books wouldn't necessarily know his Latin." He sat down in his chair again and picked up his coffee. "If I didn't blink, they'd have sold me something and left it there."

"I don't like this, Wolf," Graeme grumbled, slouching into the other chair in the corner.

Wolf smiled, hardly surprised. "You never like it when we do one of these things, Graeme — even when it's your idea!"

Graeme's lips turned up in a rueful smile. "Well, someone's got to keep a realistic eye on things," he said.

"Well at least we're meeting these guys in a pub, *not a field in Essex*," Wolf replied.

Now Graeme winced. "*Don't* remind me of Essex! What a fuck-up." He pulled out his voda. "Least let me get Shirl and her beau to be in the pub, Wolf."

Wolf nodded. "Fine. Just tell them to keep the lovey-dovey crap to a minimum — it puts people off their beer."

They were all careful, understandably, after Graeme's daughter Shirl had been abducted on a job in the not too distant past. Wolf had gone to their employer at the time for help getting her back, but it always paid to be careful — particularly when you didn't know who was involved.

Wolf found things. Always had. When he met Stanley Hopkins, all those years ago, he hadn't known what to do with this ability. Stanley had helped him, as well as introducing him to Graeme and Shirl Black. A father-and-daughter team that quickly became part of Wolf's adopted family. Graeme knew everything there was to know about antiques, legitimate and stolen. Slightly younger than Wolf, Shirl was the sister he'd never had and some kind of cross-over, taking art history courses and learning what to look for when considering books as well.

Knowing books was Wolf's other thing. Stanley had made him learn other languages, so he could study lists of ancient books; he even sent him on a retro printing course so he would understand some of the work that actually went into printing books.

Shirl's 'beau' was one Jonathan Kemp. Wolf didn't like him particularly, probably his protective side coming out, but he was a three-time champion black belt, knew something about art and, most importantly, made Shirl happy. That was all that mattered.

Wolf picked up the sheet again and slid it into the sleeve before replacing it in the envelope. "I just hope we won't need them," he muttered.

Graeme, on his voda, nodded. "Okay, see you in there." He closed the voda in one swift movement. "We're all set. It's quarter past six now — want to go?"

Sighing, Wolf picked up the envelope. "Sure, it can't be as bad as Essex."

"I told you *not* to mention Essex!" Graeme blurted.

DINNER FOR ONE GETS DEPRESSING AFTER A WHILE

A licia pushed through the front door, bags in her hands, to be nearly knocked over by two bouncy muscular forms.

"Down Porgy! Down Bess!" she commanded, and the two whirlwinds of fur, muscle and yaps temporarily abated. "Now get out the way so I can get the shopping into the kitchen." It was said to the two Staffordshire Bulls at her feet as if they should understand every word, which of course they did.

Grinning, the terriers followed her into the kitchen. Alicia put the bags down on the counter and turned around to greet them properly. She crouched down to their level and rubbed heads and jowls, the dogs' hot breath wafting around her as their excitement returned.

"Good dogs, you're such good dogs," she cooed. They were some kind of cross, as they were both larger than your average Staffy, but the breed's genes had overwritten most of their cross's contribution.

Alicia went over to put food in their bowls. The two promptly consumed the lot and Alicia let them out into the back garden. They got a daily walk from a local service, so she didn't worry about them being in the house too much.

Turning back to her kitchen, Alicia went over and emptied out the shopping.

In just a few minutes she'd boiled some linguine, heated some oil with chilli and garlic, and added a packet of fresh crab to the pan. Garlic bread went into the oven and Bob was her proverbial. She drained the pasta and added the crab mixture before pulling the hot buttery bread out. Carrying the plate, a glass of Chardonnay in her other hand, she went through to the front room, the dogs following her, hoping some tasty morsel might fall off her plate.

Alicia sat on the sofa, the vid tuned to a news station of some kind, eating the pasta, dogs curled up on the floor by her feet. The ready-made garlic bread was fine, if a bit salty. Taking a sip of the wine, her eye was caught by a headline announcer. Waving the remote, she turned up the volume a few notches.

"—London have another serial killer in our midst? We're beginning to think so. This month, a second body has been found with words carved into the chest. Both white males, both in their mid-thirties..."

Alicia's voda rang. *Great, Humphrey.* "Yes, Humphrey, I'm seeing it now."

"What the hell is going on, Alicia? Why didn't you tell me we had a serial killer running around London? I mean, how can the media have it before you've told me!" *Humphrey, playing the indignant card again.*

She muted the vid and struggled to keep her temper. "At this moment, the only people in our lab who know about *one* of the victims are me, Jack and Ace, who took his portraits. They've been in the department long enough to know better than to—"

"That's not good enough, Alicia. It'll be my head on the block in the morning when the Inspector General gets wind of this." He paused for breath. "I'm surprised he's not contacted me already!"

The two dogs lifted their heads from the floor and looked at her, wondering what all the shouting was about.

"Humphrey, I didn't know—" Alicia tried to interrupt.

The voice on the other end interrupted her, the volume and pitch of his voice increasing. "Two bodies, Alicia? And you didn't see fit to tell me? What the hell were you thinking!"

"We didn't even know there was a second body, Humphrey," she tried to interject. "No, I'm hearing about it now – on the news..." She placed the remains of her plate of *linguine con polpa di granchio* on the table beside her.

"That's not good enough!" he replied.

"Dammit Humphrey, my team have not leaked this! Talk to me tomorrow when you're feeling a bit more *civil!*"

Alicia switched the voda off and tossed it some way down the sofa. *Dammit, I hate serial killers. One was enough.*

Sighing, she picked up her pasta again and took a mouthful.

It was no good. She couldn't eat now. She put the plate down on the side again and looked at the voda. The vid cast a moving light over the furniture.

She hadn't spoken to Jaared for weeks, maybe over a month. *He's been busy, I know. So have I.*

And things haven't really been the same since Stephen died.

The voda was about all she was looking at. "Dammit Alicia, pull yourself together – just call him!"

Dean Fetzer

Alicia picked up the voda and keyed the number. "Hello, Jaared? Got a minute?"

INTERRUPTIONS ALWAYS HAPPEN AT THE WORST TIME

My head phone often rings at inopportune moments. I have tried to carry on a conversation and do things at the same time, but I'm afraid the adage about men multi-tasking is true. That said, I don't buy that women are any better at it – have you ever followed a woman down a street trying to talk on the phone? Doesn't work – they can't do both.

So I stop kissing Skeet with a sigh. "Sorry, I've got a call," I mumble. "Sen here."

Skeet leans back on the sofa with a sigh and a *nothing changes* roll of the eyes.

"Hello, Jaared? Got a minute? Sorry to bother you out of hours..." It's Alicia.

I glance at Skeet. "Don't worry about it – you know I don't sleep much. What's up?" I reach for my cigarette case and pull out a coffin nail. Skeet smiles when she sees the case. I'm distracted by that smile for a moment, having only just begun seeing them.

"—another serial killer at work. Do you know anything about it?" Alicia is asking.

"Sorry?" I ask looking away from Skeet. I don't actually have a vid, as I haven't got around to buying one. A quick check with Central confirms the story's out there. Someone's talked. "I see." Sigh. "No, Alicia, I've no idea where this came from. The other body's across London for some reason, so I don't see how the press could have put it together."

Just a moment to trace the leak... There it is: two bodies, same MO, assigned to Jaworsky. A second check shows that he met a reporter in a pub, off duty, several sheets to the wind, and discussed the case before Central could intervene. *Damn.*

"Jaared?" Alicia asks. "Are you still there?"

I finish what I'm doing and light a cigarette. "Sorry Alicia, yes. I've just authorised transfer of the second body to you – it should be on your table first thing in the morning."

"Thanks." There's a pause. "If you could check and see if it was anyone in your office, I'd appreciate it. I've got a meeting with Humphrey first thing in the morning and I'd like to be able to tell him definitively it wasn't my team."

"Already done," I reply. "It's not your team. Looks like I get to deliver a reprimand and suspension all at the same time."

I kick both up to Central for immediate action. *Just one more thing.* "And your administrator has been put on suspension for his behaviour tonight – I won't have him badgering my best pathologist. You'll have a new replacement in the morning."

"Damn – you've suspended Humphrey? How...? You didn't need to do that, Jaared. Humphrey can be an old woman, but I need him to keep track of the paper clips and handle the Company bureaucracy. All that stuff I don't want to deal with..."

I reassure her the replacement, one Felix Jerbeau, is equally proficient and willing with the red tape.

We finish the conversation on small talk.

"We ought to have dinner sometime soon – my treat."

"That sounds perfect – you going to the Christmas Ball?"

"Yes, of course." I look back to Skeet and she's looking at me, expectantly. "I've got a bit of a surprise for you there," I add.

"Okay, I'll see you there. Good night, Jaared," she finishes, hanging up.

"Good night, Alicia," I say to no one. Skeet's still looking at me when I look up. "I know you're just back, but want to go to the Christmas Ball with me?" I ask. "It's formal."

Now Skeet grimaces. "Uh, don't know right now – when is it?"

"The fifth, plenty of time to find a—" I realise I've never seen Skeet wear anything remotely feminine; well, that's the thing about being blind.

She must be thinking along the same lines. "Will you be in a tux, then?" Her eyes turn speculative and excitement flickers.

I nod. "Yep, the one time of the year the monkey suit comes out of mothballs." She starts to grin at me, and not in a good way. "I even get my nails done and everything."

That seems to increase the speculation in her eyes. "Okay, I'll go."

"Just like that?"

Skeet nods. "Why the hell not? I ain't been to a ball in, oh, years." She's not joking. "And I ain't goin' anywhere."

I stub out my cigarette in the nearest ashtray as Skeet slides closer on the sofa.

"Now, come here, Mr Sen, I don't believe I was quite finished with you." She lays on the Southern drawl nice and thick.

WHERE DID YOU SLEEP LAST NIGHT?

T he Crown was crowded but not overly so. Wolf and Graeme made their way to a table and ordered a couple of pints: real ale for Graeme, Guinness for Wolf.

Graeme spotted Shirl and Jonathan across the pub, but didn't do anything to draw attention to them. He nodded at Wolf and sipped his beer.

Wolf had seen the pair on their entry, taking a table close enough to them that, should they prove in need of backup, the two would be able to assist very quickly. Jonathan was proving an asset in more ways than Wolf liked to acknowledge sometimes. And, he was starting to grow on him.

Sphincter entered the pub, looked around for a few seconds before going back out, to be promptly followed back in by a very tall, bearded individual in wearing something like robes. The man must have been over two metres tall – *around seven feet in old money,* Wolf realised. And broad shouldered. If anything, he looked awkward and slow. Piercing black eyes stared out from under a prominent brow, assessing the pub's clientele with one searing sweep.

The unlikely pair approached their table. After his first glance, Wolf ignored them. He knew there were three other sets of eyes watching them and a 'not interested' attitude sometimes achieved better results than a seemingly attentive one.

Sphincter sat down and dialled up drinks, presumably for Goliath and himself.

Graeme spoke. "I'd stay away from the cocktails – automixer nearly killed someone in here last week."

Silence. Unusual for Sphincter. Wolf looked up and was surprised to see the kid just sitting there, mouth closed, hands on the table, hair hanging over his scabby face. It was like someone had flipped his switch to 'off'.

The giant was looking at him with intense grey-blue eyes. "So, this is the legendary Pocock Woffe." His voice had the consistency of two millstones grinding together with gravel in-between and more than a hint of Glasgow. He made a point of looking Wolf up and down. "Aren't you a bit small to play grown-up games?"

A pint of *The Crown*'s equivalent of a Weißbier showed up for the giant and a pint of the lager commonly known as 'wife-beater' for Sphincter. Wolf watched the kid for a moment to see if he'd drink it. Sphincter picked up the pint and took a steady drink. There was still something off about him.

Wolf looked back to the client. He'd long ago developed a thick skin about his stature. Besides which, he prided himself on not having an ounce of fat on his frame — it was all muscle, just not overdeveloped. Years of Tai Chi and Tae Kwon Do had given him that, at least.

"Yeah, I'm Woffe. Who are you and what do you want?" he replied, his voice pitched no higher than the murmur coming from the people around them.

The behemoth smiled. Wolf half-expected his teeth to be rotting in his jaw, looking like a row of old tombstones, but they were surprisingly normal. "I am looking for the *De Temporum Signis* you discussed with young Sphincter here."

"Huh. I was under the impression you were planning to sell it to me," Wolf responded. "Why else send me a page from a mutilated *De Umbris Idearum?*"

Still smiling, the client reached into his jacket before handing him another envelope. "This may answer some of your questions."

The envelope contained another sleeve. This one had only a fragment of a page in it. Wolf pressed the sleeve flat on the table to read it through the archival sleeve, reluctant to take it out in this environment.

The sheet was torn from a book, the words tailing off where the fragment looked burned. While his Latin was on the rusty side, there was little doubt in Wolf's mind that this must be genuine. If it was a forgery, someone was going to an awful lot of trouble.

Wolf put the sleeve back on the table. "What am I supposed to do with this?" he questioned. He'd have to get it tested. He slid it back in the envelope.

"I want the rest of that and I believe it's here in London."

Wolf considered the statement. He shook his head; they weren't ready for this. He stood up, flipping the envelope across the table. "Try the British Library; I believe they've got copies of Bruno's works. Otherwise, I think you're SOL." *Shit out of luck.*

"*S' down,* Mr Woffe," the man commanded. For the first time he looked annoyed. "I willna tolerate casual insubordination."

Wolf turned and touched Graeme on the shoulder. "Come on, I'm not sitting here listening to this nutjob."

DE TEMPORVM SIGNIS

De portentis cæli, negam ea ex-
itium nostrum significare. Immo
dicam ea ipsa ingenium Creatoris
Nostri in universitatem rerum
circum nos creando affirmare.

Quis est alius qui creaturas tam di-
versas quam aquilam, piscem,
araneam, serpentem creare
possit?

Eodem modo, cælos tamquam
machinam cælestem concepit,
planetas stellasque in orbitibus
ordinans. Deus Solus fines
operum suorum animadvertit.
Longe a me absit, superbo, affirmare orbem terrarum nostrum
centrum esse universitatis rerum.

Licet proponere cælos exemplum
modo parvum esse magnitudinis
regni Domini Nostri nolis cum
ni

Graeme made to get up too and Wolf saw Shirl and 'the beau' watching them closely.

"Wait."

Wolf looked back at him, not speaking.

"I... umm... Forgive me, Mr Woffe, I forget where I am sometimes..." the giant looked like it was a great effort to apologise.

It still didn't make Wolf want to work for him, so he stood there, waiting.

Looking down at the fragment, the colossus was silent for a moment. "Liz gave me your name, Mr Woffe," he said quietly.

Shocked, Wolf didn't move. He hadn't heard his foster sister's name in over a decade. They'd lost touch, with one thing and another. It was the way things went sometimes. For all Wolf knew she'd been dead for years.

He found his voice. "Why? What's it to do with Liz?" Wolf leaned on the back of the chair for support.

"I'm her son." He smiled at Wolf's expression. "No, not her biological son – she fostered and then adopted me. Then she worked her fingers to the bone to put me through Oxford. I got a first in Ancient Languages before going on to study the arcana of the Middle Ages and the heretics of the Catholic Church."

"What do you want from me?" Wolf asked quietly.

The giant drank a good portion of his Weißbier. "As I said, I want you to find me *De Temporum Signis*. I also find things, Mr Woffe, and I wish to... acquire the manuscript. It may well be the last copy – other than this fragment I found in the Vatican Library and... liberated."

"I can't help you... whoever you are," Wolf responded. "I do *not* deal in 'iffy' artefacts, Mr—"

"Tobias Mayweather, Mr Woffe." The titan rose as well. "At your service."

The sudden humility didn't square with the previous outburst. Wolf almost expected him to bow. Military training? Something had affected him besides his scholarly endeavours.

"Yes, well. I'm not interested in your proposition, Mayweather," Wolf returned. To Graeme, "Come on, let's go."

Mayweather didn't say anything further, merely returning to his seat as they turned to go.

"Liz said you'd refuse to help me," he grated.

Wolf had seen enough in his lifetime to tell when he was being fed a line. So he ignored the behemoth and headed for the door.

31

"Let's get out of here before I do something I regret."

Graeme nodded, glaring back at Mayweather before following Wolf out of the pub. "I know what you mean… definitely."

LIVING THE GOOD LIFE...

A licia listened to the ring tone with increasing frustration. Isn't it odd how some anachronisms continue? What used to be a manual electrical pulse sent along the telephone line to alert an early telephone owner still persisted in the UK's fairly unique double burr, obviously now generated by a computer somewhere.

I'm going to go crazy listening to this, Alicia thought, just as Jaared answered.

"Sen here."

Caught off beat, Alicia nearly didn't answer. "Hello, Jaared? Got a minute? Sorry to bother you out of hours..." she started.

"Don't worry about it – you know I don't sleep much. What's up?"

Alicia took a deep breath. "We've got a body and for some reason the press is saying we've got another serial killer at work. Do you know anything about it?" she asked, hoping it was something simple.

"Sorry?" There was a pause, Jaared no doubt accessing Central to check on the latest. "I see," he said quietly. "No, Alicia, I've no idea where this came from. The other body's across London for some reason, so I don't see how the press could have put it together." Another pause; this one much longer.

"Jaared?" Alicia asked finally. "Are you still there?"

He was another moment answering. "Sorry, Alicia, yes. I've just authorised transfer of the second body to you – it should be on your table first thing in the morning."

"Thanks," she said, not sure she wanted another killer's work to look at. *But it's Humphrey that's the problem...* she thought. "If you could check and see if it was anyone in your office, I'd appreciate it. I've got a meeting with Humphrey first thing in the morning and I'd like to be able to tell him definitively it wasn't my team."

"Already done – it's not your team. Looks like I get to deliver a reprimand and suspension all at the same time." Gap. "And your administrator has been put on suspension for his behaviour tonight – I won't have him badgering my best pathologist. You'll have a replacement in the morning."

"Damn – you've suspended Humphrey? How...?" She stopped, speechless again. "You didn't need to do that, Jaared. Humphrey can be an old woman, but I need him to keep track of the paper clips and handle the Company bureaucracy. All that stuff I don't want to deal with…"

Jaared was silent for another long moment. "Don't worry; you've got a new administrator reporting first thing in the morning. Felix Jerbeau – French Canadian, but put in ten years' work with the Company pathologist in Paris. Speaks perfect English and very efficient."

"But——" Alicia started to protest. *I don't want to train a new administrator.*

Alicia could swear that Jaared was more than a little psychic sometimes. "Don't worry, Alicia, he's very good, highly recommended and a bit of a teddy bear – according to Central. I've known him for years." He paused. The noises coming through suggested he was lighting one of those disgusting cigarettes he insisted on smoking. "And if you don't like him, you can have Humphrey back, okay?"

Smiling, Alicia shook her head. "You're incorrigible, Mr Sen. Absolutely incorrigible."

She could hear his smile in his answer. "That's why you put up with me, isn't it?" he asked.

"I didn't know you had this kind of power!" she returned. "Or I'd have asked you to sort Humphrey out years ago!"

"There's a lot to my role I can do that isn't necessary on a day-to-day basis." He paused to take another pull on his cigarette. "Don't thank me yet; let me know how you get on with Mr Jerbeau. We ought to have dinner sometime soon – my treat."

Alicia's smile grew broader. "That sounds perfect – you going to the Christmas Ball?"

"Yes, of course… I've got a bit of a surprise for you there," he replied.

"Okay," Alicia said. "I'll see you there. Good night, Jaared."

Alicia turned back to the vid and turned the sound up, wondering what Jaared's 'surprise' was. Then she started wondering about her new administrator. She flipped to the Web and did a character search on 'Felix Jerbeau'. For a worrying moment nothing came up, and then the screen filled with a long list of results.

Felix Jerbeau… awarded Légion d'Honneur for service to the French government… via the Company… humanitarian project… worked with Médecins Sans Frontières for two and a half years in Côte d'Ivoire before returning to Paris…

Sighing, Alicia finished reading the various bios and articles on her new administrator. "He sounds too good to be true, Jaared," she murmured to herself.

The two dogs raised their heads at the sound of her voice before putting their heads back on their paws with a mutual sigh.

AND YOU SHOULD SEE WHAT I CAN DO WITH JUST MY LITTLE FINGER...

I light a cigarette, the old post-coital cliché, and watch the smoke drift up to the ceiling for a moment.

Skeet stretches out luxuriously, like a cat. There's something definitely feline about her and I watch with keen interest, seeing everything for the first time. It's probably why she gets on with Dickens so well – I've never known him to jump on anyone's lap but mine, until he met Skeet.

I smile. I understand how he feels. I don't think I did a lot of things before I met her. The smile fades quickly: the memory of her absence returning. Skeet had been gone a long time and I just took her back in, no questions asked.

The pain returns for a moment. I'd thought I'd lost her for good. And she'd just left to 'find herself'.

"Did you?" I murmur into the room, the smoke curling around my fingers.

Her eyes open a fraction before closing again, a hint of breast visible under the top of the duvet. "Did I what?" she asks.

"*Find yourself*. I mean, you said you were looking..." I trail off, suddenly aware of how I sound.

One eye opens and stares at me for a moment before closing again. She nods, her head making a small sweep on the pillow. "Yeah – I was standing right there all the time," she starts. Her hand appears out of the pile of duvet and finds my free hand. "If I hadn't, I wouldn'ta come back – I realised the best place for me was right here." Her eyes open once more. "I'm just lucky you didn't stop looking for me..."

Her eyes glitter and I realise she's about to cry. "Hey, no need for that..." I stub out the cigarette and put that hand along her cheek. "Who else would have a crusty old git like me, eh?" I ask quietly.

I slide down in the duvet and take her in my arms as she weeps. Hardly the cold killer I've known longest, this softer, vulnerable Skeet is still a revelation to me.

Just holding her, I feel her sobs subside after a bit, but she doesn't raise her head to mine. I kiss the crown of her head once more and feel her relax. A moment later she's asleep.

I lie there, thinking. Sleep seems distant for me just now, and it's still fascinating to me to just lie there, staring up at the ceiling. Of course, when I was blind, I never had to see the water stain. It's from that leak a few years back. It's probably time to redecorate.

I sigh and close my eyes. Skeet's warmth is a furnace next to me. Her gentle breathing lulling me into sleep.

TGIF — THANK GRU IT'S FURDAY...

Wolf stood outside the pub for a minute, just breathing. He hadn't thought about Liz for... fifteen years, at least. He hadn't stayed in Glasgow any longer than he'd had to, running from just about everything.

Life in London hadn't exactly been the proverbial bed of roses and the streets sure as hell weren't paved with gold. But he'd survived and made a new life.

Graeme closed his voda, having let Shirl know what happened, and put a hand on his shoulder. "Come on Wolf, let's go home."

Wolf sighed. At least he had the sense to appreciate what he did have. "Okay, old man, I'll get you home so you can catch your programmes."

"A little less of the *old*," Graeme grumbled. "Fancy a few tins and the Man U match?" he asked. "Order a pizza?"

Michael was still on the road for another few days, so why not? "Sure, sounds like a plan," Wolf agreed, brooding on the scene in the pub. He rubbed his eyes and found his key for the Spider. "Let's go."

Wolf sat in Graeme's front room, staring through the large screen on the wall, a beer in his hand. The remains of the large pizza margherita they'd ordered earlier were strewn over the coffee table.

"Yes!" Graeme's sudden outcry pulled Wolf back into the room for a moment. He smothered a belch rising from the greasy pizza before taking another automatic pull at his beer.

He couldn't stop himself seeing those fanatical eyes. Liz's adopted son. *What the hell was he supposed to do with that?*

Liz knew he didn't owe her anything. Was Liz Harkins – he'd heard she had married, but couldn't remember who it was who'd told him or who it was she'd married – someone Mayweather?

The abduction of Liz's little sister, Anne, was the reason he'd gone to London in the first place, running from assault charges.

Wolf had found the little girl locked in a van across Glasgow from New Sighthill, the estate he and Liz grew up on. The girl's abductor had returned by the time Wolf had got the door to his van open and nearly got the drop on Wolf. Only youth and street-fighting reflexes saved him from something quite serious. The paedo, Kenny McMenemy hadn't been so lucky – Wolf nearly killed him.

Liz also knew that McMenemy's suicide a few months later wasn't all it appeared either. If anything, she still owed him.

Why now? Why's she sent Mayweather here? The Latin of that passage still burned in his head, the letters fiery on the page, burning with Bruno's martyrdom.

Graeme turned off the vid. Wolf looked up at the sudden silence. "Is it over?" he asked, startled.

"Yes, and has been for some time," Graeme replied.

"Who won?"

"Barcelona. Again." Graeme just looked at him. "You're still thinking about Mayweather, aren't you?" It wasn't a question.

Wolf took a sip of his warm beer. "No, the text from *De Temporum Signis*, actually." He smiled sheepishly. "You know me, Graeme, I like mysteries."

Graeme snorted, pulling a pair of fresh beers from the small fridge by his chair. "Affects your judgement," he answered. "You know you should walk away from this, regardless of his being Liz's son."

Part of his family for almost twenty-five years now, Graeme and Shirl knew about Liz Harkins and her little sister, Anne. They'd been part of his alibi when the police finally found him in London. Stanley had set it up, and they'd obviously been convincing, as the police went away and didn't come back. Besides, they weren't going to bust their arses for a damn paedo.

Wolf was annoyed. He drank some of the lager, this time releasing the accompanying belch. "I don't owe Liz anythin', you know that," he retorted. "Why would his being her son make any difference?"

Graeme shrugged, popping the top and drinking from his new beer. "It's the past – it has a funny way of getting us to do things we wouldn't normally."

Nodding, Wolf silently agreed, drinking his beer. But it wasn't about Liz or Mayweather. He hadn't lied when he'd told Graeme it was about the book. Something else Stanley was responsible for.

"So what are you going to do?" Graeme asked, although it sounded to Wolf like he already had some idea.

Sipping, Wolf smiled. "I guess I'd better speak to Mayweather again, but on my terms this time. And without Sphincter – the man seems to like having 'followers'."

It was Graeme's turn to smile. "I guess he must be paying Sphincter for his devotion. You know that kid don't believe in nothing that don't get him a fix."

Wolf nodded again, taking out his voda. "Shirl? Thanks for backing us up earlier – I need to see you tomorrow, you around?"

"Sure, Wolf, what's up?" Shirl sounded brighter than she had in a long time and he had to give the beau credit for that, at least.

"I want you to find the mutie we met earlier – Tobias Mayweather is his name." He looked across at Graeme, who nodded approval. "I'll tell you what I know about him in the morning. Come to the shop for ten o'clock?"

"Not a problem, Wolf-boy – see you in the morning." She laughed for a second. "And tell Dad not to wait up."

"That'll help his heart condition," Wolf joked back. "See you tomorrow. Night."

"Night, Wolf."

Graeme looked a bit sour. "Let me guess: she said not to wait up."

"Got it in one."

"It's what she seems to believe passes for 'wit' at the moment," Graeme griped. "Not that I mind her being happy... I'd rather that, than..." He went silent, remembering the turbulent eighteen months they'd just been through.

"Me too, old man, me too," Wolf said quietly. "I'm going to head off." He finished his beer. "Ta for the beer."

"Let me know what you find with the... What did you call him? Mutie?" He smiled. "I'd like to be there for round two."

"Not a problem, Graeme. Who else would I call?" Wolf smiled affectionately. "Talk to you tomorrow."

"Mañana," Graeme replied.

Wolf left the flat quietly and went down to find the Spider.

I DON'T WANT TO BE IN CHARGE ANYMORE

A licia stood in the morgue, clad in her greens. There were two bodies on the slabs now: one was the first victim; the second had just arrived and lay on the black body bag like a newly emerged pupae.

The smell of the cleaning fluids was strong; she must have just missed the cleaning crew with her early morning arrival.

She hadn't slept much, tossing and turning. *Damn Humphrey!* And now she had a new administrator to work with, a change Alicia wasn't sure she needed.

Shaking her head, Alicia stepped closer to the second body. It also had text carved into the shaven chest, the cuts very precise and the skin puckered around them. The incisions were only a centimetre or so deep and very little blood seemed to have leaked from them.

"Probably post-mortem," she muttered. She picked up the camera and snapped a quick shot of the chest. The large vid screen on the wall came alive with the image, and the terminal – part of the Company's Central… *intelligence* for want of a better word – immediately started analysing the text.

It was obvious that the chest had been shaved, as the person or persons involved hadn't removed all the hair, a couple of tell-tale clumps sticking out, mostly away from the centre. Alicia took a few more photos of the body *in situ* before putting the camera down and going to look for help moving the body.

By the time Alicia had roused Dennis, the morgue night porter, to help her, Central had the original text and a translation displayed in a window overlaid on the vid screen.

Tempus omnia rapit, omnia dat

Latin. Translation:

Time takes all and gives all.

Alicia stuck the mic bud to the lapel of her lab jacket. "Any attribution for that quote?" she quizzed Central.

Giordano Bruno. Seventeenth century.

"Comparison to previous quote?" *Not hopeful, but hell, you never know.*

Also Giordano Bruno seventeenth century.

"Thanks," Alicia absentmindedly said to the computer. *Who the hell is Giordano Bruno?* Not her job to know, but she bet Stephen would have. A pang as she missed him. Again.

She turned back to the task in hand and, in a few seconds, she and Dennis had the body arranged on the slab, ready for autopsy.

Dennis, a large but gentle, bearded bear of a man, helped her examine the body all over, looking for any external indicators of what might have killed him. Alicia noted the single puncture wound on the man's back, just below the left shoulder blade, and took more scans. Once they placed the cadaver back on the slab, Dennis ran the right hand of the corpse over the scanner.

Morgue gossip suggested Dennis was a member of a bike gang, which, while generating a slightly amusing image in Alicia's head, was, if true, his own business. What her people did in their own time was not her concern – at least as long as it didn't lead to their turning up on her slab.

ID: Ivan Jenkins. Further details classified. Please await assistance.

That's a new one, Alicia thought. "Damn. Just when I thought we were getting somewhere. Is the ID on the previous victim complete?" Alicia rattled off the case number with practised ease.

ID: Silvio Bartolmeo. Italian. Thirty-six. Lecturer at University College London.

"That's better," Alicia replied. "Lecturer in what?"

Religious studies – primarily spiritualism in the early twentieth century and history of the Catholic Church. Primary area of interest, Holy Office, also known as 'The Inquisition'.

"That seems a mouthful – wonder what he shortened it to at parties?" Alicia mused.

Dennis just shrugged. He never said much.

Glowering at the words on the screen, Alicia turned back to the corpse to start her autopsy. It always bothered her, having to disturb evidence. "We have scans for all that sort of thing," she muttered to herself reassuringly as she placed the scalpel in the depression just below the shoulder joint and began her incision.

With the subject's chest folded back, Alicia sliced through the sternum with a sternal saw, the whine biting into her skull. She spread the ribcage apart gently, then removing the individual organs for weights and measures. She handed the items to Dennis, who put them in sample containers labelled with the victim's name and case number.

There was nothing out of the ordinary to note until she reached the heart and the hole punched in from the back. Removing the heart from the open ribcage, they could see the opening. "Note, mark on the fourth anterior left rib suggesting glancing blow before continuing to the heart." She held the heart up for scanning before she dissected it in a metal tray. "Heart received a four centimetre incursion in the left ventricle. Death would have been practically instantaneous. Colour of tissue and wound suggests it was ante-mortem and most likely cause of death." Looking at it closer, Alicia noticed something. "Cross-section of intrusion site suggests a triangular cross-section of whatever implement was used. Note to lab: Cast incursion area immediately for weapon comparison."

Alicia handed the heart to Dennis and he packed it away, the last of the organs to be examined. Although probably superfluous, Alicia examined the skull again, feeling it first. There was a soft area that would probably bear more examination. "Soft spot on right parietal bone, posterior, further examination necessary."

She sliced around the temples before pulling the skin back. Dennis handed her the Stryker and a facemask. Alicia started up the saw with an insectile whine, which changed into a teeth-numbing buzz as it connected with the fabric of the skull. Twenty seconds later, the top of the man's skull was disconnected. Dennis handed her a tray, in which Alicia reverently placed the section of bone before examining the brain. "Brain appears undamaged *in situ*, but will remove for further exam."

Alicia carefully cut through the membrane around the brain, through the stem and slid the organ from the skull with a slight sucking sound. "Brain appears normal..." She placed it on the scale. "Weight within parameters... There's a dark discolouration at site of previously mentioned soft spot. Hmm... possible hematoma from impact with a slightly rounded object. Damage not sufficient for death, but could have immobilised the victim prior to sharp object insertion into heart muscle."

Dennis handed her another specimen tray for the brain and Alicia replaced the skull and, with a few deft stitches, reattached the scalp. She removed the chest crank and closed the flaps over the chest with her usual stitch pattern.

As she was finishing, there was a voice in the doorway. "Morning, Alicia."

She turned to find Jaared standing there, with a tall black man behind him. The other gentleman wasn't any taller than Jaared's six foot, three inches, but he was definitely broader of shoulder.

"Hello, Jaared, who's your friend?" She was still getting used to the intense blue-grey stare he greeted her with after all those years of hiding behind a pair of mirrored glasses.

Jaared gestured the man forward. "May I present Felix Jerbeau, your new administrator?"

Alicia stripped off her gloves and held out her hand. "Alicia Sampson, pleased to meet you," Alicia said formally.

"Call me *Felix*," the big man rumbled, pronouncing it with a hint of French accent. "Jaared has told me a lot about you, Alicia, and I have to say I'm looking forward to working with you." The smile accompanying the words was warm and gracious, revealing very white teeth.

"You have the advantage of me... Felix," Alicia replied with a glance at Jaared.

Jaared was smiling broadly. "I'm pretty sure you're going to get along very well," he said.

When he smiled, it was hard not to believe everything he said.

DON'T PRESS THE EJECT!

"**I**'m pretty sure you're going to get along very well," I say, more than aware of the annoyance and anger Alicia is feeling. I do my best to beam comforting thoughts at her. Everything I know about Felix suggests they will be fine – they just have to work that out.

"Ready to discuss the two cases yet?" I ask. "I thought it might be a good chance for Felix to see how you work and maybe how he can help you do your job."

She's still glaring daggers at me, but my armour holds. "Give me a second to tidy up, Jaared. Why don't you take Felix to my office and make sure Sue provides some hot drinks?"

I smile back again. "Fine, we'll see you there." I turn back to the door, gesturing Felix to proceed me back down the corridor to the office area.

Alicia's dark-haired, elfin secretary looks up as we approach and smiles at me. "Hello Commander, how are you?" she asks.

"Very well, thanks Sue." I gesture at Felix. "Meet your new administrator, Felix Jerbeau." I gesture to Sue. "Sue Franklin, who runs the place." I smile to see her dimple at the compliment. She stands up and comes around the desk to shake his hand.

"Pleased to meet you, Sue," Felix responds. "Call me Felix – everyone does." He grips her hand firmly.

"Alicia's going to be along in a second," I say to Sue. "We're going to wait in her office."

Sue gestures to us to go on through. "Coffee? Tea?"

We both agree to coffee and enter Alicia's demesne.

I met Felix over a decade ago, but I can't say I know him – beyond what Central has told me about his career and abilities. In this case, I'm hoping Central is actually helping Alicia out, because the last thing I want to do is lumber her with someone more problematical than Humphrey.

"Why'd you suggest me for this post, Jaared?" Felix asks quietly after Sue brings our coffees. "I could have spent another two years in Public Services sorting out the mess they have over there."

I think for a moment, the part of me that plays politics (badly) coming to the fore and deciding on the truth. "This department's struggled since the big C took them over – the previous administrator was a civil servant and we know they don't always make the adjustment to private sector work. At best, I'd call him a… stumbling block." I look at his dark, serious face. "You were the best choice for the job, Felix. And as I said, I think you and Alicia will get along just fine."

He doesn't stop glowering for a second before smiling wryly. "I think my husband might like this job more than he did the last."

"Why's that?" I ask.

"Hervé loves all that forensic stuff on the vids and I can almost guarantee that he'll think smelling of dead bodies will be an improvement on smelling of garbage!" There's a twinkle in his eye.

I laugh. "You may have a point."

Alicia enters the room. "What's so funny?" she asks, somewhat crossly, throwing herself down into her chair.

I let Felix answer. "We were just discussing risks of the job, Alicia," he replies. "So, what are you working on now?"

Alicia proceeds to fill him in on the John Tyler case and the two bodies on the slabs in the exam rooms and a handful of other cases, giving him an overview at the same time of the other activities of her department.

When she's done, he nods. "Now, the first question I have for you is: What do you need from me?"

Slightly taken aback, Alicia leans back. She's glad of the moment to think as Sue brings in a coffee for her; it's in a large mug, with 'Pathologists Do It In The Morgue' printed near the handle. She doesn't look at us for a minute and I work hard at blending in with the scenery – I'm only here in a facilitator's role; they are the ones who have to work together.

When she finally speaks, she says something I'm not expecting.

"You know, in all the years we worked together, I don't think Humphrey ever asked me that question. I guess it says a lot about our relationship, doesn't it?" She smiles ruefully. "I guess, to answer your question, Felix, I need you to help me do what I do best – helping people find out what caused the death of their mother, brother, friend."

Felix nods. "I think I can do that. Give me a few hours to get to grips with the systems here and I'll see if there's any way we can make your life easier – at least from a paperwork and budgets point of view."

"Thanks. And Felix," she continues, looking him in the eye. "If Jaared says you're the best man for the job, he's probably right. I won't get involved in your work as long as you don't tell me how to do mine. Deal?"

Nodding again, Felix leans forward over the desk, offering his big hand. "You've got a deal," he says, shaking her more diminutive one. "I guess I'd better get upstairs and see what the damage is." He stands, as do I, and heads for the door. He stops before he gets there. "Oh, I'm bringing over a few members of my team, as well: Julia, my manager who's very good at the numbers and Peter, who's very good with the PR side of things. If you don't mind..." He stops and swallows. "I'd like him to take over any contact with the press so you can get on with your work."

Alicia breaks into a big grin. "You mean it? I don't have to talk to the vultures anymore? Hooray!"

Smiling back, Felix turns to go again. "I thought you'd like that," he says over his shoulder.

I sit back down again, fairly sure Alicia hasn't finished with me yet. Oh yes, she's already glaring at me, again. It's marvellous, this vision thing. I pick up my coffee and let her choose her own time.

"I should be furious," she says quietly. "Of all the high-handed, imperious, breathtakingly macho things to do..."

She runs down and I wait for her to start again.

"But I think I'll just say 'thank you'," Alicia finishes, picking up her coffee cup again.

I nod. "You're welcome," I reply.

The glare comes back. "You're not allowed to be smug!" she retorts.

I hold up my hands, my serious face on. "Not smug."

The glare softening, she has to ask, "How'd you do it, anyway?"

I smile. "There are some advantages to being 'Commander Sen'. And having Central agree we had a problem with Humphrey didn't hurt."

Her answering smile fades at the mention of Humphrey. "He's going to be so angry with me..."

"What did *you* do? *I'm* the one that replaced him!" Central pings me and I put on my consoling face. "Apparently he's accepted early retirement to spend more time with his grandchildren in Spain. So no," I reach forward and take her hand, "he's not going to be angry with you."

There, the smile's back. "Now, for the clearance code, just tell it 'Cygnus Alpha 23' and you should have access to anything you need to know. Just you. No sharing the info with Jack or Dennis or Sue," I say, waving my hand vaguely at the rest of the morgue. "I'm going to look at the case details when you've finished and your new PR person Peter will be dealing with any future queries. Okay?"

Alicia nods. "I'll go and finish up. You should have my report by lunchtime."

I stand up again. "Want to meet for lunch?" I ask, thinking it's been a while.

"Fine. See you at the usual place," Alicia replies, her attention already on her screen.

"Fine." I step out the door and head for my own office.

DON'T ASK ME, I DON'T WORK HERE

Wolf sat at the counter after opening up, brooding over the giant's words and the text of *De Temporum Signis*.

True to her word, Shirl turned up promptly at ten, bearing coffee.

"Hey stud, how's it going?" she greeted him, a big grin on her face, which he couldn't help but return. She leaned over and kissed him on the cheek, surprising him. They were close, but public displays of affection were rare.

"I'm surprised you didn't ask me *how it's hanging*," Wolf responded. "To which I usually reply, 'to the left'."

Shirl made a moue of distaste. "Too much information, big boy." She pulled up the other stool to the counter and tossed her dark hair over her shoulder. Wolf had noticed she was growing it out – it used to always be in a boyish bob.

A few things had changed since she'd met Jonathan; her utilitarian clothing was another – swapped for some apparel much more colourful and stylish and... dare he think it... *feminine*.

"Triple Shot, Skinny Toffee Nut Latte. hold the cream." When she plunked herself down on the stool, she pushed a cup of coffee across to him, pulled out her voda and dropped the large bag on the floor with a loud clunk. *What the hell does she have in there?* Thinking about arsenals, Wolf shook his head; he didn't really want to know. Plausible deniability and all that.

"So, what's up?" Shirl asked, emerald green eyes set in her heart-shaped face on a level with his own.

Wolf smiled and took a sip of coffee, almost burning his tongue. He organised his thoughts. "I want to know more about Mayweather. You know the stuff: *who is he, where's he from, what's his motivation, has he got money*. That sort of thing."

"I thought you knew his Mum," she interjected.

The Black grapevine had obviously been working. Not that he minded; Graeme and Shirl were close. Wolf nodded. "So he says. I've not heard from Liz in a long time, so I've no idea. She was barely fifteen when I left Glasgow."

Shirl made a couple of notes on her voda. "Do you want me to talk to her?"

Wolf thought about this for a moment. He wasn't sure he wanted to go back to that part of his life. "I don't know. If you think it could lead to something useful, do what you think is best."

Smiling at him, Shirl punched him in the arm. "Don't worry, it's not like he's yours or anything."

"Ha ha."

Shirl looked back at her voda. "Right, usual background stuff – want anything special?"

Specials could be costly, but they'd both got a lot more cautious after a previous deal had led to Shirl disappearing for two days. "Yes," Wolf decided. "Give me a Number Three, a Number Five and a Number Eight."

"Cool."

They'd developed their own codes to save time. Besides which, who knew who was listening at any particular time?

A Number Three was a criminal records check through normal Company channels; a Number Five was a reputation check, useful when someone claimed qualifications, previous posts and so forth; and the Number Eight was a much more in-depth check of someone's background, the sort of thing authorities put in files on people they're watching.

"Anything else?" Shirl asked brightly. "You know, a fresh sandwich, more coffee, pick up your dry cleaning…"

Wolf glared at her. "No, that's all, thanks."

"Normal rates?" she asked, an innocent look on her pixie-like face.

"Cheeky mare. You know it is," he retorted. "Now go, before I reconsider."

"Yes master, I hear and obey," she replied, slipping off the stool and retrieving the bag from the floor.

This last line nearly caused Wolf to choke on his coffee. "Just go!" he gasped.

Shirl waggled a hand at him and scooted across the store and out the door. "Bye Wolfie," she called as it closed behind her. She knew how much he hated that nickname. So of course, she used it.

Janey came in moments later. "'Wolfie', huh? Shirl's working at annoying you today," she commented.

Wolf glared. "Yes, she's just too damn happy right now." He relented. "Which is also good."

Nodding, Janey deposited her bag in the office behind Wolf and returned to the counter. "Anything I need to know about, boss?" More code: Janey asking if there was any trouble she needed to be aware of.

"Only my foster sister's son trying to get us to steal a sixteenth-century manuscript – other than that, no, nothing," Wolf reported dutifully. He, Janey, and the rest of his adopted family had decided on a strict policy of no secrets. And it worked for them.

"I guess you're not talking about Shirl," Janey replied. In comparison to Shirl, Janey was tiny, blonde and wore those old-fashioned glasses, which was her preference to having her eyes replaced. She was squeamish about that sort of thing.

"No. Liz Harkins was with me in care when we were about thirteen. I found her sister when she went missing." Wolf left it at the clean version. 'No secrets' didn't always stretch to ancient history.

Janey nodded. "Had you met this son before?"

Wolf shook his head. "Nope. Haven't seen Liz since I came to London. I've never been back to Glasgow, you know that."

"I know, but people *do* come to London. And, you know, there's phones and email – they've been around for a long time now."

"Let's just say we weren't that close," Wolf growled.

He had put his childhood as an orphan in the Glasgow care system firmly behind him when he left the city of his birth. The past wasn't exactly rosy for Wolf; he rarely thought of anything before he arrived in London and met Stanley Hopkins.

His father, mentor, and best friend, Stanley had left a large hole in Wolf's life when he went quietly in his sleep, victim of a particularly painful and slow-acting cancer even the latest technology could not eradicate.

It had been Stanley who had taught him everything he could about books, art and antiquities before that bitch of a cancer had flicked the off switch.

Janey had done her usual and left him to his thoughts while she went over some new stock that had come in from one of the runners. Full title Dr Janey Small, she seemed happy to work for Wolf, publishing papers on obscure historical treatises she found at the British Library in her spare time. Wolf didn't know what he'd do without her.

They both looked up as the bell on the door dinged. Wolf just had time to register the tall blonde dancer before he was caught up in a crushing embrace.

When he could breathe again, he took a deep breath and looked into the blonde's blue eyes. "Hello Michael, guess you're back."

Michael grinned, the twinkle Wolf loved in his eyes. "You betcha, loverboy."

I DON'T MAKE HOUSE CALLS — I'M NOT THAT KIND OF DOCTOR

A licia sat in her office staring at the ceiling. Felix was already making a difference and it hadn't been twenty-four hours since he'd been assigned to her. For what seemed like the thousandth time that day, Alicia wondered why she'd put up with Humphrey for so long. *Ennui? Inertia? Better the devil you know?*

Sighing, Alicia realised it was probably all the above. Thankfully, she'd not heard from Humphrey — she didn't exactly know how to speak to him at the moment.

Lunch with Jaared had been refreshingly normal, just like old times.

"So how are you, Alicia?" Jaared had asked after she'd given him a quick update on the cases. He'd already have access to the files via Central.

"Fine, Jaared," Alicia laughed shortly. "You take me to lunch just to see how I am?"

Jaared smiled. It was disconcerting seeing his grey eyes after all the years of those mirrored glasses he used to wear. "No, but I do worry about you," he replied.

Alicia waved him away and the pain that comment caused with it. "Don't worry about me, Jaared, you've got a lot more on your plate than you used to. After today, I start to realise how much..." She sighed, looking up into those eyes. "I really *am* fine, Jaared."

He nodded, picking at the falafel on his plate. He'd suggested the place, having remembered where it was. "I didn't sort Humphrey out *just for you*," he started. "Although, helping you was a useful side effect. There's more changes coming, Alicia, but I can't say more just now." He chewed falafel for a moment before continuing. "And you're the best damn Medical Examiner I've ever met."

Alicia actually blushed. "Flatterer," she answered.

Jaared shook his head. "It's true — I don't say things like that to just anyone."

Covering her embarrassment by taking a drink of her Coke, Alicia nearly inhaled it. *Choking is not an attractive look*, she thought as she coughed into a serviette. When she'd finished spluttering she wiped her eyes and looked across at him. Damn him for looking even better than he had before.

"So I'll return the question," she said finally. "How are *you?*"

Jaared looked down at the tablecloth for a moment, tracing a pattern only he could see. "Skeet's back," he said softly.

"Oh great," Alicia said out loud, although she could have sworn.

He looked up. "I know you think she was flaky for taking off like that – and I don't disagree it was bad timing. But she's much more centred for it," he tried to explain.

"Well, if she makes you happy, that's all that matters," Alicia responded, but couldn't help putting in her two pennies' worth. "I just hope she doesn't abandon you like last time."

Jaared looked a little disconcerted for a moment. "I don't think she will – I'm seeing a whole new side of her…"

"Well, thanks for lunch," Alicia said abruptly, picking up her bag, suddenly wanting to escape. "Got to go – bodies piling up down there, you know."

"Al—no problem. We'll do something soon," he finished, standing up. He kissed her on the cheek. "You're looking well," he tried.

"Thanks. See you later." Alicia practically fled the scene.

"Good night, boss," Sue called from the door, breaking her reverie. "Don't stay all night."

"I won't – good night, Sue," Alicia responded. She'd need to get home to the dogs soon anyway. Arranging the paperwork on her desk into a neat pile, she opened her top drawer, slid the stack into it and thumbed it locked. Clear desk policy, you know, *leave nothing out for prying eyes.*

Alicia's voda went as she was putting on her coat. She nearly ignored it until she saw it was Kate's number flashing up. "Hi Kate, what's up?"

"I'm taking you shopping tomorrow, that's what. Long lunch. Bond Street. There's a particular shop there I know would suit you down to the ground."

Making a look of discontent, Alicia managed to keep her tone neutral. "Sorry, I've got a lot on at the minute, Kate – maybe next week?"

"Uh-uh-uh. A little bird tells me you have a formal on the fifth, just three days away, right?" Alicia can tell what's coming next. "Have you even thought about what you're going to wear?"

"I'm sure I've got something—" Alicia started. She could feel her resolve crumbling.

"No way – you are not wearing that mumsy lavender number you wore to Jane and Mary's wedding. That is so not you!" There was a blare of horns, followed by swearing; Kate was obviously driving and remonstrating at the same time. Multi-tasking being easier for women is such a lie.

Alicia smiled and changed her mind. It would be good to see Kate. "Okay, Kate. Here's the deal: You concentrate on driving and not getting yourself killed and I'll see you at thirteen hundred hours tomorrow. Oh, and you're buying."

Kate swore at something, probably another driver and laughed. "Okay – deal! See you sweet thing!" The line disconnected.

"Night." Alicia said to no one, before dropping the hand-held into her bag and finishing putting her coat on. How did she let herself get talked into these things?

Her trip home was uneventful, public transport being relatively glitch-free for once. The two heavy forms waiting inside the door were dancing around in anticipation, wagging their whole backsides in greeting. Alicia always laughed as their lack of tails didn't seem to stop them showing their excitement.

Alicia wasn't generally one for docking tails, but having been assaulted by a Staffy's undocked tail before, it was probably a good idea they'd been done before she and Stephen had found them at the rescue centre.

Pulling her coat off again, she spoke all the nonsense to the dogs they normally expected. Alicia talked to them a lot more since Stephen had died.

She picked up the post from the hall table and followed the two bouncy forms into the large kitchen. Having dropped the mail on the counter, she groped under it to open the bin with their biscuits in it and remove a large scoop. The two spotless bowls in the corner were soon occupied by crunching sounds and the hunched forms of two happy dogs.

Alicia turned back to the post: a bill, a renewal notice for her subscription to *Morgue Monthly*, another bill... Her hand stopped as she picked up a letter with a hand-written address on it.

It couldn't be. She brought the letter closer to her eyes. It certainly looked like Stephen's handwriting. But how could it be? He'd been dead for two years.

I LIKE MY STEAK RARE; NO, REALLY RARE

I sit at my desk a little longer, not entirely sure why I'm putting off going home.

My skullphone goes. "Hey Skeet, how are you doing?" I ask. *How are you doing? Sheesh.*

"Hey old man, I'm fine. Fancy a pint in *The George?*" she replies.

I can hear pub sounds in the background and for once it sounds inviting. A lot of things sound more inviting now she's back.

"Absolutely. Will be there in twenty minutes," I guess. "Make mine a Guinness."

She laughs. "Already ordered – should be poured by the time you get here."

My driver gets me there in ten. I hadn't allowed for a forces-trained driver weaving through traffic with judicious use of the lights and siren. I don't normally approve of that sort of behaviour, knowing what the public already think of Patrol officers and their driving, but hey, I don't often get driven to dates with beautiful women. And I'd rather not keep her waiting.

"Thanks Ellison," I say as she slides to a halt outside *The George*. "I won't need you any more tonight – have a good night."

"Thank you, sir. Enjoy your evening."

I'll never get used to being 'Sirred'. I was never an officer, always a squaddie. Well I guess those days are behind me.

I spot Skeet straight away. Sitting in the window, a pint in her hand, the spiky blonde hair as much of an attention-grabber as anything else. She spots me through the window and salutes me with the pint.

I smile and step to the door, nearly getting it in the face as a burly black man staggers out, almost tripping down the step. He catches himself before he lands in the gutter. The door to the pub swings shut on the cold.

"Commander... Sen!" he stutters. "How you doin'?"

"Great Jubal, just fine." I look him up and down, noticing the stains on his black jeans. "Been here all day?"

"You betcha ass, Commander." He starts to giggle. "Here... here's a question for you, *Commander*... what is it with the brothers and fried chicken?"

I look at him blankly. "Sorry Jubal, I don't understand."

He waves my protest away, a frown furrowing his brow as he concentrates. "Of course you do – why is it black people eat so much damn fried chicken?"

I shrug. "No idea, Jubal. Why *do* they eat so much fried chicken?"

It was Jubal's turn to shrug. "I don't know... was hopin' you could splain it to me. I mean," and he gestured wildly for emphasis, nearly overbalancing in the process, "I likes fried chicken as much as the next guy, but all t'other black people seem... *obsessed* wit' it." He leans closer, unsteadily, and whispers, "Do you tink it's genetic?"

I shake my head. I don't need diversity training to know better than to go there. "No idea, Jubal." I raise my hands. "Now, if you'll excuse me, I'm keeping a young lady waiting."

A big grin pops onto his face and he grabs my hand in one of his vice-like paws. "That'll be Miss Skeet, won't it?" He laughs, letting go of my hand. "Ya'll have a good evenin', *Commander*."

I've never worked out why he places so much emphasis on my title. Maybe he was military in a former life. I could look him up, but I try not to do that to people I know. "You too, Jubal. Get home safe."

"Oh, I ain't goin' home, just yet." He laughs again. "Maybe I'll go get m'sel' some *fried chicken*!" Cackling to himself, he weaves off down the street.

I shake my head again and half-chuckle before pulling the door open and stepping into the warmth.

A WOLF IN SHEEP'S CLOTHING? YOU HAVE TO ASK WHAT'S IN IT FOR THE SHEEP

Wolf and Michael left the shop a little early. Janey was more than capable of closing up. Besides, their security company sent someone around at closing time to ensure everything was secure. There was no such thing as *too* paranoid now.

"What do you fancy doing tonight?" Wolf asked as they stepped outside. The Spider was in a garage around the corner, but it could stay there until tomorrow if they decided to stay out.

Michael leered at him, one long hand on the case he was pulling behind him. "Why you, of course, dahhlliiing," he drawled. "Oh, did you mean something else?" he asked innocently.

Wolf smiled and wrapped one arm around Michael's waist. "Ha ha. You've obviously been hanging out with the fun crowd on tour. Seriously. Fancy that Thai place near home or getting take-out and a bottle of wine?"

"Trying to get me drunk already. I say, Mr Wolf, you are cheeky!"

Groaning, Wolf realised he wasn't going to get any sense out of his other half. "Frankie Howerd vids? Really?"

Michael nodded vigorously. "Yes, they were on all the time on the bus — our manager's a *big* fan. And I do mean *big*," he whispered in a stage whisper behind his hand.

"Great." He grabbed Michael's case and set off towards the Spider. No sense taking his comic genius out in public. Takeaway and a bottle of wine it was. "C'mon *Lurcio,* we're going home," Wolf said, showing he had some idea of Howerd's work. Everyone's seen *Up Pompeii,* right?

Keeping up a running monologue all the way to the car, Michael exhibited all the signs of that post-tour hyperactivity Wolf was familiar with. There was no way to avoid it; Wolf would just have to ride it out and hope a glass of wine would slow him down.

"Get in, Michael, I'll put your case in the boot," Wolf instructed, before wrestling the recalcitrant case into the tight boot space of the Spider. He knew it would go in eventually — he'd put it in there when he'd taken Michael to meet the bus before the tour started. He struggled for a few more minutes before the case just seemed to pop into place.

Wolf breathed a sigh of relief and turned around to find Tobias Mayweather standing behind him.

Instantly alert, Wolf realised he was virtually pinned against the boot of the Alpha. He sidled to the side until he was free of the car. "What do you want, Mayweather?" he asked brusquely. "It's not nice to sneak up on people."

Mayweather smiled, the effect more cadaverous than pleasant. "I'm sorry, I just wondered if you'd considered my... proposition," he said, the smile never leaving his face. His Glasgow accent made it *pr'poh-zi-shun*.

"I told you 'no' yesterday – didn't you hear me?" Wolf demanded.

Nodding, Mayweather seemed unperturbed by this. *Was he on some kind of medication?* Wolf wasn't in the mood to deal with him.

"Yes, I heard you. I also know you're seeking more information about me and what I know," the tall man answered.

Wolf realised he wasn't just tall; the man's hands were large and he seemed much bigger than the average tall person. He shook his head; that was irrelevant. He'd had enough for the day. "Good for you. I always want to know about people that might be a threat to me and my people." Wolf looked him up and down. "And so far, all I see is threat."

He turned and opened the door of the car and got in. Michael started talking as soon as he was seated, but Wolf tuned him out, putting the key in the old-fashioned ignition and putting the car in gear. A shadow moved along his side of the car and he could see Mayweather's waist. There was a crash as a massive fist hit the bonnet of the car directly in front of Wolf.

Wolf didn't wait around to see more. He accelerated out of the space, narrowly missing an oncoming electric Mini which blared its pathetic horn at him in protest, weaved past them and sped down the ramp to the exit.

"What the hell was all that about?" Michael demanded.

Checking the rear-view mirror, Wolf didn't answer him for a moment. "Potential client. I'm pretty sure I don't want to work for him." There was a tight grin on his face.

Michael looked from him to the new dent in the Spider's paintwork. "No, I can see he's got some issues," he said dryly.

Wolf glanced over at him, then back to the road. "He's also my foster sister's son."

"Aw shit." Michael knew what that meant.

Wolf looked at him again, shaking his head. "I don't owe her anything – that debt was paid a long time ago."

"Yeah, yeah," Michael said, waving a hand. "You forgetting I know what you're like with 'family'?"

Wolf grinned again. "I swear – I want nothing to do with that Mutant," he said firmly.

"Methinks the lady doth protest too much," Michael murmured, looking out the window into pre-Christmas London.

He's probably right, Wolf thought to himself. Still, he'd wait and see what Shirl found before he did anything else. "So, Pad Thai or Green Chicken Curry?" he asked, trying to change the subject.

LETTERS FROM THE DEAD ARE NOT EASY TO READ

A licia sat on the kitchen chair, a large glass of red wine in front of her and a letter that appeared to be from her dead fiancé on the table next to it.

Bedraggled was probably the best way to describe it. It looked like it had multiple stamps on it from more than one country and various notations in different hands, but nothing in a language she could read beyond her own name and the address of the house with 'England' as a last line underscored three times. The stamps were beautiful riots of colour, depicting small foreign vistas in a postage-stamp-sized-space.

Alicia sighed and wiped the hint of moisture from the corners of her eyes. She wasn't normally the crying sort, but Stephen had been ripped from her life so suddenly and after they had made plans…

"Stop it Al, you're a big girl now and you don't need to wallow," she told herself. "It's just a letter that got mislaid in the post." *Yeah, from Stephen*, the voice continued in her head.

Taking a large gulp of wine, Alicia picked up the envelope again and used the paper knife from the drawer to slice it open. Inside were two folded pages of fine paper, possibly rice paper, judging by the translucent quality they had. Carefully she withdrew the pages and unfolded them.

Tuesday, 12ᵗʰ of May

My darling Al,

I'm sorry I've resorted to snail mail for this — god knows if you'll even get it, as I've no idea how reliable the Vietnamese postal service is!

And it's partly because I found this beautiful paper and thought you would enjoy receiving something archaic in the post!

It's been a difficult dig, with lots of bureaucracy, paperwork and bribes involved. I feel less like an anthro-historian and more like a secretary some days. It's rather soul-destroying when I'd just rather be digging up funerary urns, but hey, I guess that's my job.

I've had a lot of time to think, all in all, and a lot of that thinking has been about you and wishing I wasn't half a world away right this minute. I miss the feel of your skin, the scent of your hair, that sparkle in your eyes when you're determined to wind me up — in short, I just wanted to say again how much I love you.

You mean the world to me, Al, and I think we should do that wedding thing when I get back. That is, of course, if you feel the same. No shotgun weddings around these here parts!

Oh, and if you get the chance, ask that mate of yours — Jaared Sen, you know who I mean — what one of the first things he said to me was.

But anyway, I've got another four reports to write and accompanying applications, so I'd best get on with things. Just know I'm thinking of you and hope to be back in London in the next couple of weeks.

Will you marry me?

All my love,

Stephen

Alicia put the paper down and let the tears flow. Damn the man. Almost two years on and he visits from the grave to ruin her fragile peace and make her think of things she'd tried to forget for all the pain they cause.

His death had been sudden and almost completely unexplained — a random attack on a professor at King's College, Cambridge. He'd died a short day and a half later from his injuries, with her at his side.

She hadn't managed to keep him from going. And that was what upset her the most.

TURN OUT THE LIGHTS, THE PARTY'S OVER...

S keet holds up my pint as I enter the pub and walk towards her table. "Hey, sailor, you new in town?"

I pull off my coat and pull out the chair next to hers before falling into it. Seems like a long day, all in all. "I don't recall ever being a sailor," I reply, taking the Guinness and raising it to my lips. Ah, nectar. "I'm not that fond of water."

Skeet leans over, leering at me. "But you *are* good at a lot of things, my dear Commander Sen." The avarice in her eyes is plain to see, and I laugh.

"Do you have plans for me tonight?" I ask in good humour, taking another sip of my stout.

"As your good friend Jubal would say, 'You betcha ass'!" She raises her glass in a mocking toast.

I raise mine in response. "I hope it's not just my ass you're thinking about," I murmur with what I hope is a wry smile.

"Hah! Nope," she answers. "I'm thinking about a lot more than that!"

"God, I've missed this."

"Me too," she replies and I startle, not realising I'd made the last comment out loud.

I take her free hand across the table. "While you've been gone, it's been pretty shit." I decide to be honest.

Skeet looks down at the table. "I know, Jaared... and I'm sorry," she says in a voice just above a whisper.

I shake my head. "I wasn't looking for an apology, Skeet – I'm big and ugly enough to know shit happens. I just wanted you to know how much I missed you." I look down at our entwined hands. "That's all. No guilt. No blame. I'm just glad you're back." I look up into her amazingly green eyes and realise I could lose myself in their depths.

Staring at me with her mouth slightly open, Skeet seems to be slightly in shock. "Wow, Commander... that's some speech. You been plannin' that one all day?"

Shrugging, I don't answer. No, I hadn't planned it, it just happened to come out that way. I take a drink of my pint, the black stuff washing the dryness from my throat. What was she going to say now?

Skeet leans in to me and rests her head on my shoulder. "What do you fancy doin' now, big boy?"

I put my pint down and smile slightly, remembering other nights. "Oh... we could go catch late night at the Portrait Gallery. Or there's always the kick-boxing in Little Bangkok. Or we could catch a drag show at *Madame Jojo's*..."

I stop because Skeet has placed her mouth over mine and is kissing me. "Shut up," she instructs, pulling away slightly before resuming her ministrations.

She pulls back just far enough to see my eyes and spends long seconds staring into them. "I like 'em," she announces finally.

"What? My new eyes?" I ask, distracted.

A nod. "Yep. Not how I pictured them, but it's definitely an improvement on the whol' mess of scar tissue." She leans back further. "In fact, I'd say you're now a very handsome man."

I laugh, a short, dry laugh, almost under my breath. "And I never dreamed I'd actually *see* you, Skeet," I say quietly. "I think I'd given up on ever seeing again." I look down at the tabletop.

Her hand tightens on mine. "Well, you do now, so that's a good thing, ain't it?" To the point, that's my Skeet.

I look back up at her, those eyes mere inches from mine. "Absolutely. I'm glad I can see you now," I reply, and can see by her expression that it's the right thing to say.

Skeet leans closer again. "Now, what say you take me home?" she says quietly. "That way you can stop undressing me with your eyes and..."

I'm distracted as my HUD flips into view, a quick status report from Central on the death of John Tyler. *Damn, just when it was getting interesting.* "Sorry Kid, gimme a minute," I say distractedly, disengaging her hand and standing up from the table. It's only a couple of steps to the door. Not a call I want to take in a crowded pub.

It's Timson. "What have you got?" I ask, although I think I can guess from the report I'm getting on my HUD.

"As you can probably see, death was an overdose of heroin, but only puncture wound was in the back of the neck — as you said, an unusual spot for a junkie to stick himself," he starts.

Nice, butter me up, youngster. I shake my head. "Verdict?" *I can see it on-screen, but it's protocol.*

"I—I think we should classify it a murder, sir," he stutters. Probably his first one.

I nod. "Very good Timson. Keep me apprised."

"Uh… Don't you want to be involved, sir?" he asks plaintively.

"I *am* involved, Timson, but you are the lead Contractor on this until I say otherwise. Understood?"

"Understood, sir!" I can practically hear the salute.

Shaking my head, I return to Skeet. "Sorry, got a newbie that needs his hand holding."

Skeet smiles, her green eyes flashing. "I'd say it's a very long time since you were a 'newbie'. Am I right?"

I smile back. *Damn those eyes!* "I've no idea how long it actually has been, to be honest," I answer, trying vainly to remember. "And I suppose it would require me working out which part of my life consisted of being the 'newbie'."

Taking a drink, I try to remember my long and busy life. It was probably the first time I joined the army; I've fought in a few wars over the years. I also moved around a lot, and it feels like I've seen most of the world. Well, the bits I *could* see until my accident.

"Which war do you want me to confess to being involved in?" I ask, half-teasing and not at all sure I want to hear the answer.

"First World War?" she teases.

I nod, drinking more Guinness. "Yes, I was there for a time."

The shock on her face is genuine and I realise I've probably gone too far.

"You're serious…" she almost whispers.

"You know how old I am; it's now a matter of public record, I suppose." I'm trying to be nonchalant, but failing, of course.

"Yes, but…" She doesn't finish. "Really?"

Putting down my pint, I take her hand across the table and stare into those gorgeous eyes. "Really." Not sure if it's wise, I continue. "You'll find my first new name, John Spencer, on the Tyne Cot Memorial near Passchendaele in Belgium amongst the missing, 1st Battalion, Duke of Wellington's West Riding Regiment."

Too far. She almost reels back from the revelation.

I smile, trying to lighten the mood. "Come on, it's not that bad, really."

Skeet's shaking her head. "It's a lot to get my head around. I mean…" She picks up her pint and drains it. "I knew you were old, but you're talking about events over a century ago… so… so… matter-of-factly." She leans back, gazing at me. Troubled.

"Another pint?" I offer, guessing a moment has passed.

She nods distractedly and I get up to see George the proprietor about two more drinks.

When I return, I half-expect to find she's disappeared – Skeet's done that a time or two before. But no, she's still at the table, but looking less bemused than she had previously. In fact, she's leaning forward, one hand on her fine chin, gazing at me with what I can only interpret as lustfulness.

I set the two pints down and resume my seat. "Well, what have you decided?" I ask quietly. "Too old for you?"

Skeet ignores the pint and takes my hand across the table. "Not at all, old m—" she starts, then shakes her head, half-laughing. "I decided it didn't matter."

I look down, relieved and pleased.

She lifts my head by placing her finger under my chin. "You hear me, in there *Commander* Sen?" she's saying loudly. "I. Don't. Give. A. Fuck."

One of the drunks at the bar applauds. "You tell 'em," he slurs.

I nod, smiling now. "Well, they say every man pays for it one way or another…"

Skeet's smiling, too. "Shut up. Take me home. Now."

"But I just got drinks…" I start.

"Now."

"Okay, your wish is my command," I reply meekly, and gather my coat and follow the girl who came back, to the door.

It's quite a bit later when my skullphone goes again. And it's not good timing either.

I apologise to Skeet and roll over to take a call from an unknown number. No one in the general population could have this number, so it's likely someone from the Company.

It's not. There's a hesitation, and then I hear a voice I'm more used to hearing in the dark. "Jaared?"

"Madeline? What's the matter?" I'm subvocalising, so Skeet doesn't know who I'm talking to.

"It is time I saw you…" She sounds nervous, which is amazing in itself.

"Okay…" *I'm not sure that's a good idea, particularly in light of Skeet's return.*

"I will meet you tomorrow night at the *Brasserie du Vin* in Old Brompton Road."

"Uh, okay, that works for me," I reply. I don't have any plans and it's probably better if I don't wait to be abducted. "Say half-past eight?"

"Very well. I will be at the back. And come alone."

"See you there."

"Who was that?" Skeet asks.

"Work. I've got an appointment tomorrow night with a witness," I reply, not entirely sure why I'm not telling her the whole truth. "Now, where was I?"

"Just over here, Mr Sen… yes, that's…mmm…"

GIMME SHELTER...

S hirl's information doesn't help much.

The freak is who he says he is. Shirl found all the adoption papers and legal bumf pertaining to one Tobias Mayweather. And she'd brought coffee again.

"It all checks out, Wolf," Shirl told him, handing him the pad with all the relevant bullets about Mayweather's past. "I can't find anything out of the ordinary on him, beyond the fact he disappeared six months ago and came back in his current get-up of sometime fanatic."

Sipping his coffee, Wolf realised he didn't understand why Liz took the kid on in the first place. "I never took Liz for the mothering type — she was never exactly maternal, as I remember."

Shirl shrugged, draining her own coffee. "People change. Just look at you," she chided him with a smile. She was way too perky for mornings and today she had her dark hair pulled back neatly into a ponytail, a minimum of make-up around her brown eyes and a touch of gloss on her lips.

Wolf grinned back, taking the ribbing in his stride. "Very funny — you're just a riot." He looked at the info on her screen again and shook his head. "Nothing on where he got that page or any hint that he's been into something dodgy?"

"Not a whisper." Shirl took the pad back and flicked across to another screen. "I *did* follow up the possibility the page had been stolen from the Vatican." She handed him back the pad.

Wolf's eyes widened as he read the article from the *International Herald Tribune*. "...and Vatican sources deny there was a break in at the Secret Archives in July... an anonymous source says the thief or thieves only took a few pages of documents, nothing of any value..." He looks up. "You think this could tie into Mayweather, then?"

"Yep," she replied. "Even if it wasn't him directly, he may have got his hands on some loot from the theft."

Nodding, Wolf agreed. "Nothing confirms his involvement beyond coincidence." He handed the pad back. "But I agree — it's a little too coincidental."

Shirl looked him in the eye. "What're we going to do now, boss?"

Wolf smiled back at her. "I think we talk to Mayweather again and try to find out what exactly he's after." He pointed to the pad. "And that might make him more talkative, at the very least."

"I agree." Shirl hopped off the corner of the desk, her ponytail swinging behind her. "I'll find Sphincter and see what he knows about Mr Mayweather." She grinned the slightly disturbing grin she'd had since the abduction. "You never know, he might just tell me what I want to know."

Wolf nodded. "I'm certain he will – particularly if you smile at him like that!" He pretended to frown. "And less of this 'boss' stuff; I don't want to be the boss!"

"Someone has to be!" Still grinning, Shirl waved at him over her shoulder and disappeared out of the office.

Wolf sat at his desk a little while longer, wondering again what he'd got them all into. He decided to call Graeme and fill him in on the situation.

"Morning," Graeme said on answering. "And how are you feeling this morning?"

Warily, Wolf looked at the voda. "Fine, why?"

"I heard Michael was back in town and figured you probably did a bit of town-painting last night."

"We had a quiet curry and went to bed," Wolf answered through gritted teeth. "Have you got spies or something, keeping tabs on me?"

Graeme laughed. "Spies? That's a good one. No, son, it's just the way it works in families, even unconventional ones like ours. Besides, Michael talks to Janey, who mentions it to Shirl, who then tells her dear old dad, so you can see I didn't do anything out of the ordinary to find out that bit of information."

"Right." Wolf remained unconvinced.

"Is it good to have the Hyperactive Kid home, then?" Graeme asked in a more sober tone.

Wolf found himself nodding. "More than you can know – I hate it when he's off touring."

"I know, but you also know he has to do it."

"Yep, I know." Wolf sighed. "I can't stop him doing what he loves any more than he can stop me finding things... Not that I love finding things... but... oh, you know what I mean." Wolf ground to a halt.

"You keep telling yourself that, son, and ignore the rush when you've found something you're looking for."

"Anyway," Wolf said, taking charge of the conversation, "that's not what I called about and you know it." He filled Graeme in on what Shirl had found so far, although, of course, the old man knew a lot of it already.

"What do you think we should do now?" Graeme asked.

"I think we talk to Mayweather again and see what we can get out of him." Wolf paused. "I think he knows where the book is, but needs help getting it out of wherever it's being kept."

"Which probably means it's dangerous."

"Yes, and it's likely he's going to try to get us to do it for a small cut when we're doing all the work."

"That sounds about right," Graeme concurred. "So you have to convince him it's in his interests to pay us more."

"Yep. And that's the easy part." Wolf sighed. "I also have to tell him I want the manuscript."

JUST WHEN YOU THINK THINGS ARE GETTING BETTER, THIS HAPPENS!

A licia went to work tired. Sleep had been furtive, at best, after reading Stephen's damn letter. She was still angry at whatever whim of fate had made it land on her doorstep now.

All it had done was reopen the old wounds and deprive her of sleep. *Just what I needed today.*

She stomped into the morgue and went into her office, trying to avoid Sue, but it was pointless.

"You've got a meeting with Administrator Jerbeau in twenty minutes, Al," Sue informed her as she placed a large cup of coffee on the blotter.

"Thanks Sue," Alicia replied. God she was tired. "I knew it was today, just couldn't quite remember when."

Sue nodded. "You okay?" she asked.

"I'm fine, Sue, just didn't sleep very well last night – too much on my mind." Alicia smiled a bit ruefully. "I could do with having an 'off' switch fitted so I can just turn it all off and sleep without thinking about things."

Sue came around the desk and leaned over to give her a hug. "It'll all work out, Al, you'll see," she whispered.

Alicia squeezed her arm and replied softly, "I know; it's just a bad day." Alicia picked up the coffee cup and sipped carefully, aware of the temperature of the contents. "I'll go see Jerbeau and get on with things. Thanks, Sue."

"Sure Al, no problem." Sue left her to her coffee.

Grimacing, Alicia looked at the stack of paperwork on the desk in front of her. *More form-filling and signing off. Great.* With a sigh, she pulled the first folder from the stack and got to work. She could at least get a few authorisations done before she met Felix.

Jerbeau had a new office, declining to take Humphrey's old one. It was a corner unit and had views across the City towards Canary Wharf and the Docklands, as well as Rotherhithe across the river.

"Come in," he called when Alicia tentatively knocked on the door frame.

He didn't yet have a secretary, and was apparently answering his own calls, judging by the earpiece he was wearing.

Alicia took an appreciative look around the office while she waited for him to finish his call.

Nothing on the walls yet, but a photo of an attractive man and two small children sat in pride of place on his desk — obviously the other half and their brood.

Feeling a momentary pain, Alicia took the seat Felix waved her to and turned the photo away from her.

Felix Jerbeau finished the call and put his voda down on the desk. He smiled, his dark eyes glowing above the very white teeth of his smile. "Okay, first meeting and all that, hope you're well and have a list of things to ask me for and a longer one of expenses you want signed off? No?"

Taken aback, Alicia smiled back at him and replied. "No, sorry, thought we'd talk about all that today."

Nodding, Felix seemed to take this in his stride. "Fine. No problem." He stood up and looked out at the view. "Okay, here's what we'll do — is there anything you could use right away?"

Alicia thought for a moment and realised they could use a new testing station for the morgue — their current version was slow and made the occasional mistake due to outdated fittings and software. She told Felix this.

"Fine, we'll get a new one in place by the end of the week." He turned back to her and that smile returned at the look of surprise on her face. "I'm sorry, Alicia, I know you're not used to working this way; it'll take time, but we'll get to know how the other works and I'm sure we'll do great things!"

"I'm sure not used to just asking for things and being told they'll arrive in a week!" Alicia acknowledged. "Are you telling me we could have worked this way before?"

Felix nodded. "From what I can see of your processes and orders, your previous administrator was very much into controlling your budgets and access to new equipment."

He frowned. "A decision was taken in a meeting two days ago that your team needs a larger budget — and more staff — to do the job that the Company requires of it. I've been charged with making sure you have all that you need to do your jobs properly."

"Wow. Why now?" Alicia asked.

"Didn't you know you've taken over most of central London's workload? No? I guess I'm not surprised, really; they probably didn't want to scare you off!" He smiled again.

Alicia looked at him in shock. "Most of central London... I knew we were busy, but I'd no idea we'd been covering more than our old patch!"

"You'll be getting some staff from the other offices very shortly — well, the ones who have been selected for your team. I hope you don't mind, but we'll also be expanding the facilities here."

"Expanding? How much larger are we talking?" Alicia demanded.

"I expect we'll be at least tripling capacity here," Felix replied.

"Triple? And who's in charge?!" She was afraid she knew the answer.

Felix looked at her soberly. "Why *you are*, my dear Alicia. Who else do you think the Company would trust with this sensitive an area?"

At her expression, he smiled again. "Don't worry, you don't have to do it all by yourself — that's why they brought me in, just to help you manage things. And your assistant, Sue, will be getting more help to cope with the admin side of things, so you won't all be swamped."

Shocked more than she'd known, Alicia sat back in her chair and thought for a moment. "I never wanted to run the place," she said. "All I've ever wanted to do was find out the mysteries a dead body contains."

Nodding, Felix seemed very prepared for her declaration. "I know you didn't, and don't worry — you won't notice much change to start with and we'll do our best to keep your workload light." That smile *was* reassuring. "Now I'll put together some proposals for you to look at and we'll talk again soon about how we progress things with the team, okay?"

Alicia nodded back. "That seems fine, Felix." She stood up. "I have to say I'm a bit overwhelmed just now — I'd no idea this was going on or that it would happen this quickly!"

"I know and I'm going to be here to help you with it every step of the way. Any questions, my door is always open to you," Felix replied.

"Thanks Felix, I'll remember that." Alicia turned to go. "Are you sure this all came out of Jaared's phone call?"

Felix smiled more broadly. "I've not known him as long as you have, I'm sure, but you may be surprised what he can do if he sets his mind to it!"

Grinning back, Alicia had to agree. "Oh, I don't think *surprised* is the right word, but I forget how formidable he can be, particularly when he wants something!"

Phew, that's a relief!

Madeline takes my hands across the table. I can't see her eyes in the dimness – small, tinted glasses hide them from me. It's a re-experience for me, looking into someone's eyes, and being able to know things about what they're thinking from them. Or expecting to look into someone's eyes.

Rather than abduct me from the street as she normally would, Madeline has been quite circumspect on this occasion, asking me to meet her in public – this is not something she's ever done before. She obviously has something to say to me and appears to be working up the courage to say it. Another difference.

The brasserie is mildly busy, with the buzz of conversations around us creating a white noise.

She starts hesitantly. "Now that you've met Nicholas, I…" She pauses and almost moves to take her cold hands from mine. "It would appear that it is time to tell you what we believe to be your destiny," she says quietly, almost whispering.

"Who's 'We'?" I ask apprehensively.

She's silent for a moment. "I think you know, Jaared," she replies quietly. "You are hardly stupid. We're a very old race and have been … 'companions'… to humanity for millennia."

I sit and stare at her again. "Uh… I know it's not polite… but how old are you?"

"Over three centuries."

My first impulse is to swear, but as she's so much faster and stronger than me it would be impolitic. So I sit for a moment, considering. "How is it…? How am I… like you, then?" I ask, changing my choice of many questions at the last second.

Madeline shakes her head. "You may well be a cross-breed – our lineage master is uncertain where your longevity comes from." She takes a drink from the wine glass in front of her, appearances, don't you know, grimacing at the taste. I'm still marvelling at these tiny things I've been missing for ninety years, when she continues. "We were surprised you managed to hide your age for so long, particularly with your ties to several government agencies on both sides of the Atlantic."

I shrug. "I moved around a lot. And when I had my 'accident' I spent a number of years in the Far East... recovering." I took a sip of my own glass, remembering my teacher, Luu Tran-Dinh, and the years I spent learning to cope without eyes. "When I returned, everyone I knew was gone or didn't recognise me. And then I came here for the Company – they've been giving me rejuv for years now and I don't know whether it's making a difference or not."

"It is... helping maintain your body, but you would probably still be alive without it," Madeline replied. "As I said, we do not know what your longevity stems from, although your ability to father a son with me suggests your blood is tied to ours."

Blood. That reminds me. "Uh... do you drink blood?"

If she could be any more unmoving, I'd swear she was made of marble. "We have... needs, *mon cheri*. And yes, one of those is blood. But we require less, the older we get. Nicholas is very greedy... we're having trouble covering his activities."

I still feel a shock at the mention of Nicholas – my son – the strange boy who understands me less than I understand him. "How is he... otherwise?"

Madeline smiles for the first time. "Destructive, dangerous, moody, and angry; all those things teenagers are supposed to be, no?" She shrugs. "But he is getting better. I can leave him unattended for a few days now and he fails to kill everyone in a ten mile radius or blow up part of London. Better."

I'm glad. I know he's been struggling to come to terms with things and he hasn't exactly had a normal 'childhood'. "Good... I'm pleased he's settling," I finish lamely.

The being across the table from me is still for a moment. "I understand the mercenary is back," she says after a moment.

Startled, I flinch. Madeline's knowledge of my activities borders on the well, I want to say 'supernatural', but that seems a tautology. "Yes, she got back from China last week."

Madeline smiles; it's not in a good way. "We are tied together Jaared, although I am far more aware of you than you are of me." She stops and takes a sip of her wine. "I am aware of your situation most of the time, mon cheri – even when it pains me."

I look down, unsure how to take this. Madeline is still so much a mystery to me. Suddenly she's in my head, a sensation I haven't felt since Stel died...

It will not always be this way, mon cheri — there will come a time for us, but it is not… yet. In the meantime, I wait and watch over you.

"How do you do that?" I murmur.

"You will be able to do it in time, I am sure," Madeline says softly. "Now, I must go – I have to meet someone before the moon rises."

For a moment, I'm transfixed with the memory of my first sight of a full moon after my operation. It had been so long, but the giant glowing orb in the sky hadn't changed. It was luminous and glorious, a wonderful thing to see after so many years.

I tear myself from the vision. "Moon rise." I can't help but chuckle. "I don't know I'll ever get to grips with the way you put things, Madeline."

I feel the eyes behind her dark glasses staring at me intently for a moment before a small smile curls the lips, the perfect blonde hair framing her cold but beautifully proportioned face. She has the face of an ancient stone goddess, beautiful, forbidding and somehow terrifying all at the same time.

"I must go, *mon cheri.*" She rises. "I will see you again soon – of that you can be certain."

I nod, standing up as well. "Of course." My hand rises to touch her arm, a sudden sense of foreboding coming over me. "Take care, Madeline," I say quietly.

"Certainly, *mon cheri,*" she says, emphasising the last. "Adieu for now."

"Adieu."

And she flows out of the brasserie, drawing looks varying from admiration to fear as she goes.

THERE GOES THE NEIGHBOURHOOD

Wolf watched Michael across the table. He'd only agreed to go out to a swanky restaurant in Mayfair to appease Michael – they seemed to see so little of each other lately.

Of course, he was distracted, thinking about Mayweather and the *De Temporum Signis*. Damn the man.

Shirl and Graeme were starting to track Mayweather's movements and see if they could work out where he'd been. Wolf didn't want to meet the man again until they knew more about him. Once Wolf was happy with the information they had on him, they'd make contact and see if it was feasible to extract the manuscript.

"Wolf? Wolfie? You in there?" Michael snapped his fingers across the table in front of Wolf's eyes. Then, in his best imitation of a space control voice: "Can you hear me? Earth to Wolfie… Please respond."

Wolf smiled and grabbed the fingers in front of his face. "Sorry, was just thinking about work," Wolf admitted.

Michael frowned, his pale features darkening. "Of course you were. Your gorgeous boyfriend is back from touring and takes you to a nice restaurant and you're thinking about work."

Those blue eyes are rather beautiful, Wolf thought. "Sorry, I'm back now, Mr Gorgeous Boyfriend. What are you going to have?"

Those eyes stared at him for a moment, before relenting. Michael wasn't good at staying angry. "Oh steak, Dahling, as always!"

"Vegetarianism never suited you, did it?" Wolf asked, mostly rhetorically. "I'm going to have the baked turbot with pea shoots; it seems the best choice for me."

"Dahling, I was never cut out to eat vegetables – all that green. Yeck!" Michael's hand found his across the table. "Got to watch your figure, eh?"

Wolf shrugged. He wasn't getting any younger and weight was getting harder to shift when it appeared. He'd had to force himself to get back into a regular fitness regime to tone those muscles up again. Too much sitting around and too little time spent actively doing things.

"Wolf, can I ask you something?" Michael looked anxious now, not so confident and brash. His blonde hair spiked up from his head, and Wolf thought he could see a little scalp peeking through.

Wolf took a drink of his water. "Sure, you know you can — whatever you want."

Michael's grip on his hand tightened and he stared into Wolf's eyes. "I've been thinking about it a lot and I think I'm going to give up touring." He looked away and then back, a little embarrassed. "I never get to see you... and I'm tired of endless bland hotel rooms... Maybe I'll start teaching — Jonno has a space for another instructor at his school..."

Confused, Wolf asked, "What are you asking me? You don't need my permission to do something else, do you?"

"No, that's not what I'm asking." Michael took Wolf's hand in both of his, those deep blue eyes boring into his muddy brown ones. "I guess... what I wanted to ask you was... Will you marry me, Pocock Woffe?"

Wolf's face broke into a smile. "Is that all? Of course I will, you nit — I was just waiting for the right time to ask you!"

Relieved, Michael smiled back. "Really? That's... that's great! We just never talked about it... and I wondered... oh, never mind. Champagne! That's what we need!" And letting Wolf's hand go, he darted over to their waiter and ordered a bottle of something sparkly and expensive.

Wolf watched him go, feeling happy. If only it were always so easy to make people feel good.

For a moment his thoughts turned to the manuscript and Mayweather, but he banished them from his mind with a rueful shake of the head. "Not tonight, Josephine," he muttered under his breath.

RETAIL THERAPY IS ALWAYS BENEFICIAL

A licia called Jaared about the autopsy results on the John Tyler case.

"So, what did you find?"

"Seems straightforward enough – simple overdose of heroin. Not something one sees much anymore, but not beyond the realm of possibility," she replied.

"Did he take it or was it given to him?" Jaared asked, getting to the crux of the matter.

"You know I can't say, Jaared. However, there is more evidence to support administered: he has ligature marks on his wrists and I could find no other marks, beyond the injector site on the back of his neck, to indicate he was a regular heroin user." Alicia flipped through some screens. "Tox report shows minute amounts of snap in his system, but that's consistent with recreational use."

"What about the hand?"

Alicia looked at her notes. "Straightforward. Lopped off with a branch cutter or something similar – no hesitation marks or the abrasions a saw would make." She thought about it. "I'd say it's someone who doesn't know his victim."

"What was the strange odour on the body?"

"You're not going to believe it: musk."

"Musk? Like from a deer or something?"

"Try Civet – 'a type of wild cat from Asia and Africa. The musk is highly prized by perfume companies. It's not something you're going to find just anywhere."

Jaared was silent for a moment. "Okay, got it. Anything else?"

Alicia took a last look at her notes. "There's a burn on the back of his left calf I can't place, but I'd say you'll find his DNA on whatever it was, probably skin."

"Okay, thanks for the call, Al."

"My pleasure – we haven't done this for a while," she replied, a smile touching her lips.

"That's the problem with desk jobs – no field work involved! I'll talk to you later, Al."

"Bye Jaared."

The rest of her day was busy with non-work activity — a welcome change. It was a long lunch with Kate, followed by shopping for a dress, which then turned into a few drinks. They talked about Kate's photography mostly and there was some refreshing chatter for both of them about various inconsequential things.

Alicia made Kate come back to her place for dinner so she could let the dogs out. It was also more relaxed that way.

The dogs fussed over Kate, who usually looked after them when Alicia was away or otherwise detained. Alicia phoned Kate's partner Morag to tell her where they were and she promised to join them when she got off work as long as they weren't "too lairy drunk by then".

Laughing at that, Alicia put together a salad while she poached some salmon fillets.

"Red or white?" Kate asked from the doorway, a mischievous grin on her face.

"Oh Kate, can't I just have a nice cup of tea?" Alicia asked, feeling a bit flushed from the several Martinis they'd drunk at *The Ritz-Carlton*.

Kate's hazel eyes flashed under her fashionable fringe. "No, you cannot! I've just put a nice Rosé in the freezer for a few moments and when it's ready we'll have that."

Alicia rolled her eyes and checked the salmon.

"Besides," Kate continued. "I need to see that dress on you outside of a cubicle at *Ferragamo's*." She pushed Alicia out of the way and shooed her towards the door. "Now go; I'll mind the fish and see where Morag is."

Alicia stood in front of the full-length, standalone mirror in her bedroom. The mirror had been a gift from Stephen, purchased for a song and carefully refinished by him as a surprise for her birthday.

The dress wasn't quite a 'little black number', but it was far more form-fitting than she normally wore. Of dark turquoise silk, with beads sewn on to accentuate its fine pattern, it hit her about mid-calf. She was glad of the little, heavily embroidered bolero jacket that went with it to cover up her arms — she shuddered at the thought of exposing her bingo wings.

A sound of clapping came from the doorway. "That's gorgeous, Al — you look fantastic," Kate enthused before turning around and picking up two glasses of wine from the table in the hall. "Here you go, all chilled."

Alicia took a sip. "Thanks, Kate." She looked at herself in the mirror again. "I don't think I'd have picked anything like this without your help."

Kate put her glass down on the dressing table. "Nonsense, you've got great taste; you just need to learn to trust it more often." She started looking through bags. "Now, where are the shoes?"

Taking another sip of wine, Alicia smiled at herself in the mirror. Maybe the pearls Stephen had given her for their last Christmas together would go with it. Or the gold chain from Crete. She shook her head, she'd decide nearer the time.

"Here they are," Kate announced, thrusting the shoes at Alicia.

Alicia put down her wine and obediently put her feet into the tiny shoes. The heels were higher than she normally wore, and she tottered slightly. But it could have been the effects of the Martinis. She somehow made it back in front of the mirror without mishap.

"Superb," Kate pronounced. "They give you a couple of inches and do lovely things for your calves." She looked up to Alicia's eyes. "Can you walk in them though Al? If not, I've got a great pair of kitten heels you can wear which might suit you better."

Waving her away, Alicia took a couple of steps around the bedroom. "No, they're fine; I just have to remember not to drink much or I'll literally fall over!"

More clapping came from the doorway. "Youse look spectacular, Al," Morag said, filling the doorway. "Sorry, no answer at the door, so I let m'sel' in." She glared briefly at Kate before smiling at Alicia.

"Thanks Morag and don't worry." Alicia walked across the carpet and gave her a quick peck on the cheek. "You know you're allowed to let yourself in – it's why I gave you both keys!"

"Ta, Al." Morag, big and bluff looked embarrassed. "I'll go get m'sel' some wine and check the fish. And where's the wee bairns?"

Laughing, Alicia replied, "They're out in the garden, but probably ready to come in, if you want to let them in."

With her glass of wine in hand, Kate took Morag's arm, gave her a quick kiss, and said, "Come on youse, let's leave the lady to change in peace." And they departed.

Alicia took another look in the mirror, smiling at her friends' enthusiasm and compliments before taking the jacket and dress off and putting on some more comfortable jeans and a blouse and a pair of flats. She hung the new items in her closet and went to join them downstairs.

"So tell us about the new guy," Kate ordered when they were mostly through with their meal at the table in the kitchen, the two dogs banished to their baskets in the corner where they watched the goings-on with careful attention.

Alicia considered Felix for a moment. "His name's Felix Jerbeau. I don't know much about him, really," she said finally. "I only met him the day before yesterday."

Morag had gone still at the name. "Jerbeau? I've heard o' him – some kind of hotshot in t' Company. Apparently he cleaned up the office in Paris in under six months. And I don' mean he was the cleaner," she said significantly.

Kate nodded. "The name does sound familiar, but I'm not sure why."

"I also heard he's a bit of a boy-killer," Morag said.

It was Alicia's turn to nod. "I'm not surprised – he's tall, dark and very handsome." She went on to tell them about her new empire and what looked like a promotion.

"Blimey, Al, you'll be running the whole thing, soon," Kate said when she was finished.

Alicia shook her head. "Not while I have Jerbeau doing all the work. It sounds like he's going to be running everything and my role won't really change much... at least to start with."

Morag poured them more wine and took a drink. "And this is all down t' Jaared?" she asked, her brow furrowed.

"I don't know that he changed the structure of the Company for me; he just got someone in who could help me," Alicia replied, defending Sen for some reason.

Shrugging, Morag took another drink. She'd had issues with Jaared since he collapsed on Alicia's floor a while back and didn't seem to trust him completely.

Kate tried to diffuse the situation. "I'm sure he didn't – the Company does its own internal restructures with little input from outsiders." She took a sip of her wine. "So when's the Christmas ball?"

"Tuesday night," Alicia said. "At *Grosvenor House*. In their ballroom, I think."

"Tell Morag who you're taking!" Kate ordered.

Her face reddening again, Alicia admitted, "Jack... from the office."

Morag frowned trying to remember Jack. "Have I met him? Oh yeah, he's the scrawny little one I scared at your barbecue last summer!"

"That's him," Alicia said, remembering the incident. Morag had heard Jack talking about the live role-playing he was involved with and had taken it into her, slightly inebriated brain, that he was a bit of a nutter. She'd proceeded to pick him up and dump him head-first into a rubbish bin – a mostly full rubbish bin. Jack had departed very quickly after that.

"Aye, why're you takin' him?" Morag said loudly. "Yuh can do better than that!"

Kate tried to intervene. "Mags, I think Alicia asked him because he was unlikely to go to the ball, otherwise."

"Tha's e'en worse! Charity case!"

"Mags!"

"I know this guy – in Admin o'er at me work. You'd like him – handsome, rugby player." Morag chuckled wickedly. "An' I bet he looks good in a tux, an' all!"

Alicia sighed. Why did people persist in trying to fix her up? She wasn't interested and hadn't really been looking since Stephen died.

"Mags! Stop now!" Kate cried.

"It's all right, Kate," Alicia intervened. "Thanks for the offer, Morag, but I'm not looking for anything like that just now. I haven't really thought seriously about it since..."

"Och, me and meh big gob," Morag said. "I know, Al, I know – fergit I said anyt'ing."

"It's okay, Morag, I know you mean well." Alicia stood up, went up to her bedroom and retrieved the letter. When she got back, she handed it to Kate. "I got this yesterday."

Kate looked at the scrawl on the envelope and blanched. "Where the hell has this been hiding?" she wondered out loud.

"What is it?" Morag enquired.

"A letter from Stephen, written sometime while he was away," Alicia replied. "And Kate's right, where the hell has it been all this time?"

"Aw, shite," Morag said softly. "Tha's jus' cruel."

Alicia nodded. "I was just starting to get on with things and he writes to me from beyond the grave." She smiled at them both and started removing dishes from the table.

Kate read it, passing the pages as she finished to Morag. They were both very quiet for a long time while Alicia sorted out the kitchen.

"Aw, Al, I'm sorry," Morag said when she'd finished. "It's a lovely letter, though."

Kate nodded, coming over to Alicia and putting both arms around her. "He loved you very much, you mustn't forget that, Al."

Alicia nodded, feeling the corners of her eyes start to prickle, and forcing herself to keep them on the washing up. "I know – I won't forget, that's the problem."

Morag joined them for a hug before saying, "I know, more wine!" making them all laugh.

The kitchen tidied, they opened another bottle of Rosé and changed the subject to something less painful, mainly Kate and Morag's upcoming holiday in Crete. They finished the bottle of wine and Alicia watched them wander off to her guest room.

Alicia was glad they didn't go home – her spare room got used again and she wasn't left on her own to brood.

She put the empties and the wine glasses in the kitchen and leaned down to hug her dogs, the two pushing close and their tail stumps vibrating almost in time. "I love you guys," she said quietly.

Then she did something she rarely did, she wiped the tears from her eyes, stood up and led the way to her bedroom. "Go on," she said, head tilted towards the bed. The two Staffys didn't need any more encouragement and were on the bed in seconds.

Alicia smiled and got ready for bed.

IF YOU'VE GOT THE MONEY, HONEY, I'VE GOT THE TIME!

I have a visitor in my office when I get in.

"Inspector General, sir... to what do I owe the pleasure?" I ask, knowing full well why he's in *my* office, rather than his.

Shorter than I am and starting to fill out a bit, the Inspector General stands up and shakes my hand. Unusual.

"I just needed to confirm a few details about the ongoing case of John Tyler... I'm sure you understand, Jaared." He gestures me to my seat behind the desk.

Oh, I understand all right. "Could it be that James Tyler's putting on pressure for us to find his son's killer and you're taking a personal interest in making sure the investigation is going well? How am I doing so far?" I ask.

"Now Jaared, it's not that simple... Mr Tyler is a person of interest in a number of cases and we need to see if we can... assist him, as much as we can." The IG doesn't fluster very easily and he's right, I've been around the block enough times to know the score.

"Of course, sir. It doesn't have anything to do with his position on the board or his pretendership to the throne." I sit down and look at him for a moment. "You can inform Mr Tyler his son's death is almost certainly the result of murder and Contractor Timson is proceeding with the investigation under my guidance."

I call up his latest reports on my HUD and grimace internally. I will have to intervene. "In fact, I'll be directing the investigation now as it *is* Contractor Timson's first major case."

"That's partly why I'm here, Jaared." The Inspector General's eyes glitter for a moment. "I've been reading his reports and I feel he needs a guiding hand... someone of your... experience... on the case would put Mr Tyler's mind at ease, I'm sure."

Dammit, he's always one step ahead of me. But then, I sometimes think he took this kind of politics with his mother's breast milk, assuming she was a 'breast-milk-is-best' kind of woman, of course.

"Yes sir, I'm sure he'll be happier with me on the case, but only just," I reply. "Particularly after our last meeting..."

The IG consults his own HUD. "Ah, yes. Unfortunate. Please be on your best behaviour, then, Jaared."

He stands up and moves to the door, turning before leaving. "I'd rather not have to clear up another one of your messes, Jaared."

"Of course, sir." I salute, something only the IG ever seems to inspire in me as I've not saluted anyone regularly for a very long time. "I'll do my best."

Timson is waiting outside my office, summoned via my HUD while I was cozying up to the IG. "You wanted to see me, sir?" he asks upon entering.

"Morning Timson," I reply. "Sit down; we've got work to do."

"Yes sir."

I flip through the reports on my desktop screen. "You've made no further progress on the John Tyler case, have you Timson?" I ask, knowing full well he hasn't.

He has the decency to look uncomfortable. "Uh, no sir, we haven't got very far." At my glance up from the case files he amends it. "Or rather, I haven't, sir."

I nod. "No. Have you reviewed John Tyler's contacts for the previous few days?"

He nods back. "Yes sir, we... or rather I... looked at his movements and didn't find much out of the ordinary." He leans forward to the desk. "May I, sir?" he asks.

I wave him on and he starts pulling different bits of the file to the front.

"Here's one of the two anomalous contacts we took from his internal GPS that deviated from his normal schedule. And if you look here, sir, we found CCTV footage of him meeting the junky we found at the scene and giving him what looks like a credit chit."

"You said there were two," I prompt, one eyebrow raised.

"Yes sir, there were." He pulls the second contact to the fore and even I can see it's sparse. "Beyond knowing he met someone, we're not sure who or where it was – his GPS was apparently disabled somehow. We know approximately where he was in London, but it's unclear as to where contact was made."

"Disabled? Isn't that difficult?" I ask, frowning at the situation, not Timson.

"Very. And it's some kind of black hole that's specific to Tyler — we've registered no similar black hole on the general public's GPS systems at that time of day or in that location to match it."

I sit back, considering. Something black market *could* do this, but I'd not heard of it happening. At least not recently. "Where's the hole in his records put him?" I ask.

"Less than half a mile from where the body was found, near Russell Square."

"What's the timeline? Could someone have injected him at that point and sent him on his way?"

Timson shakes his head. "Dr Sampson says no, sir. He disappears for about two hours and when he's back on the grid, he's moving. As near as we can tell, he was dead within three hours of his rendezvous."

Alicia; of course she was involved.

"What about CCTV around the area he disappears into? Anything?" I'm grasping at straws now.

"He's spotted coming from Russell Square tube, but I've been unable to find him coming out of the zone."

I nod. "Car, probably. See if Central can get any hits from cars going into or out of the area around that time. We're probably screwed if he took a cab..."

I think about the case for a few seconds, thinking about anything else we can do. "Any strange withdrawals from his accounts? Other than what he gives the junky, of course. Maybe something he's tried to cover up?"

Timson smiles. "I did find one odd withdrawal, but it's for athletic shoes... not exactly earth-shattering."

"Ah, but are they in his size?" I ask, thinking I'm onto something.

The smile turns into a grin. "No sir; they're a woman's size."

He's not doing that badly. "Okay, last question: Were all his cards on him when he was found?"

"No sir. All that was in his wallet was his ID and a library card. Anything of value was removed." He looks serious for a moment. "Unless we were supposed to identify him..."

"That could well be, Timson. He was supposed to be identified and probably a scandal created for his father." I smile.

Maybe it isn't as bad as I had thought. "Good work, Timson. Follow up those leads and get back to me soonest." I know he's already started the search for suspect cars from the flag that appeared on the case file as we were talking. "Dismissed."

"Yes sir," he replies and stands up. *He* doesn't salute.

NOW, TIME FOR THE SCUTWORK

Wolf sat down at the table in his workroom. The big room with high ceilings and a big window on one side had been a spare bedroom, but he and Michael had decided they didn't need two. And it gave Wolf somewhere to work on his 'projects' out of the way.

"C'mon in, he gestured to Graeme and Shirl standing in the doorway. There were two comfortable chairs for them against the wall, but moveable on the hardwood floors.

"Like what you've done with the place, Wolf," Graeme enthused as he settled into one of the chairs. "More comfortable than the old living room."

Shirl nodded. "It suits you... somehow more mature."

Wolf blushed slightly. "Thanks... I think." He glowered at Shirl. "Although I think you just said I'm old."

Shirl shrugged. "If the shit fits."

"C'mon, you too," Graeme growled. "I *am* old and getting older so let's get on with things."

"Right. Shirl, any more background on our friend Mayweather?" Wolf asked. He reached behind him to the coffee maker and picked up the tray with three cups on it and placed it on the desk.

"Well, not a lot more," she admitted. "I'd guess he already knows where the book is, but I can't guess from his recent movements." She reddened slightly. "Jonathan knows someone at the Company who took a look at his GPS records for the last two weeks."

Wolf, pouring coffee into the mugs, nodded. "Fine. I think he knows where the book is, too, but we won't know until he tells us." He added sweetener and milk to Graeme's coffee and just milk to Shirl's and his own before passing the cups round. "Graeme, any dirt we can use on him?"

Graeme smiled and blew on his coffee. "I think so. He's got an outstanding warrant for ABH up North. I'd guess that's part of the reason he's down here. Although why they've not located him by now, I'm not sure. Maybe he's paid someone off."

"Okay, could be useful as a bargaining chip." Wolf sipped at his drink. "Feels like old times, doesn't it?"

Shirl put her arm around his shoulders and gave him a brief hug. "Yep — I've missed this."

Graeme nodded agreement. "I'm watching too much telly now. Need to do something to keep me active."

Wolf grinned. "Well, guess we're back in business. Now to call Mayweather."

Mayweather agreed to meet them later in the day, at a different pub, in a different part of town.

Almost like he's worried about being spotted, Wolf thought to himself, as he told the others.

FRIDAY NEVER COMES AROUND QUICKLY ENOUGH

A licia sat at her desk again, trying to get her head around the new organisation set out on her tablet.

Jack popped his head in her door. "Got another one, boss," he reported.

"Another what, Jack?" Alicia asked without looking up, head spinning with headcounts and budget numbers.

"Another body."

"Well, this is a morgue, Jack, we do tend to accumulate bodies here," Alicia replied sarcastically.

"Ha, ha, very droll, boss." He stepped into the room. "But not all of them have Latin quotes inscribed in their chests, do they?"

"Dammit, you're telling me we've got another one of those?" Alicia threw the paper down and stood up. "Show me."

She trailed Jack down the corridor to the examination room and spotted the body immediately. Great gashes were carved into his chest, almost obscuring the words that had been carved there.

"Do you see it yet?" Jack asked.

"See what, Jack? Another violently killed man, middle-aged, average height and build, brown hair, and no distinguishing marks, if you discount the letters cut into his chest."

Jack pointed at the lettering on the chest. "Look closer at the words."

Alicia stepped closer to the body and realised what he meant. "The words were cut *after* whatever it was stripped through his insides. Otherwise, they'd be damaged and some of the letters would be missing."

"Someone went to a lot of trouble to make sure it was readable," Jack said. "I mean, that couldn't have been easy with those wounds."

"I agree. Got a translation yet?"

"Run quote analysis," Jack said into his lapel mic. The vid screen fills with letters.

Natura nihil est in rebus nisi Deus Ipse.

Latin. Translation:

Dean Fetzer

Nature is none other than God in things.

Giordano Bruno. Seventeenth century.

Alicia swore. "It is a goddamn serial killer – all the quotes tie into this Bruno." She looks at Jack. "Any idea who he is?"

Jack shrugged. "I Googled him and, basically, he was a philosopher and scientist in the 1600s." He grinned. "Google had no idea why his quotes would be turning up on bodies."

Alicia grunted, somehow annoyed another serial killer was running around London. "Flag it to Sen and we'll see what he can find out about it. And you may as well start the exam – I've got paperwork to do."

"Yes boss."

Alicia returned to her office in a foul mood. Slumped in her antique chair, she stared at nothing for a few minutes, wondering why another serial killer was affecting her so personally. "What's it got to do with you?" she muttered.

There was the sound of throat clearing from the door. "Sorry, am I interrupting?"

Looking up, she saw her new tall, dark and handsome administrator in the doorway. "Oh, Felix. No, just me talking to myself, as usual," Alicia replied, feeling flustered.

"I often find it's the best way to get a decent conversation," Felix rejoined with a smile. "Anything I can do to help?"

Alicia waved the offer away. "No, just another corpse turning up. Please, sit down," she suggested. "I hate serial killers and it looks like we've got another one."

Felix nodded. "I see. But it's not your job to investigate the crimes, just the corpses."

"Yes, but we do what we can to help the investigations," she countered. "And if the last one is anything to go by, I'd rather not get involved." She could see by the glazed look coming over Felix's face that he was accessing his HUD, and was glad once again she'd refused the implants. Bothersome things, and rude, too.

When he returned, Felix's eyes refocused. "I see; you had a mass grave to deal with in Sarajevo. Not pretty." His grimace suggested he'd seen some of the SOC photos.

"No. I'd prefer to leave that memory in the past."

94

Felix nodded again. "I understand. Now, have you seen the new structure I sent across?" he asked, all business.

"Yes, I was just going through it." Alicia waved at the tablet in front of her. "I have to admit a lot of it's beyond me, though."

"It's just the basics for outfitting all the new facilities we'll be adding to the building. Do you want to go through the details?" He was showing all courtesy; it was almost creepy.

"Not at the moment. I'll take it home over the weekend and see what I can make of it." For some reason, Alicia wanted him to leave now. She couldn't put her finger on it.

"Very well; I'll see you on Monday about it, then." Felix stood up to leave. "Oh, one other thing: Are you going to the ball on Tuesday?"

Alicia nodded. "I am."

"I was wondering if you would accompany me? You are a very attractive woman and I would be most pleased to go with you, as my other half is going to be out of town." His expression was of the 'you know how it is' variety.

"Thank you very much, but I'm afraid I already have plans for Tuesday," Alicia responded, now feeling uncomfortable, particularly after her conversation with the girls the night before.

"Have you already acquired a companion for the evening?" he asked. Again, slightly creepy.

"Yes, I have a date for Tuesday," Alicia replied firmly.

"That is too bad. I don't know who I will ask now," he replied solemnly.

"I'm sure you'll find someone to go with, a big, handsome man like you," Alicia laid it on thick.

He bowed his head slightly. "We'll see. Have a lovely weekend and I shall see you on Monday."

"Have a nice weekend," Alicia said to his retreating back. *That was weird,* she thought to herself.

ISN'T IT TIME TO GO TO THE PUB YET?

I t's Friday and I'm looking forward to the weekend – although I undoubtedly have work to do. No rest for the wicked, as they say. And I'm definitely on the wicked list.

Timson's following up the leads I teased out of him, so I have time to do other things. One of which is to start properly on the case Alicia's sent my way. Three dead bodies, all different ages, different builds and with different pathologies. But they all have phrases cut into their torsos, in Latin, and attributable to the same seventeenth-century philosopher, named Giordano Bruno who was burned at the stake by the Catholic Church as a heretic. *They do like their heretics, those Catholics.*

The case photos of the bodies are graphic and the last one is fairly shredded from three large gashes diagonally placed across the torso. Central has tried to identify the weapon which could have made such a wound, but without much success – at least attempting a match with modern weapons. "A trident, some kind of rake, or the claws of something very large."

I sigh. Antique weapons aren't out of the question. The second victim had a triangular wound through the back into his heart. Central had identified a type of stiletto with a triangular cross-section – it gives a very thin blade a great deal of strength, ideal for a stealthy weapon and suitable for the single blow to the heart.

But the first victim didn't fit this at all. A broken neck isn't exactly difficult to achieve. Alicia's team had identified a pattern of odd bruises on the temples but couldn't account for what had made them.

I stand up and look out my window. I take great pleasure in this and it hasn't worn off yet. "*Exile on Main Street*, Rolling Stones," I say out loud and the album starts playing from discrete speakers in the room at a low volume. I don't hate my neighbours enough to turn it up at this point.

Something strikes me as odd about this case. I stare out the window a moment longer, watching the wintery sunshine reflect off the tall buildings of London.

The pathology reports are still open on-screen when I turn around. "What kind of men are you?" I mutter to myself and turn to the "More Information on Deceased" pages of the reports. One of the men was no labourer, with a large beer gut and a shortage of calluses.

The other two had hard calluses on the edges of their hands and their fingers bore tough pads in several places, suggesting repeated and specific tool use. Not the same tools, mind, as Central thought one of them had used locksmiths tools on a regular basis. The other's patterns suggested something more manual, perhaps a hammer or cutting tools.

Strange. Three diverse people, nothing tying them all together. Oh wait, stomach contents on the soft one and the labourer matched – it appeared they'd eaten in the same restaurant some six to eight hours before they were found dead, although not on the same day. *Coincidence? I find that hard to believe.*

A blinking alert in my HUD catches my attention. Someone in the Research section of the Company did a search on Giordano Bruno for a private customer three weeks before. Customer name was listed as 'Mayweather'.

As I watch, another request appears on-screen from a private citizen named Graeme Black. Why all the sudden interest in a long-dead heretic?

Guess I'd better look into it.

See what I did there? Oh never mind.

Oh, if only there was an iHOP in London

T he pub they were set to meet Mayweather in was much like a lot
of pubs in Soho – overpriced, small and full of local office types
on a Friday afternoon.

Wolf and Graeme entered the bar separately, with Graeme getting a
table with a good view of the interior. And a parabolic mic he could use
to overhear all the conversations in the pub. A mic the size of an old-
style pack of cigarettes. The recorder he was using it with was virtually a
standard item in covert intelligence circles. Graeme kept in with the
intelligence community, having had the odd brush with them while he
was stationed in the Chinese conflict.

They were also using lip mics to communicate. When Wolf entered,
Shirl was propping up the bar with Jonathan, combining business with
pleasure.

"Graeme, stop pointing that thing at Shirl," Wolf sub-vocalised. He
smiled to see Graeme whip the snooper mic away from the direction of
the bar. "No sign of Mayweather yet," he reported. He grabbed a beer
from the bar and found a table.

Graeme shook his head. "*No, nor Sphincter, neither.*"

Wolf doubted Sphincter would turn up. His job was over; introducing
them to Mayweather had been his main task. Mayweather didn't need
him anymore.

"*Freak at five o'clock,*" Shirl muttered. "*And he's alone.*"

Mayweather stood in the door of the pub for a moment, as if he was
letting his eyes adjust to the gloom. It wasn't that bad and Wolf resisted
a temptation to duck under his table or wave both arms wildly in the air.
Both impulses went as quickly as they came.

Ignoring the bar completely, Mayweather strode straight over to
Wolf's table. "You are willing to help me find it?" he demanded,
without any niceties.

Wolf looked him up and down and motioned to the chair across from
him. "Hello to you, too." He sipped his beer. "I am... curious as to what
you've found and I would like more information before I commit to
anything."

With a heavy sigh, Mayweather pulled out the chair and sat down.
"What would you know?"

"I've done a little digging of my own – checking your story out for one thing," Wolf started.

A frown crossed Mayweather's face. "I know and I find it offensive. How dare you…"

Wolf sipped from his beer again. "I like to know whom I'm working with and I don't know you from Adam."

Mayweather was silent for a moment. "Did you speak to Liz?"

Wolf shook his head. "I didn't need to – we just checked on your claim to have been fostered by her. Which was as reported."

"She's not well, you know," Mayweather said quietly.

Wolf shook his head again. "I don't care, Mayweather – I don't owe her anything, as I said before."

"You saved her sister…"

"All that was a long time ago. Another lifetime." Wolf may have sounded cold, but he'd had over twenty years' work escaping from that past.

Mayweather nodded, although it was clear he didn't really understand.

"I also think you know where this item is," Wolf continued. "And don't bullshit me or I walk out that door."

"You *have* been busy," Mayweather said with a smile. "Yes, I know where it is… but it's protected."

Wolf absorbed this for a second. "Protected how?"

"I don't know," Mayweather admitted. "I met a group of men who had an interest in… other items that are in the same place."

"And…?"

"They are no longer returning my calls and I believe they are all dead," Mayweather replied.

"*Shit.*" That was Shirl in his ear.

"How many we talking about?" Wolf asked, not sure how this mattered, but trying to work out the scope of the problem.

"There were five, including my contact." Mayweather raised his hands, palms up as he shrugged. "I don't know what their main activity is, but I suspect they are professional criminals."

Wolf smiled. "Really?" *Sarcasm is the lowest form of wit*, Stanley said in his head. "Why do you think they're dead?"

Mayweather looked away. "I saw a body through a window of the House where the manuscript is kept – I believe it was my contact."

"So you want us to go into a potentially lethal situation with no knowledge of what we're up against and just waltz out with the book?

Does that sum it up?" Wolf asked, head cocked to one side, ready to evaluate Mayweather's response.

"I guess... But I have an idea," Mayweather said weakly.

Wolf nodded. "I'm sure you do. It's probably wrong." He sipped his beer again. "We come now to the crux of the issue – what's in it for me?"

Mayweather stared at him for a moment and Wolf wondered if he was going to go all self-righteous again. "I have no money..."

"Then we're finished," Wolf said, standing up.

"Wait! Wait...!" Mayweather responded, holding out a hand imploringly. "As I said before, there are more items of value in the place where the codex is – I want nothing but the Bruno manuscript!"

Wolf looked at him for a moment before getting the nod from Graeme. "*Might as well see what he thinks is in there.*"

Sitting down again, Wolf stared at Mayweather a bit longer, until the giant started to squirm. "Okay, what do you think would interest me?"

Mayweather stared back for a moment before answering. "I believe there is a codex attributed to Nicholas Flamel amongst the documents as well as what is alleged to be Flamel's copy of the *Book of Abraham the Mage*. There's a first printing of the *Malleus Maleficarum* and possibly several others which you might be interested in."

Graeme sputtered in Wolf's ear. "*The Malleus alone would be worth it...*"

Wolf didn't let any sign appear on his face. Yes, all those items would easily find wealthy buyers and would easily offset any expenses the job might entail. "How do we know they're there?"

Mayweather shrugged. "You don't."

"And if you're lying to me?" Wolf hissed. "I don't take kindly to time-wasters."

Mayweather looked him in the eye. "Alright. If you get the Bruno out of that House, I'll buy it from you..."

"You just said you didn't have any money!" Wolf replied.

"I don't, but I can get it from a benefactor who would buy the manuscript for me," Mayweather retorted, looking a little smug.

"Okay, I'll think about that for a moment. What 'house' are you talking about?" Wolf demanded.

Mayweather, confident now, pulled a data stick from his pocket and handed it to Wolf. "The details are on there. I suggest you look into its past, as that's where I saw the dead body."

Wolf took the stick. He looked at Mayweather for a long moment. "We'll look at the stick and see what we find – anything odd about it and I'll pull my people out of this deal so fast you'll need clean underwear!"

Mayweather nodded. "I understand. Let me know when you want to proceed."

"*Arrogant bastard.*" Shirl.

"You certainly are," Wolf muttered.

"What?" Mayweather asked, confused.

"Nothing." Wolf sat there, wondering what the stick held and what he'd got them into. "We'll be in touch."

Mayweather stood and bowed slightly from the waist and then turned towards the door. *Very formal for an orphan raised in Glasgow. That's what all that schooling did for him,* Wolf guessed.

Graeme came over as Shirl and her beau, Jonathan, followed Mayweather out. Wolf smiled to himself as he realised he hadn't actually met the man yet and he'd been in the same pub, twice.

"Hope we know what we're doing," Graeme said, as he sat down in the chair Mayweather had just vacated.

"Me too, old man, me too," Wolf muttered, staring at the data stick again while he sipped his beer.

TIME ALWAYS PASSES SLOWLY WHEN YOU'RE WAITING FOR SOMETHING TO HAPPEN

A licia sat in her chair, staring at the clock. All she wanted to do now was go home.

But she couldn't. She was waiting on that damnable man, Jaared Sen, to look at the results of the autopsies on the three dead men and get back to her.

Why did she always find herself waiting on him? Hadn't she done enough of that when they'd dated, however briefly – back in the days when people still dated (who knew what the youth of the day called it now?).

She thought back over the earlier conversation with Jerbeau. *Was it just her or was he a bit creepy? Besides, he's gay!*

"Get it together, Al, it's just those damn girls putting the wind up you again!" Her voda started buzzing at that moment and she answered it with some relief.

"Alicia Sampson."

"Hello Alicia, Jaared here."

"Well?" she asked, not prepared to beat around the bush this late on a Friday afternoon.

He paused. "There's been some activity concerning the three of them – I'll have to see how their movements coordinate for the last few weeks." He paused again. "As far as what you've sent me through, I think I have everything I need for now."

"Good, I'll be off for the weekend, then," Alicia said pointedly.

"Your team's done a bang-up job again, Al – you deserve the promotion and I know you'll be good at it."

"Blimey, praise from Jaared Sen. What do you want and where's the real Jaared?" Alicia demanded only half-sarcastically.

He had the decency to laugh. "I know, I know, but I'm serious. Have a great weekend, Al, and we'll catch up soon." He started to go and then she heard him say something under his breath. "I guess we'll probably see each other at the ball on Tuesday."

That damn ball. "Yes, Jaared, I'll see you there, although I can't say I'm looking forward to it," Alicia admitted. "The only consolation I'm getting is that I forced Jack to rent a tux and go with me!"

Jaared chuckled. "You *are* cruel, Alicia!"

"I know, but I have to get my kicks somehow!" It felt like old times for a minute, although Alicia knew it wasn't anything like old times.

"Okay, I'll let you go – have that weekend and see you on Tuesday."

"Yes, you too, Jaared." Alicia hung up the voda and set it on the blotter. "Now what was that all about?" she wondered aloud.

She shrugged, hung up her lab coat and pulled on her cold weather parka-like coat. It certainly didn't feel that cold out there, but she reckoned her coat was doing its job.

Weekends are made for lov— working

All plans to do something besides work go out the window when Timson calls first thing Saturday morning. At least we are up, sitting in my kitchen, Dickens curled up on the seat under the window, watching us read the newsfeeds and drink large cups of coffee.

"Sen here," I answer, pointing to my head as Skeet looks at me enquiringly. The bone phone is unobtrusive to the point of stealth.

"Timson, sir." He sounds out of breath. "I think I've located the building young John Tyler went into. It's an office block slightly off the beaten track near Russell Square. It looks like the CCTV at the convenience store three doors down caught him as he went in."

I nod. "That's good. Any sign of him leaving?"

"Not as such. CCTV may have caught a reflection of him in a private limo departing from the underground car park a little while later. The lab's trying to clean up the image and see if we can get a clean shot and maybe the registration number, too."

"Good work, Timson. Keep me posted," I say, signing off.

"Of course, sir," he replies and disconnects.

"Oh you're so professional on the phone," Skeet says when she sits down. "It's almost as if you're good at dealing with people. Not normally something I associate with your management style – isn't it normally shoot 'em all and let God sort 'em out?"

"Ha! Not anymore – civil liberties and all that," I retort. Much as I want to, I can no longer execute just anyone on little scraps of evidence or, worse, someone's word that such and such had happened.

"More coffee?" I ask, going over to the pot.

"Yes, please," Skeet replies. "Your coffee's very good, better than the crap I got in Vietnam."

"Let me guess, mostly Nescafé with condensed milk," I say with a grimace. Ah, the memories.

"Double espresso – served cold with condensed milk. You can get used to it after a while, but it's awfully cloying."

I pour more coffee into both cups and bring over the milk. "I get mine from a little boutique in Monmouth Street – they roast the beans themselves and have been sending me coffee as long as I can remember."

"Well, don't let them stop," Skeet says. "I wouldn't want to do without this!"

"Don't worry about that; I'm sure they're on Company retainer or something."

"Good."

The only thing to cause any concern over the weekend is a strange call I take from Timson on Sunday.

We haven't really left the house in twenty-four hours, unusual enough for me on my own, but it had been a while since I've had someone to lounge around the house and drink coffee with. I have to admit I'm enjoying it and Skeet seems to be, too.

So when Timson calls he doesn't really interrupt anything.

"Sir, I've found it!" Before I've even had a chance to say hello.

"Calm down – is this about Tyler?"

"The building John Tyler disappeared from!"

"Great. Call out a SOCO unit and go over it with a fine-toothed comb. Do you need me to come along?" Patronising, perhaps, but I did promise to look out for him.

"No sir, I'm just going to check access to the garage and then I'll call them all in."

"Call them first, Timson," I advise. "You want them to be on their way so you don't have to hang around waiting."

"Right sir, I've put the order in to Central—" There's a sudden loud noise from down the phone line and it sounds like he's been cut off.

"Timson?" I try, but the line is already indicating disconnect in my HUD. "Huh," I say out loud.

"Problem?" Skeet asks from her end of the sofa.

"Don't know yet." I frown. "Can't remember the last time I had a call disconnect mid-call."

So I wait a few seconds for him to ring back. When he doesn't, I try to call him. No response, not even a ring tone. I query Central who confirms he should be responding.

A ping of his GPS locator puts him in one of the buildings we discussed the day before, but Central can't determine if it's moving or stationary.

I sit back and wait for the SOCO unit to get there and order some uniforms to accompany them. Timson did send the order before going off-line, but hasn't responded to any queries since.

Of course I'm worrying. Whatever's happened to him isn't likely to be something I want to hear.

Half an hour later, I get a call from one of the uniforms. "It's not good news, sir," he starts.

"Dead?" I ask, knowing it's the worst.

"Yes sir. SOCO says he's been shot and would have died almost instantly."

"Thank you for letting me know – I'll be coming down very shortly. In the meantime, call a Resus Unit and make sure you check the rest of the building before you let the SOCOs loose, okay?" I'm already moving to the bedroom to assume my usual uniform of black suit, white shirt and Glock 66.

Skeet's standing in the doorway, watching me dress, and I have the strangest impression as I catch sight of her out of the corner of my eye, that it's Stel. I turn to look at her directly and the sensation fades.

"Guess you're going to work, then," Skeet says, eyeing up the suit.

"Yep, got a man down on one of the investigations I'm leading." I button the shirt and fumble in the drawer for cufflinks. "I don't like losing a man."

Skeet nods. "I know. I wasn't trying to start a fight. Come here," she orders, taking the cufflinks from my hand and expertly fitting them through the slots. "There you go." She looks me straight in the eye for a moment and then leans up to put both arms around me. I put my arms around her, happy to have her there.

"I love you," she says into my shirt.

"What?" I blurt without thinking, hardly expecting her to say something like that, my tough, merc-Girl Skeet.

She pulls her head back. "I said, 'I love you' – is that a problem?"

I shake my head. "No, not a problem. I love you."

Skeet nestles back against my chest again. "Be careful out there," she orders.

"I always am," I reply.

As she lets go, there's a flicker in the corner of my eye which doesn't resolve when I look at it.

KNOW ANYWHERE NICE FOR SUNDAY LUNCH?

Wolf, Graeme and Shirl had spent most of Saturday looking through the files on the stick.

The location of the House was fairly central in Kensington, part of a row of large, five-storey houses. The vid images made it stand out from the surrounding terrace. It was hardly surprising as the whole frontage appeared to be painted matt black.

Shirl had spent hours analysing the images, looking for any clues as to what the mystery of the House was. She had spotted what looked like a shadowy figure in the windows in several of the images. It wasn't always in the same window, and the figure appeared to change height and shape, suggesting multiple occupants.

Graeme had done a complete title search. "Right. The only known owner of record is a John T. Webster, who had purchased the property when it was first built in 1843. No one took ownership of the building once Webster died in 1901, by some strange coincidence on the same day as Queen Victoria, 22 January 1901." He flicked a wrist and put the original plans onto one of the screens. "This is what it looked like when it was originally built, with a standard Victorian sort of layout."

Shirl took over. "Webster amassed a fortune by fabricating iron for the massive building explosion following the early days of industrialisation in England. Apparently, once the House was finished, he'd gone around the world collecting rare artefacts, books and strange antiquities. No record of them survives, although some researchers have speculated they are all still in the House."

Back to Graeme. "The other thing he was known for was a passion for puzzles and mindbenders – the man was obsessed with them, apparently. One of the builders who worked on Webster's House over the years hinted some 'unusual' things were added to the plans. When pressed, he described hidden passages and odd rooms, but no final plans of the property have survived." He waved at the screen. "I doubt it looks like that now."

Wolf pondered this. "Right, so the layout could be completely different to these plans. Probably is completely different."

"Aye."

Shirl waved at another screen. "It's likely, from what I've read, you'll find things altered and customised."

"Okay. We go in expecting anything."

Graeme tutted, looking at the screens in front of him. "That's weird – I can't find any record that it's been kept up or owned by anyone since Webster died."

Wolf shrugged. "That's not as weird as the specs on the changes he planned which he gave to the contractor, Honor Jones, who did the last of the work. Look," he pointed at the plan on his screen.

Graeme whistled. "What's that, two sub-basements? He must have tanked the whole lot to avoid subsidence... And what's that?"

Wolf shook his head. "No idea, it's listed as BT on the schedule, but no other explanation for it." He flipped around the 3D plan he'd managed to generate. "And there's unexplained voids throughout most of the building. Following on from the builder's comments, I'd say there are some hidden rooms in there, at least."

"But what for?" Shirl asked, looking over their shoulders. "What's weirder – did you know that the contractor, Jones, and his manager both burned in a mysterious fire at their offices shortly after the work was completed? All plans and papers associated with the business were destroyed in the fire – I'm surprised you've found anything."

Graeme whistled again. "*Mysterious*, eh? Sounds peculiar." He gestured at the plans on-screen. "So where did these come from?"

Wolf smiled. "Well, apparently Jones took a copy of the plans home for further study and they were still there when his wife died. An aspiring architecture student who was a friend of the family put them in the archives of the RIBA and they were digitised in 2015 along with most of the other archives of RIBA."

Michael knocked on the workroom door. "Okay, y'all been in here for far too long – it smells like a locker room! You are all taking me to Sunday Lunch at *The Warrington*. I've been back three days and have hardly seen any of you!"

Wolf looked at Shirl and Graeme and smiled. "I doubt we've got much choice, even though there are three of us and only one of him..."

Graeme laughed and rubbed his eyes. "I guess we could do with a break, at that." He looked up at Michael. "And *The Warrington* does do a mean Sunday Roast..."

Smiling, Shirl went over and hugged Michael. "Feeling left out, again, Mikey?" Shirl was the only one that got away with calling him that and he laughed.

"No," he said, mock serious. "I just think my fiancée and my friends should come out and celebrate our engagement in style. Janey and the infamous Bernard are meeting us there in a quarter of an hour. So come on, get your coats and money and we can walk down there."

Wolf held his hands up in surrender. "Whatever you say, master!"

"I like that," Michael said. "That's Mr Master to you, plebe!"

When they returned several hours later, one of Shirl's search routines had thrown up a few other stories about the Webster place, as they'd started calling it.

"Get this: A group of spiritualists had heard about strange lights in the windows and broke in with the intention of contacting the spirits allegedly haunting the House."

"And they disappeared without a trace," Wolf guessed.

Shirl looked at him, shocked. "How d' you know?"

"I think I wrote this one," Wolf replied. "I'll bet we find a few more stories about that House along the same lines and if we question the neighbours, we'll get reports of weird lights, knocking and other 'strange' activity."

Graeme looked at him puzzled. "How d' you know?"

Wolf sighed. "Don't you guys read any of those thrillers I've given you over the years? It's what always happens."

Shirl nodded. "Yeah, but this is reality."

"I always quote the maxim that 'truth is stranger than fiction' at this point," Wolf replied. "Either there really are strange things going on there, or someone's gone to a lot of effort to manufacture a place where weird things keep happening."

Graeme nodded, smothering a belch from all the rich food. "I can see that. I did hear of a guy who built a complete haunted house out in Suffolk somewhere. Apparently one of his own traps got him and they didn't find him for three weeks."

Michael, stretched out on the settee in the corner with his eyes closed, interjected at that point. "You guys sound like you're telling ghost stories, now."

The other three stared at him for a moment. "He's right," Shirl conceded. "Hey Mikey, you're right!"

"I am, sometimes," he replied, eyes still closed. "So, what're you going to do about it?"

Wolf answered him after a few moments. "I think we need to go have a look."

JUST HANGING AROUND...

A licia used the weekend to catch up on the domestic chores she'd ignored all week and busied herself doing mundane, everyday 'life' things.

As the weather was sunny and dry, Porgy and Bess got treated to a bath in the tub she and Stephen had installed in the utility space outside the back door. Alicia thought the dogs were going to explode with happiness as she pushed Bess into the tub.

As always, the tricky part was getting the dogs clean and then back into the house without them running around in the garden making mud with their wet fur.

Stephen had rigged a little run which herded them back into the house, but Alicia couldn't remember how to put it up. She settled for putting them on their leads and attaching Porgy to the apple tree in the courtyard while she groomed Bess. Although it wasn't a small tree, she'd have to work quickly to get her clean before Porgy broke loose.

"Hold still!" Alicia laughed as she sprayed warm water over the stiff coat of the dog. "Almost done, Bess. Just let me turn the water off. Now for the towel..." she pulled the old fluffy towel from the bench and started rubbing, aiming to get Bess mostly dry before putting her back in the house. A few more seconds of vigorous rubbing and she was ready. "There you go, girl," she said, unhooking the lead and pulling her towards the open back door.

Porgy barked as Bess went past. Alicia bundled her back inside and quickly shut the door. "Now for you, young man," Alicia said sternly. Porgy barked at her as she untied his lead from the tree.

"Go on," she admonished, leading him to the bath. The dog leapt into the tub quite happily and barked at her again as she tied his lead to the hook at the end of the tub. "You're the only dog I know that *likes* being bathed!" She turned on the spray and rinsed him before spraying his back with dog-friendly soap. Once he'd been lathered, the spray made quick work of cleaning him off.

Alicia got another towel and repeated the rubdown process before he got cold. "There you go, all clean and handsome," she gushed. "Now in the house with you."

It was relatively easy to get him into the house, as Bess was inside barking at them. Alicia shoved him in and closed the door, the better to tidy up the towels and put everything away.

When she was done, she looked around the garden and decided it was mostly ready for winter. "Time for a cup of tea," she said out loud to no one.

By the time she'd gone in and made a cup of tea, the light in the garden had started to fade. The two dogs, exhausted from their bath were curled up in their beds, snoring lightly.

Alicia sat at the kitchen table with her tablet catching up on the news, most of it grim: more wars in Asia; economic instability in the New African states; and population figures for China and India continuing to explode despite enforced birth control laws and experiments with fertility dampeners in the water. Depressed, Alicia turned it off and found herself staring once again at the letter.

"Damn you, Stephen Jameson," she whispered, working hard not to cry again.

Alicia made a fresh cup of tea before taking it with her through to the living room. She put it down next to her chair by the fire, which as the light faded seemed a good thing to have on. She settled down with a sigh.

Picking up the book she'd been struggling to read, *The Miller of Mansfield*, Alicia settled in for a relaxed afternoon. Before she'd turned the page, she'd fallen asleep.

It was obvious it was a dream. The garden had a bright, sparkling quality to it that was just not natural. And there were plants growing which her dogs would never have let survive.

The sunshine was also amazingly bright with a clarity she'd never seen before. It felt like the best summer's day that Alicia had ever experienced, bees humming, the plants almost crackling with the urge to grow.

Alicia was sat on a comfortable wooden garden chair, slightly reclining and staring across the vitality of her garden.

"It's lovely, isn't it?" Stephen asked. "I come here every day."

Alicia turned and Stephen was sat in a similar chair with a small table on the grass between them. She smiled, happy to find him there. His skin glowed in the living sunshine. He looked so alive but she knew this was a dream, at best.

"Yes, it's beautiful," she replied. "We're not in my garden, are we?"

Stephen smiled back and shook his head. "It's a facsimile I create when I want to be with you... well, closer to you, as a facsimile of your consciousness doesn't really work here." He gestured around them.

"How are you Stephen?" Alicia asked.

Stephen looked at her, drinking in her skin, her hair, and eyes. "As... well as can be expected, I suppose," he replied. "How are you, Al?"

Alicia frowned. "I was fine until I got a letter from you a few days ago. Why'd you have to go and do that?" She hadn't realised how angry she actually was with him.

Stephen nodded. "I wish I could have stopped the letter, my love, but I have no influence in your world." He spread his hands. "If I could wish it away, I would gladly do so." He was silent for a moment before continuing. "While I meant every word I wrote in that letter to you, dear heart, I think the time has come for you to put away my things and think about moving on with your life."

"How am I supposed to do that?" Alicia cried, her voice loud in the vibrant garden. "Every day I'm reminded you aren't here – I can't just forget you!"

Stephen shook his head. "I don't expect you to forget, Al, but I think it's time you weren't so affected by it." He reached across the table and touched her face. "I will always love you, Al, and I will always be with you." He kissed her on the forehead, a mere hint of a touch.

"Oh Stephen," Alicia whispered as the garden faded around her.

She woke in the chair, tears streaming down her face. But something had changed, her heart felt lighter and while she was crying for Stephen, it was no longer tears of anger or regret.

I'VE ALWAYS BEEN TOLD I'M 'TOO HANDS ON'. WHAT DOES THAT EVEN MEAN?

T he SOCOs are working their way through the office where Timson was found by the time I get there.

"The Resus Team took Timson away half an hour ago, sir," the PC I'd spoken to before informed me. *Hanson?* Central confirmed it in my HUD. He's a well-built chap, with dark hair and pale complexion, standing nearly as tall as me, but broader across the beam. And not an ounce of fat on his muscular frame, I'd guess.

"Very good." I look around. "No other nasty surprises, I hope."

"No sir. We swept the entire building and found no life signs or any indication anyone had even been here." He waves one of the figures in a paper suit over. "Tell the Commander what you found, Jimmy," he instructs.

"Looks like Contractor Timson set off some kind of booby trap, sir," the young tech informs me. "Looks like he was accessing the com unit over there and some kind of nasty projectile weapon had been rigged to the unit." He looks a little pale. "And I think Contractor Timson was unlucky, sir – looked to me like whatever it was went right through his femoral artery. He'd have bled out in a matter of seconds."

Femoral – in the leg. "It was set to hit anyone sitting at the desk?"

Jimmy nods. "Yes sir, and whoever set it has a nasty sense of humour – I think he was aiming for the person's balls, sir." He blushes, realising he's said 'balls' to me.

I nod. "That *is* nasty. Thank you Jimmy. Maybe I'll make sure he's shot in the balls when we find him, for Timson – what do you think?"

Blanching now, as he realises what I mean, Jimmy nods back. "I think that's a good plan, s-s-sir. If you'll excuse me," he says as he scuttles off to carry on with his work.

"Nicely handled, sir," Hanson murmurs behind me.

"I'm not kidding with that one." I turn around. "I don't like people killing my Contractors and this one's just got on my bad side." As I turn away, a shadowy figure is in the corner, watching. As I look at it more directly, Stel nods at me and turns away.

The SOCO units end up sweeping the whole building with sniffers and thermal sensors. The heat detectors mostly return inconclusive results due to the sweep Hanson's team had performed. The sniffer finds a few interesting traces, including a trace of heroin in the drawer of the desk where Timson suffered his fatal wound.

"Sniffer can't tell if it's the same batch as we found at the Tyler dump site," Jimmy informs me. "But statistically, with the scarcity of heroin around at the moment, I'd say it's 99% probability of a match. We'll see if we can get anything else to tie it to the other scene." He looks back at the team. "Stitch is going over the com unit now and I'll let you know what we find."

"Thanks Jimmy," I reply. I turn back to Hanson, who's become my second by default. "Central confirms prognosis is good for a viable Resus on Timson, thanks to your quick response." I hold out my hand. "Thanks for your quick work."

His own HUD will show the commendation I just approved as well as a promotion to my personal team. "I don't know what to say, sir..." he splutters, taking my hand. "I just want to work in the field, sir..."

"Don't worry, Hanson," I reassure him. "You're going to get plenty of field work – you're not going to just be my driver and I reckon you'll make Contractor with a little more experience. Which it appears you're going to get with me, as I just lost a Contractor for three months' rehab."

"Thank you, sir," he says finally.

Jimmy returns with Stitch, a tiny slip of a woman who looks young enough to be Jimmy's daughter. "The com unit was hacked, sir, and by a real pro – from what I've found, it was able to send Tyler's GPS transponder to sleep for the period of time he was off grid." She smiles, blushing. "Jimmy told me what you said 'bout the perv who set up that booby trap, sir; I have to say I heartily agree!"

"I'm glad you approve... Stitch. Did you find anything that might tell us who this 'pro' is in your poking about the innards?" I ask.

"I've found a couple of snippets of code that look custom – meaning they might help us identify him," she finishes quickly at my frown. "I'll put them through the usual searches when we get back and see if we can find anything more on him from that."

"Okay, just put in your report when you know more. Any ideas why John Tyler might have been here?" I'm hoping she does so I can inform the IG.

"No sir. It doesn't look like anything that useful survived the system crash Timson started which set off the trap." She was as disappointed as I was. *Oh well, there were other avenues for investigation.*

"Never mind, we'll get him. Good work." She blushes again as I turn back to Jimmy. "You going to be much longer?"

Jimmy shakes his head. "No sir, we should be finishing up shortly."

"Okay. I'm going to go report to the IG and start following up some of the threads we've not touched yet. Maybe Timson found something he didn't know he'd found." I'm thinking out loud now as I realise the trio are looking at me a little blankly. "That's all for now, dismissed."

Jimmy and Stitch head back for the com unit and I can see a flurry of activity taking place amongst the rest of the team as they start packing up equipment.

"Hanson, I guess I need to get back to Central – find me a car?"

"Absolutely, sir!" I almost expect him to click his heels.

"Good, let's get going. I don't want to spend all day there."

"Very good, sir."

I'M NOT AFRAID OF THE DARK, BUT
SOMETIMES I GET FRIGHTENED

Wolf and Shirl pulled kit bags out of storage under the stairs in Wolf's apartment block.

"I don't think we need the armour on this one," Shirl offered.

Wolf shook his head. "Nah, it's just a reccie, so probably the chameleon suits with the infrared liners will be sufficient. Basic climbing stuff, and some night vision goggles with recorders." He grinned. "I'd rather not be too bogged down with equipment."

"Agreed," Shirl said, sorting out a couple of pouches and stuffing everything into two kit bags, one for her and one for Wolf. "We haven't done this kind of thing for a while."

"No. Hope we're not too rusty," he replied. "Graeme stays in the Rover to cover us, right?"

Shirl nodded, Graeme's last hospital visit still fresh in her mind. "I'd rather not take him at all, but you know him."

"Oh yes. And stubborn runs in this family," Wolf teased, holding up his hands in mock surrender. "You know I don't just mean you!"

Grinning, Shirl slapped his bicep. "We're all a bit stubborn, it's true – you're the worst of the lot!"

"Am I gonna have to come down there and separate you two?" Graeme calls down from the doorway. "You're supposed to be sorting gear, not bickering like a couple of five year-olds."

"We are, Dad!" Shirl called back. "But he's looking at me!" And she started laughing.

Wolf laughed too, before retorting, "Stop touching me! She's touching me!"

There was some good-natured grumbling from upstairs which just set them off again. When they had stopped laughing, Graeme was stood a few steps up glowering at them. "Are you finished? I'd like to get this over with before I die."

Wiping his eyes, Wolf looked in his kit bag. "Yep, I'm ready. You?" he directed at Shirl.

"Yessirree Bob, all present and accounted for, sir!" Shirl snapped a lazy salute at Graeme.

"Well get the bags into the Rover and let's get going, then." He pulled his coat on and plopped a flat cap down on his head.

Wolf and Shirl scrambled up and grabbed coats before picking up the bags and following him out of the flat.

"See you later, Michael," Wolf called.

"Don't do anything I wouldn't do," Michael replied from the kitchen. "Oh hell, just come back in one piece."

The door slamming was his only answer.

They got to the Webster House in no time, Graeme's knowledge of the back streets coming in handy in the stop–start Sunday traffic.

Graeme drove past it and parked across the road some fifty metres further along.

The House was dark with no light visible from the street. The blackness of the walls seemed to suck the light from its surroundings, leaving a hole in the terrace.

It was a standard plan in this part of town, four stories with a basement. There was a short series of steps up to a landing outside the front door with iron railings circling the well that went down to the basement level. Stairs went down into it behind a gate. The front door was flanked by two pillars, supporting a short portico roof.

In the back of the Land Rover, Wolf and Shirl shrugged into their tightly fitting active polymer suits, which basically made them invisible to casual observation – they would blend into the wall they were against. The infrared inserts made them even tighter, but ensured that they were virtually undetectable by scanners or night vision equipment.

They checked each other's suits like divers in the buddy system, making sure there were no bunches or gaps and that there was no chance of catching or chafing when in awkward positions.

"Ready?" Wolf asked Shirl.

She nodded. The suits weren't on yet, so he could see her head move, the eyes of two infrared torches glinting briefly at her temples. "As I'll ever be."

Wolf turned on his suit, closed the face flap and tried the throat mic. "Mic test – check."

Shirl fastened her mask and vanished in the dim light. He always found that disconcerting and tried waving his hand in front of his eyes. He could sense a vague outline of it, but couldn't even make out individual fingers.

"*Check*," he heard in his ears. "*Mine?*"

"Loud and clear," he replied. "Let's go."

"*Just a sec,*" Graeme interjected. "*Got a dog walker at two o'clock.*"

Once dog and human had passed, they gave him a few moments to carry on. Last thing they needed was a dog giving them away.

"*Go*," Graeme ordered.

Wolf popped the door and they quickly ran down the street to the black House and pressed themselves to the wall on both sides of the door. "*Anything?*" Graeme asked in their ears.

"Not so far," Wolf replied, which wasn't quite accurate. It felt like the wall was vibrating behind him.

"*You feel that?*" Shirl asked.

"Some kind of vibration... maybe a generator," Wolf replied.

"*A genny? Who maintains it?*" Graeme's voice was a bit tinny.

"No idea. Let's have a look and see what we can see from the outside."

Wolf and Shirl slipped climbing claws on their hands and toes. Wolf turned on his infrared lights and the world started glowing greenly.

Unlike the original steel claws invented in China or Japan, the 'claws' that they were using were modelled on gecko toes – staying on the surface through thousands of microscopic hairs interacting with the surface just above the atomic level.

He couldn't see her, but Wolf could sense Shirl in front of him, approaching the wall.

Shirl placed her right toe against the wall and her left hand above it. "Here goes," she said. She started climbing, easily and comfortably away from the door. In a matter of seconds, she was above one of the ground floor windows. "The curtains to the lounge are open – some furniture. Nothing else so far."

Wolf followed her, taking a breath before climbing up and around the portico roof to the window above the door. The claws held perfectly well, but his ankles and wrists started aching almost immediately. "I'm getting too old for this shit," he muttered.

"*Okay, granddad, keep checking,*" Graeme responded.

"Righto." Wolf edged his face above the sill, not expecting to see anything but dim rooms. Strangely, there didn't seem to be anything in the hall, just a staircase and what looked like four closed doors. "Nothing here," he reported.

"*Nothing from first floor window, either,*" Shirl replied. "*Going up.*"

Wolf sidled across the face of the House, the vibrations running through his fingers and toes. It didn't seem to be upsetting the claws, whatever it was. The window to the room off the hall was also empty of people, although there seemed to be a desk and bookcases from what Wolf could make out.

"Going up, too," Wolf reported, slowly moving around the window and pulling himself up the wall. His ankles were burning now. He really needed to get back to the climbing wall.

As he raised his head carefully above the window ledge, he stopped in shock. A face was staring out the window at him. "Shit!" he cursed under his breath.

"*What is it?*" Shirl asked.

"Got a visual on a person. Looks male. But wait..." He moved his head to the right. The figure's eyes tracked him. "Dammit, he can see me! You getting this?"

"*Calm down.*"

Easy for him to say, Wolf thought – *he's not hanging off a bloody wall.*

"What's he doing, other than watching you?" Graeme questioned.

"Uh, nothing at the moment." Wait, was the vibration coming through the wall stronger? "Shirl, is the vibration getting worse?"

There was a moment's pause while the figure in the room beyond regarded him with a forlorn stare. The mouth moved for a moment, but Wolf couldn't work out what he was saying.

"*I'd say so,*" Shirl replied. "*I think we should get down, Wolf – we don't want to fall on those railings.*"

"Or into that basement well, either – we've no idea what's down there."

"*Absolutely. Going down.*"

"Me too," Wolf said, slowly easing himself below the edge of the window ledge. The figure's eyes followed him down before he lost sight of them.

The vibrations seemed to recede as he went down the wall. "You behind me, Shirl?"

"No idea, big boy – where are you?"

"I'm by the door." He felt a nudge on his shoulder. "Ah, there you are." He moved over the short wall and let himself down onto the doorstep. Shirl bumped him again when she joined him.

On impulse, he touched the mail flap set in the middle of the door. It moved with a squeak. He pulled a probe out of his pouch, plugged it into the unit on his belt by feel and slid it through the slot. A Head's Up Display appeared in his goggles, showing the view into the hall. Again, it was mostly empty, barring an elephant's foot umbrella stand next to what has to be the ugliest iron hall tree with a little table in the middle.

"Odd, there's no junk mail on the mat," Wolf commented. "No pizza flyers, no clothing collection bags, nothing."

"*Someone's tidying,*" Graeme replied.

"That's what it looks like, but who?"

"*Get back here! Looks like that dog walker's coming back!*"

They didn't need any urging and quickly ran back to the Range Rover. The two of them piled into the back and switched off their suits once the car door closed.

"Did you see him?" Wolf asked Graeme. Their faceplates had cameras to record what they were looking at. It allowed them to go back later and see if they'd missed anything.

"Well, that's the weird part," Graeme replied. "Here, let me run it back." He found Wolf's feed on the monitor and moved to the timestamp he'd placed on the footage. "Here's the first room you looked in."

The hall was depicted in green on the screen.

"And this is the second," he said, moving to the second timestamp.

Again, the empty study, desk and bookshelves visible.

Graeme moved to the last timestamp. "This is what I saw when you told me you were looking at a person."

The room was empty.

"What the hell?" Wolf asked the air. "There was a guy right in front of the window, there!" He pointed at the left side of the screen. Then he saw it, just a flicker, but something on the feed definitely moved. "Wait, go back half a dozen frames, there's something in there."

Graeme obediently went back a few frames and started pacing through the still frames one at a time.

They all froze. On the screen, hand-written words appeared.

Do not come back – you will not survive next time.

EVER HAD A COWBOY SIT ON YOUR LAP?

Alicia woke with a lighter heart on Monday morning. She flew
through her morning routine before hugging both the dogs,
locking up and walking down to the tube station.

Sue was waiting for her when she arrived at the office. "You've got a
meeting with Jerbeau at half past."

"Thanks Sue – did he say what it was about?" Alicia asked, pulling her
coat off. She gratefully took the large mug of coffee.

"No, but I'm guessing it's about the changes. There's a planning
meeting this afternoon with all the shift heads."

"Mortensen's going to be there? Blimey, it must be important!" Alicia
said with a grin. Mortensen was night shift head and notorious for not
turning up at meetings during the day. His wife simply couldn't wake
him once he was asleep.

"Apparently he's in the break room mainlining espressos from the new
machine." Sue was also smiling. "I also slipped him a couple of sleep
inhibitors when he wasn't looking."

"Sue!" Alicia was shocked for a second before she started laughing.

"Don't worry, I'll slip him the antidote when the meeting's over!"

Still laughing, Alicia waved her out of the room. "Go on, I'll just
check my messages before seeing Jerbeau."

Alicia entered Jerbeau's office on the first floor at exactly nine thirty.
"Ah Alicia, just the person I wanted to see." Felix stood up behind his
desk. "Come, sit," he instructed.

"Morning Felix," Alicia replied, large mug of coffee in her hand.

"Do you want coffee? No, I see you're prepared," he called out the
door. "Evan, can I get a cappuccino, please?"

A young man stuck his head in the door. "Sure – two secs," he replied.
"Morning, Ms Sampson, can I get you anything?"

"No, I'm fine, thank you." Alicia waved her mug.

The head disappeared and Alicia turned back to Jerbeau.

"My new right hand," Felix confided. "I don't know what I'd do without him – he's only been here two days and already I'm finding him invaluable!"

Alicia nodded. "A good assistant is worth going to the trouble to keep. I have to keep fending off people trying to poach Sue!"

Jerbeau smiled ruefully. "I did consider her but realised that wouldn't have helped you!"

"I'm glad you didn't – she's already a pay grade and a half above where she should be!" Alicia replied. Then realising what she'd said, added, "But she's worth every penny."

"I'm not going to second-guess your management decisions, Alicia." He shrugged. "You need Sue and she's obviously good at what she does or you wouldn't have gone to such lengths to keep her."

Alicia nodded again. "Thanks, I was just worried I was going to have to watch personnel costs."

Felix frowned slightly. "I don't believe it's an issue at present, Alicia. I think consolidating all the MEs in one place will provide enough cost savings at this point. There has also been significant under-investment in your department for some time – which we will now be rectifying."

"I appreciate that," Alicia said. "And I've seen the initial proposals for the consolidation programme – are we going to have to move?"

"The plan is to move the other departments in this building a short distance away to slightly further down river and commit this building to being the Forensic Pathology department." He shrugged again. "We'll talk about this later at the planning meeting, but beyond some construction, I hope to keep your department pretty much as is."

Alicia let out a sigh of relief. "I was afraid it was bad news," she confessed. "Thanks for letting me know."

"Think nothing of it, Alicia – I'm here to make things work, not cause problems," Felix said with a grin. "Although I may have to move you and Sue up here for administrative purposes."

"Well, that's a small price to pay for all this change," Alicia said with a smile. "Besides, I could use the exercise!" She sipped her coffee. "Was there anything else?"

Felix shook his head. "No, I just think we should get in the habit of a Monday meeting to discuss the week's schedule and anything else that might come up."

"That's fine by me." Alicia stood up. "Sue will send you a daily report of cases and staff requirements. Obviously we never know how busy we're going to be. And Mondays can be the worst after a weekend's excesses."

"I understand. I shall see you at the planning meeting," Felix responded.

"Great!" Alicia took her notebook and coffee and headed for the stairs.

When she got to her office, the lighter mood continued. "You know, I think this is going to work," Alicia said to no one, but feeling better than she had in a long time.

I STILL HATE MONDAYS...

Monday dawns bright and early. It's still dark when I get up and wander through to the kitchen for a cup of coffee. Dickens wanders around my ankles, asking things like "Mwwrrrr?" and "Prrddt?" while trying to trip me. He's never succeeded so far, but that doesn't stop him.

I take his food out of the cupboard and put some in his bowl. He chirps gratitude and starts digging in, purring while eating – apparently it is possible. He always gets so excited and it's always the same, chicken-flavoured, dry biscuits.

I smile down at him and pour some coffee.

Sunday had been busy after I left the crime scene. Central went through all of Timson's electronic notes and I went through his cubicle, looking for anything relating to the case.

There wasn't much he hadn't told me and what he had was a name.

James Tyler.

I suppose now is as good a time as any to go into James Tyler.

New money, filthy rich and a real social climber. And another pretender to the throne. After the pandemics in the twenties, a lot of changes had to be made. It wasn't as bad as it could have been, but an estimated 2.8 billion people died across the world. We're now recovering, and Central's latest projections have the world population approaching eight billion again.

One of the side effects was the elimination of the Royal Family in the UK. The King, his children, his brother, and most of his cousins, all wiped out by the plague. Codenamed 'Odin', the altered bird flu virus was very resistant to antibiotics and impossible to treat without them. The press speculated King William had picked it up on his visit to Africa.

The result was a decimated Royal Family and a succession process plagued (pun intended) by pretenders, half-cousins and legal challenges. The surviving masters of the succession weren't helped by infighting and attempts to put this or that preferred candidate on the throne of what was left of the United Kingdom.

James Tyler had already spent millions trying to prove his claim that he was a royal by birth through his mother, some kind of fourth cousin of the dead King. Every so often there was some kind of programme on the vid about all the candidates and the likelihood of one of them becoming King or Queen. Central seemed to think he had little chance of attaining the throne, something to do with forged birth documents. Not that I care.

I met James Tyler at a function because, surprise, surprise, he's a Company shareholder.

I don't recall what the event was – I was ordered to go as usual. It was held in the ballroom of the *Grosvenor House* on Park Lane. Also unsurprising.

I had only just had my new eyes and was busy drinking in the amazing sights around me, more than a little aware of all the years I'd missed seeing people, and not just the women. Fashion has never been my passion, but I was more than a little aware of changes since I'd last seen the latest styles.

I'm leaning against the bar, enjoying the parade of half-dressed women and black tied men, nursing a very nice whisky – limited edition, cask strength and boy could I tell – when someone at the bar brushes up against me, jostling my drinking hand.

"Excuse me," the soft voice says in my ear.

I turn to look at the owner of the voice. If I could have stepped backwards, I probably would. She is stunning and looks all-natural, not body-sculpted like so many women (and a few men, I'm sure) these days. You can tell, too, am I right?

She's wearing a thin white dress that conceals and reveals at the same time and looks like it was painted on. Blonde, of course, although the darker eyebrows suggest the curtains don't match the carpets. Perfect nose, turned up in the right places, and dimpled chin. The dress accentuates her breasts which, while not huge, look perfectly formed from my point of view. And if, as I think it was, one of those that brushed me, I probably won't wash that elbow for a year! I can't help myself checking out the whole package, continuing in a downward direction; she has long legs that go all the way up to her bottom. Not as curvy as Marilyn Monroe, but she could be her sister. Now I *am* showing my age.

Then she smiles. "My apologies, Mr—"

She has me at the smile. Even at my age, all I can do is smile back like an idiot. "Commander Jaared Sen, Ma'am," I respond. Good thing I'm not wearing jackboots or those heels would probably have clicked together. "And you are...?"

"My wife, Portia, Commander," a brusque voice interrupts and I have to look away from the vision as a hand is thrust towards me. I take the hand, still stunned. "James Tyler."

I tear my gaze away. "Jaared Sen," I reply. His grip is firm and as he grips harder, I realise instantly he's trying to crush my hand. Shame that doesn't work once I adjust my grip ever so slightly to touch that nerve... there. "Pleased to meet you," I say over his gasp.

Tyler takes his hand back and would have rubbed it, were he not holding a drink in the other one. He frowns. "Is this man bothering you, Portia?"

Portia flashes me another smile, green eyes flashing. "Hardly, Jimmy, he's the first interesting person I've met here," she says lightly.

Now visibly irritated, Tyler takes her elbow. "Come my dear, we must go say hello to the Inspector General." He tries to steer her away from me.

"I want another drink, Jimmy; you go and I'll catch you up," she refuses, turning to the bar.

Tyler goes a strange sort of reddy-pink colour – I'm beginning to think I could recognise puce. "I insist, Portia," he hisses.

She waves him away. "Oh, go play, Jimmy. I'm fine here and I'm sure Commander Sen will look after me, won't you Commander?" This last is said with a flirtatious wink Tyler can't see, unless there's a mirror behind the bar.

"Absolutely, Mr Tyler," I reply, even though Central's flagged his title as being 'Lord'. Oops.

Without another word, Tyler clutches his drink, spins round and stalks off into the crowd.

I stand there, watching him go, and sip my whisky. A hand on my arm makes me turn back to the vision beside me. "May I buy you a drink, Commander?" she asks; that smile's back. She signals the bartender and he nods; he's probably got a chip in his head that tells him what everyone's drinking.

Well, what can I do? "I find it hard to refuse a beautiful woman," I reply. "Although I don't think it'll make your husband very happy."

Portia grimaces. "Very little makes Jimmy happy these days, I'm afraid – he's too overprotective and..." She stops and turns to me. "I shouldn't be telling you this, Commander. I'm sure you don't want to hear my problems."

My turn to smile. "Lady Tyler, you can tell me anything," I respond gallantly.

"Please, call me Portia – *Lady* makes me sound like someone's grandmother!" She flashes that smile again.

"Very well, Portia," I reply, bowing slightly. The bartender arrives with our drinks: kir royale for her, the whisky for me. I put down my spent glass and pick up the new one. "To happy meetings," I toast.

"To new friends," she corrects, lightly touching her champagne flute to my whisky glass before sipping the bubbly. I watch her over the rim of my glass.

"I must confess, Commander," she starts, raising her eyes to mine.

"I'm afraid I'm not a priest, Lady—Portia," I interrupt her.

She blushes slightly. "I knew who you were before I bumped into you, Commander. I—" now she looks flustered. "I've wanted to meet you for some time."

Now even more curious. I can't imagine this beautiful woman wanting to meet plain old me. "Really? Whatever for?"

Portia looks me right in the eye and the blush has faded completely. "I believe you fought with my grandfather in France, Commander," she returns, as if she meets one hundred and seventy year-old men every day.

Central flags and displays her several great-great grandfathers in my HUD. A Frenchman named Oliver Edwards would be the right age. It details his wife as well.

"I believe you mean your grandmother, as Oliver was a quartermaster sergeant she married after the war," I comment. "Claudine fought beside me at Passchendaele, it's true."

Her mouth is open in surprise. "You knew?!" she demanded.

"Of course – I think the whole company knew, eventually, but none of us mentioned it. We called her *Claude.*" I sip my whisky. "I guess she became something of a mascot for us – and no one said anything because most of us were frightened of her." I take another sip. "And she was French; no one could work out how she'd joined up with a British platoon, but hey, they took me as well."

Her eyes light up. "Really? That's fascinating Commander!" she gushes.

"Is that what you wished to speak to me about? I am rather surprised you have been able to trace me, as that was some time and several names ago." *And that worries me, too.* Central makes a note and begins tracing lines of enquiry.

"Not for someone with Jimmy's resources," she claims. "And yes, from what I gather, you knew both Oliver and Claudine, didn't you?"

I smile, remembering them both. The big, gruff Yorkshireman, Oliver, worrying endlessly about petite and boyish Claudine, with me doing my best to reassure him I was looking after her. I'd gone to Europe before the war, and when it looked like war was inevitable, I signed up, first with the Belgians, and then the French, before joining the English. I never fought with the Americans. Don't know why.

I'd had enough at Verdun, but ended up at Passchendaele, which was probably worse. I woke in a field hospital, left for dead, no clothes and no papers. No one new me and it didn't take a lot to disappear in those days.

I return to the present with a start. "I do apologise... memories," I explain. "Yes, I knew them. Oliver was always after me to look after Claudine when I went behind the lines – he worried about her a great deal, but he couldn't persuade her to stop fighting." The whisky stings. "I only heard they got married later. I had to... return to America."

That smile appears again. I wonder how many of those I've missed over the years.

"Really, Commander, I know you disappeared after the war – but not what you did next." She sips her champagne, watching me all the while. Those eyes are pools one could easily get lost in. "What did you do for the century before you turned up here?"

"That's a story for another time," I reply with a smile of my own. "I'm sorry, but I must be going – I have an early meeting and..." I shrug.

The green eyes darken for a moment before she recovers. "Of course, Commander. Thank you so much for the diversion – I would so love to speak to you about Oliver and Claudine again sometime." *Give her credit, she's not a quitter.*

"I'm sure we can manage something," I say while thinking *No way in hell*, as Central's now flagging her as a security risk. "Goodnight, m' Lady."

"Goodnight Commander Sen."

And I left her at the bar without a backward glance.

So yes, James Tyler knows who I am – he probably knows more than I want him to.

AIN'T THAT A KICK IN THE HEAD?

The trio went through all the video and other feeds they'd collected and found more anomalies.

"Jesus, Mary and Joseph on the Cross," Graeme muttered as a transparent, but recognisable, face appeared on the screen, taken from Wolf's headcam when he'd looked through the window of the lounge. "That's the fourth image of an individual we've found," he said as the figure remained on-screen for about six frames.

"Wait, go back," Shirl said, rubbing her eyes. "Is he trying to say something? Watch the lips."

Wolf and Graeme dutifully stared at the monitor. Yes, his lips were moving.

Graeme switched monitors and pulled up a menu. "Just a sec, I think I've got something for that... yes, here." He gestured and another icon lit up at the edge of the screen. The clip of video with the face ran back and forth for a few seconds before replaying the video at normal speed.

"Please... help... me," a slightly mechanical but male computer voice said.

"What the hell?" Wolf blurted.

"It's reading his lips – got shareware from somewhere that can do that. Hasn't been useful until now," Graeme admitted.

"That's spooky," Shirl proclaimed, clutching her arms across her chest. "I'll see if the database can find anything on this one." She bent over her tablet, pulling the image from Graeme's screen and uploading it to the software they had acquired with a backdoor into the Company's Central mainframe. If Central had an image, and it kept billions of images from the CCTV footage from around the city, the identity of the figure should be known very soon.

Mesmerising as it was, Wolf and Graeme soon lost interest in this new figure and went back to scanning the video feed. They didn't find any more people but the warning to keep away was repeated twice more, including on the audio of Shirl's mic in a voice that could easily have come from an open grave.

They'd played the audio three times and were almost finished with what they could do with their data when Shirl swore.

"Shit!" Shirl was staring at a new window that popped up on her screen. "Uh-oh, think I tripped something," she said softly.

Wolf looked at the little screen. "Don't worry, z3r0 is good at what he does," he reassured her. "The shells will keep Central from finding us." He sounded more confident than he felt.

Graeme nodded agreement. "It's what we pay him for, anyway."

Shirl tried to look reassured but said instead, "Well, I got a hit on him – looks like he's tied to the gang Mayweather said had looked into the House already."

Curiouser and curiouser, thought Wolf. "What was it that tripped Central?" he asked. "Do you know?"

Squinting at the tiny window that was still linked to the alert from Central, Shirl tracked it down. "Looks like he's turned up in the morgue – that guy's dead!"

Wolf nodded. "Well, that would explain his turning up on the vid rather than being visible to us." He noticed Shirl's twitch slightly. "What?"

"Can I shut this now? It feels like Central's watching me— us!"

"Take a screen grab and shut it," Wolf ordered. "There might be something else useful in there."

Graeme had been silent for a while. "What do we do now? We've been well and truly warned off this one."

Wolf stared at the face on the monitor for a moment longer. "I guess we tell Mayweather what's happened to his friends." The grin on his face became a grimace. "See if he already knows they're dead – that'll tell us quite a bit."

He turned away from the monitors and started to head for the kitchen. He stopped and looked at them over his shoulder. "Then we decide if we want to go in there or not."

DIGGIN' UP DEAD BODIES...

When Alicia arrived at her office on Tuesday morning she stored the large dress bag in the stationery cupboard next to her office. She'd had to take a cab rather than risk the tube, it was so big. Good job they'd already been authorised their expenses for the ball that evening.

Jack rushed into her office almost as soon as she'd managed to sit down, large cup of coffee poised waiting on her desk in front of her. "Guess what, boss?"

Alicia shook her head. "Too early for guessing games, Jack. Wait— you forgot to get a tux for tonight?"

Looking hurt, Jack shook his head in return. "No, I've got the monkey suit hanging in the locker room. That's not it!"

Shrugging, Alicia gave in. "I give up... What?"

He was nearly dancing with excitement. "Someone ran an image ident through CAT that matches one of the stiffs in the cooler."

This was news. "The mutilated ones?" she demanded.

"Yep. The very ones." Now Jack was grinning from ear to ear.

"Who ran the trace?"

The grin disappeared. "CAT doesn't know... no one's listed on the file details." He brightened as he thought of something. "I know! Get your mate Sen to look into it – he should be able to figure it out, if anyone can."

Alicia nodded. "Well, it's more his bailiwick than ours. I'll see what he can do." She made shooing gestures. "Now get; I've got loads to do before I get my hair done."

Jack looked mock-surprised. "You're having your hair done? You feeling all right, boss?"

Growling, Alicia pointed at the door. "Out. Or I'll have you clean out all the refrigerators for the next two weeks."

"I'm going, boss – just hadn't figured you'd be going to so much trouble..." The binder Alicia threw missed him by inches.

Jaared *was* interested to hear what they'd found. "And Central doesn't know who accessed the files?" he repeated.

Alicia shook her head. "Nope. Apparently someone's been back-dooring the system for a while now, according to the diagnostics Jack pulled out."

Jaared was silent for a moment. "That doesn't really surprise me, with a system as large as Central." He smiled, the screen filling with teeth for a moment. "I suppose we should be happy it doesn't occur more often."

"Absolutely," Alicia agreed.

"I'll see what I can find and let you know if any of it is relevant to your verdict."

"Thanks Jaared."

Jaared paused. "See you tonight?"

"Of course."

He shrugged. "Good. I *have* to be there, and it's always useful to know if there's anyone I actually want to see at these things."

"Well, I *have* to attend the damn ball, too," Alicia retorted, sticking out her tongue. "So there."

Laughing at this point, Jaared held his hands up in surrender. "Okay, I'll see you there!"

Alicia glared and waved goodbye as she cut the connection. "Everyone's a comedian," she grumbled.

YOU CAN'T TEACH AN OLD DOG NEW TRICKS (APPARENTLY)

I end the call with Alicia bemused. Oh, I've heard of hackers, but I hadn't heard of Central being compromised like this suggested. I mentally flagged it as an issue – not my area of expertise. I'd much rather someone else dealt with the problem.

I'm more concerned that someone knows who we've got in the morgue and why they're there. The number one question is: why do they have photos of them?

Putting the issue mentally to one side, I concentrate on the Tyler kid's murder. James Tyler has the influence, money and probably access to someone with the ability to kidnap his son. What isn't clear to me is why he would kill his son.

It's something more likely to happen in a moment of passion or anger – in this case, the death appears to be something that was planned. At least the 'kidnapping' was.

Maybe it wasn't Tyler himself. According to what I am reading, the kid stood to take over his dad's business. He had no record, did all kinds of charity work and had been engaged to a nice girl, one Tiffany Bowes-Lyon, from a very respectable family. I'm disappointed she's not a supermodel, but hey, you can't have everything.

It might be worth speaking to her and assessing the boy's relationship with the rest of the family through her.

Central informs me it has nothing further on our hacker, so I go down to the motor pool.

It's true, some things don't disappear without use. Driving a car in the middle of the twenty-first century is little different to driving in the twentieth, let me assure you. Okay, yes, the cars are mostly electric now, there's a lot more automation and I don't have to think too hard about where I'm going due to built-in navigation. But the principles are the same. Mostly.

I manage to get to the Bowes-Lyon mansion on the edge of Hyde Park without incident. Well, if you don't count the little old lady who had a near brush with the right front fender. I didn't hit her, honest.

The door is answered by a human butler. How extravagant in this day and age of automation.

"Yes?" The black brows over his deep-set eyes beetle at me, semaphore for 'do not enter if you aren't on the list'. He has what a lot of people would call an olive complexion, is about average height and sounds like he was educated at Harrow at the very least.

"Commander Sen, here to speak to Miss Bowes-Lyon," I reply. I have an appointment – Central's a stickler for etiquette.

"Very good, sir." He bows me into an entrance hall that might well be larger than my entire house. A huge crystal chandelier dominates the white and black space, reflected in the high polish of the tiled floor. "If you will be so kind as to wait in the drawing room to the left, I will inform Miss Bowes-Lyon you are here, Commander."

"Thank you." I've no idea what his name is and I doubt I'm going to get to know him.

The drawing room is as lavishly appointed as the entrance hall is stark. Thick, Turkish carpets cover the parquet floor, with comfortable antique furniture arranged around the large fireplace at the end of the room. A low fire is burning in the grate, of what looks like real wood. The fines they pay for this extravagance have to be enormous.

I wander the room for a minute, examining the artworks on the wall opposite the windows. It's a north-facing room, so it would appear the paintings are real. There's a Pissaro from his pointillist phase, one of Degas' ballet dancers and what appears to be one of Whistler's *Nocturnes*. I know Central will tell me the names of them all, but I don't always care, preferring to look at the work. I stop in front of the Whistler. I went to a retrospective sometime in the 1950s (but can't remember where) and remember being struck by the magic of his night paintings.

"It's beautiful, is it not?" A young woman's voice, behind me.

I haven't heard her enter and turn quickly to face the door, only to find her sat in a chair near the fireplace. "It is. I was just remembering seeing more of his work in... New York, I think," I reply, moving towards the fire.

No, not a supermodel. If anything, she's very, very plain. Dull blonde hair, slightly rounded face with few distinguishing features, and dressed in a dull, grey sweatshirt over plain blue jeans. It occurs to me that she was in the room all the time and I overlooked her.

"Please sit down, Commander." She gestures to the chair opposite her. "Coffee?" she offers.

I sink into the antique wing chair and examine her more closely. "Please."

She leans forward and picks up the coffee pot sitting on the small table in front of her. "Milk? Sugar?"

"Just milk," I reply.

Perhaps my first impression was a little off – the light of the minimal fire suggests a fineness to her skin, reminiscent of porcelain. When she raises her eyes to mine as she hands me the cup, I can see the hazel eyes would be very attractive if the spark hadn't gone from them. I can only put it down to grief.

"I am sorry for your loss, Ms Bowes-Lyon," I start.

She waves it away. "Thank you Commander, but I hardly think you came to Kensington to offer your condolences," she responds. "And please, call me Tiffany."

I nod, sipping the black coffee. *Very nice.* "No, you're right. I'm investigating your fiancé's death and was wondering if you could tell me anything about John's life." I get out my old-fashioned notebook.

A wan smile crosses her face for a moment. "I can try."

"Good. Did John have any enemies?" I ask, figuring it can't hurt to be straight with her.

"No... well, his stepmother..." She frowns. "No. Everyone loved John – he was a good, kind man and I can't believe he's... gone." She trails off to nothing on the last word. I look up from my notebook to find her staring into the fire, tears running down her face.

So. Genuine affection, it appears. Nevertheless, she's said something interesting. "His stepmother? What did she think of John?" I prompt.

A flash of anger returns the spark to those lovely eyes for a second. "She was jealous of him." Her voice is barely audible.

"Why was she jealous?" I ask quietly. "Money? Status? Something he had she didn't?"

Tiffany nods, her gaze returning to the burning wood in the fireplace. "James loved John more than anything else – probably more than he loved her. And that hurt her."

The tears start again. I need to wrap this up. I finish my coffee and place the cup back on the tray. "Could she hate him enough to want him dead?" Her pulse is up and she's flushed. There's something she wants to tell me.

She's silent for a moment, but I can almost hear her decide to tell me. Obviously no love lost between her and the stepmother.

"They had a fight... I think he refused to attend one of her charity balls... I can't remember; all I remember is what she said..." She trails off again.

"What did she say, Tiffany?" I enquire gently.

She looks at me again, anger in her eyes. "She said if he wasn't James' son, she'd kill him!"

I nod. "And you think she did?"

Her gaze returned to the fire. She nods. "I do," she whispers.

I stand up. "Thank you, Tiffany." I step nearer and take her hand. "I'll do my best to make sure John's killer is caught."

She looks up at me, her hand tightening on mine. "It won't bring him back, though, will it?"

No, that's a trick I haven't mastered yet.

DO YOU WANT THE GOOD NEWS OR THE BAD NEWS?

Mayweather seemed unsurprised by the news of his former colleagues' deaths.

"Will you enter the House?" was all he asked when Wolf phoned him.

Taken aback, Wolf thought for a second. "We're still looking at the situation, Mayweather." He glanced to the right at Shirl. "I'll let you know what we decide."

"Good – make sure you do, as I think we'll need to do it soon," Mayweather answered before hanging up.

"Arsehole!" Wolf exclaimed.

"He didn't exactly seem broken up by the deaths of his mates," Shirl observed.

Wolf turned to face her. "No, nor did he seem surprised." He toyed with his voda for a second. "But he still wants to go in – why? When it killed his first team?"

Shirl nodded. "What does he think we can do for him they couldn't?"

It was Wolf's turn to nod. "Or has he been in there already?"

"And survived?" Shirl looked shocked. "If so, how'd he survive and they didn't?"

Wolf grinned, looking more like his namesake. "That's the million dollar question. What happened in that House?"

"Something we need to ask Mr Mayweather," Shirl replied.

"Yes, I think it's time we paid him a visit."

They'd quickly worked out where Mayweather was staying after their initial encounter, a cheap tourist hotel in Victoria. It wasn't hard to find him – he didn't appear to be hiding from anyone, which was curious in itself.

Graeme pulled the Land Rover up outside the hotel. "Want me to come in, too?" he asked.

"I think we can handle Mayweather, Dad," Shirl answered.

Wolf nodded. "Yep – you can hang out here and listen to Merle Haggard. And watch for traffic wardens."

Graeme's love of country *and* western was legendary, as was his collection. He smiled back at Wolf. "You laugh, but Merle was a god!"

Shirl patted him on the shoulder. "Of course he was, Dad. We'll be back in a bit."

Wolf grinned. "You'll be listening to us as well, I presume?"

"Of course. Now go – find out what he knows."

The front desk was unattended in the middle of the afternoon. They slipped past it and up the stairs to the third floor.

The place seemed deserted.

When Wolf knocked on the door of Room 37, there was a moment of silence before footsteps approached the door. No peephole meant he had to open the door to see who it was.

As soon as the door was open a reasonable gap, Wolf put his foot in the crack to stop it closing again. "Mayweather, we've got a few more questions to ask you," he said.

"Please. Come in," Mayweather said graciously.

The room was cramped, with a small table and two chairs shoved into the corner. Wolf took one and Shirl perched on the end of the unmade bed. Mayweather ascended the remaining chair as if it were a throne.

Wolf shook his head at Mayweather's self-possession. "Okay, you weren't surprised at the news that the rest of your first team are probably dead. What happened?"

Mayweather sighed. "It went wrong almost as soon as they entered... *that place.*" He practically hissed the words. "I was still in the doorway when one of the fools tripped some kind of trap." He went quiet again, the scene replaying in his mind.

"Okay, what happened then?" Wolf asked. They needed to know before they entered what sounded more and more like a haunted house.

Mayweather looked from Wolf to Shirl and back again to stare at him. "Have you ever felt that a place was... evil, I guess... Mr Woffe?"

Wolf shrugged. "I don't think I've noticed." He paused. "How did it feel... evil?"

Lost in the grip of previous events again, Mayweather's gaze vanished into the distance. "The hall was cold. And there was the smell of... decay... possibly death." His eyes refocused on Wolf. "Don't think me a superstitious man, Mr Woffe, but there was a... presence in that hall. Something watching us all and somehow... feeding off our fear."

"Did you see anyone?"

Mayweather shook his head. "No, it was more a feeling of being watched… assessed." He took a deep breath. "It felt hungry, Mr Woffe."

"Hungry?"

"Like it would eat… our very souls."

Shirl was growing impatient with all the mumbo-jumbo. "What happened then?" she demanded.

"A… pressure shoved me through the door."

"Into the hall?" Wolf guessed.

"No, out of the House – I landed on the concrete steps. And the door slammed shut."

"That's odd, particularly if you felt it was hungry," Shirl observed.

Mayweather nodded once. "I know. I cannot explain it." His eyes sought theirs. "You do believe me, don't you?"

Unsure what to make of his insistence, Wolf nodded cautiously. "As you're here and at least some of them are lying on mortuary slabs, we don't have much choice."

"Were you in contact with them after the door closed? Did you hear anything else?" Shirl questioned.

"We had headsets all on the same frequency." He closed his eyes. "All I could hear was screaming."

Shirl looked at Wolf, disbelief in her eyes. He shared her misgivings that Mayweather was telling the truth, but remembered the way the House felt when he was clinging to the wall, like it was going to drop him. "Did you have any further contact with them?"

Mayweather nodded, his gaze on the ratty carpet that covered the floor. "Yes, Ivan… Jenkins, the man I contacted initially to retrieve the manuscript… he spoke at the last."

"What did he say?"

"One word… *run*." Mayweather looked haunted now as he looked up from his inspection of the carpet. "And I did – I ran and hid here in my room, as if that place could reach out and grab me!"

Wolf nodded. "I don't blame you for that – I'd have probably done the same."

"I'm not proud of my reaction, Mr Woffe," Mayweather said flatly, pulling his scraps of dignity back together.

"No, I don't imagine you are," Wolf replied truthfully. "And you weren't going to tell us this…"

Mayweather sighed. "I was afraid you'd think I'm even madder than you already think I am."

"I don't think you're mad, Mayweather — but I would say you're obsessed." Wolf stood up. "Okay, we're going to look into this place a bit more and see what we can find out about it. You," he pointed at Mayweather, "stay here. Don't go out and don't talk to anyone, particularly anyone from the Company."

Mayweather nodded. "Whatever you say, Mr Woffe."

Wolf and Shirl went to the door.

"I can still hear their screams," Mayweather whispered as they opened it.

Wolf nodded. "It's not easy losing people." He turned back to the door. "We'll be in touch."

"I'll be here."

SOMEONE LEFT THE CAKE OUT IN THE RAIN...

A licia spent a relaxed afternoon out of the office, being pampered at the spa she normally frequented in Covent Garden. She didn't figure it would hurt; she hated corporate 'mandatory' events and being as relaxed as possible (short of having a martini or three) beforehand was probably a good thing.

By the time she got back to the office, there wasn't a lot she could do about work. Alicia spent the three quarters of an hour catching up on administration between bouts of staring at the walls. There was something about the John Tyler case that bothered her, but she couldn't see what it was.

After reading the same paragraph five times, Alicia tossed the pad on the desk. She pulled her dress bag off the hook and retired to her cubby of a toilet to change. Fortunately, the dress fit as well as it had when she'd last tried it on. She pulled on the shoes and then added the gold necklace Stephen had given her after a trip to Greece, with a pendant in the shape of one of Crete's famous bees. The turquoise of the jacket set off her eyes in the mirror.

"Sue, can you find Jack, please? I think it's time for a drink."

Applying lipstick using the small mirror in her compact, Alicia noticed movement behind her and turned to find a man she almost didn't recognise in the doorway.

Jack was standing there, looking uncomfortable in his rented tux. His over-thin face bore none of the wispy beard or assorted piercings he normally sported and it looked like his hair had been Brylcreemed into place.

"Blimey, Jack!" Alicia cried. "I never realised you were so handsome!"

Blushing, Jack adopted an 'aw shucks' attitude and would have scuffed his polished shoes on the floor if he'd been younger. "Aw, stop it boss — you're embarrassin' me!"

Alicia stood up and went around her desk. "I mean it Jack, you brush up very well." She knocked an almost imaginary bit of dust off his shoulder before leaning up to kiss him on the cheek. "Thank you for taking me to the ball, Jack."

Amidst more blushing, Jack had the presence of mind to protest. "It wasn't like I had any choice, was it?"

Smiling, Alicia shook her head. "No, but I do appreciate the effort you've gone to. Now..." She turned back to the desk to collect her evening clutch. "Fancy a drink?"

Jack was nodding when she turned around. "I could murder a drink!" he replied. "You look pretty good yourself," he added.

Alicia put her aunt's fur wrap around her shoulders before taking his arm. "Very well, let's go get a taxi. I know a decent pub around the corner from the *Grosvenor*!"

By the time they got to the *Grosvenor House*'s Great Room, they were both feeling much more relaxed.

Alicia was beginning to think it might even turn out to be a passable night out, rather than something that needed to be endured.

Jack, well, he was thinking that he'd really like to go outside and smoke the small joint in his pocket. He also didn't think his boss would approve, regardless of its legality. Glancing sideways at Alicia and the amazing turquoise dress she was wearing ("Wait," his brain said, "that's your boss!"), he sighed, looking away and forward to his next drink.

"Come on Jack, don't look so gloomy." Alicia prodded him with her elbow.

"Sorry boss," he responded.

"Look, get me a drink and then go smoke – you've got a face like a bag full of wet spanners," Alicia chided.

"Uh, what?" he said, startled.

Alicia shook her head at him. "I can tell you're dying to have a smoke, so go have one."

"How——"

"How'd I know? You get this look like you're constipated and would much rather be somewhere else." Alicia smiled at him. "See? Easy."

Jack shook his head, half-smiling. "Here I thought I was being so cool..."

Alicia swatted his backside. "Now go get me a drink!"

THE SKY IS A POISONOUS GARDEN TONIGHT

The interview with Tiffany leaves me feeling ambivalent as I drive back to the office – something about it all rings false in my internal ear.

With a start, I realise I'm already losing the edge on the senses that took over when I didn't have my eyes to fall back on.

I find a parking space and pull in, just off Park Lane. I lean my head back on the headrest and close my eyes. I breathe deeply, in through the nose, out through the mouth, using a relaxation technique my *sensei* taught me all those years ago. I can also use this technique as an aide-mémoire to review recent events and conversations.

Behind the veil of my eyelids, I replay the conversation, ignoring the words this time.

The girl is distraught – understandably. Her body's physiological responses intrigue me, however. She's mostly collected, almost too calm. There are two points where her heart rate increases, pupils contract, and breathing speeds up.

I go back over the conversation, this time trying to match the words with what her body's telling me.

The first jump came when she first mentioned the stepmother. I shrug mentally. I'd say it's within parameters, considering the topic.

The second period of elevated pulse and other stressors is when she's building up to telling me what Portia said about John. Hmmm…

"They had a fight… I think he refused to attend one of her charity balls… I can't remember; all I remember is what she said…" She trails off again.

[PULSE ELEVATED, BREATHING ACCELERATING.]

"What did she say, Tiffany?" I inquire gently.

She looks at me again, anger in her eyes. *"She said if he wasn't James' son, she'd kill him!"*

[PULSE AT NEARLY 150BPM.]

I nod. *"And you think she did?"*

Her gaze returned to the fire. She nods. *"I do,"* she whispers.

[PULSE BEGINS TO SLOW, BUT REMAINS ELEVATED.]

It will never stand up in court, but I think the drab, plain girl is lying. I've half a mind to turn around and go back and confront her, but Central reminds me that I have other commitments this evening and should be preparing for them.

I sigh and restart the car just as one of Westminster's militant traffic wardens approaches. He taps on the window by my head and I obediently open it.

"I'm sorry, sir, but you can't park here without a permit."

What's with this guy? They normally have Heads Up Displays for this sort of thing; they're subcontracted from the Company and it should be telling him I'm in an unmarked car as well as giving him my rank and current Company Status.

I reach into my pocket for the physical ID I carry just for such eventualities just as the hand he's had at his side appears in the window. The silenced handgun, my HUD tells me, is an old model Beretta; it's always useful in moments of stress to know exactly which gun is pointed at you, I find.

Then he makes a mistake: he pushes the gun into the car, past my other hand.

It's over in nanoseconds and I'm grateful for all the training I still make myself do. He crumples to the pavement, the dent where the bodywork hit his head already swelling.

I can already hear the sirens as I get out of the car and start searching the unconscious body. No ID, no visible identifying marks or tattoos. Asian, about five foot seven, medium build. I roll up one of his sleeves, half-expecting Tong or Yak scrip on the arms, but there's nothing.

He does have a voda in his pocket, however, one call in the history and nothing else. Cheap throw-away phones are still prolific on the grey market, despite their tendency to be used for the wrong sort of activities, as in this case.

I tap it against my closed lips for a second, initiate a trace on the number and press the re-dial button.

There's an audible click (all done by software now as no mechanical switches are involved anymore). I can hear a hint of breathing, but no one speaks.

"Hello?"

Still nothing.

"Job's done," I try. *Who knows, it might work.*

There's another click and I get the dial tone. Oh well, it was worth a try. Central comes back with a trace to somewhere in Soho. And it's another throw-away voda.

I sigh and wait for the ice cream van to arrive.

TALES OF MYSTERY AND IMAGINATION

Wolf sat at his desk in the bookstore. He sighed. He was supposed to be pricing up the mixed bag of crappy paperbacks and book club versions of books *he* certainly didn't want to read and suspected a lot of others wouldn't either.

Shirl had dropped him at the shop after their interview with Mayweather. The conversation still played in his mind and the fact of his survival when it was obvious the rest of his previous team had not – that worried Wolf. He couldn't risk the others on this job; it was too dangerous.

Flicking through the box, he spotted what looked like a first edition of *Christine* (always collectible) and a good copy of *The Hobbit* (always popular) and a lot of dross, mostly *Twilight* and Potter rip-offs. Bargain table fayre for sure.

Sighing again, Wolf leaned back in his chair. His brain wouldn't stop going over what Mayweather had told them.

"Penny for your thoughts," came from the doorway. "I'm pretty sure it's not about those books in front of you." Janey was standing in the doorway with her arms crossed; all five foot nothing, blonde and impish, smiling at him.

Smiling ruefully back, Wolf shook his head. "You'd be wasting your money – nothing to report in here," he said, tapping his temple lightly.

Janey smiled back. "Well, why don't you go do what it is you need to do and stop moping around the office? You're putting the customers off."

Wolf looked past her into the main room. "We don't have any customers."

"Exactly! Now get!"

Laughing, Wolf held up his hands in surrender before picking up his voda. "One call and I'm outta here."

"You make sure that's all you do," she replied, turning back to the shop.

The voda pinged once before Graeme picked up. "Can you pick me up? Shirl took the Spider and I've got an idea."

"Sure Wolf, will be down in a minute," Graeme replied. "Want anything?"

Wolf nodded to no one. "Yep, bring the delivery box and kit. I want to try something."

"No problem. Ten minutes." Graeme hung up.

It was fully dark by the time Graeme and Wolf arrived back in the street with the House. Somewhere along the line, they had both started implying the uppercase 'H' when they spoke about it.

Graeme parked down the street from it; if there were any watchers, it was best to be careful and not give any indication that they were interested in the House. Wolf stepped out of the Land Rover with a box in his hands. He was also dressed in the livery of a well-known courier, the easier to talk to people on their doorsteps.

For appearances, he walked up to the House and up the steps to that black door. His skin was already crawling and it felt like all the hairs on his arms were standing on end. Wolf raised and let the knocker fall. The sound was peculiarly muted, not the satisfying *Boom!* one normally gets on a solid door with a hall behind it.

There was no response.

Just before he turned to go, Wolf felt a sharp pain behind his right eye, like a serious headache. Wincing, he retraced his way down the steps and turned left. "Ow," he muttered.

"*What? What happened?*" Graeme demanded over the earpiece.

Wolf shook his head. "Nothing, just coming down with a migraine or something."

"*Well, watch it... with that... place,*" Graeme advised.

"Will do."

He turned left up the next set of steps in front of the next property that almost, but not quite, touched the House. Wolf repeated the ritual, only this time pressing the buzzers beside the door for the three flats. He got no response other than a dog barking from one of the floors above his head.

Undeterred, Wolf returned to the pavement, retraced his steps past the House and went up the steps of the property on the other side.

This house was different, with a bright red door and no sign that it had been converted to flats inside. That was a rarity, with property in London at a premium.

There was a buzzer, however, and when Wolf pressed it, he heard a pleasant chime of silvery bells. The sound died away to nothing and there was no sign of occupancy. Wolf shrugged and turned to go. "Don't think there's anyone here either."

"*Damn. Thought this might turn up something.*"

"So did I."

As he turned, he noticed a net curtain twitch in a room on the same level as the door.

"Wait, someone's watching me," he sub-vocalised without moving his lips. Turning back he rang the bell again. And waited.

"*Anything?*" Graeme asked.

"Wait for it," Wolf replied.

After a very long time, the red door opened a crack to reveal a weathered old Chinese man dressed in plain Western clothes. Wolf had half-expected him to be wearing a robe or something. "What do you want?" he demanded.

"Package for next door," Wolf answered. "For a Mr—Ward."

The old man shook his head. "No one by that name there... that I know of."

"What do you mean?"

"That House has been empty as long as I've lived here – fifty years at least – and probably longer than that." He smiled at Wolf. "You're not really a delivery man, are you?"

Shaken, Wolf nearly turned around and left. But something about the man's manner reassured him. He shook his head. "No, I'm trying to find out what I can about the House next door."

Nodding, the wizened man opened the door further. "You'd better come in and have some tea, then. Talking's thirsty work at my age. Come."

Wordlessly, Wolf stepped through the door.

I DON'T WANNA DANCE...

W hile Jack was gone, Alicia took the opportunity to lean on the railing and look out over the floor of the Great Room. It was impressive in itself but the Company's party team had outdone themselves this time.

One wall of the room was hidden by a waterfall (Alicia was pretty sure it didn't come with the room) with various stills of ancient movie stars projected on the curtain of water until something within the waterfall started interrupting the flow, causing cracks to appear in the images. It was an amazing thing and was obviously fitted with some kind of suppression system to keep the water away from the guests and their expensive party clothes. It also wasn't making very much sound, only a soft hiss; odd for a waterfall.

The rest of the room was decorated with intricate lighting and a couple of brightly lit areas where people stood and chatted in pre-dinner drinks mode, the lights giving them a moment in the spotlight.

Suddenly Alicia's attention was drawn to one of the spots by the main entrance. A striking, platinum blonde had just entered the room attended by an older man who's puppyish attentions almost screamed 'husband to a much younger woman'.

Alicia almost laughed as the blonde said something through gritted teeth and the man stopped dead. If he'd had a tail, it would have certainly stopped wagging. The man meekly followed the woman until Alicia lost them in the crowd.

"Somethin' funny?" Jack asked from behind her.

Shaking her head, Alicia turned around. "Just people-watching – it's an endlessly fascinating show."

Jack handed her the vodka and tonic, and then clinked his glass against hers. "Cheers," Alicia responded before taking a sip of the cold drink.

"Cheers," Jack replied, before tasting his beer. "Blimey, decent beer at a corporate do, what's the world coming to?"

Alicia smiled. "When the Company does something like this, it tends to get things right."

"I'm just gonna—" Jack started.

Raising a hand, Alicia made shooing motions. "Go. I can cope very well without you!"

Jack ducked his head and quickly vanished in the crowd.

Alicia turned back to the railing and surveyed the gathering which was growing in size and volume. Someone else noticed, too, as the noise of the waterfall seemed to increase for a moment, before turning into white noise that effectively muted the roar of the crowd.

"Hello gorgeous," a voice murmured behind her.

"Jaared!" Alicia had known it was him before even turning around. He looked very dapper in a fitted tuxedo and dark maroon bow tie with matching cummerbund. "You're a sight for sore eyes."

"I'd say the same for you – that's a lovely dress." His eyes twinkled at her – the grey was shading towards blue in this light.

"Thank you, Commander," Alicia replied with a slight curtsey. "That colour suits you, although I never took you for a matching tie and cummerbund kind of guy."

Jaared looked pained for a moment. "You know me too well – if it's not black, I don't tend to wear it! Skeet made me branch out a bit – told me I needed some colour." He pointed at the tie. "This was the compromise."

"Where's——?" Alicia started to ask as Jaared started the same question. "Where's your date?"

"Sorry," Jaared apologised. "Skeet's at the bar, getting provisions. Yours?"

"Jack's out for a smoke. He thinks I don't know he smokes a little weed, but it's always there in his monthly drug test." Alicia smiled. "Sometimes I feel like his mother." She turned to Jaared. "When did I get old, Jaared?" she almost whispered.

"Hey, Al, you're not old – give it another century, then you can say that," he chided. "Besides, it's nothing to do with age; he works for you and you feel responsible. I know how that goes."

The tone was immediately altered as Skeet arrived. "Here ya go, Jaared," she announced, handing him a pint of real ale.

"Ta, much," he replied. "You remember Alicia, don't you Skeet?"

Alicia nodded. "Skeet, you're looking amazing in that!"

And Skeet was, in an ankle-length sheath of emerald green that offset her honey-blonde spikes. "Thanks. I don' dress like this... normally," she said, pulling at the material awkwardly.

"You should." And Alicia meant it. Skeet's height and her striking cheekbones made her look like a goddess. She wasn't conventionally beautiful, but there was something about her. Alicia felt dumpy by comparison.

"I love yer dress!" Skeet returned the compliment. Bless her, she *was* trying.

Alicia blushed. "Thanks, I was just thinking I must look dowdy next to you."

"Uh, get away! I wish I could wear that colour, I just look yeller," Skeet admitted.

Waving it away, Alicia smiled. Maybe she hadn't been giving Skeet enough credit. "I'm sure you don't, but you really should dress that way more often," she replied. "Especially judging by the effect it's having on your escort."

Jaared had been standing there motionless, a smile on his face as he watched the interplay between the two. "You two sisters or something?" he said finally.

"Watch yer mouth," Skeet advised.

Alicia nodded. "I'd say we've got great taste in men!"

Nodding, Jaared was still smiling until he saw something over Skeet's shoulder. Alicia looked that way but couldn't see anything for a moment, before spotting that platinum blonde and her puppy.

"Would you ladies excuse me for a moment, please?" Jaared murmured, still distracted. "Duty calls."

Jack chose that moment to turn up. "Evenin' Commander." He offered his hand.

Jaared's attention seemed to be elsewhere for a moment before he snapped back to his surrounds. "Jack. Good to see you. Excuse me for a minute, though; I have to see to someone." Jaared shook his hand firmly, but quickly, before heading for the group around the blonde.

"Where's the fire?" Jack asked as his gaze fell on Skeet. Even slightly stoned, her beauty registered as he gazed up at her. "And who's this?"

"This is the Commander's date, Skeet," Alicia replied. "Skeet, this is Jack, a damn good medical examiner and my assistant." Maliciously, she turned back to Jack. "Skeet kills people for a living," she said, enjoying the sight of her assistant going pale and then slightly green around the gills.

"P–pleased to meet you," Jack stuttered, offering his hand like he wasn't sure he'd get it back.

"The pleasure's all mine, Jack," Skeet answered. Her soft, southern American accent seemed to calm him. "And Al here's kidding; I don't *normally* kill 'em."

"I–I see," Jack replied, although he didn't really.

Alicia hid her smile behind her drink and glanced in the direction Jaared had gone. He'd vanished completely.

But then, so had the blonde.

WHAT DO YOU THINK PENGUINS CALL A SUIT?

Dealing with the aftermath of the homicidal traffic warden takes longer than necessary, making me late. I just manage to put on the penguin suit that only sees light once or twice a year before rushing to meet Skeet at the *Grosvenor*.

Skeet looks ravishing in emerald green — something I'd describe as a 'sheath', as it hugs her curves and accentuates her eyes. She's had her hair done, well, as much as you can with short spikey blonde hair.

"You look... amazing!"

Smiling a little shyly, Skeet leans in and gives me a kiss. "You don't look so bad yerself, handsome," she purrs.

I feign looking around. "Skeet? Where are you? I can't see you anywhere!"

Skeet slugs my shoulder — and I *do* mean slug; she's got a right like a pro boxer. "Ha, ha, very funny," she retorts.

"Bring back the real Skeet," I murmur, leaning in to kiss her again.

"Mmm," she responds, before pulling back. "Come on, we're late."

I offer my arm. "As you will, my lady."

Seeing Alicia near the bar is fortuitous. As I'd told Alicia, having someone there I want to talk to always makes these things flow more smoothly.

Then I see the very person I'd been discussing with Tiffany, only hours earlier. *Portia.*

I bring my attention back to the present, seeing Jack's outstretched hand. "Jack. Good to see you. Excuse me for a minute, though; I have to see to someone." I shake his hand. I squeeze Skeet's hand, reassuring her, although she knows Alicia already.

There's a crowd around Sir and Lady Tyler, but the attention all appears to be on Portia. Not surprising in that mother-of-pearl-coloured confection she's wearing. It practically screams 'notice me!'.

I stand there for a moment, anticipating an opening. She's laughing at a joke one of the pretty young men surrounding her has just told. James Tyler sits there a bit woodenly, a fixed grimace on his face.

There's a momentary lull and I seize the moment. "Good evening, Lady—Portia," I say quietly.

Her head snaps around and the full force of her gaze hits me like a wall. "Why, good evening Commander!" she returns. "I should have guessed you'd be here tonight – why don't you sit down?"

I shake my head. "I'm sorry to intrude, but if I could just have a word?" She frowns and James Tyler starts to get up. "Alone, if you don't mind?" I put on a wry smile and Portia puts a hand on his shoulder.

"Don't worry, darling, I'll only be a moment." She smiles back at me. "And I'm sure I'll be perfectly safe with the Commander."

She's at my side in a very short space of time and I lead the way away from her group and towards a little nook. It's near the bar, but secluded enough for my purposes.

"Whatever is so important you must call me away from those pretty boys?" Portia murmurs as we enter the alcove. She sounds piqued.

I put on my concerned face, rather than my official one and try for a light tone. "Something has come up in my enquiries today and I just thought it would be easier to clear the matter up quickly, rather than disturb you tomorrow."

Lady Tyler sips her drink, looking at me before smiling again. "I'm very touched by your solicitude Commander." She sips again. "Now, what did you want to ask me?"

I sip my beer and phrase what I want to say in my mind first. "I was speaking to your step-son's fiancée earlier today and she told me you and John had a… disagreement… on the day he disappeared."

She smiles and looks down into her drink. "You don't have to be coy with me, Commander – we argued, yes."

I nod. Fair enough. "What did you argue about, Lady Tyler?"

"Oh Commander, so formal! Please! Call me Portia!" The Lady in question appears to be playing for time and this time I pay attention to my other senses, noting an increased pulse rate, and the contraction of her pupils. When she answers, she surprises me. "We were discussing his intention to marry that… that trollop, if you must know." The surprise must have shown on my face, as she smiles more broadly. "Why? Whatever did she tell you?"

"I… I was informed you'd argued over one of your charities, L— Portia."

She laughs lightly. "That may well be what John told her, protecting her sensibilities, I'm sure."

I re-group. "You didn't think she was suitable for him to marry, then?"

She answers with a moue of distaste. "No. She's common, new money – not a single Lord or Peer in her family tree!" Sipping her wine, she continued. "As far as I was concerned, she was a money-grubbing whore sent out to find the richest prize she could!"

There's an odd note in her tone. *Like you?* I wonder. I just stare at her for the moment, hopefully expressionless. Her pulse increases again. She's definitely hiding something.

"What?" she asks defensively. "You don't believe me?"

I return to formality. "No, Lady Tyler, I do not."

Her anger is quick and probably intimidating to people who aren't used to dealing with her type. "How dare you! I make every attempt to be civil and you insinuate that I would lie about something that affects the investigation of my step-son's death!"

I shake my head. "I intimated no such thing, m' Lady." I look her in those eyes. "I merely think you are not telling me the whole truth."

Lady Portia's demeanour changes and she tries another tack. "I think this interview is over, Commander." She turns to go. "Any further questions you may have can be directed to my lawyers."

I put my hand on her arm. Firmly. "I'm not finished yet, m' Lady." I turn her back towards me. "I believe, based on what you haven't said here, that you're somehow involved in John's death."

Seething, the Lady removes my hand from her shoulder. "Don't touch me, Commander, or you'll regret it." It's delivered as a hiss.

I push her up against the wall of the alcove, one hand under her chin. "Really? Don't you know who I am?" I ask. "Of course you do – and you know where my power lies in a murder investigation, don't you?"

For the first time, she shows something like fear. "Of... of course, Commander." Her eyes dart around seeking some aid from someone behind me, but I know she can't see anyone. She looks back at me. "You wouldn't harm me at a shareholder's event, would you?" she asks softly.

I shake my head. "Whatever gives you the idea I would *harm you*, m' Lady?" I feign disgust. "But I can always have you remanded in custody, pending further enquiries."

Her hand comes up between us and she brushes my crotch. "I'm sure we can come to some arrangement, Jaared," she whispers, the offer plain between us. Her heart is racing and she's breathing fast.

Disturbed, I move my hand from her neck and remove hers from my groin. "That doesn't work on me, m' Lady, as you should know." I step back. "Rest assured I will be questioning you further, and your lawyers will not be involved."

Lady Tyler pulls her self-possession around her like a cloak. I could almost watch her change into the hard creature inside the soft shell. "Do not do something you'll regret, Commander," she bites out.

I nod. "I'm not prone to making smart decisions, m' Lady, as I'm sure you'll know from my background." Shaken, but not deterred, I turn and walk away from her.

DEAD MEN TELL NO TALES

"*W*hat the hell are you doing?*" Graeme asked in Wolf's ear.

"Having tea," Wolf replied.

The old man turned around. "And you might as well invite your friend in as well, save me repeating myself!"

"You heard the man," Wolf said to Graeme.

"*Bloody hell, this is hardly inconspicuous,*" Graeme replied.

"But hey, we might learn something."

Graeme grumbled something, but Wolf could hear him getting out of the car.

Wolf turned back to smile at the man. "I'm Wolf and that's Graeme," he offered.

"Shen Dong," the old man replied with a little bow. "Very pleased to meet you."

Wolf followed him into the house, hearing Graeme approaching up the steps behind him. "Why did you decide to come to the door?" he asked.

"I could see the light shining from your head," the old man answered cryptically.

What? "Okay."

Dong led them down the stairs into a basement kitchen that was not modern, but was clean and tidy. The little old man waved them at chairs. "Sit!"

Wolf looked at Graeme and sat down in one of the chairs. At least it wasn't cushions on the floor or something else of a suitably oriental flavour.

As if he read Wolf's mind, Dong said, "I can't get off the floor once I get down there – arthritis, you know."

Wolf and Graeme exchanged raised eyebrows across the table.

"What do you know about the House next door?" Wolf asked Dong's back.

"I think it's hungry... no, excuse my English. I believe it has something called a 'hungry ghost' inside," Dong replied as he moved about boiling the kettle and setting out a simple but elegant tea set. "Do you mind Jasmin tea? I find the tea you *gweilos* drink upsets me."

"Not a problem," Graeme said. "I drink too much tea, anyway."

"Or so your daughter tells you," Dong replied with a smile.

Graeme did a double-take and Wolf almost laughed at his expression. He shrugged a 'Who knows?' at Graeme.

"How did you know I had a daughter, Mr Dong?" Graeme asked, obviously surprised by the man's knowledge.

Dong filled the pot with boiling water before turning back to face them. "Oh, I just know things," he answered.

"What are you, Mr Dong?" Wolf asked quietly. They'd met their share of odd characters over the years and Dong was no exception.

"Actually, it's Mr Shen – in Chinese the family name is said first. But please, call me Dong." Shen picked up the tea set and made his way carefully to the table. He set it down and took the chair nearest him, settling in with a sigh. "As to what I am, I suppose you would call me a witch," Shen said with a glance at both of them. "Or a sorcerer."

Graeme spoke first. "A sorcerer."

Shen waved the words away with a careless hand. "That is not quite right and for the most part I provide herbal remedies for Chinese people. I have a shop down the road which my daughter runs for me now."

Wolf nodded. "Okay. What else do you know about the House next door?"

Shen looked him in the eye. "It leaks."

"What do you mean *it leaks*?" Wolf asked. "Water leaks?"

Shaking his head, Shen picked up the pot and poured tea. "No, not water." He handed the little porcelain cups around and looked at them both again. "It leaks evil – mostly through that wall," he said, pointing at the wall next to the table.

They both glanced at the plain white wall covered with a large silk hanging depicting a tree. Neither of them could see anything obvious.

"Is it visible?" Graeme asked. "I can't see anything."

Shen shook his head again. "No, I have contained it on this side. Mr Wolf, can you pull the hanging aside, please?"

Wolf did as he was told and it was immediately obvious that there were Chinese characters painted directly on the white wall. "What's that do?"

"I suppose you could call it a spell of repulsion, perhaps containment of the hungry ghost," the old man answered.

It was Wolf's turn to shake his head as he let the hanging drop back into place. "And that works?"

Shen shrugged. "Mostly. There are nights when nightmares bleed into my sleep, but I have a tea for that."

"What's a *hungry ghost?*" Graeme asked.

"It's a restless spirit in Chinese tradition, a spirit that was made that way due to greed, envy, or obsession." He looked at them both with no trace of a smile. "They have very small mouths and necks which do not allow them to eat, so they are always hungry."

"And the House next door has one," Graeme said.

"No, I believe the House next door *is* the hungry ghost."

Wolf had an idea. "Can we see the back of it from your garden, Mr Shen?"

Shen nodded. "There is not much to see, just a black wall with windows in it."

"The back is black as well?" Graeme asked, surprised.

"Yes. I do not believe the black is paint, but a reflection of the spirit." Shen stood up. "Come, I will show you what I can, although it is dark out there."

Graeme reached into one of the pockets on his cargo pants and pulled out a small camera. "No worries, Mr Shen, I can get most types of light with this. Maybe we'll see something useful."

Wolf had his doubts, but followed both of them out of the kitchen, through a neat utility room and out the back door of Shen's house.

As Shen had reported, the back of the House was nearly as featureless as the front, the black colour looking burned on in the dim light from the surrounding houses.

Shen stayed near the door as Wolf and Graeme made their way down the neat, and somehow Eastern, garden for a better look at it through Graeme's camera.

Looking up at the House while Graeme filmed, Wolf saw nothing but darkness. Suddenly, there was a flare of light in one of the windows near the top of the House. Then it was gone.

"Did you see that, Graeme?" Wolf asked in a low voice.

"What?" Graeme was concentrating on the screen on the back of the camera.

"A flash of light in one of the upstairs windows… second from the left, I think," Wolf replied.

Graeme shook his head. "No, didn't see it. Hopefully the camera picked it up like last time."

Wolf made a note of the time when he saw the flash, hoping he'd be able to match it up to the images on the camera.

They stood there for a few more minutes, the cold weather easily biting through their thin clothes. Nothing else happened and Wolf finally gave up. "Come on old man; let's get back inside where it's warm."

Shen had already gone back in and opened the kitchen door for them. They followed.

Wolf decided against taking any more of his time. "Is there anything else you can tell us about the House, Mr Shen?"

"I don't think so, Mr Wolf. Oh, it hums sometimes," he offered. "Not music, just a steady thrumming noise."

"Is it loud?"

"Not particularly – my daughter cannot hear it; I have wondered if it was just me." Shen smiled. "I'm not as young as I used to be and my hearing is going. Tinnitus, you know."

Graeme nodded. "I know. It's tough getting old. At least they can treat a lot more things now… and there's rejuv if you want it."

"And if you can afford it," Shen replied, the smile slipping slightly.

Wolf took out a card with just his name and contact details on it. "If you think of anything else, let me know, won't you, Mr Sh—Dong?"

It was Shen's turn to nod. "Although I think it would be better if you left the House alone, Mr Wolf." All trace of humour was gone from his face. "You know what they say about sleeping dogs."

Later Wolf would remember Shen's warning and couldn't help thinking the old man saw the future as well.

PARTIES ARE ALL THE SAME

T he evening passed remarkably quickly in the end, to Alicia's
surprise.

After Jaared returned from whatever errand had taken him away, the
group expanded to include people that Alicia knew, as well as Jaared's
old partner, whom he just referred to as 'the Fat Man' (Johannson?) –
probably irony as, if anything, the guy was on the painfully thin side.

Felix Jerbeau appeared at one point, stayed for a drink, then
disappeared, a statuesque black woman on his arm.

"She's a beard, ya know," Skeet murmured as they left.

Startled, Alicia looked at Skeet sidelong. "What do you mean, *a
beard?*"

Skeet shrugged. "He's gay, but not officially, I'd say. She's colourful
camouflage."

Alicia smiled, not surprised after her conversation with Kate and
Morag. "How the hell do you know that?"

"I can just tell," Skeet replied mysteriously. "Gaydar and all that... oh,
and I've seen her before, escorting one of my employers."

Almost spitting her drink across the group, Alicia burst out laughing.
"You had me going there for a moment!"

"Oh, he is gay," Jaared replied. "He just finds it easier with some of
the more conservative members of the Company and shareholders to
pretend otherwise."

"You guys should be on the stage," Alicia retorted. "What a double-
act!"

Skeet laughed, a pleasant sound and Alicia couldn't help smiling back.
"It's the way I tell 'em," Skeet replied. "Have you heard the one about
the one-legged hooker and the parrot? Well, this guy goes into a bar..."

About then, Alicia noticed that Jack was talking to a man she didn't
know, Skeet's joke fading into the background noise around her.

He was just above average height, reasonably trim, with dark hair,
which was starting to form a widow's peak. He looked like someone her
mother had always loved in old movies. *What was the actor's name?
Bruce... Lee? No, Willis! That was it.*

Jack caught sight of her and turned to include her in the conversation. "Boss, this is Hugh James, a guy I used to go to school with, once upon a time."

Alicia shook his hand. "Pleased to meet you, Mr James."

"Call me Hugh, everyone does," he replied, a twinkle in his eye.

"Okay... Hugh." Hugh's smile was disarming and the sparkle looked more mischievous than Alicia expected from someone at one of these parties.

"Whadda ya do, Hugh?" Skeet asked, nudging Alicia slightly. "I'm Skeet – I'm a bodyguard."

Hugh looked up at Skeet's six foot two frame, a little surprised. "A bodyguard, really? I'd have thought you were a model."

Skeet slapped his shoulder playfully and Alicia winced. "Now, don't be sayin' things like that Hugh, or Jaared here might have to do something about it."

Staggering slightly under the impact of her slap, Hugh didn't stop smiling. "Noted, Ms Skeet. I'm actually a fireman."

Alicia raised an eyebrow. *A fireman... really?*

Hugh noticed and filled in more detail. "Well, I'm a fire investigator, really – I go in after a fire's out and try to determine the cause."

"That sounds more interesting," Alicia replied. "Although I can picture you posing for one of those firemen calendars... Oh, excuse me!" She felt her skin burning, appalled at herself.

Laughing, Hugh waved her off. "Don't worry, that's probably the best thing anyone's said after I've used the fireman line." He sipped what looked like a martini. "You wouldn't believe how many people ask me if I rescue kittens!"

Skeet was smiling, but had to ask. "Well, do ya?"

This set the party laughing so loudly they nearly missed the call to take places at the tables for the dinner. Mr James joined them and soon became the life of the party.

After the meal had vanished by the power of the boring speeches from Management, Alicia excused herself to 'powder her nose', a phrase her mother had used when she was a kid.

Skeet appeared in the Ladies Room shortly after.

"He likes you," Skeet reported.

Startled, Alicia looked away from the mirror she was using to reapply her lip gloss. "Who do you mean, Skeet?"

Skeet smiled. "Oh come on, Al, you know who," she replied.

Blushing, Alicia went back to applying her gloss. "I'm sure I don't know who you mean."

Laughing, Skeet disappeared into one of the cubicles. "I'm sure you don't," echoed in the tiled room. "He hangs on yer every word and laughs in all the right places, so you couldn't miss 'im."

Alicia appraised herself in the mirror. Late thirties, morgue pallor (*English Rose*, she preferred), five foot six.

Dumpy, she thought to herself. *It's too soon.*

For a moment, she thought she saw a face in the mirror beside her. *No, it's not. Be happy Alicia.*

There was a flush from the cubicle Skeet had entered. "Did ya say somethin', Al?"

"I—I was just wondering if he's... available."

Skeet came out and checked her make-up. "No ring and interested. If he isn't, he's puttin' on a good show."

Finished, she nudged Alicia. "Jaared also checked him out: Distinguished Service medals in the military; two Medals of Honour in the fire services... running into burnin' buildings or somethin'."

Skeet winked. "And most importantly: single, ex-wife, no kids."

Alicia put her indignant face on. "You two! Can't keep your noses out..." she spluttered into silence.

Skeet did something totally out of character, at least from Alicia's experience of her – she stepped over to Alicia and put her arms around her.

"I know we're not best pals, Al, and I didn't really know ya when Stephen was around, but I do know when it's time to move on. He'd want ya to be happy."

Embarrassed, Alicia kept her cheek against Skeet's chest for a moment before returning the hug.

"Thanks Skeet. I... don't know what to say," she mumbled.

Skeet's laugh sounded softly in her ear. "Don't say nothin'," she said, stepping back. "I'll deny everythin'!"

Alicia laughed back. "Fair enough." She put her arm through Skeet's.

"Now come on, let's get back to that party!"

"Yer on!"

ALL YESTERDAY'S PARTIES

S keet and I arrive back at my house in the small hours, courtesy of a uniformed PC and an unmarked car.

Taxis were few and far to come by when we left the *Grosvenor House*, snapped up by the rest of our fellow party-goers. It was a matter of moments for me to summon a chariot; rank hath its privileges.

Dickens greets us blearily from the sofa when we turn the hall light on. "Go back to sleep; this is just a dream," I suggest softly. He chirps and puts his head back down, too tired to argue. I know how he feels, my age bearing more heavily when I'm tired.

"Drink?" I ask Skeet, weary, but not quite ready to succumb to the land of Nod.

"Jus' some water — I think I've had enough booze," she replies, sitting in a kitchen chair to pull off the heels she's worn all night. "Jesus my feet hurt!"

I nod. My clothes feel tight. I pour her a glass of water and myself some single cask whisky from my favourite supplier. We stay in the kitchen, rather than fall asleep in the comfortable chairs in the living room.

"So, what was that all about?" Skeet asks me over the rim of her glass when I sit down.

I look her in the eye. "Which part?" I'm hardly drunk; my enhanced metabolism doesn't often allow that escape and nights like tonight are a case in point.

"The part where you disappeared with that whore in the ivory sausage skin, then came back flushed and breathin' heavily," Skeet replies.

I smile. "Oh, that part!" I sip the whisky neat, savouring the burn before adding a touch of water to it.

"Yeah, *that part*," Skeet hisses.

I'm fairly certain she's armed, but I'm also sure she won't use any of that on me, preferring to kill me with her own hands should the need arise. I sigh. "*That* was work. Her stepson was killed last week and there are a number of oddities about the case which... I can't really discuss."

Skeet still looks sceptical. "A case. Who is she?"

"Lady Portia Tyler, wife of one of the pretenders to the throne, Sir James Tyler," I reply. "And she's hiding something... I'm not sure what, but I nearly snapped her neck for her." I smile at her. "Which is why I was breathing heavily when I returned to the group. I should have taken a moment longer."

"That's pretty tidy," Skeet says, eyes narrowed. Always a tough crowd. "You been thinking that up all night?"

Now I shake my head. "Nope. And I haven't been thinking about anything but you all evening — that dress does things to me I don't even know how to describe!"

"Now you're jus' trying to change the subject," Skeet complains, crossing her arms just below her cleavage.

"Sorry, what? You just distracted me."

"Perv. Is that all you think about?"

"No, just when you're dressed like that and I have to sit opposite you for an entire evening." I finish off my whisky. "Talk about blue balls…"

Skeet keeps her stern face on for another few seconds before relenting. "If you're sure nothing happened tonight…"

I stand up. "Nothing happened. I'd remember."

"Not funny," Skeet retorts. "C'mon on then, *Commander,* I need your help getting out of this thing."

"Oh, that will be my pleasure," I assure her.

"Well, you'd better make it mine as well."

"I'll do my best."

AFTER MIDNIGHT, WE GONNA LET IT ALL HANG DOWN...

B y the time Wolf and Graeme had finished going through the video, it was after midnight.

"You want the couch?" Graeme asked Wolf.

Wolf shook his head. "No, I'll walk home, I think."

"Sure?"

"Yep, it makes my back ache now," Wolf replied. "And Michael's expecting me, anyway."

Graeme grunted in an approximation of laughter. "Guess you're getting old – didn't used to phase you. You used to be able to sleep anywhere."

Smiling ruefully, Wolf nodded. "Yep, those days are gone." He picked up his bag. "All right, I'll talk to you tomorrow, old man."

The door cut off his reply of "Less of the old——" as Wolf shut it.

Wolf thought about what had turned up on the video as he walked the handful of streets to get to the apartment he and Michael had shared for almost ten years now.

The video started out innocuously enough, fading from near black to the greenish images typical of low light recording. And mostly, nothing happened. Well, nothing other than the sudden flash of light from one of the top floor windows.

It happens in slow motion.

The House seems to pulse darkly in time to some unheard but felt heartbeat.

Time passes, watching apathetically as the earth turns, its denizens screwing, eating, lying, stealing, killing, birthing...

A flash of light precedes a shower of glass from one of the upper windows, the dark shape appearing to arc out, away from the building.

The fall seems to last for minutes, the inevitable pull of gravity ensuring the body didn't float away into space.

For a split second the man's face, frozen in absolute terror, seems to fill the frame before his fall is cut short by the height of the wall between the properties.

There is no sound of impact.

It started to rain when Wolf was about a quarter mile from the flat.

"Typical," he muttered to no one, rolling up his collar as best he could to keep the freezing rain from dripping down his neck.

Walking faster over the canal, lightning flashes, almost immediately followed by a bombastic thunderclap. "Bloody hell!" Wolf swore.

Almost to the other side, he noticed the figure slumped against the railings. He was tempted to walk on by, but something stopped him. Perhaps it was the stillness of the person there, something not quite normal.

Wolf braced himself and walked over to it, rain running inevitably down his neck as he bent his head.

Up close, it was obvious the man was dead. In another flash of lightning, Wolf could see the open, staring eyes, rain starting to fill the corners, and the mouth open, in a final scream.

Wolf reached for his voda, and then swore again as he realised he knew him.

It was the man from the video.

ONE BODY, TWO BODY, FOUR...

I t was a slow start to the day. Two doggy bodies landed on the bed to wake Alicia up.

"Damn dogs," she groaned. The clock said half-past seven. "And double-damn, I'm late." She shoved the covers off her and over the dogs who scrambled out of the folds of the duvet.

Quick shower and snatched bagel and Alicia was out the door when her voda pinged. It was Jack.

"We got another one, boss."

Hurrying to the tube, Alicia was lost for a moment. *Too many Cosmos last night*, she thought. "One what, Jack?"

"Another body with words cut into it," he replied.

Damn. Just what she needed today. "Okay, prep it, and get Dennis on the photos," she ordered. "You know the drill, Jack. I'm almost at the tube; should be there in half an hour."

"Okay, boss."

"And why are you so damn chipper? You should be suffering too!" Alicia snapped.

"New hangover cure – I'll share it with you when you get in." The little bastard was smiling, she could tell.

Grumbling to herself, she thumbed the voda off and shoved it back in her bag.

The morgue was quiet when she got there, unusual for a Wednesday, but not unheard of. Sue greeted her with a smile, large coffee and two little white pills.

"What are these?"

Sue pressed them into her hand. "Don't worry, I checked with Central – it's a new hangover matrix that seems to address all the symptoms of your average hangover."

Alicia glowered a bit more before taking the tablets. "Not that I'm hungover, of course," she muttered.

"No, of course not," Sue replied. "More coffee?"

"Keep it coming."

"Sure thing, boss."

Jack was stood over the table when she got into the main examination theatre. The body was lying on its front, and Alicia could just about make out the words carved into the victim's back.

"So?"

"My, someone's a bit terse this morning," Jack replied.

Alicia glared daggers at him. "This hangover *cure* isn't working yet."

Jack made calming motions with his hands. "Calm down, boss, it'll kick in any second. Now…" He turned back to the table. "White male, tentatively identified as one Bernard 'Thicko' Barnes. Was in fine health until he fell out of a window somewhere."

"Fell out a window?" Alicia asked, curiosity piqued despite the hangover.

"Injuries are consistent with a fall of about twenty-five to thirty feet. Not far enough to pulp all the organs, but far enough to cause head and neck trauma."

"You said *somewhere*?"

"He was not found at the scene of a fall, but on a bridge over the Grand Union canal near Kensal Green."

Alicia shrugged. *Was that a bit of a tingle in her throbbing head?* "And no way he could have fallen onto the bridge?"

Jack shook his head. "None. Bridge stands alone; nothing close enough to fall off of."

"And what have we got on his back that you want to show me?" Patience was not one of her virtues this morning.

"It says, '*Si non verum est, optime fictum est*', which translates as…" Jack flicked the remote on the screen.

If it is not true, it is very well invented.

"Right." Alicia muttered. "Are these meant to be clues or what?" She looked back at the screen. "And let me guess, attributed to…"

Giordano Bruno. Seventeenth century.

Jack was watching her. Suddenly, the pressure in her head released as if someone opened a valve and let the blood back in. She felt light-headed for a moment, then her headache disappeared entirely.

"Bloody hell!" she swore. "What in the – is that the hangover cure?"

"Suddenly light-headed? Feeling like oxygen has just hit your brain? No more headache?" Jack asked, smiling. "If so, then yes, that's it."

Alicia shook her head from side to side. Nothing. "Damn, this is going to be a bestseller! Where did you get them?"

"Got a mate in R&D – it's been approved and should be in public circulation in three months."

"Can he get more?" Alicia asked, feeling a bit like an addict looking for a new fix.

Jack laughed. "Don't worry, there's a bottle in Sue's drawer with your name on it."

Alicia's mind, suddenly clear, looked back at the quote on the screen. "We're being sent messages, but what about?"

Shaking his head, Jack looked at the body again. "Do you have any idea what the cuts in his back are made with?"

Pulling the exam light closer, Alicia looked at the marks in the flesh. "No pulling at the edges, so it's sharp. Was done post-mortem – blood leakage is minimal. No tell-tale burns from a laser-scalpel. No hesitation marks." She stared at Jack. "What's your theory? I know you have one."

Jack shook his head again. "No theory, but I think whoever did this was showing passion – the cuts aren't regular enough to be machine cut. You're right, though – no hesitation marks to suggest they were doing it for the first time."

Alicia toggled her lip mic. "Comparison with previous victims? Any hesitation marks in previous cases?"

Marks consistent with one hand. No variation in execution. All marks would appear to have been done at the same time.

"At the same…" Jack breathed in. "But the bodies are all at different stages of decomp, aren't they?"

"I'd say so," Alicia replied. "But there are stasis fields that can slow decay. I don't know if we'll find it, but can you check to see if there's any kind of tell-tale symptom where they're used?"

"Will get right on it." Jack went to his cubby to do some research.

Alicia stood over the body. "So, exactly where have you been, Bernard 'Thicko' Barnes?"

HAPPINESS IS A WARM CAT

Central flags Alicia's report up when it arrives. Another body, similar condition, found on a bridge, and more quotes from Giordano Bruno cut into the back. The A.I. has no more idea what the quotes lead to than I do.

Rather than rush in, I've decided to work from home today.

Dickens is curled up in my lap and I can hear Skeet pottering around upstairs. She's promised to go out and leave me be for a bit, so I'm happy to listen to her humming something unrecognisable to herself.

I'm flicking through text and highlighted info on Bruno on my pad in the living room. It's a recent addition, as I've only needed it since the op – and I'm still getting to grips with it.

The cat grumbles as I move over-vigorously to catch a snippet I'd waved to one side. I'll never get to grips with this gestural controller, it seems.

"Dammit," I swear as the text vanishes completely.

"Don't try so hard," Skeet says from behind my chair. "May I?"

I wave at the screen. "Be my guest."

Skeet reaches over my head and with a short twirl of her hand the snippet's back.

"How'd you do that?" I ask, amazed.

"It's called *undo*," she replies. "And it can save yer ass when somethin' goes missin'."

I nod. "Okay, that's cool. I remember *undo*." I've used and been around computers since their popularity increased, but all of that experience has been without the use of my eyes. It makes for a very different experience. "You off?"

Skeet sits on the arm of my chair and strokes Dickens. His purr increases in volume and the expression on his face can only be described as smug. He almost melts when Skeet scratches him behind the ears. Traitor.

"I've got t'see someone about some work," she replies. "In a minute. Just now, I'm hanging out with ma boys."

I nod again. *Bloody nodding dog, me.* Skeet's always had a low boredom threshold and likes to be working. I understand, not having any real hobbies myself.

"Anyway, better go, can't keep ol' Sasquatch waitin'," she says, giving Dickens a final 'scritch' and leaning over to kiss me on the lips.

"You sure?" I ask. "We could always play hooky."

Skeet's chuckle is low in the throat. "Don't tempt me, big boy." She brushes her lips over mine a last time and stands up. "But if I don't get some work soon, you'll be scraping me off the ceiling."

"Okay. See you later?"

"You kin count on it," she replies. "Later."

And the door closes softly behind her.

Noticing the absence of Skeet, Dickens looks around for a moment before deciding he's got other things to do. Fickle thing. He stretches and hops down from my lap. Pretty spry for about his age.

I light a cigarette and contemplate the texts on the screen in the silence.

"Stevie Ray Vaughn, *Live at Montreux*," I say softly and the opening bars of *Hide Away* take off from the tiny speakers situated around the room. I've always loved music and my home centre has a huge selection I've collected over the years, including some rare recordings I've had to have converted from the original vinyl. No one remembers vinyl anymore, besides the extreme purists.

I sigh, my age the elephant in the room in more ways than one.

My mind drifts off to think about what Madeline said. *You may well be a cross-breed — our lineage master is uncertain...*

I suppose it would account for some of my abilities. My ability to hear and now see things no one else does.

My skullphone distracts me. "Music, mute." The music snaps quiet. "Sen."

It's Adams, a researcher from the office. Paranormal Phenomena Research that is, Central informs me via the HUD.

"I think you need to come in, s-sir..." he stutters. His voice is uncertain. My reputation obviously precedes me. "I think you'll want to see this."

"Why? What is it?"

"It's about the Bruno quotes, sir. We think there's a... an extra element involved here."

"An extra element? What are you talking about?" I demand.

He's silent for a moment, clearly uncertain as to how to continue. I can almost hear him make a decision. "We... that is, I..."

"Get on with it Adams!" I can feel blood pounding in my temples.

"Yes, sir, Commander, sir." He takes a deep breath. "We think there's a magical component in the texts. Or maybe in the way they were applied. We're not entirely sure—" And he's off.

Great. Just what I need, the Goonies involved.

I stub out my cigarette and stand up. I interrupt him. "Fine. I'll be there in half an hour."

GIVE ME BACK MY WIG

S hirl was on the phone. "What do we do now?"

Wolf shook his head. "I don't know. I don't think we dare risk going into that House – not without more than our wits and our breaking and entering skills."

"You mean we need a specialist," Shirl replied. "One that deals with haunted houses."

Exasperated, Wolf took a big breath and held it for a few seconds. He didn't feel any less tense for it. "Actually, maybe we should just call it a day. I mean, do *you* want to go into that House?"

Silence. "Well, it wouldn't be my idea of fun," Shirl said slowly. "It scared the shit out of me last time – and all we were doing was climbing the wall."

Wolf nodded. "I know. That's a bit how I feel."

"You can't quit now," a voice said from the doorway. Wolf glanced up to see Mayweather standing there, looking like he'd slept in his clothes.

"Mayweather's here; I'll call you back later," Wolf said into the voda.

"Let me know what he says," Shirl replied and hung up.

Wolf gestured at the chair opposite. He stared at Mayweather for a moment before speaking. "Do you know what's at stake here, Mayweather?"

The tall, gaunt man with the Jesus-beard gazed back at Wolf. "I– I think so, Mr Woffe."

Wolf leaned back. "You see, I don't think you do." He picked up the stills from the video that Graeme had printed off for him. "You see these? These are basically ghosts – the ghosts of the men you sent in there the first time." He found the still from the jumper/faller. "And after we recorded this, I found the guy's body."

Mayweather looked at the images askance, recoiling slightly in his chair. "But... what about the Bruno text?"

Throwing the still back on the desk, Wolf waved him away. "I'm sorry Mayweather, but I'm not really ready to die just to find a lost manuscript."

The man sat there, not getting it. Thick as shite.

Wolf decided on a different tack. "You killed those men, Mayweather! Why do you think we'd be any different?" he demanded.

Mayweather shook his head, but Wolf saw the spark that ignited behind the eyes and recognised the burning gaze of the fanatic. "I–I must know…" Mayweather whispered finally.

Shaking his head in return, Wolf did something he rarely did. "I can't help you. I won't put my fa– people at risk for a damn book." He picked up some papers from his desk. "Now get out."

He could feel Mayweather's gaze, but refused to be moved by it. He heard a rustle of clothing and when he looked up, Mayweather was gone.

Good riddance, he thought. But another part of him replied, *I would have liked to have seen it…* "Shut up," he told the voice. "You remember what happened last time…"

Shirl had called him with a status report from Edinburgh.

"Wolf! It's Shirl. I've found 'Spooky' McAllister." She sounded out of breath.

Wolf went cold. "Alive?"

Shirl laughed. "Yes, if you can call staying in a tent in the Pentland Hills 'living'. I've got him here and we'll be on the next flight to City. Put him in the usual?"

"Uh-uh. I'll meet you where I left you."

Shirl said something, but the sound snapped and popped.

Wolf had a sinking feeling. "Shirl! What did you say?"

Garbled fuzz. Nothing intelligible. The connection went dead.

"Shirl!" No reply.

Graeme was sat next to him. "What…? What did she say, Wolf?"

Wolf stared out the windscreen, a headache forming between his eyes. "She said she'd found Spooky McAllister, and was going to put them both on the next plane to City."

"If that's all, why do you look so worried?"

Wolf looked at Graeme. "I'm sorry Graeme, I hope I'm wrong." He paused. "The signal cut out." Unusual in these days with reinforced digital signals everywhere.

"You think they've got her, don't you."

Wolf's gaze lit on the phone as it went back to the view. "Aye, I guess I do."

Wolf had called their 'employer' at the time, one Jacob Euonymous, a larger than life crime boss with fingers in lots of pies. And someone – or some *thing* – working for him cleaned out a whole house of armed mercenaries without even breaking a sweat.

Everyone in the house was dead except Shirl and Spooky.

Wolf didn't like being responsible for people when it could get them killed. And he'd vowed to never let that happen again.

FIREMEN DO IT IN RUBBER

Hugh phoned just after lunch. "Did I leave it long enough?" he asked.

Alicia smiled at the voda. "Long enough for what?"

"To make it seem that I'm not desperate to see you again," he replied, a smile in his voice.

Alicia laughed. "And why would you be?"

"I really enjoyed meeting you last night, Alicia... and, I'd like to spend time with you without the distractions of your colleagues and parties..." He sighed. "Look, I'm asking if you'll go out with me – tonight – damn, I'm a little rusty..."

"I think you're doing just fine." Still smiling, she made a decision. "Look, I've got two dogs, so without organising cover, I can't really do 'spontaneous'."

Hugh sighed again. "I see. Nevermind, then..."

Alicia shook her head in exasperation. "No, not *nevermind*. Would like to come over to my place? I enjoyed meeting you last night too." Then, feeling shy, she added, "I make a mean Penne Arrabiata. Bring a bottle of Chianti or Montepulciano d'Abruzzo. See you about seven thirty?"

She gave him the address and they finished the call feeling only slightly awkward.

Still smiling, Alicia sat back in her chair for a moment, considering things.

I'm glad you're moving on. She could almost hear Stephen in her head.

"I never wanted this," she replied to herself.

We don't always get what we want, do we?

Alicia shook her head. "No, we don't."

A little later, Jack appeared in her office door. "I'm not finding anything in the research about visible side effects from those stasis fields you were talking about, but it looks like there could be alterations to the body on a cellular level."

"Right. What kind of alterations? And do you think you can spot them?" Alicia asked, getting up from behind her desk.

Jack shook his head uncertainly. "I'm not sure – it's a bit sketchy, but the researcher I found with the best info suggests that like magnetic fields, those stasis fields can affect the structure and possibly the geometry of the cells themselves."

"I'm assuming you've got pictures?" Alicia nodded towards the tablet in his hand.

"Well, I've got what he's posted online – he's in London, so we might be able to get him to come in, or something."

"Let's see how we get on, first."

Jack had been busy. In the small lab next to the main exam room, he'd set up samples from each of the bodies ready by the microscope.

Alicia waved at the setup. "Very nice – have you looked at them already?"

Sheepishly, Jack nodded, but didn't say anything.

"And? Do I have to pull teeth here?" Alicia demanded.

"Just look at the samples, boss, and see what you think." *Why was he being coy now?*

Alicia peered through the microscope lenses at the first sample. "Well, I'm seeing nothing obvious."

"That's the first one, Jenkins. And here's number two…"

Nothing. Sigh. "Still not seeing anything, Jack."

"Number three…"

Nothing on either of the last two samples, either. "You're telling me there was no stasis field?" Alicia asked, leaning back on the stool.

"Not that I can see," Jack admitted. "I really just wanted your opinion as well – make sure I wasn't imagining it."

Alicia shook her head. "No, I wouldn't say so." She stared straight at him. "Those cells aren't affected at all. But…" She stood up and moved towards the door.

Jack followed her. "What, boss?"

She turned back. "Did you notice what wasn't there?" At his shake of the head, she smiled. "I can't see any signs of decay in those cells, Jack. They could have come from a living body!"

ARE COMPUTERS TAKING OVER THE WORLD, OR IS THAT JUST ME?

L et's get something straight: I don't... well, until fairly recently... did not... believe in the supernatural. The things I've seen and experienced – well, experienced more than seen, but you know what I mean – have changed my perceptions of how the world works.

The things that happened in the south of France, Madeline, even my own blind abilities and longevity seem to come from somewhere else.

So I guess I have to be a believer. Or deny my own existence.

Adams and his colleague are waiting for me in their basement lab when I get to Company House.

Their 'lab' consists of a shoebox-sized room which seems to always be dark. Except for the candles. I understand they spend a good portion of their budget on candles and it looks like there's wax on most level surfaces. It looks like it's been trashed and vandalised and there's marks all over the walls, floors and ceiling in red, black and blue swatches, mostly indelible fat markers like the ones graffiti artists use. Other than the scent of candle wax, there's an underlying odor like the one found in teenage boys' bedrooms.

Old-fashioned computers and servers, along with a snake's nest of cable and connects fill the corners, the centre of the room taken over by a large pentangle, the obligatory candles on each point of the star and the interstices in the middle. A dark grey mist roils in the air above the middle of the diagram; moving quickly, it never resolves into anything beyond what the mind's eye suggests: an eye, a fist, part of a breast.

I shake my head and look away. I don't want to know what it is.

"Second level phantasm," Igor, Adam's colleague, informs me. They're both sitting in form-fitting chairs observing the mist. His name's not Igor, but I've always called him that and can't think of anything else when I see him. If anything, he's non-descript at best. I don't think his own mother would recognise him in a crowd. One of those people the mind instantly erases from memory as too dull. "Possibly a plague victim, but we're not sure."

I nod and look at Adams. "You rang?" There's no place to sit, so I remain standing. Near the door.

Adams looks like a geek with dark-framed glasses and a big gold earring in one ear, down to the wispy beard and what looks like a Ramones T-shirt under a grubby lab coat, protruding over a small belly. It wouldn't surprise me at all if he and Igor survive solely on instant ramen noodles and games of *Dungeons and Dragons* in their basement lair.

Anyway, Adams clears his throat as a sign he's ready to tell me what he knows. I cock an eyebrow and stare at him. I'd forgotten how useful that can be.

Disconcerted, he clears his throat again. "We… we think those marks were placed on the victim's backs…"

I wave at him. "Go on."

Adams looks at Igor, and then back at me. "I… we think whatever it was… burned the words into the flesh while they were still alive."

Now I shake my head. "No sign of burns in the wound tracks, according to Dr Sampson. Or would you like to correct her report?" I ask, only thinly veiling my opinion on such an action.

His turn to wave. "No! No! When I say *burned*, it's a general term, meaning we don't know how the marks got there – they weren't cut into the flesh… by a knife or other metal implement!"

I nod. That would make sense. "Why do you think they were alive?"

"We– we've seen the photos and their faces all look like they're in agony, suggesting they knew what was happening."

"I see." And I did. Whatever – whoever – it was that did this, they wanted anyone who saw them to know they'd died in agony. I get a message from Central:

Meeting with the Inspector General, 13:00.

Time to wrap this up. "Anything else?"

Adams looks at Igor and then back at me. "We– we want to be involved when you find what– who did this…" Adams says. He sounds unconvincing.

I shake my head. "Absolutely not. You're not cleared for field duty, either of you."

"We are! If you read paragraph 62, subsection b43: *where unknown forces are involved, a member of the Paranormal Enquiries Team can be included at the discretion of the commanding officer.*" He looks up at me, as does Igor. "That's you."

A very bad idea. You wouldn't believe how bad. "I can't risk it, even if we knew where this might be taking place."

They both look like I've punched them in the stomachs. I relent. A little.

"Look, any more of these cases and you'll be included in the investigations." I hold up a hand. "That doesn't mean field work, necessarily, but we'll see." I turn to go.

"Thanks... Commander," Adams calls after me.

What am I thinking? Well, nothing really. I need more information before we can proceed with this.

And that's not what the Inspector General wants to talk to me about.

Now is the winter... You know the rest

Wolf sat in his workroom, staring out the window at the dull day, following the rain of the night before. Bare trees did little to block the views across to the houses behind, their branches straining at the leaden sky. It wasn't raining yet, but it would be soon.

He could hear Michael in the kitchen, clattering around doing something domestic. Burning something, no doubt. His talents lay in areas other than cooking.

The dilemma of Mayweather's quest was beginning to piss Wolf off. On the one hand, there was a valuable manuscript to find. A document that shouldn't exist, and one he desperately wanted to see.

On the other, that House radiated danger. And death. He'd promised himself he wouldn't take dangerous jobs after the last time he'd put his family at risk. Shirl almost died for fuck's sake!

A cup of tea appeared in front of him along with Michael's arm.

"I can't burn tea now, can I?" Michael asked, wrapping both arms around his neck.

Smiling ruefully, Wolf nodded up at him. "Your tea's not bad. I was afraid you were rustling up a tray of scones or something."

He could feel Michael shake his head behind him. "They'd only turn out like rocks, good for breaking your teeth on."

Wolf turned towards Michael, who took the opportunity to perch on Wolf's lap and wrap his arms around Wolf's shoulders. "Penny for 'em," he muttered, placing a kiss on Wolf's forehead.

Shaking his head, Wolf didn't know where to start. "It's this damn manuscript."

"Of course it is." When Wolf didn't continue, Michael tried again. "I thought you were giving it up."

Wolf didn't answer for a moment. "I intended to. I mean, yes, I want to give it up."

"And...?"

Wolf shrugged.

"It's dangerous, isn't it?" Michael asked.

"Maybe." Wolf shook his head. "No, definitely. People have already died."

"And that's what's holding you back."

Wolf shrugged again.

Michael sighed. "You know you're going to do it, don't you?"

"But I could get someone killed," Wolf protested.

"No, you won't." Michael leaned back and looked him in the eyes. "But you will always wonder if you don't try, won't you?" He leaned over Wolf's arm and picked up the voda lying amongst the clutter of papers. "Call them."

Wolf just looked at him for a moment before taking the voda.

Shirl answered on the second ring. "I wondered when you were gonna ring." Wolf thought he heard a smile in her voice and got irritated.

"Does everyone think they know me better than I do?" he demanded.

"Wind your neck in, Wolfie, we'll be over in a few."

"Right," he said to an empty line.

What am I getting us into? he wondered to himself.

Hey wait, is that the time?

Alicia sat back down in her ancient chair with a sigh. The wood creaked comfortably beneath her.

Staring into space, she didn't even notice when Sue came in with a fresh cup of coffee.

"Boss? You okay?" Sue asked, setting the cup down in front of her.

Alicia started. "Oh! Sorry, Sue. Miles away." She picked up the coffee. "Mmm... you make the best coffee, Sue. Thanks."

Sue nodded. "No problem, boss, glad you like it." She picked up the files in Alicia's out tray. "Need anything else?"

"I don't think so, Sue, unless you can gee Commander Sen up on these bodies in my morgue," Alicia replied.

"I'll see what I can do," Sue responded, with a mischievous glint in her eye.

"Cheers, Sue."

Sue must have done something, as Alicia's voda rang mere moments later.

"You wanted to talk to me?" Jaared asked. The call was audio only, which probably meant he was using his head phone. Alicia would never get used to the idea of having a connection to anything in her head.

Alicia nodded, and then realised he couldn't see her. "I've got four bodies, now, with Latin inscriptions cut into the flesh. You doing anything about it?"

Jaared laughed. "Well, the 'Goonies' have been looking at the file and have a second opinion on those inscriptions."

"Goonies?" But the second part distracted her. "What do you mean a *second opinion?*" Alicia asked. She was piqued someone was checking up on her.

"Now, don't get your nickers in a twist, Al. The Goonies fit under the heading 'Paranormal Phenomena Research'; they may be geeks, but they could have a point." He summed up the conversation he'd had in the basement with Adams and Igor.

"So, Adams and Igor— dammit, you've got me doing it! Adams thinks the letters weren't cut, but 'burned' somehow... Interesting." Alicia scratched a note on a pad. "I'll go have a look in a minute and get back to you."

"To answer your question, yes, I'm doing something about it, Al," Jaared said. "Sorry it hasn't been the first priority, I've got a bit of a political hot potato to deal with as well."

"The Tyler case?" Alicia asked. "Isn't that who you were talking to at the party the other night?"

"Yep. There's something very strange going on with the kid's stepmother." He chuckled. "I suppose it might have something to do with the fact she's only about three years older than he was!"

"I imagine it would be a bit peculiar, at that." Alicia noticed the clock on the wall. "Shit, is that the time? Sorry Jaared, gotta go."

"Got a date?" Jaared asked. "Sounds important..."

"Well, not a date, per se," Alicia replied. "Hugh's just coming over for dinner... It's easier with the dogs... you know."

Jaared chuckled again. "I do, indeed. Have a nice night and I'll let you know where we get to tomorrow."

"Night Jaared."

I SEEM TO SPEND MY LIFE MAKING STATUS REPORTS

The Inspector General is pacing on the very expensive carpet when I reach his office.

"You wanted to see me, sir?"

"Sen! Come in. How's the Tyler case going?" No pleasantries with the staff, straight down to business.

"We're still exploring certain aspects of the case, sir," I reply. "There are anomalies that I would like to pin down."

The IG stops pacing and flops down behind his massive aircraft carrier-sized desk. Only a small forest was depleted to make it. "I want that case closed immediately."

I might be a bit stunned but hardly surprised. "Sir?"

"Close that case and let the family grieve in peace." He looks up at me. "That's an order, Commander."

"Yes sir," I reply. "May I ask—?"

He cuts me off. "No, you may not. Now get out."

I stand there for another second, not really afraid of him; I've seen too many like him over the years. "What about Timson, sir?"

He eyes me over the expanse of wood again. "What about Timson?"

"Do you not find it odd he was killed in what we think is the last location John Tyler was still alive?"

That stops him for a second and I can almost smell burning meat as his brain mulls it over. He shakes his head just before that pressure valve blows. "No, merely coincidence. Now get out!"

I nearly shake my head, and then think better of it. "Yes sir."

Hmmm… Did the stepmother get to the IG? Am I just being paranoid? I'm afraid, to quote Woody Allen, "Just because you're not paranoid doesn't mean they're not out to get you."

Something stinks about this sudden decision to close the case. Timson should be revivable in another day and then we would have more information, assuming his memory hadn't been damaged; short-term memory loss is not uncommon in trauma like this.

Central should have a good idea what Timson was up to — he was monitored like I am. Why didn't I think of it before?

The request for information on Timson's activities is blocked. A flag promptly informs me:

CASE REF: QR8975640026-0-TYLER

STATUS: CLOSED

Contact Commander Jaared Sen for further information.

Huh.

The IG knows me too well. I particularly like the bit about contacting me for further information. If only I had some.

I shrug and head for the coffee bar. Must be time for a coffee before I meet Skeet. Or something stronger.

Besides, I've got four bodies to follow up.

TURN THE MUSIC DOWN, I'M TRYING TO CONCENTRATE

T rue to her word, Shirl and Graeme turned up about ten minutes after Wolf put the voda down.

The day had closed in the meantime, the trees outside the window disappearing into darkness.

"I guess you're wondering why I gathered you all here..." Wolf quipped.

Graeme and Michael rolled their eyes and Shirl threw a pillow off the sofa at him. "Get on with it, Wolf," she commanded.

"All right, all right, pipe down," he muttered. He waved at the screen they could see. "I'm not keen on putting ourselves at risk, but you know what we're looking at."

"Go into a haunted house, get a valuable manuscript, try not to get killed," Shirl ticked the points off on her fingers. "Piece o' cake."

Wolf nodded. "I guess that's the crux of it." He looked away from them and swallowed some of his tea. "Now, anyone who doesn't want to be involved, I'll understand... I mean, I'm not willing..." he trailed off, looking back at them.

Graeme nodded. "We know the risks, Wolf," he said. "Who's going in?"

Shirl tilted her head in acknowledgement of his unasked question. "Wolf and I will make the insertion and get the manuscript out as quick as we can."

"Won't Mayweather want to go, too?" Graeme asked. "It's his party, after all."

"I don't think so – not after our last conversation with him," Wolf replied. "Trying to go in last time, getting chucked out and being the only survivor is freaking him out some."

"You can say that again," Shirl muttered.

A diagram of what they guessed the House looked like inside flashed up on the screen.

Shirl pointed at the front of the building. "There's something funky about the skin of this place – Wolf and I both felt like the claws weren't going to hold us on the wall. And that's odd, as they're rated to support half a tonne on most surfaces, even ceramics."

"Self-inserting pitons do the job?" Graeme suggested.

Wolf shook his head. "Too noisy – we don't want to attract any more attention than we have to." He glanced at Shirl again. "And we don't want to let anyone who may be inside know we're coming. If we can help it."

Shirl shrugged as if to say *over to you.*

"So, with the skin of the House behaving like it does – not exactly stable – we think we might as well try the front door."

"What, knock and hope it opens?" Michael asked.

Wolf shook his head. "Not exactly. We'll try picking the lock and see where that gets us. Should be a piece of cake." He glanced at Shirl. "If not, we'll have to try going in through a cellar window."

"When are you going?" Michael asked.

Wolf looked at Shirl and shrugged. "By the time we've checked all the equipment and made sure we've got everything, it's going to be tomorrow, at the earliest," she replied.

"I agree. We'll spend tomorrow in the workshop, checking everything and then we'll go through the plans as best we can."

They were all silent for a moment, and then Michael piped up. "What if you can't find the manuscript?"

More silence. "I guess we'll just have to call it quits at that point," Wolf managed. "I mean, we only have Mayweather's word that it's in there anyway…"

Standing, Michael nodded. "And he's not exactly what you'd call *balanced*, from what you've told me."

"No."

Michael helped Graeme off the sofa. "Anyone for pizza?"

I STARTED SOMETHING I COULDN'T FINISH

A licia had made it home with time to spare. The dogs had been walked and put out in the garden for a bit and now the sauce was bubbling away on the stove. It was her mother's recipe, a recipe she'd followed faithfully for many years – she couldn't remember when she'd first cooked it.

The table was cleared and set for two. "Candles or no candles?" she asked herself. "Too romantic for a first... something?" She felt a pang, remembering her first date with Stephen.

Stephen had just taken an assistant Anthropology chair at Cambridge when she met him in London. He was down for a conference at the same hotel where she was attending a seminar on 'Identifying Subjects by DNA Extracted from Bone Fragments'.

Finding nothing new in the seminar, she'd nipped out to the hotel bar for a drink and a chance to catch up on her office correspondence – it never quit just because she was out of the office.

Alicia had sat in a corner, away from the few other patrons of the bar. What is it about hotel bars? Why are there always people drinking in them, regardless of the hour?

Her position had put her on the route to the nearby toilets, however, and one of the patrons bumped her table on his way past.

"'Scuse me," he muttered before tripping over the chair and collapsing on the table, sending her drink, seminar papers and voda flying and pushing Alicia backward in her chair. "Shit."

With an audible sigh, Alicia rolled over and rescued her voda before the white wine reached it and started collecting her things.

"Here, let me help you," a voice said at her shoulder. A strong hand took her elbow and helped her up. When she stood up, she was looking into the most beautiful eyes she had ever seen. "Sorry for Perkins, he can't hold his drink and insists on starting early in the day at a seminar while we're still on coffee."

"I–I see," Alicia replied, unsure what she saw beyond his rugged features.

"Are you okay?" The mellifluous voice took on a concerned tone. "Are you hurt?"

She could look into those eyes all day... Alicia shook herself mentally. "Yes. And no, I'm fine," she answered both questions. Then she took a step back, physically and mentally. "I'm Alicia Sampson." She offered her hand.

"Stephen Jamieson." His grip was firm, but not crushing. He didn't have anything to prove.

"Well, thanks for your help," Alicia said, collecting her damp pack and handbag. "I'd better get back."

Stephen looked around and then back at her. "Are you sure? I would like to replace your drink, if you've got time."

Oh honey, for you I've got all the time in the world, she thought. What she said was, "I suppose they won't miss me for a bit yet."

His smile was worth it and as brilliant as she'd expected.

From never having believed in 'love at first sight', Alicia was a convert from the moment she met Stephen.

The bell interrupted her thoughts and her sauce stirring. With a curse for her daydreaming, she quickly wiped her hands before heading for the front door.

She stopped in the hall and checked her hair, tucking a stray wisp behind her ear. Bracing herself mentally, she turned to the door.

Hugh stood on the step, a bunch of flowers and a bottle of wine in his hands. "Evening," he said, looking awkward.

Alicia smiled. "Come in Hugh." She stepped back as he entered the hallway and she realised, again, how big he was.

"Thanks. These're for you." He proffered the flowers and the bottle.

Taking them both, Alicia turned and headed for the kitchen. "This way. You can keep me company. And open this."

Handing him the corkscrew and the bottle, she heard scratching at the door. When opened, the two Staffys bounded in, heading straight for the guest. "Hope you like dogs," she said ruefully.

Hugh put the bottle down and proffered hands to each dog. After they gave him a sniff, he scratched them both behind the ears. From their grins, it was obvious he had two new friends. "I love dogs, just don't have any of my own," he replied with a laugh as Bess licked his hand.

Alicia smiled at the scene and turned back to pop the garlic bread into the oven.

That's a good sign, a voice in her head said. And it was.

DARK HOPES AND EXPECTATIONS...

Morning always comes around too soon. That said, I don't know when I last slept more than five or six hours at a time. *Oh, you need less sleep when you get old…* Yeah, thanks for that.

I leave Skeet in bed and go down to the kitchen and put on some coffee in the dark. Some skills don't go away that easily.

Dickens appears by my ankles, intertwining himself and making little morning noises. Once the coffee's on, I get out his food and put some in his bowl. He immediately inserts his head and starts eating. Oh, to have such simple pleasures.

I light a cigarette, pour some coffee into a mug and head for the living room.

Making sure I've got my pad (I can't use Skeet's tablet for Company work; god knows how unsecure that would be) I go to my favourite chair and turn on the light next to it. I settle into the chair and call up the information on my collection of bodies.

There's a movement in the doorway and I glance up to see Dickens watching me for a second. He comes into the room and looks up at me. He spies the pad and frowns before turning around and exiting the way he came. Not a big fan of the pad since I got it; it encroaches on his 'me' time.

Four bodies, four inscriptions and four different ways of dying. I sigh and pick up the coffee. I close my eyes and just consider what I know about the bodies.

After a few moments, something niggles and I call up the list of the dead.

Ivan Jenkins

Silvio Bartolmeo

Bernard 'Thicko' Barnes

And the ID of the third one has just come in, one Jefferson Airplane Bolton, a specialist in mediaeval manuscripts. For some reason, the request for ID took longer to process than expected.

I flash my authority sigil at Central and it opens Ivan Jenkin's secured file. Turns out that he's a snitch for Serious Crimes. And a member of the E3 Irregulars with Thicko Barnes. Not a coincidence, I'd bet.

This leads me to wonder where their boss is.

"Last known whereabouts of Eddie Kray."

Last seen ten days ago.

That's a place to look, then.

Bolton was a specialist in mediaeval manuscripts – what was he doing with two thugs from the East End? Wait a minute, the quotes cut into the corpses have been attributed to one Giordano Bruno. "Dates of Giordano Bruno."

Giordano Bruno. 1548 to 1600.

"Brief precis of Bruno's life."

Giordano Bruno. Born Filippo Bruno.

Italian Dominican friar, philosopher, mathematician and astronomer.

Radical cosmological theories went beyond the Copernican model in proposing the Sun was essentially a star, and, moreover, that the universe contained an infinite number of inhabited worlds populated by other intelligent beings.

Burned at the stake by civil authorities in 1600 after the Roman Inquisition found him guilty of heresy for his belief in pantheism and turned him over to the state, which at that time considered heresy illegal.

Gained considerable fame after death; in the nineteenth and early twentieth centuries, commentators focusing on his astronomical beliefs regarded him as a martyr for free thought and modern scientific ideas.

Published a number of pamphlets and books, many of which are no longer in existence.

Hmmm… missing manuscripts – could explain why Bolton was involved. But wait, maybe he's the wrong period, mediaeval may not cover Bruno. "Define 'mediaeval period'."

Mediaeval period. Approximately fifth century to fifteenth century.

Hmmm. He was technically after that period. "Any specialisms to tie Jefferson Bolton to Giordano Bruno?"

Bolton specialist in authenticating late mediaeval manuscripts. Has published multiple papers on techniques for detecting fakes.

"Ah-ha!" Why would a manuscript specialist be involved with two thugs like Barnes and Jenkins? What about the other one, Silvio Bartolmeo? What was his involvement? "Silvio Bartolmeo, background." Unsurprisingly, it repeated the brief bio in the initial report.

Silvio Bartolmeo. Italian. Thirty-six. Lecturer at University College London.

Lecturer in Ecclesiastical History – primarily Spiritualism and Heresy in the Catholic Church.

Well, that ties into Bruno. I sit back in the chair and pick up my cold coffee after lighting a cigarette.

I watch the smoke curl up from my fag for a moment, revelling in my regained sight once more.

So, Giordano Bruno, monk, scientist and heretic. Could they have found a missing Bruno manuscript? Or a forgery? Going by the two experts involved, I could say 'yes'. But they're all dead. Why? And why cut the quotes into their bodies?

"It's a message," I say aloud. "A warning."

Dickens wanders in again, sees the pad is sitting on the side and jumps up into my lap. "Mwaoar?" he asks.

"No, I don't know – I can't say who the warning is for."

Hopefully not for me.

One of the benefits of being able to access just about all public records from my head is the speed with which I find things.

Of course, I don't always think of the most important item first. For instance, why didn't it occur to me that the British Library might a) have an expert on Bruno, or at least a rare books person, and b) might actually have some of his work? Well, they do. Both.

It is a simple matter of requesting a car and I'm there in less than an hour. A quick query, with my identification, sends me from reception up to the first floor: Rare Books and Music.

The tiny woman I find waiting for me at the queries desk barely reaches my elbow. I'm almost inclined to drop to knee level to speak to her. Her dark hair is cut in an efficient bowl cut and the heavy glasses she wears give her a particular gravity. That, and the fact she has a frown on her face I'm sure scares lesser mortals.

"Ms Petunia Walker?" I ask, even though Central has already identified her. I still find that a bit rude.

"That's me. What do you want?" Her tone remains as cold and uninviting as her eyes behind the thick lenses.

I see. Well I can be officious, too. "Commander Sen, Ma'am. I am looking into a possible theft of a manuscript by Giordano Bruno and I was told you are the library's expert." A bit of flattery does no harm, either. "And, I was hoping you could show me some of his work."

Apparently, this is just the spark she needs. The temperature rises from 'Ice Age' to 'Just a bit chilly'.

"Bruno? Yes, of course. I've been expecting you." For a moment, I fear she's going to flutter her eyelashes at me – she's old enough to be my mother. "Right this way, Commander."

Ms Walker leads me to a small meeting room behind the main desk. There is a leather-topped table in the centre of the room and a small pile of books sit to one side of it. The books are smaller than I expected, two of them even appear to be pocket-sized. All are old and bound in differing materials.

"What do you know of Bruno's writing, Commander?"

I shrug. "Not a great deal. His name has come up in the course of a multiple murder investigation and I'm trying to track down someone who might know of a manuscript that has come to light... I have reason to believe a missing Bruno manuscript is somewhere in London and the murders were somehow connected to it."

The dark eyes regard me somberly behind the glasses for a moment. "I see." Ms Walker picks up one of the larger books – it's still not much bigger than my hand – and shows me the frontispiece. "This is one of his more common works, *De Umbris...*"

She hands it to me. "It was published by Bruno in 1582 and is a treatise on memory – Bruno was an advocate of using mnemonics to remember critical things. It is printed on a more modern paper vellum, much higher in cloth fibres than the wood pulp paper we've been using for the last century and a half. Once printed, the pages would have been cut by hand and then bound. The binding on this copy has been replaced at least once…"

I've never held anything as old before and I doubt I will again. Ms Walker becomes positively effusive on the subject of Giordano Bruno, but I tune her out, looking at this book printed half a millennia ago. The paper has obviously aged, as there are water marks and age or mold spots, but the printing is as sharp in the twenty-first century as I imagine it was five hundred years ago. I'm surprised by the diagrams.

"The diagrams and illustrations are woodcut and then printed on the page." She picks up another volume and turns to one of the diagrams. "I love this one." I realise it actually has moving parts, two round wheels tied into the book with a thread, allowing them to turn independently. Fascinating.

When she starts to run out of steam, I figure it's time to ask her the question I came here for.

"Do you get offered books and manuscripts like this, Ms Walker?"

She stiffens. "Most certainly not, Commander." Almost an audbile 'click' as the wall goes back up again.

I look at her for a moment, remembering to listen to the other signs in the situation. "I meant no offence, Ms Walker, but if you do know anything about a missing Bruno manuscript, I do need to know."

Her pulse quickens again. Oh yes, she knows something. She looks down and starts aligning the book's edges with the straight line of the table. "I have heard… rumours… of a new Bruno manuscript that has come to light." Petunia Walker suddenly lifts her head and stares me in the eye. "But that is all, Commander. We do not deal in dodgy manuscripts at the British Library!"

I can tell Ms Walker is still hiding something. "But you might know someone who does?"

She looks away for a long minute. "There's a man called Jubal. Has a shop off Judd Street. Specialises in legal books and treatises. But I understand he has… dabbled… shall we say… in grey market documents."

Really? "Jubal? Big black guy? No last name?" I ask, not daring to hope.

Ms Walker nods. "That's him. Do you know him?" At my acknowledgement, she says, "Most unusual character to be a specialist in the law, don't you think?"

I nod again. "Jubal is unusual in more ways than you know. Thank you for your time, Ms Walker." I turn to go.

"Commander," she says behind me, "if you find it, can I see it?"

"I'll do what I can, Ms Taylor," I say over my shoulder. "I'm not even certain it exists."

THERE'S A PORTRAIT OF A SERIAL KILLER ON MY WALL

A drop of four stories would have been lethal to most mortals. As it was, Madeline hit the ground, paving stones cracking as she rolled to her feet. Running was the only option.

The thing following her was untiring and old, so old.

Madeline jinked towards the main road, and then ducked down the alleyway, which, if she remembered correctly, was covered over with stone. This was Edinburgh's old town on the hill near the castle – there were plenty of closes and covered passages to choose from. That would help for a moment – the creature didn't *have* to fly, it just normally chose to.

She'd lost her glasses somewhere along the way and now her eyes burned bloody red in the dimness. And she was angry. *Why the hell was a hellhound pursuing her?* She could hear Reynard in her head saying, *It is simple – who have you pissed off, this time?*

She'd only been in Scotland for a week and she'd had no end of problems. This was just the latest.

The passage was about thirty feet long and sloped down at one end. Madeline stopped in the middle and waited. A length of iron piping was attached to the wall as a handrail. She pulled on it and a section of tubing tore free from the stone, leaving her with an iron staff about five feet tall. It was old iron, too, which would lend it some potency and, hopefully, strength.

A slight scrabbling noise sounded at the upper end of the passage and Madeline moved into a defensive crouch, facing it. The disturbance subsided and she tensed, sensing the creature was still there.

With a guttural roar, it charged down the tunnel towards her. For a split-second, Madeline stood there, able to see the flow of the air around it, judging her moment before spinning and racing towards the other end of the close.

Near the opening, she whirled and thrust upward with the iron pipe. With a cry of "SEPARO!" she hit the roof of the tunnel and ducked out of the way.

The stones and masonry that composed the ceiling of the passageway didn't stand a hope in hell and parted with a loud *Crack!*

Surprised by the suddenly falling ceiling, the thing behind her tried to stop. It was unsuccessful and roared angrily over the noise of the cave-in.

Still clutching the length of iron, Madeline backed towards the open end of the close, wary that it hadn't been trapped by the stonework. It wasn't likely she'd damaged it, as they're nigh indestructible. But you never knew.

Behind her, a low growl started.

Merde! There were two!

Pausing just for a moment, Madeline readied herself. She whirled, aiming the iron pipe at what she hoped was the throat of the hellhound.

She was too slow.

BLACK HOLES AND REVELATIONS

J ubal's shop is only a rare book's-throw from the British Library, so I
walked it.

I've known Jubal for about fifteen years after one of his competitors
trumped up a first degree disturbing the peace charge to get him offed
by a Contractor. Me.

Fortunately for Jubal, I worked out what was going on. Besides, a
First Degree Peace Disturbance charge means you've incited a riot or set
up a rock concert in the middle of a residential area. While he's
annoying, Jubal's never been that offensive.

He's also very security conscious; you can't get into his shop without
ringing the bell and being scanned so he can decide if he likes your looks
or not. And one of his scanners plays with the implants in my head, as
something buzzes in my phone like a small cluster of angry wasps. Then
a momentary feeling of dizziness. *Dammit, my implants are supposed to be
shielded!*

After the scan, and probably a visual inspection, Jubal decides that he's
feeling friendly as he buzzes me straight in. I like that.

"Afternoon, Commander... What can I do for you?" he asks, straight
to the point, no joking around, or strange observations today. The
whites of his eyes seem inordinately pale against the darkness of his skin,
iris and pupils nearly black. His usual jovial mood seems to be missing
today. *Wonder why that is?*

"Is it something I said, Jubal?" I ask.

He looks at me blankly for a moment. "What." It doesn't sound like a
question.

"You've gone quiet, Jubal, for some reason. No idle banter or
discourses on 'fried chicken'."

A smile crosses his lips for a moment. "I was very drunk, *Commander* —
my apologies for anything offensive I may have said."

I look around the shop. It's full of large books and there are a lot of
identical covers. I idly scan a few of the bindings, but the actual titles
aren't visible on the older books. And I don't know much about
historical law works. Can't see anything unusual, besides a handful of
rare books in the glass cabinet at the front of the shop. *So why does he need
so much security?*

Maybe a change of tack. "Business good, Jubal?"

He's guarded again. "Can't complain – much."

Oh well, I'm not one for subtlety. "Have you heard anything about a very rare Giordano Bruno manuscript coming on the market, Jubal?"

"No."

I look at him and it looks like there's never been the trace of a smile on his face. "Now Jubal, you're not playing the game." Those dark eyes in the brilliant whites stare at me. "You're supposed to say something like, 'What Bruno manuscript?' or, 'Is there?' or even better, 'Who's Gordon Burno?' But you didn't say anything like that."

He's looking at me like he wants me to disappear. "Sorry, Commander, you've lost me."

The rare books in the glass cabinet – I've no idea what they are, but probably legal books if Jubal's got them – look dusty as I peer through the glass at them.

"You see, Jubal, I think you know exactly what I'm talking about." I stand up straight and face him across the counter. I shake my head, listening to the racing of the blood through his veins and his heavy breathing. "Pulse is up..."

A searing pain hits me behind the eyes. I smell the scent Madeline always wears. And burning. For a moment I see only darkness then realise there are two flaming red eyes looking at me. What the...?

I shake my head and whatever it was fades. *A vision? Was I just in Madeline's head?* Jubal's looking at me oddly.

"You okay, Commander?" he asks.

"Fine Jubal, fine." I shake my head again. "Where was I?"

"I could have sworn you faded for a moment, Commander – I could see through you for just a second," he adds.

I ignore him, not wanting to think about it. "Back to you, Jubal; you're breathing heavily, and I dare say you're perspiring, too."

"Not as much as you, Commander..."

"I don't think you *have* the book in question, Jubal, but I think you know where it is or maybe who's looking for it." I lean over the counter. "Don't you?"

Unconsciously, he backs into the counter behind him. And I'm not even being threatening yet.

"Well, Jubal?"

His eyes dart around the shop, looking for someone who isn't there or for some kind of *Candid Camera* setup. These days, pinhead cameras make the whole surveillance game even more complicated – you would never notice someone is watching you until it's too late.

I drum my fingers on the countertop. "I'm waiting, Jubal."

He comes to some kind of internal decision. "Okay, but you never heard nothin' from me."

"I understand."

Eyes still zooming over everything in the room, he leans forward. "I have heard somethin' about a Bruno manuscript." He's speaking very quietly now, confiding, as if that will help. "It's supposed to be one of those missing books – you know, the ones no one's seen since they were published, kind of thing."

"Right."

His eyes meet mine, boring in. "Of course, they say the Vatican's got loads of books that're supposed to be missing." He leans closer still, so I can smell the onion on his breath from his lunch. "And I wouldn't put it past 'em."

"The Bruno manuscript, Jubal." I sigh; trying to keep him on track is proving difficult.

"Right, right." He seems a bit more animated now. "Anyway, I heard some mutant is looking for the Bruno – he's over two metres tall!" And Jubal's not a small bloke himself.

I circle my finger in the air, telling him to get on with it.

Jubal leans closer again. "You need to go to *Hopkins' Rarities & Antiquities* on the Charing Cross Road. Talk to Pocock Woffe – or 'Wolf' as his friends call him."

Wait a minute, I know that name from somewhere. "Who is Pocock Woffe?"

I swear Jubal looks over his shoulder. And I thought *I* was paranoid. "He's a book dealer who finds things. It's his shop."

Central takes the opportunity to put more information up in my HUD.

Pocock Woffe, aka Wolf: antiquarian bookseller, *Hopkins' Rarities & Antiquities*, 80 Charing Cross Road.

Bingo. Now I remember. It had a strange fire a little while back. "Thank you Jubal." I turn to go. "That wasn't so hard now, was it?"

"*I ain't a snitch Commander!* Don't you be tellin' no one 'bout this!" He does sound worried.

I look over my shoulder. "Your secret's safe with me, Jubal." I smile at him while he unlocks the door and I pull it open. "Bye."

Dean Fetzer

Time to go pay Mr Woffe a visit.

Although whether he'll help me after our last encounter, I'm not sure.

JUST WHEN YOU THINK EVERYTHING'S GOING TO PLAN

Wolf and Shirl spent a good portion of the day going through their kit for the night's excursion.

"Wolf, is this pack working to spec?" Shirl asked, breaking through his reverie.

He took the powerpack from her and plugged it into the diagnostic unit. There was a flicker on the screen, which was almost imperceptible, before it stabilised into the green. Wolf frowned and popped a new one out of its protective bubble. He plugged it into the unit. No flicker.

"Something's off – try this one," he said, handing her the new one. "Got backups?"

Shirl nodded, brushing hair from her face. "Yep, all systems have at least one backup, with another set in the car with Da."

Wolf pushed the armour he'd been repairing to one side. "Beer?"

Smiling, Shirl nodded. "Wouldn't say no. But don't we need to keep sharp?"

"We're only having the one and it's not likely to affect us by the time we're in place to do this thing." He grinned back. "Besides, we can always take a little snap to make us more alert."

"Jesus, Wolf! Don't let Da know – you know what he's like about drugs!"

Wolf popped the tops from two micro-brew ales from the shop's fridge and handed her one. He clinked his against hers and raised it. "To successful breaking and entering."

"Cheers," Shirl replied.

They drank their beers in silence for a moment. The shop was around the corner from Wolf and Michael's flat, converted from a private garage stuck in between two properties. With land so expensive in London, every spare inch seems to get used for something.

When he'd found it, Wolf had spent two months adding lights, a heating unit and a small toilet as well as proper insulation and a security system. Even at this time of year, it was relatively warm.

Shirl had been peeling the label from her bottle, concentrating intensely. Wolf knew she was building up to something, but didn't want to ask. She'd get to it in her own time. He took another sip of his beer.

"Do you think we'll get it, Wolf?" she asked.

Wolf nodded. "Yep."

"What about the protections? I mean, the last team got fried, why not us?"

Shirl always asked the hard questions. But then, someone had to. And after her abduction when they were working for Euonymus, it was hardly surprising. Wolf still didn't know what had happened and suspected it was something she had barely told her therapist about.

Wolf considered the question before answering. *How did he know they'd make it. Instinct? Gut feeling? Hope?* "We're different – we've done this sort of thing before."

"We're talking about magic here, Wolf – we're not experienced in that," she reminded him.

"No, but I think there's a way around it."

"What 'way'?"

"Mayweather survived it."

Shirl shook her head and sipped her beer. "Only because the House kicked him out the door. We don't know what happened there."

"We could take him with us," Wolf suggested.

Mid-drink, Shirl snorted, choking on her beer. "We haven't got the gear to fit him – I mean, he's almost seven foot tall! How do you propose we get him in?"

"And not exactly coordinated," Wolf said.

"No."

Wolf drank his beer, thinking. *What was he thinking? It was a suicide mission.*

Then his voda rang. Janey.

"Hey Janey, something wrong at the shop?" She didn't normally ring him in the day-to-day.

"Wolf, there's a Commander Sen from the Company here to see you," Janey replied.

Sen? Wait a minute, wasn't that the guy he'd run into when they were looking for Euonymus's Amber Room? "What's he want?" Wolf asked, not sure he'd like the answer.

"Says he needs an opinion on a missing manuscript – something by Giordano Bruno?"

What the fuck? "Sorry? Has he got a Bruno manuscript?" Play dumb, it always works with the Plod.

"No, he wants your opinion on the whereabouts of a Bruno manuscript. I said you were in tomorrow, but he insists it's urgent."

"Big ugly guy? Wrap around shades?"

"Actually, no – big, handsome bloke with very pretty grey eyes," Janey replied.

Wolf thought for a moment, before shrugging mentally. *The guy could have had surgery or something. Whatever.*

Anyway, they could use a diversion. "What time is it?" He took the voda away from his face and looked at the time displayed there. 16:34. "Okay, we'll pop down and see him – tell him it'll be about forty-five minutes."

"Okay boss. See you in a bit."

Shirl was looking at him. "What was that all about?"

Wolf shook his head. "No idea. We've got a nosy copper asking about missing Bruno manuscripts the very day we're going into a haunted house to retrieve one."

"That can't be a coincidence," Shirl said.

"I don't believe in them for a start," Wolf replied. "So you're going to drive us down and I'm going to have a chat with the Commander."

"Okay…"

"Let's just hope the conversation doesn't end up like last time – he had me in a little room for twelve hours, asking about Euonymus."

He saw Shirl blanch out of the corner of his eye. "He was involved in that?"

"He didn't know anything and I didn't enlighten him," Wolf answered. "Though I heard he took out Euonymus all by himself."

Shirl's grin wasn't exactly humorous – too many teeth. "He gets points for that in my book."

Wolf smiled back. "And mine. I never liked that twat, Euonymus." He flicked on the security and pulled on his jacket. "Come on, the sooner we get there, the sooner we'll know what he wants."

It's just like riding a bike, well, almost

Alicia pushed paper around on her desk, not even thinking about work.

"Boss? You going to sign those requisitions before I go home?" Sue asked from the doorway.

"What?" Alicia looked up. "Oh, yes, of course." She found the appropriate lines and signed each one with her heavy Mont Blanc. Another gift from Stephen.

"You okay, boss?"

Alicia finished the last one and looked up. "I'm fine, Sue, just a bit preoccupied with—" *Hugh*, her brain finished. "...*things*," she substituted.

Sue picked up the papers. "Hmm, I think I can guess what kind of *things*."

Alicia pinked. "Why? Has Jack been talking?"

Sue almost smirked. "No, but I have other sources. Let's just say your time with the fireman the other night was remarked upon."

Great. They were all gossiping about her.

Seeing the look on Alicia's face, Sue was quick to correct her. "Not like that, boss!" She came around the desk, depositing the pile of requisitions, and put her arm around Alicia's shoulders. "Everyone is pleased that you've found someone since... you know..."

Yes, Alicia did know. Stephen had been a regular visitor to the department when he wasn't off digging up China, or South America. "Thanks, Sue."

"No problem, boss." Sue released her and picked the papers up again. "We only want you to be happy, you know?"

Alicia nodded. "I know. Me too."

She sat staring into space again after Sue's departure before shaking her head in annoyance. She picked up her voda and hit the preset for Kate. "Hey Trouble, got time for a drink tonight?"

There was a burst of noise in the background. Kate was in PR and her team was often a bit rambunctious. "Sorry about that – the children are ready to go to the pub." There was the sound of a door closing. "A drink? Sure Al. Shall we meet at the *Narrow* in about an hour? Then you can bring the kids."

"Okay, sounds good – I'll see you there." Alicia hung up and stared into the distance for a moment before shaking her head again and standing up to get her coat.

MEETING PREVIOUS INTERROGATION SUBJECTS CAN BE AWKWARD

I t's dark and getting cold when I get back to *Hopkins' Rarities & Antiquities* at five thirty and knock on the door. The petite blonde lets me in – *Janey?* – and I enter the shop for the second time today.

"Thanks. Is Mr Woffe here?" I ask.

The blonde nods. "Yes, he's in the office at the back. Just go on through."

"Thanks," I say again. I pull my long leather coat off and drape it over one arm.

The office is the one of two doors on the back wall of the office and stands open. Unsurprisingly, the walls are covered in yet more books. I don't know anything about books beyond remembering reading a lot of them when I was younger.

When I step into the doorway, Woffe, seated at the desk, and another woman standing looking at something over his shoulder, glance up at me. Woffe stands up and nods at me. "Commander Sen."

"Mr Woffe." My HUD has already ran the girls identity. Shirl Black, known associate.

He gestures at the chair in front of the desk. "This is my... friend... Shirl," he offers by way of introduction.

I nod to the attractive brunette and sit down, draping my coat over the back of the chair. The brown-haired lady looks like she's in good condition – lots of muscle tone – but a bit shorter than I prefer. *This vision thing is quite distracting sometimes.*

"It's been a while, Commander," Woffe offers. "I almost didn't recognise you."

"Yes. I do apologise if I was... over-zealous... last time we met." I'd been looking for Skeet and a friend's niece when we met before. And I was pretty sure his employer at the time, Mr Jacob Euonymus, had them both. It was a mess and I lost a good man getting them back.

Mentally shaking myself, I return to the present. "I'll get straight to the point, Mr Woffe, to save your time and mine." I lean forward, deliberately listening to their heartbeats and respiration. "I've got four dead bodies in the morgue and I'm thinking they tie into a missing

Giordano Bruno manuscript. Would you know anything about such an item?"

Both their heartbeats speed up as soon as I mention the bodies and again when I mention Bruno.

Woffe looks at me steadily, though. *Give him credit for that.* "Any particular manuscript? There are a few missing manuscripts attributed to Bruno."

I shake my head. "I've no idea, Mr Woffe. And all I've got to go on is four dead bodies – one of which I've just been informed, you found – with Latin quotations from Bruno carved into their skin." I watch them for a moment; the girl blanches, Woffe just looks at me. "Would you have any idea why that could be?"

Woffe shakes his head. "I've no idea, Commander. I didn't know the body I found on the bridge had any kind of... mutilation."

Heartbeats still elevated. I nod. "I see." I make a show of looking at my voda, even though I don't need it. "The quotes aren't from one particular document, so it's difficult to say which manuscript might be involved. Besides, if it's a missing book, it's hardly going to be quotable, is it?"

They both look at me, not giving anything more than increased pulses away. Central's been monitoring Mr Woffe for some time, as he's been involved in a few cases that haven't been entirely above board.

"I believe there's a fifth body to be found, but we've yet to discover it."

At this announcement, they look at each other and the woman shakes her head. He raises an eyebrow. "Can you give us a minute, Shirl?"

She doesn't want to, but she nods and slips past me, out into the shop.

I don't say anything, letting him take his time.

Finally, he looks me in the eye and seems to come to some decision. "I... you may be right about the other body."

I lean forward, pressing any advantage I have. "Yes? What exactly do you know, Mr Woffe?"

He stares at me a moment longer. "Let's just say I may know someone who was... involved in what happened."

"Go on."

Reluctant now, he hesitates. "Well, I don't know what happened, but I know someone involved." He picks up a cup of coffee and swallows.

I didn't get offered a drink. Huh. "Do you know about a Bruno manuscript?" I press him.

"I… have been informed about a particular… 'item' that is attributed to Bruno, yes," he answers. "I have no way of verifying it at this point, as I don't know its exact whereabouts."

I nod. "But you know approximately where it is, then?"

"I… may." He leans forward as well. "Look Commander, what are you after here?"

I shrug. "I don't actually give a shit about the manuscript, Mr Woffe – I'm trying to solve four, perhaps five, murders. Any ties to the manuscript are coincidental. If you know anything about their murders, I need to know what it is."

He sighs and leans back in his chair. "You won't believe me, Commander." He looks up at me again. "I'm not entirely sure I believe it."

"Try me."

His reluctance is tangible. "I believe that they were killed by a… a House."

Okay, my interest is definitely piqued. "A house?" There's a knock at the external door, followed by a murmured exchange. I turn my head and see a tall man standing inside the door talking to Shirl and Janey. Distracted, I turn back to Wolf. "What do you mean, 'a house' ?"

"There's a House in London that is very… protective of its contents. I was approached by someone who had been involved in an attempt to acquire the manuscript you're talking about."

I smile. "So you do know which manuscript we're talking about, then?" My HUD identifies the figure at the door as one Tobias Mayweather, petty crook, part-time lunatic and cult leader.

Woffe nods. "I do. I believe it's a manuscript attributed to Bruno called *De Temporum Signis*, or *On the Signs of the Times*." He takes another drink. "There are a number of 'missing' Bruno manuscripts, but that is the one I've been led to believe is in the House."

"And this House… killed my four bodies?"

Woffe nodded. "Yes, I think so."

"How do you know? I mean, it's not exactly something we can check, is it?" I ask, angry now.

"I know I'm going to regret this," Woffe mutters, pulling a tablet out of a bag. "Okay, let me pull up some video we shot." He fiddles around with it for a moment and points at a screen set in the wall of books. "Here are just some clips from video we shot a few days ago."

The first image appears to be a man staring out of a window, followed by three more images of men not doing anything. The last image is of a body being thrown from the top floor window of the House, which would be consistent with the injuries of the fourth body in Alicia's morgue.

I shake my head. My HUD has confirmed the bodies in the morgue are the men in the video images. And Eddie Kray's number five. So where's his body?

Woffe is looking at me expectantly. "Well? What do ya think? Is that any help to your investigation?"

I nod, but I'm not in the mood to share, just now. "Where's the House, Mr Woffe?"

"I can't tell you."

My turn to sigh. "You're interfering in an ongoing investigation, Mr Woffe. I would tread carefully."

He gets angry. "I tell you and any chance I have of recovering that manuscript goes out the window — what do you expect me to do?"

"I expect you to cooperate, Mr Woffe." I jab a finger at the screen. "That's a crime scene and I need access to it. At the very least I can lock you up for obstruction — and anyone else who knows what or where that House is."

Woffe closes up. I know the type and know I'll get nothing else from him. Damn.

"Wolf," Shirl says from the doorway. "You'd better tell him — I think we'll need him."

Don't you hate it when that happens?

Wolf looks at Shirl in the doorway and frowns. "We'll need him?" Shirl sighed and waved at Mayweather behind her. "He's got an idea about why he was kicked out of the House that night."

Commander Sen stiffened across from him.

Wolf could have sworn he was blind when they met before; it was almost disconcerting to see those pale grey eyes.

"Mayweather knows what happened at the House?" Sen demanded. He turned back to Wolf. "Why didn't you tell me you had a witness?"

It was Wolf's turn to sigh. This was turning into a right mess. "What's he want now?" He gestured at the hulking figure of Mayweather.

Shirl was leaning against the doorframe. "He thinks the reason the House kicked him out was it would only allow five people in at once."

She glanced over her shoulder at Mayweather. "And now he thinks we'll need five to go in again. The number has some kind of significance."

Wolf thought about it.

That was far more people than he wanted to risk. And he'd rather not risk any more of his team; he needed Graeme outside, monitoring things, and there was no way he'd get Michael involved...

Mayweather, as much as Commander Sen, was an unknown quantity. How would he function under pressure?

"I can furnish another body, if Mayweather joins us," Sen offered. Mayweather nodded, some kind of resolve in his eye.

Looking Sen up and down, Wolf snorted. "Not sure an old man like you can keep up with us," he replied.

"Try me." Sen stood up. "When were you planning on going in?"

Wolf glanced at Shirl and shrugged. "We were going in tonight."

Sen looked at them both and nodded. "Give me until tomorrow night and I'll make sure we have backup."

"No. No backup – we do this my way or not at all," Wolf said.

He could see Sen struggle for a moment with that one before acquiescing.

"Okay, but I need to get equipment together. What are you taking? Chameleon polymers? Armour?"

Wolf shrugged again. "You okay to wait until tomorrow night?" he asked Shirl. She nodded, face grim. "I'll give you a list," he said to Sen.

Sen stood up, eyeing Mayweather, probably considering arresting him as a witness. He looked back at Wolf. "I'm only going along with this as I need to see inside that House. As it is, I'll have to explain things to my superiors."

Grinning, Wolf couldn't help but stick the knife in. "Well, you could always arrest us, but you won't get anything."

Sen looked at him for a moment. "You'd be surprised what we can do these days, Mr Woffe."

"Call me 'Wolf' – everyone else does." He watched Sen put on his leather coat and head for the door. "No backup, Commander Sen," he called after him. "I mean it."

"Very well, Mr... Wolf. We'll play it your way." The bell on the door tinkled as the tall Contractor left the shop.

"Be at my studio tomorrow at six, Mayweather," Wolf said to the hovering giant before handing him a scrap of paper with the address.

"Thank you Mr Woffe," he rumbled.

Wolf waved it away. "Yeah, yeah. Get out of here." He felt out of sorts, as if Sen had blindsided him.

Uninvited visitors gone, Shirl slumped down in the chair opposite the desk, a cup of tea in her hands. She'd already slipped a new cup of coffee across the desk to Wolf.

"What the hell was that all about?" she asked.

"I've no idea," Wolf replied. "I just know we've now got Mayweather, the Commander and another unknown to worry about when we go into that House."

"We'll be lucky if they don't all get killed," Shirl observed.

Wolf snorted. "I wouldn't mind, but I bet there's a lot of paperwork if you get a Contractor killed."

Shirl nodded. "I'll bet. Wonder who else he'll bring?"

"We'll find out tomorrow, I guess." Wolf sipped his coffee. There was a dash of whisky in it, no bad thing. "Oh, better ring your dad and let him know we're not working tonight."

"Already done." Shirl drained her tea. "Come on, I'll run you home – we've got all day tomorrow now to finish sorting equipment."

Groaning, Wolf finished his coffee. "What are we going to put Mayweather in? I don't think we've got anything big enough."

Shirl shrugged. "Add it to the Commander's list. He can sort it out."

"Good idea." Wolf stood up and grabbed his jacket. "Come on, let's get out of here."

WE'RE ALL GOIN' DOWN THE PUB...

Porgy and Bess strained on their leads, having already worked out in their doggy brains where they were going. They liked the pub by the river; the landlord always made a fuss of them and made sure they got treats and bowls of water.

Alicia smiled, letting the dogs pull her along. The air was crisp and clear, no clouds, meaning it would be a cold night.

The pub was bright and warm, a buzz of conversation greeting them when she got the door open. "Hi Mike," she greeted the burly man behind the bar. "Red wine for me and a bowl of water for the monsters, please."

"Coming right up," he replied with a lopsided grin. "Good to see you, Alicia – how are you doing?"

"Oh, you know, overworked and underpaid." Her stock answer.

"Same here," he joked. "All the time I spend serving these reprobates when I could be on my yacht in the Bahamas!"

The door behind Alicia banged open and the dogs recognised Kate before Alicia even turned around.

"Hi puppies!" Kate said loudly, getting down on their level and hugging them, receiving big sloppy kisses from both dogs. "Hey Al," she added, standing up and wiping dog slobber from her face.

"Red wine?" Alicia asked.

"Sure."

"Make it a bottle of the Tempranillo, Mike," Alicia said to the barman.

"On its way."

They squeezed through the chairs and tables to a corner spot near the open fire. The dogs settled under the table until Mike came over with a bottle, two glasses and a big metal bowl of water.

"Here you go," he said.

"Cheers Mike," Kate replied.

"Yes, thanks Mike," Alicia put in. "And whatever you're drinking as well."

"Thanks, Ma'am," he drawled. "Don't mind if I do."

When he'd gone, they poured the wine and clinked glasses. "Cheers," Alicia said.

"Yes, cheers." Kate sipped the hearty red and looked across the table at Alicia. "So, how's things?"

Alicia blushed, trying to cover her embarrassment by sipping her own wine. She succeeded in drinking too quickly and coughed, going even redder.

"That tells me something's up," Kate said with a smile.

Somewhat recovered, Alicia nodded. "I've... met someone."

Kate raised an eyebrow. "A male someone, I presume?"

Alicia couldn't meet her eyes for a second. "Yes." She looked up and carried on quickly. "His name's Hugh and he's a fire scene investigator."

It seemed unlikely that Kate's perfectly plucked eyebrows would go any higher in her surprise. "A fireman! Well, that's a turn up for the books after that stuffy old academic."

Smiling, Alicia took another drink of her wine. She knew Kate had loved Stephen and didn't take offence at her description of him. "I– I think Stephen would have liked him."

Kate nodded. "As long as *you* do, that's the main thing." She leaned forward, conspiratorially. "So, spill – where'd you meet him? When are you seeing him again? What are you doing next?"

Alicia laughed. "I've no idea – he came over for dinner last night and we haven't made any plans."

"Dinner! You are a fast worker!"

Slapping Kate on the shoulder, Alicia laughed again. "Nothing happened!"

Kate leaned around the table and hugged her with one arm. "I know, I'm just joking!"

Alicia sobered slightly. "I'm not entirely sure I want it to..."

"It'll happen when you want it to," Kate replied, picking up her wine glass again. "I'm glad you've found someone, Al. It's good to see you smiling like this."

Blushing again, Alicia took another drink. *Time to change the subject.* "How's Morag?"

"She's fine – and a bit miffed she's got to work while we're in the pub!" Kate smiled.

"Well, she's Scottish – she likes a drink!" Alicia laughed.

"True, very true," Kate concurred. "She sends her love, anyway."

The conversation wended its way through several different topics, the level of the wine in the bottle dropping in parallel. Food was ordered and the two dogs under the table managed to snaffle a few treats from the plates above their heads.

Wine gone and feeling sated, they decided it was time to go home.

Outside the pub, dogs winding around their knees, Alicia hugged her friend. "Thanks Kate, I needed that."

"My pleasure – you know you only have to ring me any time," Kate replied.

"Thanks." Alicia hugged her again. "I'll let you know what happens."

"Good." Kate stepped back and leaned down to hug the dogs. "You look after your Mum, you two." Two doggie grins greeted her and Porgy gave a low woof. "We'll want to meet this Hugh, too."

Alicia laughed again. "As soon as I know something, you'll know. See you soon."

"You can count on it."

Opening the door and turning off the security system, Alicia let the dogs enter the house before her. "Go on! Bedtime." The two looked at her before trundling down the hall and settling in their baskets in the kitchen.

Alicia smiled and reset the system before going up to bed.

As she closed her eyes, a warmth that had nothing to do with the wine she'd drunk suffused her.

Sleep well Alicia.

ON AGAIN, OFF AGAIN — MAKE UP YOUR MIND!

My skullphone rings as I head for home. "Sen."

"Commander… Jaared, help me."

"Who is this?"

There's a pause, sounds of swallowing. Then, "It's Portia Tyler, Jaared."

Great. Just what I need right now. "What do you want from me, Lady Tyler?" *Keep it professional.*

Another swallow. "Call me Portia – I want you to find who killed John."

You mean you had nothing to do with it? "I'm sorry, I've been removed from your stepson's case, Lady Tyler – you'll have to take it up with the Inspector General."

Now there are sounds that could be crying. *She knows all the tricks.* "I– I know you think I had something to do with John's death, Jaared… but I didn't… you have to believe me." Pleading now.

I don't believe a thing you say. "As I've said, Lady Tyler, I have no jurisdiction in the case any more."

And that's when the flag appears in my HUD. The Tyler case has been reopened with me as lead Contractor, flagged as *immediate priority*. Sigh.

"I think you'll find that has changed, Jaared." She's practically purring now.

"Yes, Lady Tyler, I now have lead authority in John's case." I check the time. "Are you available to answer some questions now, Lady Tyler?"

"Certainly, Jaared, I was hoping you could come straight over." Central flags me an address in Mayfair while she stumbles over the same information. *Drunk subjects are a pain, even if they're sometimes useful.*

"Very well, Lady Tyler, I will be over shortly." Rather than requisition a car, I flag a cab.

On the way to the Tylers' apartment, I call Skeet. "Hiya."

"Hey big boy, you gonna be home soon?"

I grimace. "If only. I'm off to the Tylers' place; I've just been reassigned to their son's case."

"Awww. I had plans…"

"I figured. Listen, you got anything on tomorrow night?"

"I'm supposed to be meeting Dekker – he's got something lined up for me. Why? What did you have in mind?" She chuckles. "I can postpone, particularly if it involves you, me and that chocolate in the fridge."

I'm smiling now. "Well, it involves you and me, but the chocolate will have to wait."

"Awww… Mr No-Fun." She sighs, and then gets back to business. "What's up, then?"

I fill her in on the House and its role in the murders. "I'm not sure I want you going in, but I want you with their guy, monitoring things from outside."

"You'll need a fifth if Mayweather's right about numbers."

I nod. "I know, but I think this might be more up Madeline's alley – supernatural effects and all that."

"Do you have to get that bitch involved?" *Mee–ow.*

"And she says such nice things about you," I reply.

"I don't think you can trust her, Jaared."

"She's saved my life, Skeet. I'd have never made it back from France without her." I'd told her about Stel and the trip to the south of France. It hadn't exactly elicited the sympathy factor I'd been looking for.

Silence. Then a sigh. "Okay, if you think *she'll* watch your back more closely than I will…"

"That's not it at all, but she's hard to kill."

"So am I, big boy, so am I."

"I know, but I don't want to risk you – I doubt I'd be able to do my job if you were in there with me." Truth. Well, mostly.

More silence. "Okay, call the bitch."

"I'll let you know when I'm on my way home."

"I'll get my gear together. See you later."

Ouch. "Okay, bye."

Click.

I ring the number Madeline gave me but there's no answer. There's not even a personal message when it goes to voicemail. I leave a message anyway, asking her to call me.

As I hang up, Central informs me that Timson's been revived and is asking for me. Huh.

The cab stops outside an older, but still impressive, apartment building in the heart of Mayfair. I pay the cab and step onto the curb.

I pass a big guy with shoe-polish black hair and a thousand yard stare on the steps of the building.

Edward Alamo, fixer and general dogsbody for the Tylers. Or at least he is when he's not in prison.

I'm not supposed to know him, so I ignore him.

When I get into the lobby, there's even a human on the reception desk and a security guard in the corner next to the door. I don't imagine for a moment they aren't backed up by the latest security systems, but it shows a particular level of wealth being willing to keep people hanging around the lobby of your apartment building.

The receptionist looks up, his eyes sizing me up even as I detect the flicker of a HUD in his right eye. Probably knows my underwear size by the time he says, "Yes? How may I help you?"

"I'm here to see Mrs Tyler."

"Of course, Commander Sen. Take the lift to the top floor and turn left when you leave it."

"Thanks." I still find it disconcerting when they do that.

Following his instructions, I find myself outside an understated door that says a lot more about the expense and opulence of the place than gold-plated taps ever did.

It opens as I approach, another human servant framed in the doorway. *Possibly Philippino this time.*

"Come in, Commander. Lady Tyler is expecting you in the salon." He takes my coat and gestures for me to precede him down the hall.

I enter the only door that's open and find myself in a large room with floor to ceiling windows looking over Green Park. 'Expecting' me evidently doesn't mean she's waiting for me, as the room is empty. I wander over to the windows and inspect the view.

"Would you like a drink, Commander?" the butler, or whatever he is, asks me.

"I'll have a double whisky, single malt, no ice." *What the hell, I'm on overtime now anyway.*

"Very good."

The view is amazing; the lights of the buildings surround the dark area that is the park defining it. It's bigger than I remember.

"It's a great view, isn't it?"

I turn and it's Lady Tyler herself. "Yes, it is. You have a lovely home."

She waves my compliment away with the hand not holding my whisky. "Here you go, Jaared, this whisky comes from James's private reserve. There's water on the sideboard if you find the cask strength overpowering."

I take the drink and she settles herself on a sofa looking towards the window. The butler places a long cocktail on the side table near her and then leaves the room.

I sip the whisky and examine her for a moment. She's wearing something floaty and diaphanous – a peignoir? I can't say I'm very good at identifying women's lingerie.

The whisky is superb and does need a little water. I walk over and add a drop or two, not wanting to dilute it too much. I'm also letting the silence build as she seems happy to let it grow between us.

When I turn back to her, she's watching me intently. Her heartbeat is normal, but her respiration is up slightly.

I decide on a diplomatic tack first. Maybe it will wrong-foot her. "I'm sorry about our… disagreement the other evening."

She waves it away in the manner of a grand patron ignoring a small slight by an underling. "Think nothing of it, Jaared." She smiles coyly. "Perhaps it was the drink."

I let that go. I knew exactly what I was doing. "Why would your stepson's intention to marry 'that trollop' be any concern of yours, Lady Tyler?"

"Call me Portia," she instructs. She looks away for the first time. *Deception? Getting her story straight?*

Heart rate still in same general area, although slightly dilated pupils could show evidence of tranquillisers. "If John had married her it could have affected James's bid for the throne."

Ah, the pretender's case for the succession. "By showing he was human or by associating your family name with the wrong sort of people?"

"Exactly Jaared, I knew you'd understand." She beams at me. She didn't answer the question. "We are expected to maintain a certain… level… in our society, Jaared. And that would have compromised our position."

"So why not kill the girl?"

"Jaared! How can you imagine I'd kill anyone?" *Pretending to be scandalised now.*

I smile. "I don't know, Lady Tyler, but I have several cases associated with you where Contractors were involved in, shall we say 'discrediting', people you didn't like."

Her gaze is steely now and the heart rate has increased slightly. "That was a long time ago, Commander." More formal now.

I shake my head. "The most recent case associated with you was only about three months ago, Lady Tyler. A Peer of the Realm was dangled off his balcony overlooking Hyde Park during rush hour."

I pause for effect. And it had been Eddie Alamo, again. "Witnesses claim he was instructed to vote for a bill your husband was backing or he might find himself taking unscheduled flying lessons."

Lady Tyler has the decency to blush. "I'm sure I don't know what you're talking about, Commander."

"At least that incident didn't involve a Contractor, I'm happy to say. I'd hate to think you were using the Company as some kind of private security firm, Lady Tyler." I sip the whisky.

She stares at me for a moment before picking up her glass and sipping the contents. "What is your point, Commander?"

I shrug. "I was merely pointing out you are not above suspicion in your stepson's death, Lady Tyler."

Icy now, the temperature having dropped by ten degrees at least. "Do you have any questions, Commander, or are you wasting my time?"

"Did you have John killed, Lady Tyler?"

Her respiration and heartbeat are indicating some attempt on her part to subvert my investigation.

"Well, Lady Tyler?"

"No. I had nothing to do with John's death." Cold, emotionless, stated as flatly as she could manage.

I nod and finish my whisky. "Very well, that's all I had to ask you this evening, Lady Tyler."

I place my glass on the sideboard. "I'll see myself out."

I get to the salon's door before she speaks.

"I don't know why you don't believe me, Jaared... I really didn't have anything to do with John's death." Her voice is much quieter now.

I turn back. She's staring out the window at the view. Or maybe looking at her reflection in the glass. I can't tell.

I sigh. "I'm fairly sure you are telling the truth, Lady Tyler."

Her eyes meet mine in the reflections on the glass. "But you are hiding something that has bearing on my investigation. That's definite."

She stares at me a moment longer before looking away.

The butler is standing behind me and wordlessly guides me back to the door.

As I take the lift down, I wonder just what I've achieved, if anything.

THE WAITING IS ALWAYS THE WORST

It was bad enough Sen had found out about the job, but now he intended to come along!

Gritting his teeth and turning away from his workroom window, Wolf looked at their plans for the House again. They had no idea what had been modified since the original builder's plans had been put together. Besides which, all these houses were slightly different; some were wider, some narrower.

And by all accounts Webster had been something of an eccentric. Okay, barking mad.

"Wolf?" Graeme stood in the doorway. "I had an idea."

Wolf picked up his beer and swivelled in his chair. "Uh-oh. What kind of idea?"

Graeme brought his tea in and sank down in the other chair. He studied the milky liquid for a moment before answering. "Well, I've been thinking about Deng."

It took Wolf a moment to place the name. "The neighbour?"

Nodding, Graeme took a sip of his tea. "Yeah." He was silent again and Wolf just waited, knowing better than to try to draw him out. "I think I'll go see him."

Wolf took a drink of his beer. "Okay."

Looking uncomfortable now, Graeme continued in a rush. "You know I don't believe none of that magic crap, don't you? Well, that House worries me and I think we can use all the help we can get on this one. Whaddya say?"

"Your call, old man – and I know what you mean about that House." He looked Graeme in the eye. "It worries me a lot."

Graeme looked back down at his tea. "So, I... I'll go see Deng in the morning and see if he can help."

Wolf nodded. "Fine."

"She's all I got, Wolf," the old man whispered.

"I know." Wolf got up and went over to Graeme and did something he rarely did; he put his arms around the bony shoulders. "But you and I both know we can't change her mind once she's made it up."

Graeme laughed, a soundless 'huff'. "Got that right; takes after her mother, there."

Wolf squeezed the old man once and let go. "And her father," he corrected. "I promise I'll do everything I can to keep her safe. You can count on me."

Squeezing his arm with one hand, Graeme stood up and made for the door.

I just hope I can keep us all safe, Wolf thought.

I NEVER LIKE THE SMELL OF HOSPITALS

Outside the Tylers' palatial apartment, I grab another cab and go to see Timson. Talk about a contrast.

The duty nurse directs me to the Extreme Care ward where cases like Timson's go. Resuscitation is more commonplace than it used to be, but still traumatic as far as its impact on the body.

And, while the trauma to the body is easily repaired, the damage to the brain from lack of oxygen is harder to fix; contrary to popular belief, we Contractors don't have a backup of our brains on Central somewhere – that would have to be some facility. Our egos alone would take up a lot of room.

I'm not expecting a lot of coherence from Timson.

He's still in the repair bath when I reach his cubby. His face is the only part exposed above the milky fluid, which contains millions of microscopic, well, robots, I guess, specially designed to repair the body and assist healing.

Timson looks mostly normal, aside from being submerged in the bath, and his eyes are closed.

His nurse looks at me as I approach, that officious frown on his face (you know the one; they've had it from time immemorial). "Yes, can I help you?" His nametag says 'Brendon'.

"I'm Commander Sen, Brendon. I understand Timson's been asking for me." My identification wreaks a marvellous change.

"Ah, yes, Commander. Let me see if he'll wake up." He turns to the panel beside the bed and looks at the incomprehensible numbers for a moment. "This should help." Brendon turns back to me and smiles. "He's been quite insistent when we've had him awake. Normally sets off the stress alarms."

Huh. "He's a good Contractor – he'll go far…" I had no idea he was so driven and Brendon seems to sense this.

"Just a second, here you go." He steps away from the bed. "I doubt he'll be lucid for long – he's still half-frozen from the Resus Unit."

"Thanks Brendon." I move closer to Timson. "Timson, Commander Sen here."

His eyes haven't opened, but he suddenly sighs. "Got to…"

"Got to what, Timson?"

Nothing. Then, "...tell the Commander it was Edalamo..." He fades again.

What? "Sorry Timson, please repeat."

Another sigh. "Tyler... killed... Edalamo..."

Edalamo? Edward Alamo?

Central's responses on 'Edalamo' turn up several possibilities: a long dead actor, a Tex-Mex place over on High Street Kensington, and some kind of Aggravating Yoga done in a cold room. I think I know which one I'd choose.

The one that seems most likely is the Edward Alamo — just released from Wormwood Scrubs. Reading his file, I'm surprised he wasn't terminated a long time ago. He's been suspected of just about everything from arson to GBH to extortion. A lovely guy.

I also just passed him coming out of the Tylers' building.

I examine his file on Central and try to work out how he's survived termination so long. *Ah, there it is.* He's been in suspended animation for five of the last ten years as part of his sentence. An odd twist, as I don't know any Contractors who would authorise this. A quick check of the file lists a fictional Contractor.

"Who the hell is that?" I ask Central and something very strange happens: Central glitches. I've been tied into it for at least fifteen of the last twenty years and I've never seen it do this.

All contact with Central stops for only the briefest of moments, hardly something to write home about, right? The issue is more to do with the fact Central never glitches like this.

When Central returns to normal after a few heartbeats, I flag it to the IG with a recommendation for a Priority One deepscan of the Central core.

The IG calls me immediately. "What the hell are you playing at, Commander? Do you know how much a diagnostic like this will cost us?" Formal title and mention of budgets in the first breath — not a good thing.

"There appear to be... anomalous entries in the database attached to Central, which could compromise our ability to do our jobs, sir." I flash him over a personal data sample of the event.

"So Central glitched for a nanosecond — that's hardly the end of the world," he grumbles.

I nod. "Of course, sir. Except it's never done that before."

A moment of silence. "Are you sure?"

I nod again, and then remember he can't see me. "I've only been plugged into Central for fifteen years, sir, but I don't recall it ever happening before." I think back. "Not even in the beginning."

Another lull. "Why now?" he demands.

"I don't know, sir. But I just requested some information on a file that appears to be damaged. I had heard rumours of someone accessing the system by a back door, but I didn't have enough to authorise an investigation. Until now."

A priority flag flashes across my vision. "I've authorised the investigation, Commander – under your supervision and on a need-to-know basis." He pauses.

Great, more work. "Right, sir," I reply.

"I don't think I need to impress upon you the delicacy of the situation here, Jaared, do I?" I can hear him lighting one of his cigars. "If this got out, our judgement for the last decade could be questioned."

"Yes, sir, I understand, sir."

"Well, get on with it, Commander. And I expect regular progress reports on this."

"Absolutely, sir." He closes the connection and I'm listening to the space inside my head for a moment before my phone shuts down.

Amazingly, after what I've just discovered – and a sudden lack of trust of Central – it's a matter of moments for Central to locate Alamo and arrange for his pickup and detention.

Good. Something to do first thing in the morning. A car has turned up while I was visiting Timson, so I slump into the seat. "Home, James."

"It's Carson, sir."

That's the problem with recruits these days, no sense of humour.

YOU ALWAYS DO YOUR BEST TO KEEP THE OLD FOLKS OUT OF TROUBLE

Nicholas hesitated outside the door. He'd never been here before. Well, not exactly like this. He'd watched Jaared through the windows once or twice, after Madeline had shown him where his father lived – but never with the intention of going in.

He nearly turned away before remembering what was at stake. Oddly, he couldn't sense the man inside the house. Perhaps because he was his father. He hadn't tried before.

Raising his hand, he knocked on the door.

There were steps, and a shadow crossed the peephole. The door opened. A tall blonde woman stood in the doorway and, for a moment, he thought it was Madeline. The hair was too short and he realised she was taller, as well. The illusion passed.

"Yes?" she asked.

Nick stared at her for a moment. "Is– is Sen here?"

"No, he's not." She glanced over his shoulder. "He should be here any minute."

He turned to go.

"Wait. Who are you?"

"I am his son, Nicholas."

The woman doesn't react to that. She obviously knows about him. "Do you want to wait for him?"

He waved one hand. "It doesn't matter."

"You can still wait."

"I will find him later."

At that moment, they both heard footsteps coming down the mews. Jaared appeared in the light spilling from the doorway. Nicholas had a sudden sense of a power – it was obviously his father.

"Here he is now," the woman observed.

"Hello Nicholas," Jaared said. "Did you want to see me?"

Nicholas looked at him for a moment. "Hello Father." He wondered how best to say what needed to be said.

Jaared stepped towards him. "Do you want to come in?"

"No." He looked at his father. "Madeline is missing."

"What do you mean, *missing*?" Jaared did look concerned.

"Madeline was performing an errand for the Elders and has not been heard from since." *Now the difficult part.* "I... I need your help."

Jaared looked at him blankly. "I don't know what I can do – surely your 'Elders' are looking for her."

Nicholas's lips curled up in disgust. "They are doing nothing," he spat. "She is old enough to look after herself, in their opinion."

"Do you know where she's gone?"

"No, but I know someone who does," Nicholas answered.

Jaared was silent.

Nicholas's frustration burst out. "I'm worried about her, Father."

At this, Jaared at least had the decency to look surprised.

WHO HAS TIME FOR CHILDREN WHEN YOU'RE MY AGE?

I'm surprised to see Nicholas, to say the least. His news that Madeline may be in trouble is even more surprising.

"I don't know how I can help you, Nicholas."

The boy, for that is what he is, stands between me and Skeet. I can't see the expression on his face, the light from the doorway casting strong shadows. Even with my other senses, I don't really 'see' him.

"How long has she been missing?" I will help the boy, but I can't work without data.

"She will have been gone a week, tomorrow."

Not that long, in my experience, but I had never seen her every day. The fact that I had been thinking about Madeline earlier – to the extent of even ringing her number – plays on my mind. *Maybe Nicholas can...* "Nicholas, come in for a moment. I need your help, too."

The boy laughs under his breath. "What? I help you, and you help me find Madeline?"

"If you like, but that wasn't my intention." I step towards him. "I will do what I can to assist your search for her, but I have a more immediate need of your help."

He turns towards the door and Skeet steps back into the hall. She looks at me and I shake my head. She disappears into the kitchen.

Nicholas enters and turns the other way into the living room. He's standing by the fire after I close the door and follow him.

"What do you want of me?" he asks.

I wonder for a moment if I'm doing the right thing. *Oh well, not a lot of choice.* "I need you to accompany me tomorrow night into a... House... that we believe has some kind of supernatural influence."

The boy looks at me again. "Why do you need me?"

I sit down in a chair and look up at him. *He's very tall.* "Your speed and strength may be of use to our party."

He relents and sits in the chair opposite. "I am not indestructible you know."

"No, I know, but you are stronger, faster and younger than me. That is a benefit."

He stares at me again. *That intense gaze isn't Madeline's. Is it mine?*

Dean Fetzer

"And you will help me look for her after?" he asks. I can hear the impatience in his voice – Madeline must really be missing.

"Of course. It's the least I can do."

More silent scrutiny. Finally, "Very well, I will see you tomorrow night."

"We're meeting at—" I start.

"I will find you." And he's gone.

I sit there in silence for a moment when he's gone. "Skeet?"

Skeet enters, hands me a glass – whisky – and sits down on the arm of the chair. "What'd the kid want?"

I look up at her. "He's more than a child – don't ever underestimate him." I sigh. "He thinks Madeline, his mother, is missing."

Skeet looks at me more closely. "And is she?"

I rub my eyes, but the headache doesn't cease. "I don't know. Probably. Maybe. I've said I'd help him, so I will." I look at her and shrug. "He's going to help us go into the House tomorrow night."

"Uh, you're going into that House with a teenage vampire? Do you know how crazy that sounds?"

"Yes, but having someone like him might give us an edge." I sip my whisky. "He's got talents and abilities I can only dream of."

"I thought... I was going to go with you..." There's hurt in her eyes.

I pull her down into my lap. "Hey, the last thing I want to do is exclude you – but if that House is as dangerous as I think it is, I don't need the distraction." We haven't worked together since we first got together, so I don't know what it'd be like. I think Skeet sees that. Doesn't help, though.

Skeet looks at me for a moment before sipping my whisky. She makes a face. "I can take care of myself, you know. And Nicholas's your son."

I nod. "I know, but he... doesn't worry me, not like you do. Fuck, I'm making a real hash of this." I take my whisky back.

Suddenly she wraps both arms around me and squeezes. Skeet's not dainty; she manages to squeeze the breath out of me.

"What was that for?" I ask when I get it back.

Skeet smiles. "You know."

I shake my head. "No, I don't."

She sighs and puts my empty glass on the side table. "Yes you do." More silence. "Okay, I'll help monitor the situation from the outside

236

tomorrow." Skeet stands up. "Now come to bed. I don't want you down here brooding…"

I smile and stand up. "By your command."

WOLVES MATE FOR LIFE, DON'T THEY?

Wolf swore and threw the faulty clip from one of his equipment pods onto the workbench. The catch wouldn't hold for some reason. He was having trouble concentrating and the longer they waited, the worse it got.

He'd been awake hours before the alarm and had lain there, listening to Michael's breathing on the other side of the bed. Wolf's temples throbbed with a headache, as much sleep-related as anything else.

The buzzer on the door went. *Who could that be?* He checked the wall clock. *No, Shirl wasn't coming around until later.*

He flicked the button on the screen and saw Michael hovering on the pavement, looking around at the neighbourhood. *Odd, he didn't normally come to the workshop.*

Wolf buzzed him in. "Hey."

Michael smiled at him. "Hey yourself, big boy."

Smiling back, Wolf was glad of the distraction. "What brings you to the salubrious surroundings of my workshop?"

Holding up a bag, Michael stepped towards the workbench. "Just thought I'd bring you a coffee and almond croissant – and a distraction."

Wolf took the bag. "Thanks. Why the distraction?"

"I can feel you fretting all the way from the flat," Michael said. "You never like the waiting and I thought the least I could do was help take your mind off it."

Cracking the coffee open, Wolf nodded. "Well, you're right about the waiting. Never did like it." He sipped the bitter brew. Must be from the coffee place on the corner.

Michael came up behind him and put his arms around him. "You're going to be safe tonight, aren't you Wolf?"

Wolf made light of the question. "Always am." *And I'll do my best to keep everyone safe.*

Seeming to sense the subtext in Wolf's answer, Michael whispered, "You will – you always do."

That made Wolf suddenly angry. No he didn't keep them safe. Shirl had been kidnapped working on one of Wolf's 'jobs'. Graeme had ended up in hospital, too. He pulled away from Michael, turning the anger away from his lover. "I almost killed them both — I don't want that to happen again."

Michael turned him around. "No, you didn't. Blame yourself all you like, but it wasn't your decisions — or your actions — in either case." He looked angry now. "Shit happens and you get up and go on. If you don't, you're dead."

Wolf shook his head. "I can't ignore what happened. I won't let it happen again."

"I'm not saying you should, but channel that anger into doing what you guys always do — your best."

"My best? Is that it?" Wolf sounded bitter to himself.

"You know it is, honey." Michael lifted his chin. "You and Shirl are highly trained, experienced in doing what you do and yes, you've had setbacks. Doesn't mean you don't know what you're doing."

Wolf nodded, acknowledging the truth in Michael's words. "What if it happens again?"

Michael shook his head. "You can't play the 'what if' game — I fall over onstage if I start second-guessing myself. Be confident." He took Wolf's hand. "Now, come on, stop brooding here in your lair and come back to the flat and watch some crap daytime programmes with me."

Smiling in spite of himself, Wolf let himself be dragged towards the door.

TIDE AND TIME — AND BODIES — WAIT FOR NO MAN

A licia sighed and rubbed her eyes. The budget reports seemed to be getting longer. Hardly surprising if her department was growing by two-thirds. "Why did I agree to this?" she muttered.

Her voda rang. "Sampson."

"Hi Alicia, it's Jaared."

"Morning, Commander — what can I do for you?" *All business.*

"That's a bit formal," Jaared said. When she didn't respond, he continued. "I was wondering if you'd got the tox report on John Tyler?"

"I'll check." She flicked through a couple of screens and found the report. *What the hell?* "Yes, the results are back, but you already know that."

Jaared had the decency to be embarrassed. "Sorry, I guess I didn't phrase that correctly. Can you tell me more about the results on…" She could almost hear him mentally flipping through the pages of the report. "Line fifty-four. What's that indicate?"

Alicia found the line he was on about and read it. "Elevated levels of potassium and sodium hydroxide found in the victim's bloodstream. Well, that indicates something out of the normal in this case. Why? What are you thinking?" Her curiosity was piqued in spite of herself.

"I'm not sure, but I think he was drugged before the heroin made it into his body," Jaared replied. "Why else would a normal, straight, white male be found in a squat, dead of an overdose?"

"Why indeed? Particularly one with a Peer for a father and just about anything he wanted on a silver platter."

Jaared was silent. "I just can't find the motive on this one, Al — generally liked, except by his stepmother. But I don't get the feeling she'd kill him."

Alicia sighed. "I don't know, Jaared. That's your department." She looked at the screen again. "Wait a second. There is an odd result on line sixty-three — elevated levels of serotonin — that shouldn't be there…"

"What do you mean?"

"I mean, it's not something occurring that high naturally — I'd say it bears out your theory that something was done to him before he was injected with the heroin."

"Okay, thanks Al." He was silent again. "At least I know he was killed now."

"Glad I could be of help," Alicia replied.

"Are you all right, Al?"

It was Alicia's turn for silence. She wasn't sure why, but she felt a bit cranky. She sighed. "Sorry Jaared, just feeling a bit off today."

"Anything I can do?"

Alicia shook her head. "No, I don't think so." *I've met someone, Jaared.* But no, he wasn't interested in her life anymore.

"It wouldn't have anything to do with a handsome fire investigator, would it?" She could hear the smile in his voice and couldn't help smiling back.

"You bastard! Have you been following me?"

Jaared chuckled. "No, I just saw the way he was looking at you the other night – *and* the way you were looking at him."

"Thanks Jaared." She wasn't sure what she was thanking him for, but she suddenly felt happier.

"My pleasure." He didn't say anything for a moment. "You deserve to be happy, Al."

Alicia felt her eyes well up and couldn't say anything for a moment. "Thanks," she whispered.

"I'll talk to you soon – maybe we can meet up for dinner when I get this case sorted out."

"That'd be good."

"Okay, got to go – I'll talk to you soon."

"Bye."

Coffee isn't a drug, it's a necessity

S o there's these two guys walking their dogs, a black Labrador and a Chihuahua. Passing a bar, the guy with the Labrador says, "Let's get a beer."

The other: "We can't take our dogs in there."

The first: "Watch." In he goes and orders a beer.

"Sorry, you can't bring your dog in here."

"He's my seeing eye dog."

"Oh. Sorry. Here's your beer."

The other guy follows. He orders a beer. Same response: No dogs allowed.

"He's my seeing eye dog."

"Yeah, right. A Chihuahua? Give me a break."

"They gave me a CHIHUAHUA?!"

I used to feel like I'd been given the Chihuahua most days. Now, I have to confess to being a bit confused.

I've spent a very long time not being able to see the nose on my face, much less anything else and I adapted pretty well, over the years. My teacher, a tiny man living in a swamp in Cambodia, spent six years correcting my blunders until I could walk across the world without tripping or bumping into things. As an added bonus, I learned to defend myself.

Then my eyes came back and I've been drunk on sight ever since. And much as I hate to admit it, a lot of my best successes come from the times I use my other senses, rather than my eyes. Finding a balance is beginning to wear me down.

I hang up the phone with Alicia. I'm in two minds about how I feel. On the one hand, I'm glad she's moved on. Stephen was a good man, but the last thing he'd want her to do was close down and be a widow for however long she lived.

On the other, I can't help feeling nostalgic for the relationship we once had. Nostalgia's an inevitable hazard when you're my age, although I know not everything about the past was wonderful.

The kicker (and probably salient point) is Alicia dumped *me*; I always knew she was intelligent. I just hope Skeet's as smart.

I shake my head at these maudlin ramblings and go in to see Alamo before my crisis team meeting.

Taller than I had expected, he's got very black hair, which is cut reasonably short, and a widow's peak. I'm more than a little reminded of Bela Lugosi, the best on-screen vampire, although his face is gaunter, his cheeks almost sunken.

"Whaddya want?" he demands when I enter the interrogation room. He's already restrained in the Chair, which has a few 'accessories' for easier interrogation of subjects.

I sit down, ignoring him for the moment. It's obvious I'm not going to get a lot out of him without some help. "Ten ccs of fast-pentha," I murmur into the bead mic I put on as I enter the room. The Chair administers the drug and he stiffens.

"Bastard — you won't... get... anything... that... way..." he tries to say through a suddenly clenched jaw, his dark eyes hard, the muscle contraction an initial side effect of the fast-pentha.

I shrug, slumping into a chair. "I don't care if you say anything, Alamo — I'm enjoying the show already."

For the first time, I see fear in his eyes. "What do you want?"

I sip my coffee, ignoring him.

"C'mon man, I can't feel my toes — whaddya want?" He sounds desperate now.

I look up at him and he's straining to get out of the restraints. Strange, the fast-pentha shouldn't allow him that much movement. "Shock burst, ten seconds," I order.

His body spasms violently and the leather straps creak. When the electricity stops flowing, he sags against the restraints for a moment before renewing his fight against the straps.

"Ten ccs phenobarbital." This kind of interrogation is as much about knowing how the different chemicals tend to react in conjunction as it is about getting the subject to talk. Alamo's still fighting me, somehow, so I need to break down his resistance.

His body slumps as the second drug enters his system. A smile crawls onto his thin face. "Really? A sedative?"

I ignore him. "Who hired you to kill John Tyler?"

The smile remains. No answer.

"Another five ccs of fast-pentha." I sip my coffee and pretend to ignore him again. Interesting that his vitals aren't registering within the normal parameters. Something's off here. I get the Chair to do a scan on him and discover why.

There's a natural drug supply in the human body called the hippocampus, at the base of the brain. This is where things like adrenalin and endorphins get manufactured and then shoved into the bloodstream at need. Several decades ago, advances were made to augment this useful part of human evolution and put it more under our control. I say 'our', but it's not really available to most people – the surgery's hardly cheap. I have the ability to 'gland' different substances when needed, a very helpful addition.

And it's obvious on looking at his scan, that Alamo has one too, but one allowing him to circumvent fast-pentha and ameliorate the effects of the phenobarbital.

I go to the equipment locker on the wall. We humans have spent a very long time torturing one another and I have an encyclopaedia of techniques at my disposal which comes in useful. I select a shock probe and slip it into my pocket without him seeing. Don't want him preparing for what's coming.

"I know you want something, man – just tell me what it is," he wheedles, still straining at the restraints.

I move around behind him and he tries to turn his head, but can't because of the head clamp. I slip the probe into the slot already prepared for it and press it up against the back of his neck. He must sense it somehow, because he stiffens as 50,000 volts shoot into the base of his skull. *Shame; he'll have very sore muscles in the morning.*

That should incapacitate his augmented hippo for the moment. "Fifty ccs fast-pentha." It shouldn't be enough to kill him, but I want it overriding anything else in his veins.

He slumps in the chair, resistance gone for the time being.

I turn the Chair and stand directly in front of him, my face mere inches away from his. "Who paid you to kill Tyler?"

"Uh... the Council... Tyler..." he mumbles.

"What 'council'? C'mon Alamo, who's *the council?*"

"The... the Council... of... the... Seven..."

I've never heard of a 'Council of the Seven'. "Who hired you? Personally? Who was your contact?"

"No... one..." *I can't believe it, he's fighting it again.*

"Twenty ccs of fast-pentha." He's going back to being flash frozen again in a minute, so he's not going to die on me. "Who was your contact?"

His eyes are totally unfocused and there's saliva dripping down his chin. "Tyler…"

"Yes. Who paid you to kill John Tyler?"

A look of frustration passes over his face and he frowns. "No, no, no…" he mumbles. "James… Tyler…"

James Tyler — what the hell? And then it all clicks into place.

The blaring of the crash alarm brings me back into the room. "Crash cart in Interrogation Room 4, stat," I say aloud. The combo of drugs has temporarily caused his body to shut down. But we can fix that. "You're not getting away that easily," I promise him.

WHY ARE DUNGEONS ALWAYS DANK AND COLD?

Madeline regained consciousness gradually. A new experience, unconsciousness. Doesn't happen to the long-lived very often, sleep is but a memory.

The cellar is cold and unfinished, the bare stone covered in moisture and growing things, some of which have a faint bioluminescence. Stone steps led off to the upper floor to her left. There was very little other light.

Able to see in most conditions, Madeline moved, a hint of a cramp in her cold legs. She hissed as the cold silver of the manacles moved on her skin. Someone who knew what she was put her here.

That someone would die horribly.

The manacles were bolted into the stone. Madeline ignored the continued discomfort of the silver touching her skin and tested the strength of them. It felt secure, probably titanium under the silver, but she felt it wouldn't take much to dislodge them.

A step on the stone stairs alerted her to the other's presence before she felt it. A dim light shone down from above. It wasn't human, judging by its size, and it felt old. Not worried she would escape either, judging by the fact it had left the door at the top of the stairs open.

"Ah, back with us," the hulking figure grated.

"Release me and I will kill you quickly," Madeline retorted, her voice hoarse with lack of use.

This brought out a laugh, the sound of boulders rubbing one another in a rock fall. "I don't think so, child. The Council has uses for you."

Madeline spat, trying to conjure some moisture into her dry mouth. *Why had she waited to feed?* She was weaker than she should be. "I don't recognise your 'council'."

"Tsk," the giant said. "That's irrelevant – they are more than capable of controlling one of your kind." It gestured at the chains and the cellar. "As you can see."

"What do you want from me?" Madeline demanded.

The rock giant, for that is what it was, paused, one foot on the bottom step. "All in good time, Madeline, all in good time."

"Wait! You know me, but who are you?" She tried to keep desperation from her voice.

"That is also unimportant. I have merely been tasked with looking after you." Halfway up the stone stair, it paused again. "You are hungry, yes? But you will last for a while longer?"

Madeline sighed. Yes, she would last, but not happily. "I will. And when I am free, I will kill you."

It laughed again. "Well, we shall see. But first you would have to be free." With that, it left her in the darkness.

ARS MEMORIÆ

My skullphone interrupts my maudlin ramblings. "Sen."
"Co-commander, it's Adams."

"Yes, Adams, I know." I struggle to keep the exasperation out of my voice and fail. "What is it?"

There's a moment of silence before he answers – I didn't think I scared him that much. "I... I have some supplementary equipment for your..."

"Incursion," I supply.

"Okay, 'incursion'. Is now a good time?" he asks.

"As you're standing outside my door, Adams, you may as well come in."

I can hear him mutter, "How's he do that?" as the door to my office opens.

"Easy," I reply. "Your shadow was on the glass and I could hear your heartbeat, as well as a good portion of your side of the conversation. Now come in."

Looking more nervous than ever (with a heart rate approaching one hundred and twenty beats per minute) he approaches the desk.

"What have you got for me?"

He places a small packet on the desk which, when I empty it out, contains something looking like a carved lump of coal.

"It's a ward which should protect you against things like psychic attack, possession or just plain daemonic attack."

I look at him for a moment, my mouth hanging open. "Are you serious?"

Adams nods. "De-deadly serious, sir."

I pick it up.

As soon as I do, a hum spikes in my head before fading back to a dull background noise. I put it down and the hum stops. I pick it up again and the same thing happens. Sounds guaranteed to give me a headache.

"Does this work?" He seems to melt a little further under my gaze.

He nods again. "Yessir. Rab was attacked by an incubus a few weeks ago and had the presence of mind to push this into its face. Apparently it burned the thing's nose off."

Rab? Oh yes, Igor. "Okay." I think for a moment. "Can I get four more? No, make it six." *Observers might be affected too, you never know.*

Adams reached in his courier bag and pulled out six more packets.

"Here you go– oh," he says, finding something else in his bag. "You may need this, too." He leans forward and places an item wrapped in what looks like old linen.

"What's this?" I pick it up and nearly drop it again. I've unwrapped what appears to be a withered hand, severed at the wrist.

"Hand of Glory," he replies, still cool and collected. "You light it and it gives light only to you or anyone touching you. It also works in magical darkness where normal light doesn't."

"*Jesus, Adams.* Where the hell did you get this?" I re-wrap the hand. "What is it?"

Adams shrugs. "We got a consignment from China a while back and this is the first case where it might actually be useful." He looks sheepish. "It's the hand of a hanged man, or so they claim. It does work, as I tried one to make sure we weren't getting ripped off."

I nod. I don't knock it as I've seen stranger things. "Fine." I sigh, knowing I'll regret asking. "Anything else?"

He surprises me. "I'd like to come along, sir." Adding quickly, "Only in an observational capacity."

Frowning, I check his file in my HUD. "You're still not cleared for field work, Adams."

He nods, looking at the floor. "Yes sir. I just hoped to observe this one…"

I let him stand there for a moment before relenting.

What the hell, Skeet and Graeme could look after him. And (famous last words) he shouldn't be in any danger.

"Okay, you can observe, but you'll be with the external team."

His head comes up and I swear, if he'd been a dog, his tail would have been going fast enough to take off.

"Thank you, sir! I'll be quiet and keep out of the way…"

I frown at him. "You will, Adams. Don't make me regret adding you to the team."

"I won't, Sir. You can count on me!"

"Adams."

"Sir?"

"Shut up and get out."

"Yessir!" He mock salutes me and makes his escape.

I sigh again. *I hope I'm not going to regret this.*

WAITING AROUND SUCKS

Wolf threw the last bit of kit in his bag and slouched back on the sofa. They were waiting for the others to turn up and Graeme had gone to pick up a van from a mate with an eye for spy gadgets. And it would be more comfortable than the Land Rover, particularly if this took longer than an hour or two.

There was nothing more to do in preparation. He and Shirl had spent the last hour and a half practicing capoeira, letting the movement unwind their muscles and relax them. He felt very relaxed and just about ready for anything. Well, almost anything.

He sighed, wishing he could have a beer, but knowing he needed to stay sharp. A single mistake could kill them all.

Shirl nudged him. "Don't sigh like that; you're making me thirsty, too."

Wolf grinned. "After this one's over, the beer's on me – promise."

"They better be."

"What'd you tell Jonno?" Wolf was still getting used to Shirl having a full-time boyfriend. First one in a long time and it looked promising.

"I told him I had a date with you and he rolled his eyes."

Wolf laughed. "Didn't he want to come along?"

"Yes, but I told him you weren't his type." Shirl was grinning as well now.

Silent after that, Wolf wished he could have kept her out of it for the thousandth time. "I'm glad he... and you... are doing so well."

It was Shirl's turn to laugh. "*That* sounded awkward! You don't half sound like Da, sometimes."

"Can't help it – he was a formative influence on the little shit I used to be."

Shirl shook her head. "You weren't ever a little shit – not to us, anyway."

"Oh, you just missed out on the best bits. I was an arsehole when I met Stanley." His eyes unfocused, thinking of Stanley. "There are still days when I wonder what he saw in that fucked-up street kid."

"He was good at seeing people, our Stan," Shirl replied, then shrugged. "You can't ask me, anyway – I knew him all my life and I've got no idea what he was really like, beyond the jolly uncle who always gave me books."

Wolf looked down at the floor. "I still miss him."

"We all do, Wolfie, we all do," Shirl murmured.

After a long moment, Wolf changed the subject by standing up and stepping over to the practice mat. "Come on, show me what you got!"

Shirl laughed. "Oh, you want some of this, do you? Just you wait!"

LIFE'S A BITCH, AND THEN YOU DIE

J ames Tyler is not difficult to find.
He doesn't work that I can tell, but he's always busy. What he calls his 'office' is in his penthouse apartment. And I'm in said flat for the second time in two days. I must be travelling in more affluent circles.

Tyler doesn't look up as I'm escorted in, staring at something on one of his screens. "Yes? What do you want, Commander? I'm very busy."

I'm sure. "It's about your son, Sir James."

At this, he looks up. "You've found out who killed him?" Tyler looks almost hopeful on one hand, but I can see some tension there, now I'm looking for it. His heart rate is up, too.

I nod. "Yes, we know who did it, Sir James."

"Who? Who killed my son?" he demands.

"You did, Sir James."

The look on his face. I'm glad of my new eyes just for moments like this.

He tries to deny it, of course. "That's preposterous! I've never heard anything more outrageous! Get out of my office now – as a Peer of the Realm, I do *not* have to listen to this!"

I sit down on one of the Louis XV chairs, carefully. I'm pretty sure it's original.

Tyler's almost frothing now. "I said, get out!"

I stare at him. "No."

He picks up a voda and starts dialling. "Let me speak to the Inspector General, now!" he shouts when someone picks up on the other end. "I don't care if he's in a meeting – put him on *now!*"

"That won't be necessary, Sir James."

The Inspector General steps into the office, followed by Lady Tyler. She appears to have been crying, but I have little sympathy for her.

"You wished to speak to me, Sir James?" The IG takes the other fragile chair. Lady Tyler moves around the desk to be beside her husband.

Tyler looks at Portia and then at the IG before slumping back into his chair. "You believe him, then?" he says to the IG, waving in my general direction.

The IG sighs. "Sir James, when Commander Sen started looking at you as a suspect, the trail was fairly obvious – to Central, at least." He sighs again. "The transaction to Alamo that you tried to bury in a subsidiary holding's accounts, while a good ploy, still left a paper trail."

Tyler starts to protest, but the IG isn't having it. "And don't start claiming you were framed, Sir James – it's highly unlikely that the method used to pay Alamo for your son's death was anything but intentional. Our analysts find no evidence the payment could have been made by anyone but you."

Lady Tyler speaks up. "I can't believe you think James could do such a thing!"

I stare at her. "Yes, you do. Which is why you've been trying to distract me, all along. I *did* warn you that I was not like that, Lady Tyler."

Oh, if looks could kill. Without another word, she stalks to the door and out of the room.

"Portia!" Tyler calls. "Wait..." His voice trails off as he realises the futility of trying to stop her. "So, that's it then? I'm guilty? Off with his head!" He cackles, an edge of hysteria creeping in.

The IG shakes his head. "While I would be delighted for Commander Sen to execute that order, Sir James, I'm afraid we do not have the authority. You will be remanded in custody until such time as a court of your peers can be initiated."

Tyler snorts. "Don't you mean 'a court of Peers', Inspector General?"

The IG inclines his head. Two officers enter the office and move to either side of Sir James Tyler. He stands up, apparently resigned to his fate.

"One thing, Sir James," I say. "Have you any information on the Council of Seven?"

As the IG gives me a sideways glance, Sir James starts to answer. "Of course, they are..." He slumps to the floor.

Dammit. "Get a med team in here, pronto!" I shout at the uniforms. I kneel next to his body. No pulse. I turn him onto his back and start compressions. I'm pretty certain it's futile, but you never know.

"Jaared, that was... unwise," the IG says. He's looking out the window at the view over the park. He sighs again. "I should have warned you that asking about the Council would not be... beneficial."

Still pressing on Sir James's chest, I look at the IG, astonished. "You *knew* about the Council of the Seven?"

The IG holds up a hand. "I cannot tell you anything or talk about them directly, Jaared. We don't want another one of those in here now, do we?" He waves at the body.

Still compressing, I look down. "No sir."

Sighing a last time, he says, "I will make certain... documents... available to you, Jaared, but I cannot help you with this." He looks at me before leaving the room. "I may be able to shield you to some extent, but we will not be speaking of this again."

I nod, evidence of what could happen beneath my hands. "Thank you, sir."

The IG smiles, a hint of sadness in his piercing eyes. "Oh, I wouldn't thank me, Jaared. This is only likely to end one way."

You ain't nothin' but trouble and a pretty smile...

There was a sharp rap on the door.

"Company," they said together, and then, "Snap!"

Wolf stood up and went to the door. It was dark outside, the early pre-winter night setting in with a vengeance.

Sen and a tall blonde woman stood outside the door.

Wolf waved them in. "Come on in."

Both the Commander and the blonde had to duck slightly to get through the priest's door set into the larger door. Sen carried two large duffle bags and the blonde had a pack to go with the assault shotgun she carried easily in the other hand.

"Whoa, whoa, whoa! Who said anything about firepower?" Wolf protested.

The blonde grinned. "I don't leave home without it."

Sen nodded. "This is Skeet. And..."

Wolf had been about to push the door to when a smaller figure in an anorak and ski hat pushed through the opening.

"Who the fuck are you?" Wolf demanded. He looked at Sen. "Who's he?"

"I'm Adams."

"That's Adams – he's here as an observer," Sen said. He didn't look happy about it. "And he's an occult specialist... which may come in useful. Skeet and Adams will be with your man as observers, possibly experts, should the situation call for it." He paused again. "Our 'fifth' will be meeting us at the rendezvous."

Adams stuck out his hand. "Pleased to meet you, Mr Woffe."

Wolf shook his hand absently. "Yeah, whatever." He looked at Sen and back at Adams. "Occult specialist, eh?" He was more concerned about the missing fifth person; Wolf didn't like unknowns – or surprises.

Nodding like one of those noddy dogs in the back of a crap car, Adams was smiling. "I'm looking forward to seeing what happens at the site tonight!"

"Fine, just stay out of the way." Still unsettled, he looked back at Sen. "You ready?"

Sen smiled. "As we'll ever be."

There was another knock at the door. When Wolf saw Mayweather, his eyes narrowed.

"Mr Woffe."

"Come in, Mayweather – you need to try on your kit before we go."

Mayweather nodded and ducked through the priest's door.

"This is Mayweather; he'll be joining our little party tonight," Wolf said by way of introduction. Sen nodded and the tall blonde just stared. Wolf picked up the second kit bag Sen had brought and led Mayweather over to the workbench.

The next half an hour was spent getting Mayweather into the polycarbs and adjusting them so he didn't accidentally come undone, or worse, turn the suit off. When Wolf was satisfied with the fit (Mayweather didn't really get a say) they packed another bag for Mayweather.

Wolf looked at Sen before saying a few words. "We're going in for two things. We need to try to locate the manuscript we've been led to believe is in that place."

"And I need to try to locate the crime scenes where five men have died," Sen followed on. "If that's possible."

Nodding, Wolf looked at the people in the room. "Number one priority is getting all of us out again. No heroics, no stupid moves and you listen to me at all times – I've done this kind of thing before and I *do* know what I'm doing. It could save your life or, more importantly, mine." He looked at all of them in turn. "Any questions?"

Mayweather's hand went up. "Not a question, Mr Woffe… I just wanted to say thank you for your help."

Wolf looked at him in the following awkward silence. It was broken by the sound of a horn outside the workshop. "That'll be Graeme," Wolf said. "Saddle up."

They grabbed kit bags and filed out through the priest's door before piling into the waiting van.

ONCE MORE INTO THE BREACH

The van that Woffe's team has acquired is bigger than I expected. All seven of us fit quite comfortably in it, even though it's stuffed to the gills with all the latest surveillance equipment. I don't want to know what that means, although Central is probably happily chasing down the owner right now. I get a pain, thinking about Central – how trustworthy was it now?

Windows are only in the front of the van, so the rest of us ride oblivious to the passing streetscape.

The old man, Graeme Black, drives easily around the roadworks that seem to be endless in London. Down through Notting Hill and Kensington and into Earl's Court where the House is. Central tracks us and a map of our route is displayed on my HUD.

We are mostly silent on the journey, everyone thinking about what comes next.

When I say 'mostly', that would be all of us but Adams, who seems to be suffering a bout of nerves.

"So then I said, you can't use that charm on a Wendigo, you moron – it'll chop you up and eat the pieces for breakfast!" He laughs, sounding a bit edgy.

"Adams."

"Yessir?" He looks at me.

"Give it a rest."

"Yessir." Adams settles back in his jumpseat. "So then he said—"

"Shut up Adams!"

I get the hurt puppy look, but that's easily ignored. And miracle of miracles, he actually stays quiet.

My head phone rings and I glance at the others before taking it.

"Commander Sen?"

"Yes, how can I help you?"

"It's Tiffany Bowes-Lyon." A beat, then I hear her take a deep breath. "I understand Sir James was behind it – and you killed him for it."

I realise I'm shaking my head. "No, Ms Bowes-Lyon, I didn't. His death was unrelated to John Tyler's case."

Silence. "I know it won't bring John back, but I'm glad he's dead." The line goes dead.

People are funny and when it comes to grieving are entirely unpredictable.

The van makes a few more turns before it slows and goes through the manoeuvres of parking. Once it stops, those of us going into the House strip down to our skivvies before pulling on the mimetic polycarbons that will conceal us as we approach the House.

Graeme slips through from the cab of the van and starts prepping the equipment around us. Skeet watches him with interest, but keeps out of the way.

There's a tap at the back of the van. Wolf looks at me. "Your fifth man?"

I nod. "Yes, that'll be the last of the party."

At Wolf's signal, Graeme cuts lights. Wolf cracks the door. "Yes?"

"Jaared Sen requires me," a low voice says.

"Climb in Nick," I reply.

Nicholas's head appears in the gap, a dark object in the dim light from the doorway. "I will wait out here, if you do not mind." He wrinkles his nose. "I am not sure I can stand the stench."

"Okay." I hold up one of Adams's charms. "Want one of these?"

Wrinkling his nose again, Nicholas backs away, shaking his head. "I do not think so."

I shrug.

"The stench?" Wolf closes the van door again and stares at me a moment as the lighting comes up to dim, before finishing pulling his suit on.

"What the hell was that!" Adams hisses, voda in hand. "It lit up several wards by itself..."

"Shut up Adams," I repeat. I hand out the wards to everyone, including Graeme and Skeet. "I think you should put these on under your suits, right Adams?"

He gulps. ""Y-y-yes. They should be in contact with your skin."

"What is it?" Wolf asks.

"Level 5 ward: should keep you safe through most standard magical attacks and traps. Anything above Level 5 and you're on your own!" Adams answers, far too cheerfully.

I drop mine over my head before concentrating on putting on the skintight suit. It warms for a moment before adjusting to my body temperature, the hum fading quickly.

Think of a wetsuit, but one covered in microscopic cells, like a chameleon's skin. We can be almost invisible in these suits as they even vent heat in such a way that infrared sensors can't see us. It's also tight.

Skeet helps me pull the suit up to my neck, closes the seals at the back and fits the hood. There's a moment of quiet before the polymer of the suit adapts over my ears and I can hear again. I leave the facemask dangling for the moment – they can get sweaty as I recall.

Wolf and the girl, Shirl, are pulling on thin layers of armour, before sliding the chameleon polymers on over it. Obviously an older model.

"You should upgrade," I say. "This does what that does without the extra bulk." My suit has a built-in layer that stiffens and blocks the impact of projectiles or knives but stays supple the rest of the time.

I get glared at by Wolf. Shirl answers. "We weren't planning on using them again..."

Nodding, I do understand, probably more than they think. "And yet, here we are." I smile, to take some tension out of the situation.

"You lot ready yet?" Graeme asks. He sets up a folding chair for Skeet, directing her to it with a flourish before settling into what is obviously his command chair. He glares at the hovering Adams, before turning back to his console.

"Nearly," Wolf replies, as Shirl helps him fit his hood, facemask dangling.

"I need status checks on your suits," Graeme states. "Where's number five?"

I shake my head. "He won't be needing a suit, nor will you be able to follow him when we're in the House."

Adams looks puzzled for a moment before twigging. "I knew it! He's a..."

Skeet and I both say "Shut up Adams!" at the same time. How cute.

Graeme looks at Wolf for a second, and then Mayweather, who shrugs, lost. The big man's not said a word since we got in the van and seems a bit dazed.

I mentally thumb a switch and Central shoots my suit's status signal to Graeme's boards. I know, mid-twenty first century and I still think of things in terms of 'switches', 'boards' and 'consoles', mechanical things filled with tubes and the smell of hot electronics. Believe me, nothing in that van smelled hot or had a tube in it.

"Got it." Graeme nods at me. "You're number three." He slid his fingers through the air like a maestro. "Which makes Mayweather number four." He'd obviously already pulled in the signals of the other two while we were suiting up, I'd guess making Wolf number one and Shirl number two.

"Okay," Wolf adjusted the wrist fastenings of his suit. "I guess this is it. No heroics, grandstanding or anything else." He looked at the three of us. "Follow my orders, dammit."

I throw him a mock salute. "*Ja wohl, mein Herr.*" Everyone looks puzzled. Another age-related joke, obviously.

Mayweather just nods.

Wolf looks at us all again for a long moment. The group catches the same case of nerves and the quiet is a sober one. I can hear the van's skin contracting as it cools, small pings and creaks.

"Okay, let's go." Wolf sighs. "Sooner we go, the sooner we come back…"

I slip my mask on, ready now, the familiar fight chemicals beginning to sing in my bloodstream. I can almost hear something else and suddenly wonder where Madeline is. It's not like her to miss a party.

"*Comms check,*" sounds in my ear.

"*Number one, check,*" Wolf replies.

Shirl follows. "*Number two check.*"

"Number three, check," I say when she's done.

"*Number four, check,*" from Mayweather.

"*All comms functional, you've got an open window — you're clear to go.*"

The interior lights dim again to darkness before the back door of the van opens and we melt into the cold night.

NOCTURNE WITH STARS

What is sentience? At what point does something become 'alive'? We have definitions for humans and animals, but what about *things*? Computers have been mimicking sentience for nearly half a century and we created them.

What about places? The fey have talked about ley lines for centuries, but what about places of emotion? Arenas, churches, execution sites… where does all that emotion go?

The House is still brooding.

Annoyed with the recent intrusions, the House elbows the sorcerer's home, making the hanging on the wall of the kitchen bang and a few more cracks appear in the plasterwork.

Cold, blue fire runs through the walls and along all the metal in the House, but nothing burns. The fire cleanses as it runs, not destroying but purifying, the dark rooms momentarily bathed in the azure glow.

The rooms are decontaminated, all bar one. That one remains closed, sacrosanct, its guardian stirring uneasily as the fire nears it. The treasure it guards is too precious for fire to touch.

Next door, Shen sees a blue flame follow the path of the cracks in the adjoining wall, mutters a phrase and the flame disappears. He shakes his head and watches the wall, more than aware of the House's unease. He goes back to his chanting, hoping his efforts will assist the strange white people he'd agreed to help.

And now it senses others approaching. What is this? Another intrusion?

Four hot people and a cold one. For a moment, the House shudders, remembering another cold one. One the Master had brought to the House to help prepare some of the defences now extant in the House.

The House had been barely aware when the Cold One had pulled at the very fabric of the building and settled the entity calling itself 'House' more firmly into the stones and mortar of the structure. Whatever he did strengthend and twisted the material until it would take a significant force to destroy the building.

The quintet, invisible on many levels, approaches the front of the House and it knows it is only a matter of time before they enter.

Satisfaction enters the aura of the House.

Entering the House is acceptable, new blood is always welcome and sustaining for the entities calling it home.

Leaving the House, on the other hand, is far more difficult.

I DON'T LIKE TO WATCH

T he three left in the van looked at one another for a moment. Skeet pulled the folding chair over and dropped into it. "Skeet," she said, holding out a hand to Graeme.

"Graeme, but I guess you knew that," he responded.

Nodding, Skeet hooked a thumb over her shoulder at Adams. "That's Adams. He's a geek."

Graeme smiled as Adams protested. "Hey, I'm an 'Occult Specialist', I'll have you know."

"Keep your underwear on," Skeet said without looking at him.

Hurt, Adams leaned over her and offered a hand to the older man. "Adams."

"I heard." Graeme looked back to the screens. The four were not visible on the camera pointed at the House. Another screen was split into four windows, numbered one to four and showing the forward vid inputs from the masks. The biosensors in the suits were also reporting. Two and Four had elevated pulse rates and were apparently starting to sweat already.

Graeme clicked his mic. "Shirl, you need to gland five cc of Neo. Mayweather, you too, if you've got it."

The suits had mics at the throat which picked up sub-vocal responses. A 'yessir' from Shirl; little more than a grunt from Mayweather.

Skeet nodded. "Keeps 'em calmer but they can still function," she explained to Adams.

Adams nodded. "Right." He looked around behind him and found a plastic crate of odds and ends which he managed to spill under one of the consoles. He righted it and sat down gingerly. When he caught Graeme glowering at him, he smiled back and shrugged.

Graeme turned back to the screens. "I don't like having our fifth man uncovered," he muttered.

"Don't think he functions like the others," Skeet replied. "I'd even guess that suit would hinder him more than help."

"Especially if he's..." Adams spoke up.

"Shut up Adams," Skeet said without looking at him.

"Why does everyone keep telling me to shut up? I only said he's—" he gasped

"Yeah Adams, that's why we keep telling you to shut up." Skeet had turned and put one hand on his shoulder, near the neck. The pressure point under her thumb wouldn't kill him, but he'd got the message. Skeet tapped her nose and let him go. "Need t'know, Adams."

Graeme watched this, seemingly amused. "It's okay, I know what he is – I've seen his kind before. Once or twice."

Skeet eyed him warily. "That's more'n most and not somethin' most people survive."

Shrugging, Graeme watched the screens. "Luckily it wasn't looking for me."

Nodding, Skeet looked back at the screens. The team was pressed up against a garden wall, waiting for a jogger – a jogger? – to make his or her way past.

"Heat signature says woman," Graeme muttered. "Come on, come on, come on, come on…"

"I don't like the waitin', either," Skeet replied. "Doesn't suit ma' personality much."

Graeme chuckled in appreciation. "And gets you into trouble?"

Skeet nodded again. "Yep." She toggled her headset. "Number three, you stay frosty, ya hear?"

There was a single click, which she smiled at. *"Frosty."*

The team was just visible on the monitors moving to the front door. At least that way they'd know what had happened to the previous group.

Up the stairs, a few moments at the door while the locks were disengaged, and they were in.

"All team in and accounted for."

"Acknowledged," Graeme replied.

"What now?" Adams asked from his crate.

Skeet sighed and crossed her arms. "Now, we wait."

EVER HAD THAT FEELING YOU'RE BEING WATCHED?

T he interior of the House is oppressive. It's not hot, but there's some kind of pressure or maybe a sound compressing us all as we step into the foyer. Even through the nose filters on the mask there's a smell of dust and decay. Age.

"*All team in and accounted for.*" That'll be Wolf, in my earpiece.

"*Acknowledged.*"

We'd decided on strict radio silence to begin with, at least until we'd established what was going on with the House. And as Nicholas wasn't on the comms, it wouldn't hurt to do things the old-fashioned way.

"*Disengage suits.*"

It also seemed sensible to be able to see one another once we were in – save the power packs and allow us to communicate without the comms.

We're all clustered just in the door. I can still hear their heartbeats through the polymers – that's harder to disguise than our heat signatures.

Wolf uses the agreed hand signals, saying we should move forward down the hall.

We all turn and the floor drops from under us.

"*Shit.*" That'll be Mayweather. His heart rate is up again.

It's dark and by lucky chance I seem to be on top of the pile. I can feel Nick's colder skin, so guess he fell as well. I had half hoped he might have avoided the drop.

"What now?" he murmurs in my ear.

"*I thought we agreed radio silence,*" Wolf said in my ear.

"*Fuck that shite – it knows we're here!*"

"I think we can probably dispense with that," I reply, pulling my mouth cover back. "As Mayweather has observed, it's obvious it knows we're here." I start to stand up and Nicholas pulls me to my feet in one motion. I still can't believe how fast he is.

"Is everyone okay?" Wolf asks. Everyone responds in the positive. A few bumps and a bit of bruising, but nothing show-stopping.

I can't see anything with my goggles, not even trace heat signatures from the bodies around me. I trigger the infrared light between my eyes and can't see that either. "Can anyone see anything? Infrared or otherwise?"

A body bumps me. Shirl, I'd guess, from the size and stature. Nick steadies her on one side and I on the other. Such gentlemen. He must have fed before he came as he seems quite calm.

"*Not a thing,*" in the earpiece, echoes her sub-vocalisations. The air is cool and damp, although the moisture makes it feel a bit cloying, even through the mask. All sound is dead, like the walls are covered in acoustic tile.

"*Nope.*" Wolf all business.

"*Not a fuckin' thin'.*" Mayweather obviously swears under stressful conditions.

This is beginning to seem all too familiar. It's amazing how much one starts to depend on one's eyes when you've got them. I relax and let my mind work out the space around me as it used to do. It's not large, but it does seem empty. Maybe a hall?

"*Adams said to remind you about that item he gave you, number three.*"

I remember. The 'Hand of Glory'. Didn't think I'd be using it quite so soon. I fumble in my belly pack for it and nearly drop it when one of the fingers catches on the pocket. While I may not need it — we're in a corridor leading towards the back of the House — it might be useful for someone else to be able to see our surroundings.

I click the lighter I put in with the dead man's hand. I can hear the flame, but not see it. I move it to the end of one of the fingers by touch and am rewarded with a flicker of light.

Nick, who is still touching my arm, inhales sharply. "What's that?"

"Hand of Glory. Apparently dispels magical darkness. Does that mean you can see, too?" I can see a rough sphere of light showing me a brick-lined corridor. The walls are wet in patches, something black growing in the damp mortar. The ceiling is quite high above our heads, as I can't actually see it from the glow of the Hand.

"Yes." He removes his hand from my arm. "But only while I'm touching you."

The others don't appear to be able to see me. I wave my hand in front of Shirl's face and she nearly falls backward as the slight breeze hits her mask. I catch her arm and she gasps.

"What's that light?" She can see now she's touching me. Wish Adams had included an instruction manual.

"Hand of Glory," I repeat. "I guess it only works by touch." I put it in her hand. "Here, you hold this for a moment, I want to check something."

She nearly drops it when she realises what it is. I close her fingers more tightly around the stump and place Nick's hand on her arm before letting both of them go.

I'm instantly plunged back into darkness and disoriented for a moment. This sight thing is unreliable after so many years without it.

I take a deep breath in through my nose and let it out slowly through my mouth, finding my centre. Letting my eyes go, my sense of the space expands, telling me more about the hallway than I'd been able to see. It's about six feet wide, twenty feet long and level, flagstone floor. The door at the far end is closed. The rest is blank wall.

I step away from the group towards the only exit from the corridor, letting my senses tell me where to step. The floor doesn't appear to have any traps or pressure points and I get to the door without incident.

There's a tingling on the back of my neck, suggesting I'm being watched. I can only assume it's the House.

"Commander, what are you doing?" Wolf calls. He's obviously touching the light now.

"Just checking our options."

"Can you see anything?"

"Not a thing." I smile at the sudden flood of concern behind me. "But I was blind for a very long time, Mr Woffe – I know a thing or two about complete darkness."

"Any chance someone could reach the trap we came through?"

I doubt it. "I would think the House would stop us going that way, even if we could." I don't like touching the walls, even with gloves.

"Just don't set off any traps," he replies.

"There don't appear to be any in this corridor, but I haven't examined the door yet."

"We'll come to you."

"Okay, when you're ready." I glance at the walls. "Just stay in the middle of the corridor, if you can."

Some muttering, then I can hear them shuffling towards me, obviously all touching to get the benefit of the Hand. Maybe not Nick as he should be able to do a lot of what I do, naturally.

I ignore them for the moment and turn my attention to the door. I can't sense anything untoward in the door. It just appears to be a door. I run my fingers up and down the join, but there's no catch or other way to open it.

I press my fingers against the door and push. Nothing. Then I try pushing it from side to side with my fingers and feel it give slightly when I push to the left. Hmmm...

I can feel the others behind me and someone touches my shoulder, instantly bathing me in the ghostly glow from the Hand. I blink at them, one naked and three masked faces visible in the dim light.

The finger I had lit is almost gone and a second one has started guttering. Adams also didn't tell me about the smell, which is fairly putrid. I close my nose filters, but it's too late.

"Whatcha got?" Wolf asks.

"I think the door slides to the left," I reply, turning back around.

Nick is beside me, pressing against the door and attempting to slide it. It doesn't move.

"It appears to have a latch of some kind," he mutters, exerting himself. I don't know how strong he is, but Madeline has warned me not to spar with him because the young can be much stronger than they or we realise.

There's a loud *snap!* and the door moves. Whatever it is, he's managed to open the door in spite of it.

The darkness is unchanged and I sigh. I never expected this to be easy, but this is getting silly.

Puzzles, puzzles, why is it always goddamn puzzles

Wolf's nerves had been on edge since they'd fallen into the darkness.

All the technology they had at their fingertips and no one could see anything. Then Commander Sen lit the fingers of what looked like a desiccated hand and there's light as long as they're all touching.

He was sweating in his suit, the wicking liner working overtime to keep the moisture from building up. Wolf took a sip from the small reservoir, just enough to wet his mouth. No idea when the next bathroom break could be.

Opening the door into the next room was disappointing, in that the darkness continued.

The Commander, with his strange ability to see in the dark, led the way. *Or not so strange if you consider he used to be blind*, Wolf thought to himself.

"Nothing in here but a table. Well, a plinth, really. It's too tall for a table. About two foot square. Appears to be some kind of stone." They could barely hear him moving about the room, the darkness dulling and muting the sound. "The walls are the same brick. I'd say it's about fifteen feet square."

The human chain went through the door when Sen pronounced it all clear. And partly as they had expected, the door behind them snapped shut. Wolf shrugged in his suit. "Not a lot we can do about that now. The only way is forward."

Shirl was holding the Hand of Glory with some distaste, but not protesting. The ghostly glow it gave off was still enough to make them feel better about the unnatural dark.

"Whatcha got?" Wolf repeated, examining the table in the dim light.

Sen, Mayweather and the young man called Nicholas were staring at the tabletop. It appeared to be one of those sliding puzzles kids played with, but made of stone and embedded in the top of the plinth.

"We've got a puzzle to solve," Sen replied. "And it's not a simple one. Four tiles on a side, makes it fifteen tiles, with a gap. Let's see, that's about 20,922,789,888,000 possible combinations of the fifteen tiles."

"Shite." That from Mayweather.

"Why do we have to solve it?" Mayweather asked before Wolf could.

"No other door." Nicholas spoke for the second time.

Wolf couldn't see the walls, but guessed they'd already been around the room. "No door? Damn. Stay here." He took the Hand from Shirl and went around the walls. Not that he didn't trust Sen, but he liked to be on top of things.

And no door. He found two fine lines in the brick, on the same wall as the door they had entered, which might have been the edge of an opening, but it was very tightly fitted if so. No obvious way to open it – not even hinges they could lift. He sighed and returned to the table. "No door."

He tried to hand the burning Hand back to Shirl, but she shook her head. Wolf shrugged. Whatever worked.

"We obviously have to solve the puzzle to get out of this room." Sen was staring down at the pattern on the table, trying to make sense of it.

"Graeme, can you see this?" Wolf asked.

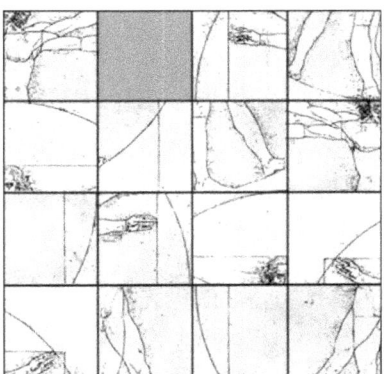

"*That's a 'no'*," Graeme replied. "We've seen nothing since you went through the front door."

But they could still communicate. Weird. "We've got a puzzle to solve."

"*Yeah, heard that bit – sounds like Webster's idea of fun.*"

"How hard can it be?" Shirl asked no one. She started sliding the pieces around on the table. There was a grinding sound from one side. Shirl stopped.

"What the hell was that?" Mayweather demanded.

Sen looked at Nicholas. "I believe the wall behind me moved," Nicholas said.

"Yes, I'd say it's now about an inche closer to the table than it was when we entered the room," the Commander added.

"What've you got? Bat senses?" Wolf asked, to cover his worry.

Sen shrugged. "More or less. Let's just call it a heightened sense of spatial awareness."

Mayweather broke in. "Whatever. So you're saying the walls move if we move the pieces around?"

"Let's find out." Wolf moved one piece and there was another grating sound, this time from another side.

Head cocked to one side, the Commander appeared to be listening. "I'd say that was the other wall."

"Shite." Mayweather repeated.

"From what I remember about these puzzles, a solution can be found in 43-81 moves."

"Yer just a walkin' google," Mayweather replied.

They were all silent for a long moment, weighing the options.

Sen had been staring at the board. "At the risk of stating the obvious, if we don't solve the puzzle fast enough, I suspect we'll be rather compact."

More silence.

"I ken do it," Mayweather stated.

Wolf looked at him in the ghostlight. "Are you sure?"

"I used t' do these all the time," he replied. Wolf suspected he was laying claim to a confidence he didn't really feel.

Wolf shrugged. "What have we got to lose? We're not getting out any other way."

They studied the tiles, looking for a pattern.

"What is it supposed to be?" Shirl wondered. Then she looked at the Hand. "And you'd better hurry; I don't think we've got a lot of light left."

The image was unclear, but there was definitely an image in the tiles.

Mayweather concentrated before moving anything. He seemed to come to some conclusion. "Got it."

Wolf reported in. "Mayweather's going to attempt the puzzle. You been monitoring the conversation?"

"*Yes.*" There was a pause. "*You'll all be a lot thinner if he gets it wrong.*"

"Ha ha, very funny. Keep monitoring and I'll report when he's finished."

"Copy that."

He started sliding the tiles around and the sound of the moving walls started almost instantly. Mayweather whipped the tiles around in a frenzy, trying to block out the grating. Wolf started a timer with a press on his wrist buttons. The countdown started ticking away just to the edge of his vision.

The Hand flickered, but didn't go out. They couldn't see one another's faces behind their masks, but the tension in the room was almost tangible, the sound of the walls tearing at their nerve ends.

Sen and Nicholas suddenly turned away from the group. It took Wolf a moment to work out what they were doing. When they vanished he realised they were monitoring the wall's progress.

"The wall we came in doesn't move," Nicholas reported over the noise.

"How can they all move?" Shirl asked. "It doesn't make any sense – it'd be physically impossible for the three walls to do that…" Her voice trails off.

Sen's voice carries, although he seems closer. "I don't think we're dealing with simply a physical phenomenon, Ms Black."

"Call me Shirl," she said to the grinding darkness. "Everyone else does, Commander."

There's a barely heard chuckle. *How does the man keep so damn cool?* Wolf wondered.

"Very well, call me Jaared. 'Commander' makes me feel so… old."

The noise went on unabated. "Half the distance from the walls has disappeared." Nicholas had raised his voice to report.

Mayweather was whipping the tiles back and forth and around, frenziedly trying to get the image to match up. "There, no, not that one," he muttered as he concentrated on the moving tiles.

Wolf caught a glimpse of the image. "*Vitruvian Man*," he said aloud.

"You're right," Shirl replied. "Why would Webster use that?"

Shrugging, Wolf watched as the image became clearer. "It's one of Leonardo's most famous drawings and incredibly important. Maybe he used it because we'd know what it was."

"Based on the rate the walls are moving, we've probably got about two minutes of space left," Sen reported. "Everyone but Mayweather and Wolf, move to the space behind the plinth – I'm not sure what'll happen when the walls reach the plinth, but I'm not convinced it'll stop."

Shirl jostled Wolf's elbow as she squeezed past. Sen watched Mayweather for a moment before he and Nicholas slipped past. Wolf moved around so he was nearly behind Mayweather, trying not to burn the man with the Hand.

Mayweather went to wipe sweat from his face and then stopped, thwarted by the facemask. "Dammit," he swore softly. "Just three more…"

Wolf found himself trying to calm him. "Easy, just take it easy. Lots of time."

Then he caught sight of the bricks moving towards him from the other side of the table.

The sliding of the tiles made no noise over the approaching walls. If anything, Mayweather's flicking tiles was happening faster. He didn't seem to see the moving partitions, engrossed in finishing the puzzle.

Wolf looked left and right: the walls seemed much too close. Sen had said two minutes. The timer in his mask said it had already been almost ten since Mayweather started. "C'mon," he muttered under his breath.

"I'm workin' as fast as I ken," Mayweather replied.

"Sorry."

The walls were nearly on them now. Gauging the distance, he figured it was only a matter of seconds before the bricks touched the plinth. Shirl's touch on his back was suddenly reassuring.

"One more…" The movement of the tiles was passing in a blur.

With a *clunk!*, the walls touched the pedestal.

Wolf expected the sound of tortured stone. What he saw in the dim light was either supernatural or a very clever bit of engineering.

The walls seemed to flow around the grey stone of the plinth, gradually consuming it.

"Mayweather!"

"Almost there!"

"Brace yourselves!" he shouted at the others.

Wolf could see the edges of the plinth disappearing, only centimetres between the puzzle and brick. Then his view was suddenly cut off as he was pushed behind Mayweather by the wall. He tensed, waiting.

"Got it!"

There was a loud *snick!* and the brick stopped pushing on Wolf's shoulders. Instantly, they snapped back to their original positions. It was so fast, he wasn't sure if he'd imagined the whole thing.

Shaking, Mayweather sank to the floor.

Shirl moved around Wolf and bent down next to him. She whispered to him and he braced himself, raising his head. He used the edge of the plinth to lever himself up.

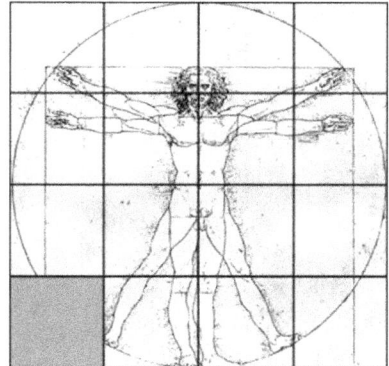

Sen and Nicholas moved into the glow.

"Second door is open," Nicholas reported.

"And we're not thinner." Sen was smiling. "Thank you, Mr Mayweather. I believe you've done it."

"Yes, thanks Mayweather," Wolf added. To the listeners he said, "All okay, Mayweather did it!"

"We gathered from the lack of screaming — good job, Mayweather."

"Well, what are we waiting for?" Wolf asked.

At that moment, the Hand guttered and almost went out.

ASK ANY LONDONER AND THEY'LL TELL YOU IT RAINS ALL THE TIME

A licia closed the curtains in her sitting room on the sudden rainstorm.

Pulling her cardigan closer around her, she shivered, the old house feeling draughty. Alicia knelt in front of the fireplace, fiddling with the new insert Stephen had put in…

"We are *not* going there tonight," she informed the two furry bodies pressed up against her.

Two smiling faces peered up at her, their back ends almost rotating as they wagged their stumps. They loved the fire and would sit as close to it as they could.

"There," Alicia announced as the induction coil in the fireplace started glowing. The hologram appeared, projecting the illusion of a fire. "I told him it's not the same," she muttered, remembering the arguments about changing the old fire. They'd had no choice really, with all the new contaminant regulations introduced – far too late – to deal with London's air quality and the planet's warming.

Alicia returned to the sofa with a sigh and settled back into the cushions. The had the vid on, with Sky News rolling in the background and the sound almost muted. She was only planning on doing some paperwork on her tablet, with a glass of wine.

Sipping her wine, one of the news items caught her eye. She picked up the remote and flicked the volume up.

"… a series of explosions have been reported in mostly uninhabited parts of Russia, China, the Congo, Brazil and New Colorado. They were detected by PPS satellites as they were limited to remote areas."

The scene changed to slow motion spouts of earth, trees and rock obviously shot at high resolution from the orbiting protection satellites put up by the media channels as yet another way to invade people's privacy.

"No eyewitness accounts have yet been reported.

"In other news…"

Alicia turned the sound down again. She shrugged and sipped more wine before returning to her papers and tablet.

Her voda went off and she looked at the ID on the screen. Alicia smiled, almost involuntarily. It was Hugh. She felt giddy as a schoolgirl, waiting for him to call.

"Hello?"

"Alicia, it's me. Hugh."

"Yes, hello." *A bit stiff, Al*, she thought.

"I was just wondering what you're doing tonight," he said after a short silence, possibly put off by her formalness.

Alicia thought about it. Mentally shrugged. "I'm sitting on the sofa with a glass of red wine in one hand and my tablet in the other. The fire's on and the dogs are just settling in to warm a side at a time."

Hugh laughed. "That sounds pretty good." He inhaled and let it out. "Don't suppose I can tempt you out for a drink?"

It didn't take much thought, given her reaction when she'd seen it was him calling. "Why don't you come over here? I've got some leftover stew on the stove, if you fancy it."

He laughed again. "Sounds good — I'll see you in about half an hour."

Alicia couldn't help smiling. He made her feel special. "Goo— great! See you shortly."

"Bye."

Putting the voda down on the sofa arm, Alicia sipped her wine. She could have told him not tonight, but she realised she wanted to see him. She almost threw the wine glass down on the table in her haste to go check her make-up. And maybe change the top. *Definitely change the top!* The dogs watched, bemused as she darted out of the room.

Alicia was halfway up the stairs when a fine vibration went down her spine and the hair on the back of her neck stood up. She stopped.

She'd suddenly had the strangest feeling something wasn't right with Jaared. He might even be in serious trouble. Shaking her head, she carried on up the stairs.

"Come on Al, snap out of it," she muttered to herself. "Don't crack up now – the gorgeous Hugh is on his way!"

And with that, the premonition faded.

C'MON IN HERE BOYS, HAVE A CIGAR...

I can only describe the feeling when the walls snap back as *relief*. Rooms getting smaller has long been a part of movies and books, probably since Alice and her experiments with size in Wonderland. What is it about the walls closing in that worries us so? Is it some primitive claustrophobia, gradually shifted from the psyche as we got used to living in caves, but which returns at times of stress?

The Hand gutters and I fear it's going to go out.

"Adams, how long have we got on that Hand of Glory?" I ask quietly.

Graeme's reply isn't reassuring. "*He says about half an hour.*" There's some off-channel muttering, suddenly cut off. Then he's back. "*We reckon you've been using it for twenty minutes.*"

I nod. Central's calculations show that, too. "Thanks."

Across the small, touching circle, Wolf is looking at me, that much I can tell, even with most of his faceplate in place. "What?" he asks.

"I think we should get a move on if we want to get out of this dark before that Hand goes out," I reply. "I'm happy to take point with Nicholas, as I think we're both better adapted for darkness."

Wolf nods. "Fine, you two take point and we'll follow your lead."

Still touching, the five of us snake through the new door. Just beyond the door is a set of stairs. The ceiling of the stairway follows the stair down, making it feel like a tunnel.

We head down and I'm at the bottom when I start to feel light-headed. Suddenly the floor rushes up to meet me and then, nothing.

Nicholas is slapping my face, none too gently, when I wake up. "Jaared! Wake up!"

I wave him away, feeling groggy, a pounding in my head. "Okay, okay, keep your shirt on... I'm almost ready, Mom..."

My head hurts like there's a spike in it. I still can't see, but I struggle to my feet anyway and stagger slightly as I reach vertical. Nick's hand is like a vise on my arm. Then it all comes back, a cascade of emotion and darkness.

"What happened?" I ask. "Where are the others?"

"Everyone's accounted for. There was a tunnel – remember the steps going down? It is about ten feet long, and then there are some steps going up again."

"Why'd I pass out?"

"I would say the tunnel was filled with carbon monoxide. Lack of oxygen to the lungs and Robert is your father's brother." His grip shifts on my arm. "I was unaffected and had to carry you all up the other steps."

"Did you just make a joke?" I ask, glanding a few substances to counteract the effects of whatever it was. "Is everyone else okay?" I call a bit louder, intending to rouse them if they can hear me.

Muffled, I hear responses. *Damn this darkness.* It sounds like someone's reporting what happened to Graeme.

"Is that Hand still burning?"

"I don't think so."

I find the speaker, leaning against a trunk or something. Not entirely sure as I crouch down beside her.

"Shirl? Have you still got the Hand?"

"Yep, I've got that nasty thing," she replies. "But it's not giving off any light."

"Let's see what I can get out of it. Hold it here..." I place her hand with the object on my knee while I find my lighter and a pen in the pouch. It's a good thing I stick with one of those old-fashioned Zippos. I pull the insert from the brass case and position it over the Hand. Pushing the pen into the body of the lighter, I squeeze as much of the fuel onto the hand as I can.

Before it can evaporate, I run my thumb over the striker. I can't tell by sight, but warmth on my hand tells me the fuel catches and then the Hand is burning again. The fingers are mostly gone, but what's left emits that dim glow. I put the lighter back together and return it to the pouch.

"We'd better get going," Shirl says to me. "I don't think we've got a lot of that left."

"I think you're right. Where are the others?"

Wolf suddenly appears on her other side as he touches Shirl's shoulder. Then Mayweather is visible. I can just make out piles of random garbage around us. There seems to be an assortment of brass and wood steamer trunks around us, with old chairs, lamps and what looks like a chamber pot stacked on top of them.

"Okay, same plan as before, Nick and I in front, finding a way out of this mess." I stand up, my head clearing with the effects of the drugs and endorphins. "Actually, I think I'll take that, this time." I hold my hand out and Shirl hands me the rest of the Hand.

The area we're in is just full of Victorian tat. I'm sure a collector would be in orgasms but I am more irritated than anything else. "Can you see a path through this, Nick?"

"I think... this way."

As we wind our way through the piles of stored mirrors, hatboxes and various side tables, a feeling of something not quite right seeps into me.

"I don't like this," Shirl whispers from behind me.

"Ignore it, kid. It's this damn House," Wolf responds.

"Easy for you to say," she retorts.

Nick is finding a narrow channel or maze through the stacked and discarded history. The Hand is still casting a dim glow, but it gutters and spits.

As we round an elephant leg umbrella stand and a hideous hall tree that could be the duplicates of the ones in the hall upstairs, a glint of gold catches my eye. On the shelf of a tall, thin bookcase, it's one of those damn toy monkeys with the cymbals and the vacant expression. I hated them the first time around.

It suddenly starts bashing its cymbals together and the noise nearly makes me drop the Hand.

All I see is a blur and the monkey is sailing through the air, the final crash as it hits something solid satisfying.

"Nice."

Nick turns back to me, looking young. "Sorry... I– overreacted..." he said quietly.

I shake my head, still feeling that foreboding of something bad about to happen. "I'd have done it if you didn't."

Silently he starts leading again.

After what seems like hours, although the chron on my HUD insists it's only minutes, I'm convinced the Hand is about to go out when the lights come on.

"What the...?" I can see the light from my head torch all at once. I turn around and it's like watching the rest of them break the surface of a black stretch of water. I blow out the Hand and stuff it back in my pouch. Never know, it might be useful again.

"We're out of the dark," Wolf reports in.

"Good to hear it. Watch yourselves," Graeme replies.

We're in another hall. There's nothing on the walls, just more of that red brick. At the end of the hall is a cast iron staircase. The kitchens must be down here somewhere, but I haven't seen any sign of them. That said, the map being displayed in my head suggests we've only covered a bit more than half the basement we'd expect from a normal house. *Where's the rest of it?*

"The only way is up," Shirl says beside me. I can see why she and Wolf are thought to be brother and sister – they're both five foot two or three and compact. Her head barely reaches my chest.

I make a quick check on the others. Central is continuing to monitor, but I'm getting no sense of interference. "I think Shirl's right. Let's get going."

Wolf looks at us and then almost bounds onto the steps. His footsteps ring on the iron.

Hissing, I make *slow down* motions. "Quietly, if we can."

He shrugs. "It already knows where here – what difference will it make?"

The sense of dread seems to build for a moment and I can't help but agree. "Go on, then."

I can feel the House watching as we start filing up the stairs.

IF THERE'S ONE THING I HATE, IT'S MAZES

It felt like they'd been walking up the stairs for hours.

"It must distort things," Wolf muttered to himself.

"What?" Mayweather said below him.

"Nothing, just wondering how long this staircase is," Wolf answered.

"I lost track after a hundred and twenty," Mayweather offered. "And by my calculations that would put us on the sixth floor of your average tower block."

Wolf nodded. "I was just thinking the House distorts space somehow."

"That or the staircase moves too."

"That's a horrible thought," Wolf rejoined, stopping. The staircase wasn't moving. It would have to be acting like a treadmill, keeping pace with their steps if it were moving. And they'd have spotted that by now.

"Nope, guess not," Mayweather observed.

After what seemed like hours, but the chron in his mask told him was only fourteen minutes and thirty-nine seconds, they reached the top of the stairs.

A featureless room greeted them. Instead of brick, the walls were unpainted plaster, dull brown in colour.

But the most startling feature was the skylight. The ancient glass, encrusted with years of pigeon droppings, was letting in rays of bright sunshine.

When all five of them had reached the top, they stood there for a moment.

"How——?" Shirl started to ask. Then: "Da, what time have you got?"

"*Nineteen forty-two. Why?*"

"It's still dark out there, isn't it?"

"*Don't be daft, of course it is. What're you on about?*" Graeme's voice was suddenly concerned.

"Never mind, Da. Out."

Sen was staring up at the skylight. "Some kind of localised time acceleration?"

Nicholas was also staring up. "Or a recording," he suggested.

They all looked at him at the same time, realising that somehow they knew he was right. Wolf looked back up at the sunshine streaming through the smeary glass. "A recording…"

"Come on then, whatever it is, let's get on with it." Sen, taking charge again.

Wolf felt a moment's irritation at Sen's presumption before realising he was actually glad someone else was leading this time. A weight lifted from his shoulders and he smiled. "Yes, come on, we've got a manuscript to find."

LA, LA, LA, I CAN'T HEAR YOU...

I n the van, the three exchanged glances.

"What the hell was that all about?" Skeet asked. "All their vitals just spiked."

Graeme leaned forward and tapped a few links, looking into the data they were getting. "Hmmm... their bodies are reacting like they've stepped into daylight. See." He pointed to the screen. "Pupils have contracted; blood vessels in the skin are open. All the sorts of thing I'd expect if they were in bright sunshine."

Adams leaned forward, excited. "I think they're experiencing some kind of temporal distortion – not time travel, as we all know *that's* impossible! I'd agree with the idea that it's some kind of recording, obviously from a previous day in the House's history."

Graeme and Skeet both looked at him like he was a new species of bug.

"Oooohhhhhh-kkkkaaay," Graeme replied, and then shrugged, raising his craggy eyebrows at the same time. "It's as good an answer as any."

They watched the readouts silently for a moment. The video channels still hissed with the static they had picked up as soon as the quintet entered the House.

Adams inevitably broke the quiet. "But isn't that cool? I mean, they're experiencing psychic phenomena we've only speculated about!"

Skeet regarded him coolly for about ten seconds. "Do you have a girlfriend, Adams?"

He reddened, suddenly embarrassed. "No."

"You see, I could say, 'That's hardly a surprise, is it?' or 'How did I know?'" she responded. "But I think I'll settle for 'Can you see the issue here, Adams?' I think that's more constructive."

Adams slouched on his crate, staring at the screens, jaw clenched.

"I wish we could see what was going on," Graeme muttered.

Skeet patted him on the shoulder. "They're fine..." she started to say.

Then the screens went blank.

"Fuck."

Graeme's choice of words was much more creative and forceful as he checked every system and routine, making sure it wasn't something he'd done.

"C'mon – bring it back!" Skeet had hold of Graeme's shoulder, her fingers like iron talons.

"Wolf! Shirl! Can you hear me?" he was practically shouting in the mic. Nothing.

Skeet watched his every move, double-checking over his shoulder, her fingers twitching to get involved. "Dammit! I can't afford to lose him now…" she muttered, starting at the blank screens.

The signal did not come back.

THIS SHIP WAS BUILT TO LAST

T he sunlight is welcome after the thick, soupy darkness. And, as things keep getting weirder in this place, I'm not going to sweat this one.

The air smells of hot dust, like my grandparents' attic when I was a kid.

I flip the top part up as the goggles aren't telling me anything in the sunshine. I walk to the door and try the old-fashioned brass handle. Nothing. It's a plain four-panel door, any paint it once had now flaked away.

I glance at Nick who shrugs. Nodding, I reach in my pouch and pull out a slightly large thimble-shaped object. Placing it over the lock activates it.

There's a quiet whirring followed by a click as the bolt on the door disengages. "Et voila!" I say, glancing at the others before turning the handle.

It rotates, like all door furniture. But the door doesn't move.

"Let me try," Nick suggests. He grasps the lever and turns it. I can see him straining, and he's much stronger than I am.

For a long moment, I think he's going to pull the handle off the door and we'll somehow have to break through it. Then the door groans loudly, as if it's not been opened in years, and opens with the *pop!* you get with different air pressures between chambers.

I swallow to adjust the sudden discomfort in my ears.

"A pressure differential? What's that all about?" Wolf murmurs.

I shrug. "There's so much going on here we don't understand, what's one more thing?"

Nick steps through the door into darkness. I glance at the others before following. I can feel them right behind me.

The door slams behind us, cutting off the light. I flip the visor of my mask down and realise it's only normal darkness this time. And find myself on the edge of a pit.

A thin pipe runs across the pit, rusted and showing obvious signs of deterioration, like rusty lace.

Nick is studying the pit carefully and I follow suit. I nudge Central to get an analysis and find there's nothing there. "I– I'm cut off," I say, suddenly at a loss after all these years of having its presence in my head.

I can hear the others checking things, but it's as if I'm at the end of a long tunnel, the sounds barely registering. Suddenly a sub-process kicks in and a simulacrum of Central I didn't know was there kicks in. Not full connectivity, but recording capabilities and basic functions, according to the data running across my HUD.

"I can't get Da," Shirl is saying. "There's no response on any channel."

"Let me see."

"You won' be able to reach anyone." Mayweather's voice.

We all look at him. "How do you know?" Shirl asks.

"This happened to my team." He is leaning against the wall, not at ease, but in the grip of some memory. "I never heard from them again."

"Great." Wolf swears, loudly and longly.

I'm studying the pit again, trying to discern what is at the bottom. It's got to be twenty feet deep.

"Rusty spikes, clawing metal, large springs, possibly glass and what looks like wooden stakes," Nick says in my ear.

"Lovely." I nod at that pipe. "I don't think that pipe will hold one of us, much less all five."

I can feel his nod in my ear. He leans forward, placing one foot on the pipe. It groans loudly before a *crack!* signals some kind of structural failure. It sags now.

Switching settings on my mask, I get a hint of something. I point at the floor under our feet and beyond it to the floor of the pit. There's a flicker in the corner of my eye. Stel is standing amidst the rubble in the far corner of the pit. I get the feeling she's been standing there for some time. "Nick…"

"I see it," Nick says. Before I can say or do anything, he has lowered himself over the edge of the pit, legs dangling into space. He disappears.

The others have stopped trying to get hold of anyone outside. We'll get contact back when the House decides we should and not before.

Nick reappears, levering himself up as if it was nothing. I don't help him, knowing he's at least several times stronger than I am and proud with it.

"Well?"

He nods. "You were right, there's a ledge around two sides and then a drop to the floor below." He waves at the rest of what I'm guessing is the top floor of the House. "I do not think we can get back to that from here."

I shrug. "It doesn't matter – I think the House is leading us to where it wants us to go." I glance back at the others. "And I'm happy to let it lead... for now."

I turn back to the others. "Did you hear Nick? We have to go around this pit on our fingers to the far corner." I can see the anxiety on their faces. "There's a clear space on the floor below there where you should drop and it should allow you to leave the pit unharmed."

Wolf and Shirl look at each other and shrug. "Piece of cake," Wolf says, and I can tell he means it.

"No. No way," Mayweather protests. "I canna do that – my god, are you people mad? It's a pit full of spikes and broken glass!"

I step towards him. "Mayweather, it's the only way past it..." I might as well be talking to a wall, all the good it's doing.

He's shaking his head, lower mask flapping back and forth. "No! I'll chance the pipe and meet you down there!"

"It won't hold you, Mayweather," Wolf interjects. "The gloves will help you grip the ledge..."

Mayweather sneers. "So yeh say – I canna risk ma neck on that ledge."

Nick is standing next to me and we block access to the pipe. "I can't let you do that, Mayweather," I say quietly.

Suddenly he shoves me. Hard. I feel myself overbalancing towards the pit and steel myself for the impact. It's gonna hurt.

Nick's hand shoots out and catches my arm. I feel his fingers scrabble for purchase for a moment before his grip hardens, inertia and gravity thwarted and reversed.

"Thanks," I gasp, rubbing my arm. My shoulder feels wrenched.

Mayweather has dropped down onto the pipe and is slowly and jerkily moving along it, crawling along it. The metal groans ominously.

"Mayweather, come back!" I call, knowing it's futile. Fear has him. We can do nothing but watch, none of us prepared to risk trying to physically bring him back.

He gets about five feet from the lip of the pit when there's an almighty *crack!* and the pipe buckles. Mayweather vanishes instantly into the tangle of the floor below. The impact must have activated his suit – I can't even pick up his heat signature.

I sigh. One down. How many more will the House demand before we're done.

Wolf is beside me. "He didn't stand a chance, did he?"

I shake my head. "No. I don't think so."

Wolf turns and I think for a moment that he's preparing to go back. But he lowers himself over the pit edge. "C'mon, then. What're ya all standing around for?"

I USED TO BE IN THE CIRCUS, RAN AWAY TO BE A CLOWN

Wolf hung over the pit by his fingertips. The ledge he was holding onto was only a few centimetres deep. He'd shuffled along it for about four feet and his fingertips were already on fire. He probably had another ten to go, and then another twenty on the next wall. The climbing aids, all those gecko hairs, were keeping him firmly attached to the small shelf he was inching down. They could hold twice his weight no problem.

"Why the hell did I have to be first?" he asked himself, *sotto voce*.

"Get a move on Wolf, some of us have things to do," Shirl chided. She was waiting to let him get a lead on her before following.

"Or waiting for me to fall to my death," he grumbled. His shoulders already ached. Wolf had a slight case of bodybuilder's shoulder, meaning his arms no longer reached above his head naturally. He was still limber enough – he didn't spend all that time keeping shape for nothing – there was just the issue of upper body muscle to deal with.

After what seemed like an eternity, shoulders burning with the effort, he reached the corner.

"Halfway there, Mr Woffe – Shirl's following on now," Sen called.

"Ta," Wolf gritted out. For a moment, he hung by one hand as he moved to the ledge on the next wall.

Is all this worth it? Why don't you just let go?

"Fuck. Off." Fingers on the other ledge, he quickly moved his other hand to the new ridge.

It could all be over so easily, the voice in his head repeated.

It didn't sound like anyone he knew.

Biting his tongue with the effort, he kept shuffling along, knowing Shirl was behind him. Last thing he wanted to do was slow her down. And, damn her, she was probably faster than he was.

You are always in the way, aren't you?

Wolf huffed a short laugh. Whoever it was, they didn't know him very well. He didn't waste any more breath on it, concentrating in moving and not falling onto the large spike he knew was waiting below him.

Suddenly he hit the wall. In surprise, he dropped, and, contrary to normal reaction, let his legs relax. When he touched the floor, his legs acted as springs, cushioning the landing in a small open space. He turned around and could see a narrow path through the debris leading away from the corner.

"I'm down," he called. "Watch the wall on your left, Shirl – it surprised me."

"Ta," she replied, concentrating on her movement as she traversed the corner. He could see her approaching. As he watched, the Commander dropped to the ledge and began the same journey. Nicholas stood impassively at the start, his eyes just shadows in the dim light. Then the (boy?) man turned to look straight at him and Wolf caught the spark of an eye. Something about it was threatening and he glanced away.

Shuddering, he moved along the path, wanting to get out of the way before the others arrived.

Shirl joined him moments later. "I hope we don't have to go back that way," she quipped. "Don't think my shoulders could take it."

"Here." Wolf turned her so her back was to him and massaged her shoulders through the suit for a moment. There wasn't a lot he could do, but it might ease the burn.

"Cheers, that's better." She turned around. "Now you."

Shirl's strong thumbs went to work on the muscles around his neck where the tightest muscle groups lay.

"Aaaahhh," he almost moaned as she found a particularly knotty bit. "Thanks. You're a sadist."

"My pleasure, Wolfie." He could tell she was smiling and he found himself chuckling.

"What are you two giggling about?" Commander Sen was behind them, doing isometric stretches to relieve some of his own muscle aches.

"Nothing, Commander," Wolf replied. He wasn't about to volunteer to massage Sen's shoulders. The man still scared him. *I just hope I'm in as good a shape when I'm his age – however old he is.*

Nicholas appeared behind Sen moments later, having made quick work of the ledge and for a second time.

"What are we going to do about Mayweather?" Shirl asked.

There was silence for a moment as they all considered the problem.

Sen cleared his throat. "I'm afraid there isn't a lot we can do for him. He's out there somewhere." He gestured at the dense pile of rubble and spikes in the pit around them. There was no obvious way to get into it that wasn't guaranteed to hurt them.

More silence.

"Ready?" Wolf eyed them up. With a nod from Sen, nothing from Nicholas, and a shrug from Shirl, he turned and led the way out of the pit.

The way out was just a normal door, no locks, bars or other oddities to make life difficult. It opened on the first try. The room beyond was dimly lit by a few stray bars of streetlight that slipped through the heavy curtains.

They found themselves in a bedroom. A large canopied bed stood in the middle of the room, the canopy deteriorating into shreds of dusty cloth. It was impossible to tell what colour they had been in the dim light. The heavy curtains were equally dusty and deteriorating. The gaps letting in light were the result of the fabric falling apart.

Shirl gasped and Wolf followed her gaze. In the middle of the bed was a body. In the dim light, he couldn't make out any detail. It could have been as old as the fabric in the room. There certainly wasn't the smell of a dead body.

"Partly mummified, I'd guess," Sen said aloud, as if in answer to their unspoken questions. "No recent decay."

"How can you tell," Shirl said in a hushed voice.

"Lack of insect life, mainly flies. No discernible smell – well, besides dust." His tone turned musing. "Although I'm surprised it mummified as this country's so humid. It normally requires much dryer and warmer conditions to achieve this state."

Wolf smiled. "Chalk another oddity up to this House."

Sen looked at him and smiled. "True, Mr Woffe, very true."

A cursory inspection showed nothing else in the room.

"Well, shall we?" Sen asked, gesturing at the second door.

Shirl looked at Wolf. "Do you think it can be that simple?"

Wolf shrugged. "Why not? Maybe it's trying to catch us off guard." He strode over to the door and turned the crystal knob. With a squeak, the door opened and he stepped through into a hallway. "See? Not a problem."

A staircase led down to the next floor. Well, part of one did. There were gaping holes in the stairs, like large stones had crashed through to the basement. And where there should have been a return staircase to the upper floor was only a blank wall. They didn't waste time looking for a door; as the Commander had already pointed out, what they were looking for wasn't likely to be up there.

So, Wolf in the lead, they began picking their way past the holes down to the first floor.

WHAT DO YOU DO IN A CRISIS? NOT PANIC!

S keet stared at the blank screens, willing them back into life.
Part of her, the normal part, wanted to rush in there and find
Jaared and get him back out. Safe.

The rational part – which got ignored a lot of the time – was keeping
her sitting in the chair, staring at the dark screens.

Graeme's lower half was sticking out from under the console, with
him checking and rechecking connections. Sensibly, Adams was sitting
quietly in the corner staring intently at his voda, occasionally poking at
the screen.

With a heavy sigh, Graeme pushed himself out from under the desk. "I
can't find anything wrong under there."

Skeet just looked at him, the rational part of her brain managing to
clamp down on the scream that threatened to burst from her throat.
"What the hell just happened?" she managed.

Adams interrupted. "I don't think it's your equipment."

He held up the voda so they could see the screen. An
incomprehensible diagram of squiggles and runes danced around on it.
"The etheric energy fields around the House are probably blocking most
transmissions."

The voda pinged and he quickly whipped it back to stare at the
patterns. "Odd, there was just a spike of some kind."

The screens chose that moment to reboot. It wasn't full video, but the
screen with the team's vitals was doing something.

When it cleared, there were only three sets of telemetry coming
through.

"There's one missing," Skeet said, gritting her teeth.

Graeme nodded. "Yes, seem to have lost one. It's..." He squinted at
the screen. "Looks like it's Mayweather."

"Could it be a malfunction?"

"I don't think so."

"And—?"

Graeme looked at her first, and then Adams, before looking back at
the screen. "I'd say he's dead."

He tapped a couple of keys. "Although why aren't we getting flatline
telemetry...? There's nothing."

Skeet thought about that. "Would damage to his suit cause that?"

A shrug. "Would have to be pretty massive – it's got a backup power supply and redundant systems. Even for an old suit like Wolf's we'd get more than this."

"The House took him," Adams whispered.

Skeet glared at him, hardly believing her ears. "Ya think that pile of bricks just– what? Ate him? C'mon Adams."

Adams stared back at her, the patterns on his voda ignored. "I think it's making an exchange... whatever they want balanced by six lives now. All the original party."

Graeme nodded. "He's right, that's all the group who entered the House before."

He returned to the screens. "Well, I guess Mayweather didn't actually enter last time, or he would've been dead too."

"The House doesn't forget..." Adams was practically rocking back and forth. The voda had dropped from his fingers.

"Shut up Adams!" Skeet and Graeme said in unison.

Shen Deng sat on his cushion, staring at the wall. Something had happened in the House; he could feel it in the dark energies flowing through the bricks.

I could have moved away years ago, he thought to himself with a heavy sigh.

He continued chanting, closing his eyes to concentrate on the bindings he was weaving around whatever it was possessing the House next door.

But he couldn't leave.

Not when he realised his purpose was to monitor the House. His granddaughter was showing promise to take his place. She might be more powerful; it was difficult to judge at her young age.

Shen drew breath and interrupted the chanting to add a ward in red on the wall. It was a pictogram of a young woman drawing water from a well.

The wall in front of him shuddered and white paint fragments drifted down towards the floor.

The House adjusts itself.

Minor shifts on its foundations. Creaks and groans as it settles again.

Its current collection is complete now. There is just the last body to be removed.

Almost replete, it might even give these new intruders what they want.

I SEEM TO HAVE LOST MY STRING IN THIS MAZE

"Lulling us into a false sense of security," Shirl mutters as she struggles to cling to the faded wallpaper. Her palms and boots are using their gecko traits, at least keeping her on the wall. "Then, when we're least expecting it, it'll take another member of our party."

Wolf looks at her like she's mad. "I always told Graeme he let you watch too many vids."

Shirl turns her head back from concentrating on the stairs and sticks her tongue out at him.

"Now children," I start, "let's worry about what happens next, okay?" Shirl is right, though. Now we're past the pit, it's been too easy, even this stair that isn't there. The skin between my shoulder blades is taut and itchy, waiting for a new blow to fall.

Nicholas is silent at the bottom of the stairs. All he'd done was jump over the obstacles and float down. Bastard.

He's a lot more controlled than I had expected from Madeline's reports.

Wolf is on the wall now. He's not as lithe as Shirl, however acrobatic he is. I stretch my shoulders and start to follow him.

The feelings of impending doom hanging over us all don't dissipate when we're all on the first floor landing. There's a window, and one door on the wall opposite the one we just traversed. Again, no sign of another staircase.

I sigh. "I'm beginning to tire of these games."

Wolf nods. "Me too, but I don't think we've got much choice at the moment." He motions at the door. "Shall we?"

I'm armed, but I don't know what I'd shoot right now. I may need the bullets later to avoid a Donner party scenario. "Very well. I'll lead."

This door squeaks as we open it. Odd, that's the first part of the House that doesn't appear well-oiled and maintained. A smell of damp and rot greets us.

On the other side of the door is a room spanning the rest of the floor with a large desk in the middle. There is no other furniture visible. To the right is a door set squarely in the wall.

The desk is mostly clear, other than something that looks like a very old Scrabble board and a set of letters scattered around it.

Nicholas is already trying the door. Again, it opens easily. He and Wolf enter the next room without a backward glance, impatience evident in their movements.

I glance back at Shirl who seems pre-occupied with the letters on the desk.

"Coming?" I ask, stepping to the door. "I don't think we should get separated – you know what this place is like for slamming doors!"

My attempt at humour barely registers. She half-smiles, not taking her eyes from the blotter. "Just a… yeah, okay." She moves to follow me.

I step through the door and there's a bang. The door is gone and it's dark again. I flick on my lights, rewarded with another bedroom to look at. There's a sagging bed in the middle of the room, but it looks like it could fall apart at any moment. A wet odour dominates and the black pattern on the wall is most likely mildew or something worse.

There's no other door out of the room, either. "What the hell?"

Wolf shrugs. "We can't work it out either, but *he*—" He gestures to Nick, standing by the wall, wearing his impassive face. "He figures it's another puzzle or test or whatever you want to call it."

I nod. "I guess it must be. Particularly as Shirl is out there and we're in here. Shirl, can you hear me?"

There's an audible click and then static. "*…just hear…*" Click.

"We're locked in, Shirl!" Wolf says after the click.

Then what is on the desk hits me. "Shirl! The letters on the desktop must be the next puzzle – there must be something you need to spell."

More static. Click. "*…spell…what…*" Click.

"I think you need to spell a particular phrase…" My head is starting to throb. "But you'll need a clue as to what," I say to myself.

"What? I'll need…"

"There should be a clue – do you understand? Can you see any word or phrase that would give you an idea of what letters to use?"

Click. "*…think…hold tight…*" It fades into static again. Click.

I sigh. I've no idea if she understands what I'm trying to say and it appears we don't have much in the way of comms. I slide down the wall to the floor next to where the door was. I look up at the black patch of growth on the wall. "Hope that doesn't contain airborne spores…"

Wolf looks at mold on the wall, and then at the bed. I can almost hear him thinking about sitting on it. He decides against chancing the spongy-looking furniture. He slides down the wall between Nick and I.

"Well, it could be worse," Wolf ventures.

I tense. "I wish you hadn't said that."

He frowns. "Why?"

I point at the wall behind the bed. Water has started pouring down the wall. *That'll be why it smells damp.*

"Shite."

Oranges and Lemons, say the bells of St Clement's...

Shirl fiddled with the settings on the com unit. "Bloody thing! Never works properly when I need it..." Giving up, static hissed from her headset.

"Give me a minute, boys – hang tight and I'll see what I can do."

More static.

"Guys? Can you hear me?"

Nothing.

Shirl flicked the comms channel off transmit and stared at the blank wall for a moment. "This is getting real old," she said under her breath. With a sigh, she turned back to the desk.

She looked down at the tiles and swore. She'd never been very good at Scrabble.

Actually, it didn't look that much like Scrabble, just letters on tiles and a plain grid. None of that other stuff like *Triple Word Score* on the dull white board.

Picking up one of the letters, Shirl wondered if it could be ivory. The surface was uneven and seemed to be yellowing. The letter *T* stood out in an antique typeface of some kind, carved into the ivory. She put the tile back down and poked the letters on the board with one finger.

"Shit," she said out load as the tiles started moving, rearranging themselves into a sentence. If she hadn't already seen ten impossible things today...

She shook her head. What the hell did that mean?

Her com clicked on. "*...Shirl...hurry...water... the room...*"

"What? Wolf! Say again!" *What did he mean – water?*

"*You need...hurry...water...up to...knees...*"

"Water's filling the room? Shit – copy that."

"The water is up to our knees," Wolf shouts into his mic again, but all he gets in return is static.

"Dammit." The water pouring down the wall is coming in faster than I'd thought possible. At this rate, the room will be full in about ten minutes.

I'm standing in water now. The suit is waterproof so far, but I don't think it was intended to be. I look over at Nick who shrugs. He's inherited his mother's inherent Gallicness in a single shrug. Only the French can make one movement so expressive.

"Can you point your light in here?" I ask Wolf. He obliges by pointing his wrist torch into my pouch.

I look into the tiny pouch, wondering what I have that might help us. In the bottom, underneath my pick thimble, the remains of the Hand, a pack of cigarettes and lighter, there's a trio of conical lumps.

Wolf has obviously been watching. "What're those?" he asks quietly.

I heft the heavy objects. "Limpet mines. Forgot they were in there."

He whistles. "Well, those should blow a hole in that wall."

I shake my head. "They might, but..." I point to the wall behind Nicholas. "We need to get through that wall. I don't think three of these will be enough."

"Two would do the job: one there, and one here," he replies, also pointing.

"Think about it, Wolf – this room is capable of holding a room-full of water. Do you know how much pressure that exerts? These walls are reinforced with steel or concrete. I'd probably need three to get through just the one wall." I put the tiny explosives back in the pouch. "Without knowing what the walls are strengthened with, I could waste two and not make a dent."

Wolf looks resigned. "We have to hope Shirl can work out how to open it, then."

I nod. "I'm afraid so."

Shirl was still staring at the board, but something was nagging her. A tickle at the back of her memory. *What was it? Where had she seen that phrase before? Wait a minute... hadn't it been on that video Graeme had shown them?*

She clicked on her mic. "Wolf, I've got a phrase here that I know I've heard somewhere – in Latin: '*Tempus omnia rapit, omnia dat*'."

Static. Then: "*Repeat that?*"

A flood of relief. Now if only they could make sense of each other.

"I said it's a phrase: '*Tempus omnia rapit, omnia dat*'. Any idea what that means?"

A howl screeches across the com channel. Shirl could almost swear it sounded like a banshee. "Stop jumping at shadows," she muttered to herself.

More static. "*Say again?*"

"It says, '*Tempus omnia rapit, omnia dat*'." Shit this wasn't going to work.

"...like... Bruno..."

Bruno? Yes, of course, that was it – a quote by Giordano Bruno! Her com channel came on again. "...*need... translate...*"

Translate? What did he mean? Then the lightbulb went off in her head. "Translate the phrase from the Latin! If only I knew Latin!" Shirl wanted to batter that blank wall in her frustration. "Calm down," she advised herself. "This isn't helping." Something dawned on her. "Wait a minute..."

Shirl pulled her voda from her pouch and started flicking through her notes. *She didn't have the video capture... what about the notes... nope.* She said, "Dad," to the voda. It dialled, doing its best to connect her.

There was a click and then nothing. *Dammit!*

"What... about... a... message?" She typed out the phrase onscreen, along with what she needed, and sent it. Hopefully, whatever the House was doing, her message would get through. And one back in, of course.

Wolf gasped as the water reached his privates. He always hated that part of getting in the pool. The genitals always seemed overly sensitive to cold.

"Shite! I hope she under-rr-st-st-ood m-m-me." His teeth had begun to chatter, the suit no insulation against the cold water.

The water had a brackish smell as if it had been in the holding tank a long time. There also seemed to be bits of plant material in the water, like moss or something.

Then how did that explain the smell of damp and decay in the room when they arrived? It hadn't been wet, of course, but who knew when it had last been used.

Nicholas stood impassively by the wall. Wolf wondered what it took to get a rise out of the guy. *What are you?* he wondered to himself.

Commander Sen was waving his arms to generate some body heat. "I'm sure she'll solve it, she's a bright girl."

Wolf snorted. "Yeah, sh-sh-she's always been a pain th-that way."

Sen smiled. "You've known her a long time, then?"

"You could say that." Wolf didn't want to think about that, though. "Do you think she understood what I meant about the Latin?"

"I hope so, Mr Woffe, I sincerely hope so," Sen replied. "Otherwise, we're likely to get even more uncomfortable."

Graeme looked down at his voda as it pinged, a sign of a message arriving. He read the message, thinking *What the hell?*

"What is it?" Skeet asked. Adams was sitting in the corner, quietly, his lips moving. He seemed to be weaving some kind of incantation.

Frowning, Graeme flicked his fingers across the screens, looking for something in particular. "Message from Shirl – she needs a translation of what she thinks is a Giordano Bruno quote."

Skeet huffed a short laugh. "Is that all? What the hell?"

Graeme shook his head. "No idea. I don't even know how that worked as we haven't had comms since they dropped out." He found the file with the notes on the autopsies and flicked through it on screen until he found the quote. "*Tempus omnia rapit, omnia dat...* that's it." He hit 'translate' and waited.

Copying the resultant text from one screen to another, he sent it back to Shirl's voda. Graeme turned and looked at Skeet and Adams. "Now let's hope that went."

In the room, the black, brackish water is reaching Wolf's chin level. He's quite a bit shorter than me – will need to keep an eye on that. Actually, something occurs to me.

"Nick, c-c-can you come nearer, please?"

He approaches, seemingly untroubled by the rising water. Nicholas raises an eyebrow.

"M-Mr Woffe is going to be in trouble shortly – and we'll need t-t-to keep his h-h-head above water." I point out the obvious.

Nick nods acknowledgement.

"W-w-we're going to support him in a m-mo-moment." I turn to Wolf. "If you give me your ha-hand and one t-t-to Nicholas, you can brace your feet on our l-l-legs, which should give you a chance to catch your b-b-breath."

It also has the side effect of reducing our heights – not a problem for Nicholas whom I don't believe can drown – but it could prove a difficulty for me.

I'm just hoping Shirl can get us out before then.

Contact with Wolf and the others appeared totally severed. Shirl's com just spat static when she tried to contact them. Or howled at her, which was more disconcerting.

"I don't even know if they're still alive," she whispered. The voda was in her right hand, her knuckles white as she willed the message from Graeme to arrive.

The voda remained silent, no signal.

"Dammit, give me a signal!" Shirl almost shouted.

For a moment, nothing happened. Then another. Just as she was about to hurl it against a wall in frustration, the screen lit up. Signal!

It pinged to tell her a message had arrived.

"Yes!"

Shirl bent to the tiles on the table, hoping they were still alive.

The water is almost in my mouth. I don't want to swallow any, the colour and smell suggesting that wouldn't be pleasant. Or do anything for one's health.

Wolf is braced on our legs and Nick is impassively holding him. Both Wolf and I are suffering the coldness of the water, teeth chattering almost non-stop. There's no point in trying to speak; the girl will either get us out or she won't. Simple as that.

I close my mouth and breathe through my nose, trying to stave off the moment as long as possible. My leg is cramping where Wolf's standing on it – the cold and my strange stance combining to stress the muscle.

Water laps at my lips and I resist any temptation to open them. I close my eyes and concentrate on surviving just a little longer.

"C-co-commander, l-l-let me down – we c-c-can swim. T-t-t-tread water, at least..."

He's got a point; there's still a few feet above our heads free of water. "O-o-k-k-kay," I stutter against the cold. "M-m-might as well give it a s-sh-shot."

He lets go and starts treading water. The cramp in my leg intensifies. I lift it and start massaging it, trying to get some feeling back into the limb before I have to use it.

A strong hand grips my harness and lifts me free of the water. I look down and Nick is holding me up by one hand, the water nearly in his eyes.

"I w-w-wish you'd done that earlier," I grumble. His smile is almost visible under the disgusting water.

The circulation returning to my leg is like fire for a few moments, but my rubbing seems to be restoring it. It feels like it will work normally now.

"Y-y-you can let me go now, if you want to try to t-t-tread w-w-water." I know he probably won't drown, but for some reason I can't bear the thought of him standing under this awful water.

He shakes his head and lets go of my harness. I start treading water. He pops above the surface for a moment. "I have never learned to swim." He sinks back down.

"E-ea-easy. Just move your legs and arms around. Y-y-you'll figure it out."

He looks dubious, but then tries it. Next thing I know, he's thrashing about in a poor approximation of treading water.

"T-th-th-that's it," Wolf encourages him.

I smile, as Nick's gyrations become more rhythmical. He actually smiles with pleasure, an expression I haven't seen before.

"C-c-c'mon Shirl," Wolf grits out, comfortably keeping his head above water.

I whole-heartedly agree. The ceiling is getting closer and the cramp in my leg is back.

Shirl glanced from her voda to the tiles and back to the voda. "That's right, isn't it?" she asked no one. She'd arranged the tiles to show:

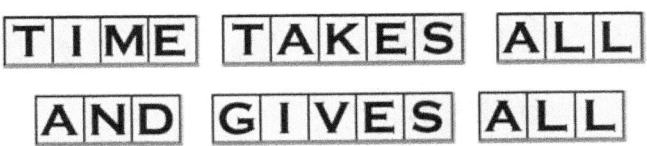

TIME TAKES ALL
AND GIVES ALL

For a long moment, nothing happened. Shirl glanced at the voda again, just to make sure. Yep, that's how it looked onscreen. She remembered that Latin didn't have any accents or other funny characters just for this reason.

After what seemed like years had passed, Shirl noticed the tiles were glowing and appeared fused into a single strip on the board.

A very loud *clunk!* sounded somewhere behind the walls, followed by the noise of rushing water.

Shirl tried the com. "Wolf? Commander? You there?"

For a long moment, nothing. Then a burst of static that tore through her head. *"Shirl! You did it — the water's going down!"*

Shirl slouched back against the edge of the desk, suddenly drained. "Thank god," she said to the empty room.

IT'S NEVER A GOOD IDEA TO POKE THAT TIGER

When the door opens and Shirl is standing there, I want to hug her. Obviously, I can't, as I don't know her that well...

Wolf does it for the rest of us. "Ya beauty!" he shouts, throwing his wet arms around her. "I knew you could do it."

Shirl's smiling, but it looks a bit strained. "I'd rather not do that again, if I can avoid it," she replies, wrinkling her nose. "You stink."

"I know, but at least we're not drowned!"

I nod. "Amen to that – I'm glad we avoided it, too."

Nicholas stands at the other door that has opened. "I suggest we stay together, as much as is possible."

Wolf nods. "Absolutely." Then he glances sideways. "Of course, if we had done that before, we'd all have been in the room when the water started coming in."

I shake my head. "I think the House is more devious than that – if we'd all died without a chance at solving the puzzle, well... what would be the fun in that?"

"I think he's right," Shirl adds. "I was almost right behind you when it shut the door. I don't think it would have let me enter the room as well." The ward around my neck pulses once, a heavy tug on an invisible chain.

There's so much happening here I can't comprehend. I like to consider myself at least somewhat spiritual, with all my training in the Far East. But this sort of phenomena is much closer to my distant Catholic roots, shit *The Exorcist* and *The Omen* brought into the light, however briefly.

"C'mon, let's find this manuscript and get the hell out of here," Wolf mutters.

I don't point out we're running out of places to look. The House seems to be sharing all its secrets with us; I find this more than a little worrying. Unless we've missed something completely.

The fact it's no longer trying to obstruct our every move is also a concern. The stairs are easily accessible now and appear intact.

"Do you realise we're almost where we came in?" Shirl asks in the silence as we carefully take the stairs. I'm alert to any changes that might happen or traps we've failed to spot. "So watch that spot by the door, Wolfie."

"I agree. The last thing we want to do is have to start the whole maze over again."

It's a matter of moments to get down the intact stairs and, following Wolf's example, avoiding the trap just inside the door.

The Hall looks perfectly innocuous, with the awful hall tree and elephant's foot umbrella stand we saw before.

"That's horrible." Shirl's pointing at the elephant's foot.

I nod. "Those Victorians, eh? Such jokers."

Wolf, already in front of the door at the end of the hall, flashed a smile. "Yeah, who else would have thought of taking an elephant's leg and making an umbrella stand out of it?"

We all gather in front of the door for a moment. "Well, what are we waiting for?" I ask. "I can't see any obvious traps or triggers."

"Me either." Wolf reaches out and touches the knob. His body spasms for a moment.

"Wolf!" Shirl reaches towards him but Nick pulls her back.

Then we realise he's laughing. "Sorry, couldn't help myself!" he gasps.

Shirl punches his shoulder. "You bastard! For that, I'm not going to save your arse next time!"

Still chuckling, he turns the knob and enters the next room.

"What's an elephant?" Nick asks me quietly.

I glance at him, only remembering how young he is at that moment. "It was a large animal from Africa and India, I think." *How to describe an elephant to someone who has never seen one?* "That," I say, pointing at the umbrella stand, "was just the bottom part of one of four legs and its skin was like that all over. An elephant would fill this hall. It had big floppy ears and a trunk where its nose would be, which it used to pick things up or spray water..." I trail off, guessing from his expression, he's not seeing it. "I'll find you a photo when we get out of here."

We follow the others into the next room. It takes up most of the ground floor, running all the way from the front of the House to the back, ending in what looks to be a Victorian sunroom. The glass in the conservatory is fogged with a mixture of pollution, pigeon shit and leaves. A few panes are cracked or missing, a cold breeze blowing through the room from somewhere.

"Lovely. Let's buy it and fix it up, Wolf!" Shirl sounds much brighter than I feel.

Wolf looks back at her and frowns. I guess I can see what he's frowning at: the walls are covered in bookshelves – *empty* bookshelves. Above the oak bookcases, what looks like some kind of bas relief decorates the walls. The ceiling is an ornate composition of various carved and stained woods. It reminds me of something, but I can't think what.

Where lights should hang in the centres of the two rooms, there are simply blank octagonal areas. I can't see any evidence that lights were ever installed in this room. Come to think of it, I haven't seen lights in any of the other rooms, either. How strange.

Now we're in, I can see it's two rooms, plus conservatory, separated by pocket doors – the ones that disappear into the walls.

As we step into the back part of the room, following Wolf's lead, the pocket doors slam together behind us.

"Shite! Seriously?" Wolf asks no one. "I'm getting a little tired of this."

I nod.

Nicholas seems to be listening to something. I step towards the glass at the back of the House and stop.

Stel's appeared just inside the glass. I can see her trying to say something, but it's unclear. Then she waves at the right side of the room, where Nicholas is standing, looking at the empty bookcase.

I glance back at her and she just nods. I step up next to Nicholas and look at the shelving. "Anything?" I ask.

He doesn't speak immediately. "There is something…"

When I look back, Stel's *phii* has gone.

Nicholas starts feeling the shelves, checking corners, mouldings, anything he can touch. Near the bottom, he pauses for a moment. "Naughty, naughty," he mutters as he gestures with his left hand.

My ward pulses, feeling very heavy for a moment before returning to normal.

With his right hand, he presses down on a part of the shelf that looks like all the rest. There's a click and the whole shelving unit swings away from the wall, revealing a passage.

And it looks normal, at least to the unaided eye.

"Finally, something that doesnae involve a test!" Wolf says, stepping forward.

I flick through the settings on my goggles and Stel's *phii* is in front of me again. I put an arm out to stop Wolf. "Hang on, think I've got something." Stel is pointing down now. Must be something wrong with the floor. "Are your boots non-conductive?" I ask Wolf, glancing at Shirl. She nods; he doesn't.

"Well, yes, as long as they're intact."

Shirl and I both look at him. "What do you mean, 'intact'?" she asks.

Wolf shrugs. "I stepped on something a while back – there's a hole in my right boot and my feet are wet. Why?"

I sigh. There's no way things were going to go perfectly and this just keeps getting better. "I think there's a charge running through the floor." I root through my pouch and find a two pence piece. Copper conducts. I show it to them. I toss it onto the floor of the hall.

There's a *crack!* and the smell of ozone fills my nostrils. The coin, blackened now, is lying in the middle of the passage. Stel disappeared as soon as the coin hit the floor.

"There's no way you can walk down that hall," I say. "I'll have to carry you past it." I examine my own footwear and thank procurement silently for providing top of the range equipment on such short notice. Shirl does the same.

"Great. This just gets better," Wolf mutters.

I look at Nicholas, standing next to the doorway. "Will you be able to walk it?"

He shrugs. Ah, the eloquence of teenagers. I never thought I'd experience it from one of my own. Nicholas steps in front of the door and then leaps forward.

There's no time to do or say anything. He makes it about two-thirds down the hall, because of the relatively low ceiling. Seemingly unaffected by the electrical current, he continues walking down the hall and turns a corner. "The current stops here," he calls.

"Want us to go first?" I ask Shirl.

In response, she steps tentatively into the passage. Nothing. Without a backward glance, she hurries down the hall. Probably not a good idea to linger.

I turn to Wolf and move to just beside the threshold. "Ready?"

"As I'll ever be," he answers. I crouch down slightly and he places both hands on my shoulders before hopping up to wrap his thighs around my waist. "Giddyup!"

"I'll drop your ass if you kick me," I reply. Thankfully his weight is easy enough to balance. I step onto the floor ahead of me. Nothing. Not even a tickle.

I release the breath I am holding and taking a firmer grip on Wolf's legs, stride down the hall and turn the corner. Nick and Shirl are standing in front of an ancient lift, the sort with a screen you have to slide to one side before entering.

I crouch slightly to let Wolf alight. "Well, what are we waiting for?" he asks. "We're not leaving without finding something." He slides back the grate and steps in.

Shirl follows him. I look at Nick and shrug, before following.

The lift was a tight fit. Panelled on two sides in what looked like oak with solid brass fittings, only slightly tarnished with age. If Wolf didn't know better, he'd guess someone had been cleaning the brass and recently. The back of the lift was another screen like the one on the front.

Sen slid the front grate closed and Wolf punched the single button, marked 'Library'. For a long moment, nothing happened.

"Gre—" he started. Then, with a solid *thunk!*, the light over their heads came on as the lift engaged and started creeping upward. The slowness of the lift was almost agonising. Funny how none of them had even debated whether or not taking the lift was safe. It was the only choice.

The exposed wall of the lift shaft wasn't blank on the other side of the grill, but they could just make out the decoration by the light of the lift. In what Wolf recognised as Arts and Crafts (which would fit the period of some of the work on the House), were figures of workers and various worthy crafts, all marked out with gilt highlights.

After what seemed an eternity, Wolf realised the sound behind him had changed and turned to find they had reached the 'Library'. The lift stopped with a judder and the light over their heads went out again.

Wolf reached forward with trembling hands and found the handle for the grate in front of him. He slid it to one side and, taking a deep breath, stepped forward.

A golden light came on, shining straight down at a pedestal in the centre of the room and Wolf gasped.

You close my eyes and I can see everything

T he atmosphere in the van was tense.

Graeme was staring at the readouts, trying to decipher what was happening merely by scanning the lines of data coming from the three remaining suits worn by Wolf, Shirl and Sen.

Still sitting on his crate, Adams seemed to be almost catatonic. He hadn't picked up his voda. It lay on the floor of the van, a ghostly halo of almost-seen glyphs hovering in the air over it.

Skeet was pretty sure she hadn't seen a voda do that before.

And Skeet was thinking about Jaared. While watching the other two do, well, nothing.

I never meant for this to happen, Skeet thought in the silence of the van. *He was only supposed to be a job.*

She'd never said it, hell, hadn't even thought it. But there it was.

Her client wanted access to Jaared, paid her to get close to the old man. Skeet didn't know what they wanted from him – that was above her pay grade. But she had her suspicions.

She'd been approached through an old contact, Tony Shonin. Not Japanese, English, but he had a fondness for old Jap girl bands.

Tony'd found her in Pa Tong, Phuket, drunk in a ping-pong bar. Skeet couldn't even remember why she'd gone in there; girls doing things with ping-pong balls weren't really her thing.

"Got a job for you, Skeet-meister," he'd started.

Skeet had waved him away, glass in hand. "Only interested in another Chang, 'mate' – don' need a job."

Tony leaned across the table and, for a moment, she thought he was going to try to kiss her. He didn't. The hypospray penetrated the back of her hand and was whipped into her bloodstream. In moments, she was nearly sober.

"Dammit, Tony, I've been working on that drunk all day!" she protested.

He nodded and smiled. It wasn't a friendly smile at all. "Yeah, I know. Sorry to be a buzz kill, but you've got a meeting and I need you sharp."

"What the fuck, Tony? I told you I don't want a job!"

Tony stopped smiling. "Afraid you haven't got a choice, Skeet, my dear." He gestured at two figures standing just inside the bar. Skeet wondered why she hadn't seen them before – they seemed to be standing completely still while the bar's activity moved around them like currents around rocks in a stream.

"Oh shit." The Sato twins. Bad news in any language.

"You see what I mean, then?" Tony stood up. "C'mon, you've got a meeting."

The 'meeting' turned out to be in the Presidential Suite of the *Coral Beach Hotel*, with amazing views over the Andaman Sea.

Her new boss was not someone she'd ever met before. English again, but a small and intense woman, as opposed to Tony's bearish figure.

"Ms Skeet, how kind of you to join us," she said by way of introduction.

Skeet opened her mouth to point out she hadn't really had a choice, but stopped short as Tony shook his head. "Just 'Skeet' 'll do."

"I am Ms Watson," the small woman continued, nodding. On closer examination, she was obviously older than Skeet had thought, the telltale whiteness around the eyes the only sign of more than one rejuvenation treatment.

Ms Watson led the way to a small table on a balcony shaded by an umbrella. Once they were both seated, Ms Watson poured Skeet a glass of cold mineral water. "You must be dehydrated after a day of drinking."

Skeet nodded, accepting the glass. The water was cold and on the verge of giving her ice cream head.

Taking a sip, Ms Watson got straight to business.

"You know Mr Jaared Sen, don't you… Skeet?"

"Commander Sen? Yeah, I know him." *What was this?*

"We want you to… introduce us," Mrs Watson said.

"Why? What's he to you?" *Why am I defending him?*

Ms Watson shook her head. "That is not your concern, Skeet." She took another sip of her water. "We have a business proposition to put to him." She set her glass down and looked Skeet straight in the eye. "All you have to do is arrange for us to get close to him and we will do the rest."

Covering her confusion, Skeet took another drink and thought: *What's it worth?*

Tony named a sum that nearly took her breath away. *All that just to get you near the man?* The sirens in her head were loud, but she could use that money. Retire. Stop merc-ing around.

She put down her glass. "Okay, what do you want me to do?"

Skeet realised she'd been staring at the symbols hovering over Adams' voda for too long; she had a spiking pain behind her left eye. "Dammit."

Graeme glanced her way. "You okay? You zoned out there."

Rubbing her eyes, Skeet nearly shook her head. *No, not okay.* "Yeah, just a bit of a headache."

He handed her a tube. "Try this – rub on your temples and it goes away."

"Thanks."

There was a sudden spike on the monitors of the remaining team members. "Wonder what that was?" Graeme mused.

"They've found what they're looking for," Adams answered.

They both looked at him, and then each other.

"Okay, I'll bite. How do you know?" Graeme asked.

Adams looked at them with shadowed eyes. "Cause the House just got a lot more active. I don't know if they're going to make it out alive."

"I SEE WONDERFUL THINGS..."

The room wasn't that big, but the walls were covered in shelves, floor to ceiling. One inset panel had a painting that was nearly invisible in the dim light, but it was obviously old, even so.

Wolf nearly stepped forward. Shirl's hand on his arm stopped him.

Sen quirked an eyebrow. "Are we going in or not?"

Shirl shook her head. "Not until we've worked out if there's more games to play."

Staring intently at the floor ahead of him in the light from his head torch, Wolf couldn't help adding, "You wouldn't want to get this far and lose a leg now, would you Commander?"

"True, that would be unfortunate."

Wolf took a pocket torch from his pouch and leaned down towards the floor. He shone it just above the surface of the floor, looking for any sign of further traps or just lifted boards that might prove to be some kind of trigger. He flicked through the coloured filters on the flashlight, watching for changes in the patterns of the floor.

For a moment, he didn't see anything. Then he noticed one of the parquet floor areas was slightly off-pattern. Flicking the light around, he spotted two more similarly off.

"Right, there's a few areas on the floor that appear to be different. I'm going to put some pressure on one and see what happens."

Wolf reached forward, still crouched, and pressed on the mismatched tile. Nothing happened. He was surprised. "Wait a minute..." he muttered. He looked at the 'normal' area. Reaching forward, he put pressure on it.

There was a soft *ppphhhhtttt* sound. He looked up and stopped, his head torch catching the end of a short bolt sticking out of a book spine to his right. If he'd stood on the trigger, it would have hit him about chest high.

Wolf glanced back at the others and Sen made a slight bowing motion.

Smiling, Wolf looked back at the floor. "Looks like these odd-patterned bits are stepping stones. You lot stay here a mo'."

He stepped forward onto the first 'stone' and waited. Still nothing happened. He breathed in slowly and stepped to the next one. Then the next. Flashing the light ahead of him, he spotted three more to take him right up to the pedestal.

Avoiding the other areas, he made his way to the golden light and what lay on the lectern. Pocketing the torch, he examined it.

"What is it, Wolf?" Shirl called from the doorway.

It was a small book, scarcely more than a leaflet, but bound on both sides with heavy leather-bound boards. Wolf didn't pick it up, but pulled a knife from his pouch. He opened the blade and carefully opened the cover. The frontispiece had an inscription in a beautiful hand, in Italian. "From the Library of Peter Cardomel, 1643," he read aloud. His heart leapt. Cardomel had been a minor collector of rare works, with a particular interest in alchemy and the occult.

"Is that good?" Sen asked.

"Cardomel was a collector, so yes – means he found it sometime after Bruno's death. It could be authentic." Wolf turned the next page, holding his breath. The title page was there.

IORDANVS

BRVNVS NOLANVS
DE TEMPORVM SIGNIS

Hoc in libello res in caelo nostro
gestas eventusque horum temporum signorum explicare conor.

Wolf closed his eyes, relief passing over him like a wave. "Well, it's here, all right," he informed the others. He turned to the first page and excitement made his fingers tingle where he was touching the page.

DE TEMPORVM SIGNIS

PRAEFATIO

Sine dubio illam stellam novam
quae in caelo nocturno apparuit
vidisti, sine dubio quid significet
meditatus es?

Hoc confirmo, o amice, multi sunt
alii qui ipsi de origine illius sid-
eris, de momento quod occasus
talis posuerit, quaerunt, in-
quirunt, cogitant. Num in tempo-
ribus finalibus sumus, Christi ad-
ventum secundum exspectantes?
Haec est interpretatio una quam
tibi credere licet.

Aliter visum, nonne alium argu-
mentum validum est totam universitatem rerum circum nos

i

"What? Out there, waiting for you?" Shirl asked.

"Yep."

"That's spooky."

"You can say that again," Wolf replied. Curiosity got the better of him and setting the Bruno manuscript back down, he turned away from the lectern. Shining his light across the walls around him, he could see the walls were covered in books, scrolls and papers tied up with ribbon. Looking at the floor carefully, he stepped towards the shelves.

Just looking at the titles, he could see several books on display he could sell and retire on the profits. Amongst the titles he saw a copy of what could only be the *Book of Abraham the Mage*, an early alchemist's text. There was also a folio that appeared to be a rebound copy of the *Malleus Maleficarum*, a fifteenth century treatise on witches by a Roman Catholic Inquisitor.

On display on a nearby shelf was what looked like a music score. Wolf wasn't remotely musical – it could be by Bach, Liszt or Joe the piano player for all he knew. There were too many things to look at, so Wolf gave up trying to see it all.

He reached out a hand towards the *Book of Abraham*. Before it reached the binding, the book started trembling. Wolf pulled his hand back and the movement ceased. He repeated the motion and got closer. Not only the book he was aiming for, but all of the items on that shelf started jittering in their slots. As his fingers brushed the spine, the book leapt out and crashed to the floor. The golden light above the podium pulsed, almost going out before returning to its previous intensity.

Wolf winced, hoping it hadn't activated another bolt. When he remained unperforated, he relaxed again. Then he noticed the tall figure standing to his left, between him and further treasures. The figure was indistinct, almost vapour, but there were two embers where the eyes would be. And they were watching him with a familiar inensity. "*Mayweather?*"

"I don't think you'll be able to look at anything else," Sen said behind him. "I'd say the House is willing to let you look at the Bruno, maybe take it, but it seems to be very protective of its treasure."

The Guardian – which had been Tobias Mayweather – didn't move, but the message was clear: *You may only look at what is intended for you.*

Wolf nodded, reaching the same conclusion as the Commander. "Shame, as I'd like to see what else it has on those shelves."

"C'mon Wolfie, get the Bruno and let's go!" Shirl answered. "I think I've had enough of this place."

Finding himself agreeing, Wolf carefully stepped back to the lectern and, more boldly, turned another page of the book there. It certainly looked authentic, but he couldn't help feeling there was something off.

Gritting his teeth, he closed the book and picked it up. The golden light pulsed once and then vanished, as did the shadowy Guardian. No more darts flew across the room, so he took that as permission to take it.

Carefully, watching the floor as he went, he retraced his steps to the lift where the others waited.

The gate slammed shut behind him and the engine engaged with a jerk. Wolf was thrown against the others as the car seemed to descend much faster than it had gone up.

They were almost forcibly ejected when the lift reached the ground floor.

Tales of Mystery and Imagination

I f Nicholas wasn't in front of me, we'd all have fallen down. He stands there just outside the lift like a rock, implacable.

There is almost a palpable force pushing us towards the entrance of the House. "I guess it wants us to leave," I quip.

The others don't seem to find it funny. We quickly move back through the rooms on the ground floor, the pocket doors open once again, to the entrance hall.

"Time to turn the suits back on," Wolf says.

One by one, the three of us vanish, only vague hints of bodies arranged around Nick.

As a group, we do our best to skirt the trapdoor just inside the front door, but it doesn't seem interested in opening for us, this time.

The door flies open and before we know it, we're lying in a heap on the step.

"*Wolf? Shirl? What's going on?*" Graeme's voice crackles over our comms. Contact regained.

"We're fine and we've got the Bruno," Wolf replies. "We lost Mayweather, though."

"*We figured, when his stats went black. C'mon don't hang around on the step like that,*" Graeme chides.

It's not that big a deal, as our suits are mostly camouflaging us. We pick ourselves up and make our way to the van, the door gaping open in the dimness.

"Father, will we look for Madeline now?" Nick asks as we approach the van.

It's not that late, considering it feels like we were in there all night. But I'm exhausted, so I shake my head. "Not tonight, Nick – we'll have to start tomorrow."

For a moment, I can see something on his face. *Anger? Disgust?* Then it's gone. "Very well. I will be at your house after dusk."

"Okay, Nick." I reach out to touch his arm, but don't quite. "Don't worry, Nick, we'll find her."

He nods and vanishes.

A small and very old Chinese man steps out of the shadows near the van.

"Shen!" Wolf says, deactivating his suit. Shirl and I follow suit, as it's not a big deal in the dark of the street.

"I think you have done something to the House," Shen replies. "The... agitation I have felt recently has calmed itself."

Wolf shakes his head, glancing at me. "We didn't do anything."

I shrug. "Didn't we? We left Mayweather in there."

Shirl nods agreement.

Shen smiles. "Ah, perhaps that was what it was looking for all along." He bows formally, once. "Good health and happiness to you all."

"And to you," Wolf responds.

The little man turns and crosses the road to the door of the house next door. I watch him disappear and wonder briefly if he'll have less trouble with the House now.

The others are already in the van and I step up into it, pulling the door shut behind me. I barely get turned around before I'm being crushed in Skeet's vise-like grip.

"What, were you worried?" I ask softly.

If anything, the pressure increases then releases. "'Course I was – that place is a killer," she replies.

I spy Adams over her shoulder, looking pale in the corner. "You all right, Adams?" Skeet lets go of me and rolls her eyes.

He nods. Starts to speak, then clears his throat. "I don't think I like field work, Commander," he said finally.

I don't laugh or do anything else patronising. "Thanks for your help, Adams – the things you provided did come in useful." I pull the remains of the Hand out of my pouch. "This got us through a room that was unnaturally dark and I have to say I'd never have thought of it."

Adams brightens. "Really? What happened? I need the details for my report..."

I make calming motions. "Tomorrow, Adams, I'll give you a full account, okay?"

"Yes sir – thanks!"

"C'mon, we're getting out of here," Graeme grates, slipping into the driver's seat.

We brace ourselves as he pulls out into the quiet street, quickly but not enough to draw attention.

When we reach Wolf's workshop, Graeme puts the van in front of the doors and opens the side door, the easier to move equipment and bags out of the van.

We all pitch in, even Adams, moving bags and boxes into the workshop. We'd stripped off the camo gear in the van, stowing it in the kit bags.

All the equipment out of the van, Graeme shakes my hand. "Thanks for your help, Commander."

"You're welcome, Graeme," I reply, not entirely sure why he's thanking me.

His gaze flicks to Wolf and Shirl, bent over the book on the worktop. "Let's just not do it again soon, eh?"

I grin. "You got it."

He slams the van door and climbs back into the driver's seat.

I go over to the other two by the workbench. "So, what'd we get?"

Wolf frowns at me.

"I was kidding – I don't think I could explain what I was doing with that old book if I wanted to!"

Shirl nudges him and picks up the book. "This is it." She hands it to me. "Sixteenth century. Looks to have been rebound at least once, but the paper's original and purports to be from the library of one Peter Cardomel, a collector in Milan in the early part of the seventeenth century."

I take it gingerly. "You're handing me a sixteenth-century book with no gloves or anything else?"

Wolf shook his head. "The British Library believes that more damage is caused to books by people wearing gloves than by not wearing them. This book's lasted almost five hundred years because the paper's made of things besides wood pulp. Go on, have a look."

I gingerly open the book. I can almost sense the age of the book, from the colour of the paper to the slightly irregular printing on the pages. As I turn the pages, I realise there are illustrations to go with the text. There's something crude about them, not helped by the fact I've no idea what they're about.

Seeming to sense this, Wolf fills me in. "It was a response to the appearance in the night sky of a very bright star – a supernova – in 1572. A lot of people thought it was the end of the world, but to people like Bruno, it was confirmation that there was more to the stars than pinpricks in the celestial sky. And it ultimately got him burned at the stake."

Wincing, I close the book and hand it back to him. "What will you do with it now?"

"Not sure. I will probably spend some time studying it before I take it to some experts for verification." His eyes flicked to Shirl. "It's invaluable as the only remaining copy." He places the book back on the worktop. "Thanks, Commander. We couldn't have done it without you." He holds out his hand.

I shake his hand. "I'd like to say it was my pleasure, but I'm with Graeme – I don't want to do *that* again anytime soon!"

Shirl, standing to the side, suddenly leans up and kisses my cheek. "Thanks."

Wolf frowns as something else occurs to him. "We also didn't find that other body – shouldn't there be a fifth man somewhere?"

"Not something I'm going to lose a lot of sleep about. It's probably in there somewhere, but I'm not going back to find out. We're going to go now and I have no idea what I'm going to tell my superiors." I shrug. "Goodbye, Mr Woffe."

"Goodbye, Commander."

I collect Skeet who has been leaning by the door during all this and we step through the priest's door onto the pavement.

"Shall I call a car or do you want to get a cab?" I ask. I glance across the street and Stel's *phii* is watching me from a doorway. I nod and she lifts her hand in an approximation of a wave before fading into the shadows for what I feel is probably the last time. "What?"

Skeet takes my arm. "I said, let's walk for a bit."

I shoulder the kit bag on the other arm. "Okay, you're the boss." It's not that far from Maida Vale to my house, but it *is* a walk.

In the company of Skeet, I could probably walk for a long time.

"Jaared," she starts. "I've got something to tell you…"

Acknowledgements

Firstly, I have taken liberties with Giordano Bruno's writing. While I have made every effort to get his quotations and my interpretations of his work, any mistakes are mine. Apologies to any purists out there who I may have inadvertently upset, but please don't write in.

That old adage about writing what you know would make life easier! For help with my (poor) Latin, thanks have to go to Robin Peach, from the Language and Linguistic Science department at the University of York for translating my efforts at Latin.

Thanks to Ellen Kardell for her cover design and Ben Locker for his help with my promotional material.

Thanks go to all the fans, particularly Theresa Dunlap – Jaared's No. 1 Fan! – at Just One More Paragraph (tweezlereads.blogspot.com), Kirsty Bower at Book Love Bug (booklovebug.blogspot.com) and two of my biggest supporters Alison Barclay and Sharon Mazel. The rest of you know who you are and I'll be adding names on a regular basis.

I have to thank my folks, after the launch of my last book in my hometown.

And last, but most importantly, Debra – thanks.

London, March 2012

If you enjoyed Book of the Dead,
read on for an exclusive preview of

Dead Silent

*the final book in the
Jaared Sen Quartet*

Dead Silent

221 Baker Street

I hit the wall as a projectile smacks the bricks in front of me. Flinching, I duck back, trying to make as small a target as possible.

Nick's body impacts the surface behind me.

"You okay?" I hiss.

"Of course," he replies.

I shake my head in exasperation, catching my breath, wiping the sweat from my forehead. He's still immaculate.

"It helps they do not know how to use projectile weapons," he continues.

Laughing under my breath, I take a quick peek around the corner. Another bullet kicks up some brick dust. "I think they're learning."

It's been a long time since I've been in this kind of firefight. Thankfully that kind of training never quite disappears. I'm carrying a modified late generation Hechler and Koch MP5 (MP5SD5-XXD, for the gun nuts out there). It hasn't really changed that much since I first used one but it's fewer moving parts requires more technology to support it now.

I actually have a readout in the corner of the Heads Up Display (HUD) running in front of my eyes, telling me barrel temp, type of ammo and how much ammunition I've got left — and if I let it get too hot, a red warning light tells me to stop.

I usually listen.

We're pinned down by some nasty things Nick assures me aren't human. Nice. I always like the supernatural to get involved in my day-to-day life.

And the fact they've picked up assault weapons worries me more than a little.

At least we've managed to kill or lose those damn hell hounds.

Hunting for Nick's mother (and my... whatever), Madeline, hasn't been as straightforward as I'd have liked it to be. But I promised the kid I'd help him find her.

Madeline disappeared sometime in the last two and a half weeks.

I don't normally worry about Madeline, as she's nigh indestructible. Being a vampire, it's much easier for her to heal an injury than for your average human; all she needs to do is drink some blood.

But Nick is nothing, if not persistent. And as I used him to get us through that damn House, helping him find her is the least I can do.

The last time anyone heard from Madeline was over a week ago when she checked in with the vampire equivalent of the local council, The Elders. (I don't know much about them, just what Nick's let slip; I get the feeling he's not supposed to tell me anything about them at all.)

Anyway, Madeline was in Edinburgh, looking for someone called the "Devakantaka". Central looked it up for me and found it's something to do with the Bhagavad Gita — Hindu scripture — but beyond a reference to 'mighty warrior of Ravana', I know nothing.

Nick found her hidey-hole here in the 'burgh, but she hadn't been there for a while. Even I could tell that.

I think that's when the hell hounds found us.

* * * * * *

I'm waiting for my man...

Skeet pushed the drooping fringe of her spiky hair back from her eyes and shook her head.

The meeting with Tony Shonin hadn't gone well.

"What the hell do you mean we have to wait?" Tony demanded. He was hissing in the crowded confines of a coffee shop off Regent Street. His Thai tan looked out of place in grey old London.

Skeet hadn't wanted to meet him anywhere more private.

"I mean, you ain't gonna find him in London, Tony," Skeet replied. "He's gone up north on a job."

Tony sat back. The Sato twins were with him, uncomfortable in their warm clothes. They looked totally out of their element. Probably had never been anywhere this cold.

"That wasn't the deal, Skeet." His eyes were cold, dead.

Skeet held her hands palms out. "I ain't shittin' you, Ton, he's off bonding with his kid in Scotland." *Hunting for that bitch.* "I can't help it if you's can't lift him now."

Those icy eyes stared at her a few beats longer. "If you're lying to me, Skeet, I'll do more than kill you, you know that."

Nodding, Skeet picked up her coffee. "I know, Tony — I ain't lying."

Sipping the last of his coffee, Tony looked away from her for the first time. Skeet nearly sighed in relief, the snap she'd glanded hyping her senses, not calming her down.

"Okay, Skeet, here's the situation: you let us know when he's back and we'll take care of things from there." Tony reached across the small table and patted her cheek with a hand like a slab of corned beef. "No need to get your pretty blonde head in a tizz." The smile accompanying the pat almost made her scream.

Gritting her teeth, Skeet smiled. "No worries, Ton, we'll get the bastard!"

Tony stood up. "For your sake, we'd better, kid — the boss don't like time-wasters." He nodded at the Satos. "And I think they'd like to get back to the islands; this cold weather's not good for them."

Skeet nodded again. "I know how they feel."

"Be in touch, Skeet," Tony threw over his shoulder. "I'd hate anything to happen to that pretty face of yours."

"You betcha, Tony," Skeet replied, stomach flip-flopping.

Skeet pulled a flask from her boot top and surreptitiously added it to her lukewarm coffee. The whisky hit her nostrils before the cup reached her lips. She shuddered and tossed the drink back.

Dammit Jaared, of all the times to go off with your scary kid.

* * * * * *

Jonesing for your touch

Jonesy's stomach lurched as he dropped out of the data cloud into the canyon of Central's normal processes.

The Grid flew by, glimpses of stray data nodes just registering in the corner of his eye.

Always night in the Grid, the only light comes from the construct's datasets and drone functions.

It was difficult to move through Central's architecture slowly, so Jonsey only had a sense of massive city sprawl, artificial intelligences more organic than planned creations — and no one had a street map.

This is hopeless.

Shaking his head, Jonesy pulled the jack out of his socket and sat up with a sigh. His eyesight took a moment to adjust to reality, lines of code ghosting over the dull paint of the walls in his flat.

He rubbed his eyes and wished the throbbing at the base of his skull would slow down. He glanded some *chill* and the throbbing subsided to a dull thud.

"Call Sen," he said to his voda, his voice hoarse from lack of use. There was a 'click' and it went straight to voicemail.

"*...Sen. I'm currently unavailable, but if your enquiry is urgent you can reach the duty controller by saying* connect me *after the tone.*"

Jonesy sighed. He hadn't reached Sen in days, hadn't really spoken to him since the quick meeting with an analyst at Company House. He stood up and went to the bathroom.

That was the problem with code checking, left little time for amenities like going to the toilet. He knew a guy, had a whole setup out of a spacesuit built into a chair so he didn't have to leave it; took care of all his biologicals. One day, the chair broke down and the guy starved to death in a pool of his own shit and piss.

Jonesy shuddered at the memory.

When he returned from the head, Jonesy took a pull on the energy drink in the clip next to his work chair.

This job felt like a pointless exercise. He was never going to spot a single incursion in Central's matrix. Even multiples wouldn't be that obvious, unless the intruder left some kind of glaring error behind him.

He jacked in again and initiated the intricate one-time codes that let him access Central. His terminal had some kind of arrangement with Central to give him access codes when he needed to enter and not before. That kind of security wasn't really Jonesy's area.

Unsure what to do next, Jonesy cruised over the vast amalgamation of processes and data that made up Central's 'mind'. Occasional details leapt out at him, but nothing out of the ordinary.

Damn.

Jonesy was about to jack out again when he thought of something he hadn't tried yet. With a mental shrug, he initiated a filter programme he'd been tinkering with. Designed to help him find bugs, it would hide a lot of the normal functions of the matrix. Hopefully, not seeing the busy data streams would expose the intruder.

The filter immediately cancelled a lot of the visual information he was getting patched into his brain, leaving the matrix in near darkness. The only things left were current activities — things Central was 'thinking' about at the moment.

Shit. It all looked normal. He added a couple lines of code to the filter on the fly, basically asking it to show him a little more detail, but not too much.

For a few minutes there was nothing. Disappointed, he almost jacked back out to tell Sen he couldn't spot anything out of the ordinary.

Out of the corner of his mind's eye, Jonesy saw a sudden outgoing data spur light up like a geyser.

"Ka-*ching*!" he shouted in the quiet of his apartment. "Got ya!

He mapped the spur and slipped up to it with a stealth programme a mate of his in Specials, the tame hacker quadrant, had given him. With a flick of his ghostly wrist, a tracer jumped into the stream of data and disappears, one end stuck to the edge of the hole whoever it was left in Central's security.

It probably wouldn't last long, but it might allow him to triangulate where and what was accessing Central. All he could do for now. Well, other than assessing what damage the link was doing to Central's normal thought processes.

Back in the real world, Jonesy told his voda to ring Sen again. There was the burr of the electronic ring then *"This is Commander Jaared Sen. I'm currently unavailable..."*

"Code B-two-theta," Jonesy intoned. "Message for Commander Sen: I've got something for you, Commander — I think I've got a lead on what or whom is messing with Central." He looked at the voda again, shook his head. "Call me."

Tossing the voda onto a cushion, he took a long pull from the energy drink in the holder by his chair and sat down again. "Now, let's see where that goes..." he muttered.

The jack slipped into his socket like a familiar lover and he was back in the Grid.

* * * * * * *

Dead Silent

Coming Autumn 2012

You can find more information on Dean's books and sign up for the monthly newsletter – letting you know about new releases and news about what he's up to on his website at

www.deanfetzer.com